"I remember Eil
long after the
—Kay Hooper, *New Y*

PRAISE FOR EILEEN WILKS'S NOVELS OF THE LUPI

"Grabs you on the first page and never lets go. Strong characters, believable world building, and terrific storytelling . . . I really, really loved this book."
—Patricia Briggs, #1 *New York Times* bestselling author

"As intense as it is sophisticated, a wonderful novel of strange magic, fantastic realms, and murderous vengeance that blend together to test the limits of fate-bound lovers."
—Lynn Viehl, *New York Times* bestselling author of the Darkyn series

"Full of intrigue, danger, and romance." —*Fresh Fiction*

"An intense and suspenseful tale . . . A must-read . . . Eileen Wilks is a truly gifted writer." —*Romance Junkies*

"There is no better way to escape reality than with a Wilks adventure!" —*RT Book Reviews*

"An engaging paranormal tale full of action and adventure that should not be missed!" —*Romance Reviews Today*

"Held me enthralled and kept me glued to my seat."
—*Errant Dreams Reviews*

"Fabulous . . . The plot just sucked me in and didn't let me go until the end . . . Another great addition to the World of Lupi series." —*Literary Escapism*

"Intriguing . . . A masterful pen and sharp wit hone this third book in the Moon Children series into a work of art. Enjoy!"
—*A Romance Review*

"Quite enjoyable . . . with plenty of danger and intrigue."
—*The Green Man Review*

Books by Eileen Wilks

TEMPTING DANGER
MORTAL DANGER
BLOOD LINES
NIGHT SEASON
MORTAL SINS
BLOOD MAGIC
BLOOD CHALLENGE
DEATH MAGIC
MORTAL TIES
RITUAL MAGIC
UNBINDING

Anthologies

CHARMED
(with Jayne Ann Krentz writing as Jayne Castle, Julie Beard, and Lori Foster)

LOVER BEWARE
(with Christine Feehan, Katherine Sutcliffe, and Fiona Brand)

CRAVINGS
(with Laurell K. Hamilton, MaryJanice Davidson, and Rebecca York)

ON THE PROWL
(with Patricia Briggs, Karen Chance, and Sunny)

INKED
(with Karen Chance, Marjorie M. Liu, and Yasmine Galenorn)

TIED WITH A BOW
(with Lora Leigh, Virginia Kantra, and Kimberly Frost)

Specials

ORIGINALLY HUMAN
INHUMAN

UNBINDING

EILEEN WILKS

BERKLEY SENSATION, NEW YORK

THE BERKLEY PUBLISHING GROUP
Published by the Penguin Group
Penguin Group (USA) LLC
375 Hudson Street, New York, New York 10014

USA • Canada • UK • Ireland • Australia • New Zealand • India • South Africa • China

penguin.com

A Penguin Random House Company

UNBINDING

A Berkley Sensation Book / published by arrangement with the author

For information, address: The Berkley Publishing Group,
a division of Penguin Group (USA) LLC,
375 Hudson Street, New York, New York 10014.

ISBN: 978-0-425-26337-2

PUBLISHING HISTORY
Berkley Sensation mass-market edition / October 2014

PRINTED IN THE UNITED STATES OF AMERICA

10 9 8 7 6 5 4 3 2 1

Cover art by Tony Mauro.
Cover design by George Long.

UNBINDING

PROLOGUE

Aléri in Winter

KAI hadn't had a cup of coffee in eighteen months.

That's what she was thinking about when the Queen of Winter's emissary came to see her—about coffee and her favorite mug, the purple-blue one with little speckles that she'd bought at a pottery shop in Oklahoma City. As she followed the emissary out into the streets of Aléri, she thought about that mug and the coffee table she'd painted turquoise and the necklace her grandfather had given her for Christmas four years ago. The Queen had arranged for her things to be put in storage while she was gone, and she appreciated that, but she missed that table. And her grandfather. And cell phones. She missed cell phones and the people she could call on one.

She missed home.

Aléri was one of the largest cities in Iath. Kai had been here several times since traveling to the sidhe realms, aka Faerie. Her mindhealing teacher lived here, in a stilted treehouse not far from the human quarter. Elves hated being crowded, and they loved trees and fields, lakes and gardens, so Aléri was more like a broad scattering of towns and villages than the kind of city Kai was used to. Incredibly lovely towns and villages, that is. Every structure, small or large, stone or wood, low to the ground or perched in the limbs of a huge tree, was meant to add to the city's beauty.

But Aléri as she'd seen it before was nothing compared to the city when it hosted the court of the Winter Queen—which did not involve a Disneyesque snow castle or fantastical ice sculptures. Those images had lurked at the back of her mind until she arrived at court. Reality had been a real pop in the face.

Nathan suggested that she think of Winter's court as an ongoing creation, a composition in time and people, as well as space. It was certainly beautiful, an unpredictable tumble of art and artifice through what seemed to be untouched nature. But Winter's court was as hard to pin down as the elves who mostly populated it.

Parts were stable; parts were sheer illusion; and parts of it shifted with the wind, or on a whim, including its location. When Kai first arrived at court, her bedroom window had overlooked a slate-gray ocean with a slim crust of beach separating the sea from her cottage. She'd woken four days later to find the same window looking out on a forest of towering conifers. Last week, the scene had shifted yet again—this time to the top of a hill overlooking the white roofs of Aléri, the largest city on the continent of Bá, in the realm of Iath.

Iath, home to the Queens of Summer and Winter. And way too many elves.

The structures of court mostly occupied a low, craggy butte on the western edge of Aléri. Kai's guide led her even further west until they met with a beaten-earth path that wound through waist-high grass set to whispers by a steady breeze. The sound reminded her of the ocean's endless murmurs. But this was a pale ocean, sere and shallow, edged in gold where the slanted breath of sunset stroked color along the blades of grass. Kai walked smooth and easy, with no trace of a limp.

That astounded her. The first time Dell had healed her surely ought to be the real marvel, but it was the more recent healing that boggled her brain. But that first time—over a year ago now—she hadn't been paying attention, being too close to the darkest of edges to be aware of more than the easing of pain. Plus, she'd hadn't known how to pay attention that time; it had taken her months to learn how to observe her body from the inside. She still had a lot to learn, but fourteen days ago she'd been able to watch while the chameleon reknit her crushed knee . . . and today she walked painlessly on the hard ground of Iath's central plains, following a white rabbit.

That's what her guide looked like, anyway. The colors of its thoughts proclaimed it something much different. Definitely sidhe, and probably an elf. A few of the Wild Sidhe could wear other seemings, but most couldn't. It was the elves who'd mastered illusion.

She was so bloody damn sick of elves.

Elves were not human. This was both true and obvious, but it was a truth Kai sometimes tripped over. Human and elf were, she thought, like water and vodka—two clear liquids that shared many qualities, but heaven help you if you threw the wrong one on a fire. The very existence of a court and the courtiers who peopled it underlined some of the similarities. Sidhe from multiple races and realms came here to show off, to exert their power or connect with the powerful, which made it not much different from Washington, D.C., the court of Henry VIII, or Caesar's Rome. Some came as guests. Some held positions in the court.

Kai was a guest. Her partner and lover was not. Nathan was no elf, however. He was Wild Sidhe. If the other sidhe races were like planets orbiting the elves, the Wild Sidhe were comets—affected by the gravitational pull of the most powerful race in their system, but living mostly apart and on their own terms. Nathan's position was as unique as he was. He was the Queen's Hound.

That was a position of power. Nathan had his own, innate power, too, and elves respected power. Kai, on the other hand, was pretty much nobody. Sure, there was a trace of sidhe blood in her ancestry, but not enough for her to register as sidhe. Not that she wanted to, but being human in Faerie could be a pain in the ass.

The cute little bunny had stopped a few yards ahead. One ear twitched. It looked back at her.

At least it didn't pull out a pocket watch and exclaim about being late. Maybe the Queen of Winter had never read *Alice in Wonderland*? Or maybe this particular minion didn't know how to play to the joke. From what Kai could tell, most elves didn't have much of a sense of humor. A sense of amusement, maybe, but that wasn't the same thing.

"I suppose not," a silvery voice said from behind her in flawless American English.

Kai jumped and spun. Ten paces back along the path stood a luminous woman dressed in white. The Queen of Winter always wore either white or black.

Beyond the color, Kai never noticed what the Queen's clothing looked like. Who would? Her presence overwhelmed even as her beauty pierced—a stark, inhuman beauty like the translucent glory of ice or a single wolf's call in the dead of winter. Her hair was black. Her skin was white. Truly white, not merely Caucasian, but a white that changed with the light, or maybe with her mood. Sometimes it made Kai think of camellia petals, inexpressibly pure and soft. Other times it was more like pearls, hard, and hinting at rainbows.

It took Kai a moment to gather herself after her first stunned reaction. It always did. Not that they'd met often. The first time they met, Winter had decided to send her on a three-part quest instead of killing her. They'd spoken each time Kai completed the first two parts of her quest, and again just as the last segment of her quest went so horribly wrong. The Queen hadn't held her to blame. There'd been too much wrong in that realm for any two people to fix, even when one of them was Nathan. So much wrong that, for the first time in over three thousand years, the two Queens had left their home realm at the same time.

Kai had seen what Winter and Summer could do, acting together. What they would do if lords of the sidhe broke Queens' Law. She shuddered at the memory and knelt on one knee, lowering her head.

"You may rise," the Queen told her.

Kai did, and found an extraordinary pair of eyes studying her. Winter's eyes were the color of water—no color and every color. At the moment they looked ash gray. Her skin, caressed by sunset, reminded Kai of an orange-kissed moon, and today her midnight hair fell to her hips, straight as rain. Small silver bells had been braided into it. They chimed sweetly when she tilted her head. "I thought the bunny shape might amuse you, but perhaps you're too irked with us to find amusement in such a conceit."

Why hadn't Kai heard those bells until this moment? Maybe the Queen had just now arrived. Maybe she'd been following Kai all along, but cloaked from any sense Kai possessed. Either was possible. "Perhaps I am," she agreed.

"You have been offered no discourtesy here."

No, she'd been courtesied half to death. Sometimes barbs lay beneath the exquisite politeness of the courtiers. Sometimes curiosity. Such an oddity Winter had chosen to invite to her court! And why? No doubt it was meant as a courtesy to her Hound, but Winter seldom acted from only one cause. "I'm sure the fault lies with me. This doesn't lessen my discomfort."

"Or your annoyance." The Queen's voice was light, her lips curved in a smile. "My court is difficult for a human. There are other humans here, however. Has not Malek made you welcome, as I asked?"

"He's been very helpful."

Winter tipped her head. "You dislike Malek."

She disliked most slimy little weasels, but it wouldn't do to say that. Kai didn't know if the Queen liked Malek, but she found him useful, mostly as a messenger. Like Kai, he was a one-off, with a Gift so rare it was thought to be unique among humans: he could cross between realms without a gate. Naturally, the sidhe believed this meant he had a trace of sidhe blood in his ancestry. The one thing she did like about the man was his quiet but firm insistence that he was human, period. "Malek is embarrassed by me. He's trying to help me overcome my deplorably human manners so I won't stick out so much at court. He hasn't had much success."

"Ah, I understand. Most humans wish to blend in when they are among us. You do not."

Anger that Kai had been suppressing for too long burst to the surface. "Blend in? Humans can't blend in with elves. No matter what we do, you will all remain more beautiful, more graceful, more steeped in power and art than we can ever hope to be. *Blending in* is a cheat. It blinds us to what is genuinely ours."

"True, though you may want to consider the utility of camouflage." She paused, her eyebrows lifting delicately. "I do have the right word? I refer to a nonmagical illusion that allows one to take on the seeming of one's surroundings."

Kai suspected she'd been gaping. "That's the right word. I was surprised that you agreed with me."

"Yes, that was obvious." Winter turned away. "The young always believe they've stumbled upon concepts their elders have never dreamed of. Walk with me."

Kai hurried to catch up. As she reached the Queen, the path obligingly widened to allow them to walk side by side. It was disconcerting.

For several minutes they simply walked. Kai wondered why she was here, what the Queen wanted . . . because she wanted something. Kai couldn't see Winter's colors, but she felt sure the Queen had a purpose.

A small smile touched Winter's lips. "You think I am without whim?"

"I think even your whims have purpose."

"It bothers you when I read your thoughts."

"It's a bit one-sided, isn't it?" Not that Kai could read thoughts, but she saw them. With almost everyone else, she saw the colors and patterns of their thoughts. Not with Winter.

"It bothers you," she repeated, "but it doesn't frighten you. I don't frighten you."

Kai, too, could repeat herself. "Because even your whims have purpose. You're unlikely to kill me or seriously harm me. You love Nathan and wouldn't lightly bring him the pain of—of such sundered loyalties. You might turn my life upside down again, but not for a small reason. Not out of pettiness. And while I can't hide my thoughts from you, you don't require or expect me to be anything other than what I am." It was oddly relaxing, in fact, to walk and talk with this queen.

"Has Nathan not told you that truth is part of my domain?"

Kai frowned. It was hard to conceive of truth as a domain, yet if it were, it would belong to Winter, wouldn't it? Truth was hard, uncompromising, even ruthless at times. It's what was left when everything else was stripped away. And it explained why Kai found it necessary—even easy—to speak candidly with a woman who'd ruled for longer than any human civilization had existed. A woman who, with her sister, could rearrange continents. "How do your courtiers manage?" she blurted. The words "candid" and "elf" normally didn't belong in the same sentence, and the courtiers she'd met had mastered the art of the oblique.

The Queen's expression didn't change, but a spark of—amusement? Glee?—lit those changeable eyes. "I am not easy to serve."

Kai surprised herself with a quick grin.

They walked on without speaking. Kai held her tongue both because she was supposed to—one didn't speak until the Queen indicated a desire for speech—and from sheer intimidation. But they walked side by side, so she wasn't looking directly at that heart-stuttering beauty. The awe factor faded, and their silence grew easy. It reminded Kai of walks she'd taken with her grandfather, who'd taught her the value of sharing silence.

At one point Winter crouched and for several minutes watched a thin string of ants cross the path, her fascination as keen as any three-year-old's. At another, their footsteps startled a flock of birds into the air, and Kai paused to watch their dark shapes rise like smoke into the sky. That time, the Queen waited for her. Eventually Kai realized that their path did have a goal—a pool, dark and still and round. An island of water in the ocean of grass. At the pool, the path transformed from earth to small, pale stones to encircle it, forming a perfect frame for the dark water. Four benches sat at the cardinal points around the pool.

Winter sat on one bench—the one at due north—and motioned for Kai to sit, too. As if there had been no break in their conversation, the Queen went on, "Because truth is my domain, I am concerned with the effect my people have on yours. The human skill at mimicry renders you more vulnerable than other races. Malek is a good example. He has grown almost elfishly subtle over the years. He would be devastated to learn that his skill failed with you. I suppose he didn't allow for your Gift . . . ?" The barest hint of a question lifted her voice at the end.

Was that a trick question? The Queen had asked that Kai not reveal to anyone at court what her Gift was. Some of them had the Sight, of course, but seeing Kai's magic wouldn't tell them much. She had it on good authority that she looked like a binder, but the Queen would have killed a binder, not invited her to court, so even those able to see her magic wouldn't understand what they saw. "As far as I know, Malek has no idea what my Gift is."

The Queen chuckled. It was a surprisingly human sound, quite unlike the wind-chime beauty of elfin laughter. "Had you not realized why I asked you not to speak of your Gift? It's been amusing, watching everyone scramble around, trying to figure you out. I would be very disappointed in Malek if he hadn't located your teacher by now."

That was a jolt. She'd known the elves were curious about her, but that they—and Malek—might have been surreptitiously investigating her—

"Nathan doesn't care for court, either," Winter said, "though he enjoys the hunts. You dislike Malek."

Mental whiplash could be a problem in conversations with elves. Kai took a moment to sort out her thoughts. "You used him as an example. I suppose he's just that for me—an example of what I fear could happen to me, if I were around your people too long."

"No, you wouldn't become like Malek. You're more likely to suffer a mysterious accident caused by, but not traceable to, your human passion for what you consider honesty."

That startled a laugh from Kai. "Wouldn't someone who claims truth as her domain value honesty?"

"The human desire to pen truth up in words makes little sense to me. Truth is vast, minute, immutable, and ever-changing. It is certainly too vast to express itself through a single race—something my people at times forget." She leaned forward and picked up one of the smooth, pale stones and studied it—then abruptly chucked it at Kai.

Without thinking, Kai caught it.

"What would you do with that stone?"

Kai looked down at it and ran her thumb over the smooth surface. "Probably put it back where it was. It looks good here."

The Queen nodded. "There is beauty in the stone on its own, but it is especially pleasing set with others like it. Yet if I were to set it in some places—on a mosaic floor, perhaps, or among the pillows on a divan—it would look out of place, even ugly."

"Are you telling me that I belong with my own kind?"

"Children are often prickly and self-conscious. It leads to false assumptions."

"I'm prickly about being called a child, too." In sidhe eyes, humans were all children—young, boisterous, unpredictable. And sidhe law treated them as such.

"If it were in your power to change your status, would you do so?"

Kai went still. "How?"

"Malek is adept at elfish ways, yet he is not elf. As you noted, such mimicry has a cost. This cost was one reason your realm was interdicted until recently—to allow humans to develop away from our overwhelming example, that you might express your own truths."

"Um," Kai said, that being as much as she could manage while her view of human history reshuffled itself.

"But not all humans live in your realm. There are many and many of you scattered throughout my realms as well. If we are a problem for your people, you can be a problem for mine, as well." She turned her unearthly eyes on Kai. "I have a proposition for you, Kai Tallman Michalski."

ONE

San Diego, Two Months Later

MURPHY'S Law cuts across barriers of class, creed, species, and realm, Kai reflected as she stepped out of the clinic. She reached up to adjust the glasses she'd brought with her to the appointment, which had light-adaptive lenses. It didn't help.

"Over here!"

Kai squinted in the direction of the woman's voice. The bright blue of Arjenie's Prius was visible several yards away, but its shape was obscured by shifting blobs of pale color, as if the air were inhabited by zillions of translucent jellyfish bobbing merrily along. Kai sighed and looked down. The sidewalk was close, so there were fewer thought-remnants between it and her eyes. She could see the curb, so she aimed for it.

She made it to the end of what she was pretty sure was a white car, then had to look up again to get a bead on the Prius. And saw the man headed for her.

At least she thought it was a man. She only got glimpses of him. His thoughts were much more vivid than his physical form, clearer than the jelly-fish remnants. Almost solid, in fact—tawny gold laced with green and deep purple, with licks of wary pewter. It was that on-alert pewter that jacked up her heartbeat. The assassin who'd nearly killed her in Annabaka had thought in just that color. She dropped into a crouch and reached for Teacher.

Which, of course, wasn't there. She was in San Diego, not Annabaka, and people here tended to notice over a foot of steel sheathed at your hip. Especially cops.

"Hey." The man stopped. "You okay?"

She closed her eyes briefly in embarrassment. She knew that voice. Doug was one of Arjenie's guards. One of Kai's first patients here, too. She should have recognized his thought patterns. She'd worked on them. "Doug. Right. I'm, uh, not seeing properly."

"You said you might not. Need a hand?"

Want and need sometimes lived in different neighborhoods entirely. "Probably." She sounded surly. Try again. "Yes, thank you."

Doug took her arm and steered her to Arjenie's car. She climbed in. He left, no doubt headed for the car he and the other guard had used. Kai grabbed the seatbelt and pulled it around her.

"No stopping for coffee, I'm guessing," Arjenie said.

All Kai could see of the other woman was a dim shape topped by the red blur of her hair. Arjenie's colors were lovely, though—lots of shifting yellow, blue, and lavender at the moment, with a few disappointed or worried gray tendrils. Lovely and intricate and . . . engrossing.

Kai made herself look away. "Better not. Dammit, I hate having my eyes dilated. I was really looking forward to the best mocha in the city, too."

"We'll do it another time. Maybe after you get back from that visit to your grandfather?"

"Sure. If I'm still in the same realm, that is."

"There is that."

Finding a day when she and Arjenie could both get away hadn't been easy. Arjenie worked from home, which made flex-time possible, but a lot of her work was urgent. When someone in the FBI's Magical Crimes Division needed something researched, they usually needed the information thirty minutes ago. And for a while after she arrived, Kai had been flooded with patients.

Nathan's job had been over the moment he killed the artifact linked to the god of chaos. Kai's had begun that same moment. The knife had been used to force obedience on a lot of people, and that kind of compulsion damaged minds. Not everyone affected by the knife had wanted Kai's help, but enough had. She hadn't been able to leave to see her grandfather.

But she would, she reminded herself as Arjenie backed out of her parking spot. The most immediate healing was done. Several of her patients needed another session or two, and all of them should have follow-ups, but no one needed her right now. In three days, she and Nathan would head for Arizona to see the old man who was her only living relative.

Arjenie gave her a quick glance. "That dial-it-down technique of yours isn't working, I take it."

"Obviously I'm not as far along in my training as I thought." It had been over two years since the last time she'd had her eyes dilated at an exam. A lot had happened since then. She'd been sure this time would be different—sure, but not cocksure, which was why she'd asked for a ride.

"Or maybe it isn't you. Maybe the drops affect your Gift directly."

"I'm told that isn't likely."

"Oh, yes. By that woman who holds her nose oh-so-politely while she's teaching you."

Kai grinned. The phrase she'd used was, "the most polite disdain possible," when she told Arjenie about her teacher. "By Eharin, yes."

Arjenie snorted. "If she—shoot, I need to get that." She tapped the steering wheel to answer her phone. It was Doug, wanting an update on where they were going.

Much as Eharin made Kai grit her teeth, she was glad to have a teacher. Finding someone to help her learn how to manage her Gift hadn't been easy. Fact was, there simply weren't many mindhealers, and Kai had two knocks against her: she was human and she wasn't willing to apprentice. The top mindhealers hadn't been interested. Oh, a couple of them might have done it as a favor to Nathan, but she did not want him going into favor-debt on her behalf.

Price had been a factor, too, with the least important part of the cost being counted in currency. Information was the true coin of the Queens' realms. Nathan had handled that negotiation, of course. Under sidhe law, Kai was a minor, so the contract had to be between her teacher and Nathan. Kai didn't mind. No one unused to the Machiavellian nature of elves should try to cut a deal with one of them. Kai's form of the mindhealing Gift had complicated matters. As far as they'd been able to determine, she was the only mindhealer ever who actually saw thoughts. In sidhe terms, that made her a one-off, someone of mixed blood with a rare or unique Gift that was unlikely to breed true.

Finding out she had a bit of elf blood in her veins had been almost as much of a shock as learning she wasn't some kind of weird telepath the way she'd thought all her life. Kai didn't read thoughts. She saw them. She could change them. For twenty-seven years she'd tried her damnedest not to dabble around in other people's heads, and mostly she'd succeeded.

Now, though, she was supposed to dabble. Carefully. Very carefully.

Arjenie tapped the wheel again to disconnect. "I should've let Doug know our plans changed. I keep forgetting I have guards now. But what I was about to say is, how would Eharin know if those drops affect your Gift? Her mindhealing doesn't work like yours and she's never been to Earth, much less experienced tropicamide."

"Tropical who?"

"Tropicamide. It's the most commonly used mydriatic for eye exams." Arjenie stopped at the parking lot's exit. Traffic was heavy, and she'd need a big enough gap for her guards to follow in their white Toyota. At least Kai assumed that's what the blurry white shape behind them was. She couldn't see much of the car for the colors . . . fascinating colors.

Dammit. Having her eyes dilated had never been this bad before. Kai made herself focus on what Arjenie was saying.

". . . though it's possible they used phenylephrine today. You should probably find out, because if you get the surgery you'll be using drops for several days, and you don't want to use whatever they gave you today. Probably the surgeon will prescribe something that lasts longer than tropicamide, but still. You'll want to be sure. Assuming you got a green light for the surgery?"

Kai had to grin. Arjenie insisted she wasn't a genius, but

she came close enough for most purposes. "You knew all that right off the top of your head."

"I looked into Lasik surgery for myself at one point." At last a large enough gap in the traffic flow appeared and Arjenie pulled out. "That was mostly wishful thinking. My peculiar healing would just put my eyes back the way they are now. It might take a couple years, but that's likely what would happen."

"Because changing the setting for a part of the body takes body magic, not healing."

"Right, and I've got zero body magic. So did the surgeon consider you a good candidate for the surgery?"

"It's a go if I decide to do it." The pretty blue of Arjenie's thoughts had sharpened to an eye-popping turquoise that danced with the yellow and green in such an intricate way, it was hard not to watch. Hard not to . . . hell. If she wasn't careful, she was going to fall into fugue. She hadn't had that problem in a long time.

"If?" Arjenie said. "I thought you'd made up your mind."

"I thought I had, too." Kai sighed and closed her eyes and leaned her head against the headrest.

These days she could dial her Gift up or down, depending on the needs of the moment. Mostly she left it dialed down enough that thought-remnants weren't visible and current thoughts were the merest watercolor overlay. That sure wasn't working now. Having her eyes dilated had always sharpened her Gift to a distracting intensity, but it had never been this bad before.

Eharin was wrong, dammit. The problem wasn't with Kai's perception of how her Gift worked. The problem was with the drops themselves. They'd screwed with her Gift.

There *was* another option . . .

"What happened? You were pretty keen on getting your eyes fixed."

"It's the timing. Dr. Piresh won't be able to schedule me for another month."

"And you don't know if you'll be here that long."

Kai nodded. "I could go ahead and set it up, I suppose, and cancel if Nathan gets sent somewhere." Or she could just stay here while he did his Queen's bidding. The idea of waving goodbye as he went off to who-knows-where to do God-knew-what did not sit well, which was just silly. Nathan had managed to keep himself alive for a few hundred years before they met. He'd be fine without her.

She wasn't sure she'd be fine without him. Unhappy with herself, she sought a distraction. "Coffee. I want some. We should go in search of mochas like we'd planned."

"You think that's a good idea?" Arjenie clearly didn't.

"I know a way to shut my Gift off."

"Oh?" Her voice brightened with curiosity. "Is it hard to do?"

"Not really. I'll need Dell's help to turn it back on, so I won't be able to do that until we get back to Clanhome." Kai's familiar could have come into San Diego with her, but it was easier if she didn't. Cities were hard on Dell. "But that shouldn't matter."

"If it's easy, why didn't you already do it?"

"Well . . . being without my Gift is weird. And, uh, Eharin told me not to."

"If it's dangerous—"

"She didn't say that. She taught me how to turn it off, how to turn it back on, then told me not to do it until I'd had more advanced training that was not included in our deal. Then wouldn't explain why."

"She's an intellectual tease."

"Yeah." That was typical of Eharin's approach to teaching. She didn't object to Kai asking questions. She just ignored them. "Um. I should explain. This technique doesn't literally shut my Gift off. It sets up a loop so my Gift doesn't reach my awareness. If there is any danger, I'd guess that it lies in leaving the loop running too long."

"That makes sense. Some spells use loops to build up power. I've never heard of doing that with a Gift, but theoretically you might build up more power than you can handle and damage your channels."

"That's pretty much what I've been thinking." And it pleased her to have her guess seconded. "Eharin wouldn't confirm my theory, but she didn't say it was wrong. Though the sidhe talk about *kish*, not channels. *Kish* means matrix—an innate, unalterable ground that determines the form our magic takes—what kind of a Gift we have, what elements we've an affinity for, all kinds of things."

"Oh, I like that! Kish is not so much a pattern as the ground for a pattern?"

Arjenie had grasped the concept about ten times faster than Kai had. "That's right. It's the essence from which a pattern grows."

"That's a better model than channels. We tend to think of channels as mostly two-dimensional, like the patterns water makes as it gathers in rivulets and streams. Even if we see them as three-dimensional, like blood vessels, it's not all that helpful a model when magic is really more multidimensional and antidimensional."

"You just zoomed way past me."

"Sorry. What I mean is that the unquantifiable nature of spatial references inherent in true chaos combined with the inversion of—"

Kai laughed. That startled her eyes open. She squeezed them shut again. The colors were now so bright they hurt. It had never been this bad before, not even during a big thunderstorm. "You're not helping, though you did provide me with a new fantasy. I'd love to see you go up against Eharin."

"I wish I could talk to her, even if she is a pain in the butt." Arjenie sounded wistful. "I could learn so much. But maybe looping your Gift isn't a great idea, given the potential risk."

"I've done it before, and left it looped for hours with no problem. We'll have plenty of time for coffee."

"If we're right about the problem. It seems like Eharin would have at least nodded when you suggested that, even if she didn't want to take the time to explain."

Kai snorted. "What, and admit the pathetic little human is right about something? Aside from how much she'd dislike that, I don't think she ignores my questions to save herself the bother of explaining. I think her plan is to honor our deal to the letter while leaving me so frustrated I'll agree to renegotiate. Probably she wants something she didn't get in our initial deal. Probably something from Nathan." They all wanted something from Nathan, and were happy to use Kai to try and get it.

All except one, that is. The Queen of Winter already had Nathan's service. Now she wanted Kai's.

"Devious," Arjenie commented. "But elves dote on devious, don't they?"

"Oh, yeah. Give them a choice between straight and twisty and they'll take twisty every time."

"Are the other sidhe like that?"

"Some. The elves are sort of the United States of the sidhe realms. They aren't the only ones with power, but they've got more of it than anyone else, and their culture pervades the realms. Not everyone adopts it, but no one is untouched by it." Kai frowned at the darkness behind her closed lids . . . which wasn't entirely dark anymore. "Arjenie, my eyes are closed."

"Um, yes."

"I'm seeing colors anyway." Colors that brightened even as she spoke. Sharpened. And *pulled.*

"Did that ever happen before?"

"No. It's not supposed to. I'm going to loop my Gift."

"Are you sure—"

"I'm sure that being pulled into fugue is a bad idea." The fugue state was almost identical to the one she entered to heal—the same kind of "almost" that separated flying from falling.

"Oh." A beat of silence. "Do you need me to pull over?"

"Nope. I just have to focus." While she still could.

Until Kai was catapulted into Faerie eighteen months ago, all her training had come from her grandfather. Joseph Tallman was a Navajo shaman, and his techniques were very different from those of the sidhe. Eharin considered Kai's method of centering slow and inelegant, but she'd admitted that it worked. So first Kai prayed silently, asking the Powers for their aid and blessing. When she felt centered, she touched her lower belly, her chest, and her lips, whispering a word with each touch, feathering power into the touch through the word. She did that three times.

Kai opened her eyes. And grinned at the crisp, clear world around her. "Better call Doug and tell him we changed our minds again."

TWO

FAGIOLI—which meant "beans" in Italian, according to Arjenie—was noisy, crowded, and charming, with a large patio to catch the overflow. The stone walls enclosing the patio were mostly hidden by an enthusiastic vine smothered in bright pink flowers. Kai and Arjenie sat on that patio in air soft with spring and heady with the mixed scents of flowers and brewing coffee.

Also chocolate. Kai inhaled deeply before sipping on the best knock-off mocha Frappuccino in the world, which made it the best in all the worlds. Coming home had been wonderful, but kind of weird, too. Not what she'd expected. She'd changed on her journey, of course, but she hadn't expected those changes to make everything here look so . . . different.

But her mocha coffee drink was everything it was supposed to be.

Across from her, her new friend was sipping her own mocha. Aside from her hair, Arjenie Fox looked like the geek she was. Her eyes were an unusual aquamarine color, but hidden as they were behind her glasses, they didn't draw attention. Her face was narrow, her skin pale with a scatter of freckles. She was short and thin and had a small limp when she walked, due to a long-ago injury.

But that hair! It wasn't just red. It was RED. That shout of color burst into curls the way birds burst into song or fireworks erupt in temporary stars. Today Arjenie had set a dam in place—a headband that held back that wild froth of curls.

Kai sipped again. "And you claim this is only the third-best coffee shop in the city?"

Arjenie grinned. "According to the coffee snobs I hang out with these days, anyway. You should hear a bunch of lupi arguing about coffee. Is the subtle balance of Ethiopian beans superior to the aromatic acidity of Kenyan, or is it a tad bland? Or maybe it's Costa Rican beans with the subtle balance. Whatever. They can't agree on who grows the best coffee, who roasts the best coffee, or who brews the best coffee, but they have reached consensus on the third-best place in San Diego to buy a cup, and this is it."

"But with the very best mochas."

"Amen. I guess they don't have mochas in the sidhe realms?"

"There is no coffee in the sidhe realms," Kai said gloomily.

Arjenie's eyebrows shot up. "None?"

"Not in any of the realms I was in. Mostly people hadn't ever heard of it."

"That's so sad. How many realms did you visit, anyway? Unless that's one of the things you can't talk about—"

"Oh, that's no secret. Four. Well, five if you count Edge. Some don't consider it a true realm, since it's so small—more of a between-place. Though I wonder if that's the real reason it gets demoted. Edge is more about gnomes, not so much about elves."

"Count Edge," Arjenie said firmly, then paused to lick whipped cream off her upper lip. "Just in case it bothers a snooty elf or two."

Kai grinned. "I like the way you think."

Arjenie cocked her head. "Which was your favorite realm? Not Iath, I'm guessing."

"Definitely not." The Queens' realm was all about elves.

"But you didn't dislike them all."

"No . . . I do have some good memories." Absently Kai's hand went to the silver cuff on her left wrist and the cabochon jewels set there. She thought of an old man and a most uncanny child and smiled. "I liked Deredon. It's more rugged than most—more primitive, I guess, if you consider wilderness primitive. A lot of Wild Sidhe live there. A fair number of humans, too. It's a chancy place, but all the realms are chancy."

"Isn't that where you got your amulet, the one Cullen's so eager to study?"

Kai nodded. "He wanted me to leave it with him, but the amulet's tuned to me. If I take it off, it starts losing that tuning right away. I've let him look at it while I'm wearing it a couple times. That gets pretty boring, just sitting there while he stares and scribbles notes in the air, but—"

Frenzied yapping broke into their conversation. Kai twisted around to see.

A few tables away, a small dog was trying desperately to attack Doug and his partner. The dog's flustered owner tugged on the leash attached to his harness. She finally picked him up. "I am so sorry. He's usually such a friendly thing."

"Smells my dogs on me, I bet," Doug said easily. "I've got three."

"Terriers," Arjenie whispered, "do not like the way lupi smell. Most dogs react to them, but terriers tend to consider their smell a challenge. My aunt has a Jack Russell named Havoc, which is the perfect name for him. When Havoc and Benedict first met—did I tell you about that already?"

"No, and I want to hear."

"It was soon after Benedict and I became a couple. We drove back to Virginia to spend Christmas with my family. Now, this was the first time for him to meet them, and vice versa. Poor baby. He was so anxious, and things didn't go at all the way he'd hoped."

Arjenie's "poor baby" was over six feet of pure warrior. "And you can tell Benedict is anxious . . . how?"

Arjenie grinned. "He looks even more grimly determined than usual. Anyway, we pulled up out front . . ."

She went on to tell a story involving Havoc, a skinwalker, at least two native Powers and several members of her family. Kai wouldn't have believed it coming from someone else—not with her Gift shut down, anyway—but Arjenie was painfully honest. It was one of the things Kai liked best about her.

"You think it was really Coyote?" she said when Arjenie finished.

"Oh, yes. Benedict was sure of it."

"And if he's sure, you are." And that, Kai thought, was the other thing the two of them had in common. They were both in love with someone they trusted all the way down—

"Hey, it's not like he's never wrong. But he was wearing his knowing face, not the stubborn one. I saw the stubborn face this morning when he insisted that I bring guards with me today. He might be right, he might not, but he was surely stubborn."

Someone who could be unbelievably pigheaded—

"His knowing face, though—that's how he looks when he talks about running four-footed. He *knows* what that's like. Stubborn doesn't come into the picture."

—someone who wasn't human. Nathan couldn't turn furry the way Arjenie's lover did. He had only one shape, and that was very much a man's shape, but he'd been born a hellhound. "What do you do when he's being stubborn?"

"Depends on if it's stubborn-reasonable or stubborn-idiotic. The guards, now, I have to admit that's reasonable. Someone could try to grab me to use against Benedict. I'm not much of a threat to the Enemy, but he is."

Kai's lupi hosts were at war. So were the humans around them, but mostly they didn't know it. Their enemy was an Old One they usually referred to as the Great Bitch or the Great Enemy. Battling an Old One would have made for a short and lopsided war if *she* had been able to conduct her battles in person. But *she* had been locked out of the realms when the Great War ended over three thousand years ago, so she had to fight through proxies—like the one whose possession of a forbidden artifact had brought Kai and Nathan back to Earth a few weeks ago.

Kai wondered if Arjenie felt as matter-of-fact about the possibility of being kidnapped as she sounded. She couldn't, could she? Without her Gift, Kai couldn't tell. It was disconcerting. "And if he's being stubborn and unreasonable?"

Arjenie's eyebrows lifted. "You might as well tell me, you know."

"Ah . . ."

"Nathan seems like a reasonable guy, but no one is reasonable about everything all the time."

Reluctantly Kai smiled. "I'm being obvious, huh?"

"Oh, yes."

"It's this business about getting my eyes fixed. Nathan thinks surgery is barbaric. He . . . I told you why Dell can't help me, didn't I?"

"She doesn't know how to change just one part of a body."

"Pretty much, yeah. But there are people who could fix my eyes in a blink. No surgery, no pain, no problems. I'd go from 20/200 to 20/20. Maybe better than 20/20." Kai paused. Nathan expected her to keep this secret. But the offer had been made to her, not him, right? So it was up to her to decide how much of a secret it should be. "People like the Winter Queen."

"I'm sure she could, but—wait. You mean she'd do that?"

"For a price. She wants me to take service with her."

"Well, that bitch."

Kai laughed. Arjenie never cursed, not even the occasional "damn," which made it even funnier. "It's not like she's being evil to make the offer, but I don't like the idea of putting myself in her hands. I'd have to vow to her, you see. And she to me," Kai added, wanting to be fair. "And there are some strong benefits to that. I'd get the very best training, for one. I'd also become a legal adult, which—"

"Wait, you aren't one now?"

"Not in sidhe eyes. I'm human. The trace of sidhe blood in my makeup may be the reason for my Gift—they certainly think so—but it's not enough to make me sidhe, so I'm not one of the grownups. Not in the realms." Kai paused. And blinked. The flowers on the vine behind Arjenie were moving. Fluttering. But there wasn't any wind. "That is so weird."

The flowers burst up into the air.

Not flowers. Butterflies. Hundreds of bright pink butterflies exploded silently from the leaves of the vine where, a moment ago, they'd been growing. They blossomed up into the air in a cloud of frothing pink.

People exclaimed. Four tables away, two chairs scraped. "Arjenie—wink out!" Doug called.

Kai didn't remember standing, but she was on her feet when Arjenie vanished. One second the redhead was sitting in her chair, looking up at butterflies that shouldn't exist. The next, that chair was empty.

A lone butterfly landed on Kai's arm.

"Ouch!" Without thinking, she slapped it—then stared at her arm. Pink dust from the slaughtered butterfly smeared her skin. A bright bead of blood glistened amid the pink. The pretty little butterfly had *bit* her.

The pink cloud descended.

NATHAN moved to the free throw line, having been thoroughly fouled by a wiry fellow named Carl who could jump like a bullfrog.

Nathan hadn't played basketball until three weeks ago, but he'd watched the game often and thought he was catching on pretty well. For a very long time he'd avoided playing any sport because of the difficulty in holding himself to a human level of competence, but he no longer had to hide what he was. Since they arrived at Nokolai Clanhome he'd played pickup with his hosts several times. He liked it. Werewolves were as fast as he was and almost as strong.

They were also highly competitive. Nathan grinned as the ball sailed smoothly through the hoop. So was he.

Cheers and jeers rang out from both teams and from those who'd gathered to watch. There were several women among the watchers. None of them were werewolves, of course, that being a sex-linked inheritance.

Lupi, not werewolves, he corrected himself, using his T-shirt to mop his face. They preferred to be called lupi, and any people should be allowed to name themselves. But the habits of years are hard to break, and he'd thought of them as werewolves for roughly four centuries now. Avoided them for that long, too, since they could sniff out what he was—or at least that he wasn't human—and passing for human had been important during his long stranding here. Plus his scent was inherently challenging to a lupus, which could cause trouble.

But now he was here openly, no longer pretending to a humanity he didn't possess, and the Nokolai leader—their Rho—had named him *ospi*. That meant clan-guest. These particular lupi seemed to be dealing well with the provocation of his scent.

Turned out he really liked playing with werewolves.

Over on the sidelines, his phone trilled. "It's Kai," he explained, and headed that way.

"Hey, what about our game?" someone on the other team called. Another one jeered, "She calls, you come running?"

Since that was self-evidently true, Nathan didn't bother to answer. If the man didn't understand that Kai was more important, words wouldn't convince him.

"Shut up, Harris," a big man said.

The big man was watching the game, not playing in it, mainly because no one wanted to be on the team that played against him. So Nathan had been told, and he believed it. Benedict Jones—whose Native American features didn't go with the surname—was in charge of security and training at Nokolai Clanhome, and he was more than simply good at his job.

The first time Nathan sparred with Benedict, he'd lost.

That had gotten his attention. This form wasn't as deadly as his original body, but he hadn't been defeated in unarmed combat in nearly three hundred years. Then it had been a pair of Chinese monks, and he'd promptly joined their order so he could learn from them. He hadn't had the opportunity to train with anyone who posed a challenge in a very long time, but hadn't thought it mattered. One of his Gifts was what might be called perfect muscle memory. Once he learned how to do something, his body *knew* that move.

He saw now that he'd been wrong. His body remembered everything he'd taught it, but training was about the mind as well as the body. His speed had suffered, too, from the lack of a real challenge.

When Nathan and Benedict fought their second match, they'd used knives. Nathan won that one. It would have been amazing if he hadn't. The long knife was his weapon, and he was very good with smaller knives, too. He knew of one person, a crotchety old elf named Samision, who could defeat him with a sword and might be his equal with a knife, but there was only one being who could definitely best him, knife-to-knife. The Huntsman could not be defeated by any weapon.

For their third bout, he and Benedict had returned to unarmed fighting. That match had lasted over two hours before they decided to call it a draw. Nathan was confident he could kill Benedict if he had to. That was his Gift, after all. He wasn't sure he could defeat the man short of killing him. It was really very intriguing.

As Nathan reached the place he'd left his phone, Benedict's phone rang. The back of Nathan's neck prickled with alarm. Benedict's Arjenie was with Kai. If they were both calling at the same time . . . he answered his phone. "What's wrong?"

"Now, don't freak out. I'm fine. Arjenie's fine, too—she's busy telling Benedict that right now. She wasn't even bitten."

Nathan's heartbeat didn't pick up. It settled as his senses sharpened. He spoke very evenly. "But you were."

"I've got a lot of little bitty owies, that's all. There's no real damage, but I did bleed, and you know how Dell is about my blood being anywhere but inside my body. She's determined to come to me, no matter how much reassurance I send. I think I managed to persuade her to wait for you by the gate, so could you pick her up on your way?"

"What bit you?"

Kai sighed. "Carnivorous butterflies."

THREE

"**DOESN'T** bloody make sense," the man in the passenger seat muttered . . . not for the first time.

"Not yet," Nathan said, slowing as he approached the gate. Lupi lived in clans; each clan claimed some amount of land which they called a clanhome. Nokolai Clanhome, where he and Kai were guests, lay forty minutes from San Diego. Its boundaries were marked by both a fence and an immaterial claiming bearing some resemblance to a sidhe lord's land-tie. Guards patrolled the fence, with one pair always near the gate. "It will."

Several of those playing basketball had been guards, so Benedict hadn't had to wait to collect a squad to take with him. He would have had to wait for the clan's sorcerer, however, if Nathan hadn't offered to. Nathan had several reasons to make that offer.

First, time wasn't a major factor. Kai wasn't really damaged, and the guards who'd been with Arjenie had killed all of the butterflies. At least they thought they had. It wouldn't have been easy. Small prey like that could be hard to catch, but apparently the butterflies had been so intent on biting people that they hadn't tried to get away.

Second, a sorcerer was apt to be useful. Nathan might

know more than most in this realm about magic, but he lacked the Sight. That was an uncommon Gift among his people, and even more rare in humans.

Not that Cullen Seabourne was human. He went beyond rare to unique, being the only Gifted lupus on Earth, and therefore the only one in existence. Cullen was also a consultant for the FBI, though the Unit agent he usually worked with was currently on her honeymoon. Still, Cullen had worked with the local office several times, and that should help them gain access to the scene.

Third, and most important, Nathan had offered to wait for Cullen because of Dell. He needed to pick her up, which meant he needed to take his own vehicle. While the chameleon had excellent control for a relatively new sentient, it was best not to trap her in a small space with half a dozen lupi. She didn't like the way they smelled.

Yet she did like Cullen Seabourne.

It had taken Nathan months to work his way from toleration to real trust with Kai's familiar. Within thirty minutes of meeting Cullen, Dell had allowed the sorcerer to pet her. When Nathan asked Kai about it, she'd shrugged. "She thinks he's funny."

Nathan stopped a few yards short of the gate. The two guards wore matching stony expressions. They were clearly very conscious of the smoke-colored feline stretched out on the sandy ground twenty feet away, her tail twitching. In this, her true form, Dell was over eight feet long, nose to tail-tip. Her oversize pads hid claws that would do a grizzly proud. She needed those claws; the teeth in her oddly shaped muzzle weren't made for biting. Chameleons consumed blood and magic, not flesh.

The blood part of her diet had been provided for by a small herd of sheep. The magic part was augmented now by the Winter Queen's gift: a dusky purple gem set into a band around one ankle, a gem capable of storing a vast amount of magic and disgorging it at whatever rate Dell required. Such a talisman, made by Winter herself, was literally priceless in Faerie. Here on Earth, no one had any idea what it was, although Cullen Seabourne had asked. Three times.

Nathan put the vehicle in park and got out. Dell flowed to

her feet and started for him. He shook his head at her. "Kai is in the city."

Dell stopped. Her ears flattened. Her lips lifted in a snarl.

Nathan waited. Dell knew very well she couldn't go into a crowded human city looking like that.

"She understands you?" one of the guards asked.

"Dell understands a fair amount of English, but language doesn't come easily for her. She's a gestalt thinker."

"Gestalt?"

From the car came Cullen's voice. "Like a new wolf. She doesn't think in words."

The chameleon cast a snarling glance at the guards.

"I'm here," Nathan told her. Meaning that he would guard her during her transformation, when she was vulnerable. He thought a moment and added, "*Not* Cynna. She would stand out too much."

Dell gave him a haughty look meant to say that *of course* she wouldn't choose such a distinctive form, but Nathan suspected she might have. Dell loved what she thought of as Cynna's markings—the tattoos that covered most of her skin. A couple times now she'd disconcerted people at Clanhome by wearing Cynna's form when she came down from the node to see Kai.

Dell huffed out a breath and began her change.

The chameleon's transformation looked nothing like those of the lupi. Took longer, too. Her fur went first, soaked up into skin the same shade of gray. Then muscle, flesh, bone, and sinew melted into a thick gray ooze that briefly held Dell's original shape before flowing into a new one.

One of those stoic lupi guards made an "ewww" sound.

It was probably the eyeballs, Nathan thought. They'd disconcerted him at first, too. Dell always left them for last, so they bobbed around on the viscous gray surface of her transforming body until she had the shape she wanted. Then they wandered to the front of the reshaped head.

That head was rapidly sprouting hair now. The rest of the details shaped themselves, and a few moments later an apparently human woman stood there, holding out one hand imperatively. She wore the Queen's gift around her right wrist and nothing else.

Dell had chosen one of her favorite "hiding" forms, a blended-race woman with features that managed to be unremarkable rather than exotic. Here she'd probably be taken for Mexican with a trace of Asian ancestry. "Pass me the dress, will you?" Nathan said to Cullen.

A cotton dress came sailing out the window. Nathan caught it and tossed it to Dell. Dell preferred dresses or robes to pants and refused to wear underwear. After they arrived, Kai had bought her a few loose dresses so the omission wouldn't be too noticeable.

A moment later, the chameleon slid into the backseat wearing a demure brown dress with tiny blue flowers. Nathan closed the door and got back behind the wheel.

Dell looked at Cullen. Her nostrils flared. "Smell Cynna."

Cullen heaved a sigh. "Ryder's napping. Cynna and I were taking advantage of that, but we hadn't gotten very far. You look nice, Dell, but I like your other form better."

"So does she," Nathan said, putting the SUV in gear and accelerating through the open gate. "Human forms feel weak to her."

"She loses strength when she changes?"

That would seem odd to a lupus. "It's a matter of innate abilities versus learned skills. Shifting her coloring, now, that's innate, like those colorful lizards you have here. The ability to change her entire form is innate, too, but she has to have a pattern to copy, and she can't edit those patterns. She has to use all or nothing."

"So if the person she copies has a mole, she will, too?"

Nathan nodded. "This form isn't as fully human as it looks, which is why her sense of smell remains good. That's one reason she likes this form even if it does feel weak to her. She retains a few things regardless of her form. Her blood stays the same, as does her cells' ability to hold magic. Kai thinks she must retain her brain structure, too. She thinks the same way no matter how she's shaped."

"Huh." Cullen thought that over briefly, then shook his head. "Her brain must transform to some degree. The skull's a different shape."

Nathan shrugged. Cullen wanted details he didn't have.

"Go fast," Dell said suddenly. "Heal Kai."

"Wait a minute," Cullen said, looking at Nathan. "You can heal? Someone other than yourself, I mean."

"Not me," Nathan explained. "Dell. She can do it with Kai because of their bond, and it's really body magic, not healing. The result is the same, but it takes a lot more power." Which Dell had now, thanks to the Queen's gift, though she still stayed near the node much of the time, saving the gem's power for an emergency.

Nathan used to think that the mage who'd originally created the familiar bond in Dell had been a touch crazy. A chameleon seemed a peculiar choice. But the obvious drawback—Dell's need for magic—turned out to also be a plus. That need had caused her species to develop the ability to store an enormous amount of power, which could be drawn upon through the familiar bond.

The other plus was her body magic . . . and what that meant.

Most mages didn't take familiars because the risk outweighed the benefits. The death of a familiar would, at best, magically cripple the mage for days or weeks. At worst, it killed. The reverse was true, too. Dell had survived the breaking of the familiar bond with her mage when she was hurled to Earth when the realms collided at the Turning, but she'd been in bad shape by the time Kai found her. She'd used up her vast reserves of magic, and her hunger had been deep and terrible—and not just for magic. She'd been so alone. So very alone.

Until Kai. When the familiar bond broke, it didn't go away. Some combination of Dell's knowledge, Kai's Gift, and the mystery of affinity had made it possible for Kai and Dell to anchor the raw, bleeding end of that bond in Kai. Later, that bond and Dell's frantic need to keep Kai alive had made it possible for the chameleon to use her body magic to save Kai's life . . . body magic that operated instinctively, rebuilding according to whatever pattern Dell had. The pattern she had for Kai was of a thirty-year-old human woman in excellent health.

No one knew exactly how long chameleons lived, but Dell's lifespan would likely be counted in centuries, not decades. Which meant, Nathan thought smugly, that Kai's likely would be, too. *If* she didn't get herself killed in some mundane or uncanny fashion that Dell couldn't fix in time. "Dell, has something else happened to Kai?"

"Bug bites. Blood. Go fast."

"Can't go very fast on this road. I'll speed up when we hit the highway." Dell hated it when Kai bled. Blood was food and life to the chameleon. Still, her level of anxiety bothered Nathan. Kai might downplay an injury to keep him from worrying, but she wouldn't outright lie about it. Could she be hurt worse than she realized?

"Bug bites," Cullen muttered. "How does that make sense? The Great Bitch has tried assassination, hellgates, demon-possessed doppelgangers, explosives, dworg, destroying the U.S. through mob rule, and destabilizing the entire realm. Those didn't work, so now she's using butterflies? I don't get it. Unless they're infected in some way—"

Nathan broke in as a thought occurred to him. "Dell, do the bug bites have poison? *Eriahu,*" he added, using the most general term for poison in the elfin tongue. Dell had known elfin longer than she had English, but her connection with Kai usually made English easier for her.

Dell growled.

"What does that mean?" Cullen said. "No, yes, maybe, shut up?"

"That's frustration. Either she doesn't know or she isn't sure what I mean." Gestalt thinkers sometimes showed amazing insight, but they processed information so differently that communication was difficult.

Nathan thought about the context of the last time he and Kai had discussed poison around Dell. Dell would understand that when he said "poison" just now, he hadn't meant "colorless, odorless liquid added to the Devrai ambassador's wine at an equinox celebration by an agent of the Osiga which killed him in thirty seconds," but she'd be puzzled by which attributes of that event he wanted her to apply to the current situation. Was he talking about a substance consumed at a particular time? One administered at a celebration, or one used by Osiga agents? Something that killed, something that lacked odor, something added to wine, or something frequently given to Devrai ambassadors?

Or maybe she was trying to sort through elements of that

event he'd never noticed. Dell's process was *different*. "Eh. Yes, I've confused her. I phrased my question badly. Dell, will the bug bites make Kai sick?"

A growl. Then, "Not now sick."

"Later sick?"

Silence.

"Dei're het ahm Kai *insit?"*

More silence. Then: "Dots, dots, dots!" She hissed, sounding very much as she did in her other form. *"Jisen dá, oranahmni!* Go fast."

"Dots?" Cullen repeated.

"Dots are what she calls words," Nathan explained.

"And the rest of it?"

"Roughly translated, 'shut up, dot-eater.' I think I've exhausted her patience with language."

None of them spoke again until they left the gravel road for the highway, where Nathan could, as promised, speed up. Eighty wouldn't be conspicuous along this stretch, he decided. "Arjenie has some skill with magic."

Cullen shook his head. "If you're wondering if she could check out Kai, the answer is no. She and I have talked spellcraft enough for me to be sure she doesn't have anything that would help."

"Arjenie wasn't bitten." Arjenie's Gift was far more useful than invisibility, as it extended to all the senses except touch and made her impossible to notice, but . . . "Normally, mind magic doesn't work on insects."

Cullen snorted. "And you think there's something normal about carnivorous butterflies?"

"Not," Dell said.

Cullen twisted to look at her. "They're not normal? Or they're not carnivorous?"

"Like Dell."

"Blood drinkers," Nathan said. "They drank Kai's blood?"

"Go fast," she said.

Maybe a hundred would be better.

"NO one is being admitted to the scene. Move away now to keep our access clear."

Nathan had nothing against cops. He'd been one himself for a time. But the officer stationed at the police cordon near the coffee shop was beginning to annoy him. "If you lack the authority to admit us, you need to contact your superior."

"No, sir, I do not. Orders are clear. The three of you need to move away."

"Look," Cullen said, "you've seen my ID. If the FBI is here—"

"I can't give you that information, but if they were here and if they wanted you to join them, they'd have let me know, wouldn't they?" There was a definite touch of smirk to his mouth.

Cullen's scowl should have melted the officious young officer into a puddle of cooperation. Instead the man stood even stiffer. "I've told you twice now to move on."

"It's a public goddamn sidewalk, asshole."

A sidewalk currently crowded with curiosity seekers and a couple reporters, one of whom was eyeing Cullen. He was certainly photogenic, but it was also possible the woman recognized him. Nathan touched Cullen's arm to get his attention and jerked his head to the left, where Benedict waited. For a moment he thought Cullen was going to stay and argue himself into getting arrested, but Benedict said his name. Cullen huffed out an impatient breath and obeyed.

Benedict and his men had arrived a bare five minutes ahead of Nathan. They'd been told to move along, too, and Benedict had chosen to seem to obey. Though he'd deployed his squad, only two of them were visible, and Benedict himself was waiting about twenty feet away. It was a good decision. This young cop was the type to react to intimidation by doubling down, and all Benedict had to do to look intimidating was breathe.

"I'm going to call Kai," Nathan said as they headed for Benedict. "Cullen, maybe you should call Ruben."

"Damn straight I will. I'm betting the FBI hasn't been called in at all. Whatever idiot is in charge decided to shut them out for some stupid reason, though this is clearly a Unit 12 matter. If—"

Dell spoke suddenly. "Kai pissed. Wants us come in."

Nathan glanced at her. "I imagine so. But she doesn't want

you to do anything, does she?" Such as break the young officer's neck so she could get inside.

Dell growled softly. Nathan took that for an affirmative.

They'd reached Benedict. Cullen pulled his phone out. "Dell, you going to be okay waiting a little longer? Ruben can get us in, but it may take—"

"No need," Benedict said. "Arjenie already called him." He nodded at the barricade, where a dirty white Ford was pulling up. "Guess he sent us this guy, since Lily's in France."

Cullen stopped and shook his head. "Huh. Who'd have thought I'd ever be glad to see the Big A?"

"He'll admit us?" Nathan asked.

"Yeah. He's an asshole, but he's not stupid."

The four of them headed back toward the barricade, where three people were getting out of the car—two men and a woman. It was obvious which one was in charge, but not because he looked the part. Derwin Ackleford, the special agent in charge of the FBI's local office, was a middle-aged Anglo, neither short nor tall, fat nor thin. He wore a suit the color of bland and a grade-A scowl.

Nathan had met Ackleford during the legal sort-out of the events that brought him and Kai back to Earth. The man was regular FBI, not part of their Magical Crimes Division, much less the special unit that investigated the most serious magical problems. While he had a smidgeon of a Gift, he preferred to think of himself as a null. He didn't like magic, didn't trust it, and knew damn little about it. Still, if he was reasonable about using the resources at hand—i.e., Nathan and Cullen—his ignorance didn't have to be a major problem.

"Ackleford," Cullen called as they drew near. "We need to get in there, and Dickhead over there isn't listening."

Ackleford, as usual, stank of cigarette smoke. He aimed his scowl at Cullen. "I know why you're here. But you two—" He pointed at Benedict, then at Nathan. "You two can go away. Believe it or not, I'm not here to reunite everyone with their girlfriends."

Benedict said, "You might find my nose helpful."

Ackleford considered that. The idea didn't make him any happier, but he said, "All right. But it's my turf, so my rules. As for you." He turned the scowl on Nathan. "Your girlfriend doesn't need you to hold her hand while someone sticks on a bandage or two. If she even needs bandages. Didn't sound like it. You can wait out here with—"

"Now, that's short-sighted," Nathan said. "I know a lot about magic."

"I've got Seabourne for the woo-woo stuff."

"I have knowledge that Cullen doesn't."

Ackleford knew that Nathan was sidhe and that he served the Queen of Winter. Not that he understood who and what Winter was, no more than he knew what exactly Nathan was. But he had at least been told about her. "This have something to do with your elf queen?"

"I don't know yet."

"You get your visa problem straightened out?"

"I'm all official now." Nathan had a passport issued by the Queen of Winter, but getting an entry stamp had been a bit of a problem. He hadn't come into the U.S. in the usual way, for one thing. For another, other realms had been myth to the people here for a long time. That had changed, but while the U.S. had recently altered the legal definition of "country" to include nation-states not part of Earth, the rest of the legal apparatus hadn't caught up yet. In the end, the secretary of state had had to issue a special allowance.

"That helps, but—" Ackleford looked at Cullen. "Seabourne? You want him underfoot?"

"Hell, yes. Were you really considering not using him?"

"Hell, yes. But if you want him, I can live with it. You." He jabbed a finger at Dell. "Who are you, and why are you here?"

She didn't answer, though she studied Ackleford intently. Nathan spoke for her. "She's called Dell. She needs to see Kai, too. It's important."

"Dell. That your first name or last?"

"Just Dell," Nathan said.

"She can answer for herself, Hunter."

"Actually, she can't," Cullen said. "Not easily. She doesn't use language well. And no, I won't explain here—see the reporter headed our way?—but you need to let her see Kai."

Dell must have figured out that this man was the key to getting to Kai. She spoke to him. "Kai pissed. Needs me."

"So you do talk. What does she need you for?"

"Bug bites. Needs me fast." She looked at Nathan. "Fast, fast, fast!"

"Special Agent," Nathan said, "I need to get Dell to Kai. Dell hasn't been able to tell me why, but if she says 'fast,' I believe her."

Behind Ackleford's abrasive manner lay a sharp mind. The man looked sour enough to curdle milk, but he said, "All right. Don't make me regret this. I probably will, but you can at least try not to turn this into a complete clusterfuck. Come on."

At the barricade he treated the young cop to his scowl. "Where the hell's your sign-in sheet? You letting people on-scene without them signing in? Burns, stay here and show the dickhead how to set up a sign-in sheet. See if he's got any clue who has already entered. Probably not, but—"

"Sir," the cop interrupted desperately, "a sign-in sheet isn't needed because no one is allowed to enter the scene at this time. We're treating it as a biohazard zone, so—"

"Yeah?" Ackleford pulled out his ID case. "Well, I'm Special Agent Derwin Ackleford. This is now my fucking scene, and I want a fucking sign-in sheet."

FOUR

A police lieutenant with coarse gray hair, sixty extra pounds, and breasts lay in wait for Ackleford just inside Fagioli. Battle was joined immediately. Nathan didn't wait to watch Ackleford dispose of his opponent. His ability to go unnoticed was minor, but it worked a treat in situations like this. People would see him just fine as he edged past the combatants. They just wouldn't pay any attention.

Once inside, he stopped and looked for Kai.

The long, narrow room was mobbed with dazed, excited, angry, and frightened people talking at each other. Add in EMTs, paramedics, and a handful of cops and you had a standing-room-only crowd. He glimpsed a bright red head moving their way through the crowd—Arjenie Fox, no doubt heading for Benedict. No Kai.

On his left, the wall was punctuated by two arches that gave access to the patio. Or would have, had the cast iron doors been open. Looked like the patio had been evacuated, save for a couple cops who seemed to be sweeping the flagstones. That's why the place was so crowded.

"Gods!" Seabourne groaned. "Those idiots! Sweeping up the—you!" He grabbed one of the silent agents. The man, as it turned out. The woman had been left behind to explain about sign-in sheets. "Come with me and get rid of those clowns!"

"Uh—I don't know if—"

"Do it," Ackleford snapped.

"Don't you be telling my people—" the lieutenant began. "Hey, you! Stop!"

Dell had waited as long as she was going to. The chameleon darted past the lieutenant, who tried to grab her. Fortunately for everyone, he missed.

Nathan followed Dell. That was the easiest way to find Kai.

One thing about this particular hiding-form. It might not be as powerful as Dell's original body, but it was not really weak. Dell shoved, elbowed, and—once—lifted people out of her way. Nathan had to pause when Dell knocked one young man to the floor right in front of him, so he heard Kai before he saw her. "I told you I was fine. And you cannot just yank the EMT out of—sorry, sorry, she's a trifle anxious. You're done, though, right? There's nothing more to check . . . all right, Dell, you're here, so see for yourself that I'm fine."

Nathan helped the young man to his feet, apologized quickly, and at last saw Kai.

She sat at a tiny round table against the west wall. Dell sat across from her, holding Kai's hands with both of hers, her eyes closed and her face blank. An irritated young woman—the EMT who'd been evicted from the chair Dell now occupied—crouched nearby, packing a blood pressure cuff back into her kit.

Kai's jeans and tank shirt were still tidy, aside from some pink smears. So was the hair she'd pulled into its usual braid. Her glasses were intact. But her beautiful, coppery skin was covered in some shiny ointment . . . and in tiny red welts. Hundreds of them, looked like. Arms, cheeks, throat, hands. They were everywhere.

She looked up. "Hi, there. Do I look that bad?"

"Like you have a bad case of measles." He moved close and squatted down beside her, wishing he could hold her hands instead of Dell, which was silly of him. He couldn't do what Dell could. He smiled at his own nonsense, and Kai smiled back. He loved her smile. The corners of her wide mouth curled up at the ends like quotation marks, giving her the look of a satisfied cat. It was adorable, an adjective he'd learned she did not care for, so he didn't mention it now. "A really bad case of measles. Do they hurt?"

"No, and they haven't raised my temperature or my blood pressure, but they itch. Clara—she's the EMT—gave me some ointment that's supposed to help. So far it hasn't."

"Itching can drive you mad," he agreed, and frowned. "You smell funny."

"You do know you aren't supposed to tell a woman that?"

"Could be I'm smelling the butterflies on you."

"Could be. A lot of them got smushed against my skin. Clara washed off the pink dust and butterfly guts, but the smell probably lingers enough for your nose. Um, Dell thinks that since you're here, I should pay attention. She expects this to be tricky, so would you watch over us both?"

Tricky? Nathan frowned, but there didn't seem much point in questioning Dell. He stood and laid one hand on Kai's shoulder. "Of course."

Her breathing slowed. So did her heartbeat, which he could hear when he stood this close. His Kai. She felt *safe* with him. Safe on a level thought couldn't reach. Even in a room this crowded with noise and strangers, she could trance deeply when he was touching her.

Nathan called up power and settled himself to guard. He took a slow breath, carefully noting the scents, then scanned the room so he'd have a baseline image—out, around, up, down. It amazed him how often people forgot to look up or down. He did the same with the sounds, then with the tactile messages the room offered—temperature, airflow. The part of him that watched would note all changes, although only a few would be brought to his conscious attention.

Then he took a slower survey to gather information. To his right, three young women sat at a small table—two blondes and a redhead. The two blondes were spotted like Kai, though not as extensively. The redhead had her back to him, so he couldn't tell about her for sure, but she was scratching one hand with the other one. A uniformed officer was questioning them, but they insisted they hadn't seen anything except butterflies, and for God's sake, couldn't they go home?

There were three reasons for their demand, all under the

age of three. The redhead held a squirming toddler who kept trying to scratch her arm. One of the blondes was nursing a baby, and the other jiggled a stroller. Nathan couldn't see the stroller's occupant, but he could hear him or her. Very soon those whimpers would become a wail.

No visible threats. He kept scanning.

The EMT had finished repacking her kit and moved to a pair of young men standing against the back wall. She asked if either of them needed treatment. Neither had visible bite marks, and both shook their heads. On the other side of Kai's table were the restrooms and a door that probably led to storage. He focused carefully, tuning out the other sounds . . . two people in Ladies', no one in Men's.

A pair of uniformed officers came into the room from the patio, closing the iron gate behind them. The cops with the brooms, he thought. Cullen must have succeeded in evicting them. Ackleford was still at the front of the room. Not that Nathan could see him, but a moment's concentration let him sort Ackleford's voice from the rest. The shifting of people between him and the door marked someone moving toward the back of the room. He glimpsed a dark head . . . Benedict.

Nathan took a moment to check on Kai. Still deeply tranced. The red spots from the bites hadn't faded. He frowned and bent so he could sniff the skin of her bare shoulder. That faint trace of not-Kai scent on her skin bothered him, tickled at his memory. He'd smelled something similar once. Not the same, but similar . . .

"Why didn't I see you head back this way?" Benedict demanded as he reached Nathan. Arjenie was with him.

Nathan straightened. "You saw. You just didn't notice."

"I'm in the habit of noticing. What did you do?" Benedict didn't raise his voice, but he put some demand into it.

Did Benedict realize how often he tried to place Nathan under his authority, or was it so instinctive he hadn't noticed? "I'll ask you to keep your voice calm so you don't disturb Kai."

"She's in a healing trance?" Arjenie asked, tilting her head. "In this noisy place?"

"Kai's good at trance."

Benedict gave Kai and Dell a quick glance, but repeated,

"I'm in the habit of noticing, but the moment I took my eyes off you, you were gone."

Nathan sighed. Clearly Benedict wasn't going to let it drop. "It's a trick of mine, similar to what Arjenie does, but less powerful. Had you been paying attention to me, it wouldn't have worked."

"You're like me?" Arjenie said, delighted. "I've never met anyone who had even a teensy trace of my Gift."

One of the women exited the Ladies'—tall, dark-skinned, about forty. "I don't know that it's the same Gift, but the effect is similar. Although, like I said, mine isn't as effective as yours."

Benedict wasn't done yet. "You didn't use this trick of yours to get past the cop at the barrier."

"Wouldn't have worked. He was paying attention."

"Any more tricks I should know about?"

Arjenie elbowed him in the ribs.

He frowned at her. "What?"

"That's rude. It's rude here because it's pushy, and it's even more rude where Nathan comes from. You don't go around asking people how powerful they are."

"Be good to know, though." He looked at Nathan. "Seabourne says you've got a whole tangle of Gifts."

"That's one way to look at it."

"You've got a dagger that disappears when you aren't using it."

"True. Have your people already healed their bites?"

Benedict's eyebrows twitched down in dissatisfaction, but he answered. "I assume so. I haven't seen them yet. They made the lieutenant nervous, so she stuck them out back with a couple officers."

"I'd like to know."

Benedict frowned and looked at Kai again, this time carefully. "How fast does she usually heal when Dell does this?"

Nathan forbore to explain again that it wasn't healing, it was body magic. "Faster than you."

"You think something's wrong." Benedict didn't wait for an answer, already turning away as he said, "We need Seabourne."

The redhead at the next table screamed.

FIVE

BEING jerked out of deep trance was a lot like being sound asleep and having a bucket of ice water dumped on you. Kai's body jolted along with her mind. She blinked stupidly. Her veins sang with heat. Her heart pounded. Her mouth was dry.

The heat came from Dell. The other two sensations came from fear.

Her body thought she should be afraid? Why?

No one was leaping at her with a knife or gun or club. Dell hadn't reacted, but it took a sledgehammer to get her attention when she was working body magic. But Nathan wasn't alarmed, either.

Of course, it took rather a lot to alarm Nathan. She was just craning her head around to see if he'd drawn Claw when a chair crashed to the floor. "She was here!" a high, hysterical voice cried out. "Right here in my lap, and then she wasn't! She just vanished!"

Kai couldn't see clearly—Benedict was in the way—but there were three women at the table to her right, along with a cop. The cop was standing. One of the women was, too. She looked frantic.

"Now, now," the cop said. "She must've climbed down and

you didn't notice. She can't have gotten far. We'll find her, don't worry."

"Your little girl's missing?" Nathan asked sharply. "Two or two-and-a-half, short red-blond hair, dark shorts, white shirt with a yellow cartoon duck on the front?"

"Yes, yes, that's her. Do you see her? She was in my lap, then all of a sudden she wasn't. Cammy!" she called suddenly, straightening. "Cammy, Mommy needs you to come here. Cammy!"

All around them, people were exclaiming. Some of the sitters stood; some of those already on their feet started to move.

Benedict's voice boomed out. "Everyone, listen up! Stay where you are. We've got a little girl missing. She's two or two-and-half—no, dammit, I said *stay put.* The little girl's name is Cammy. She's wearing dark shorts and a white T-shirt with a duck on it. Look around you. Look under your table."

The marvel was that they did. Not quietly—everyone seemed to be asking everyone else if they saw her, how old did he say she was, what had happened, and a dozen more pointless things. But they stayed where they were and most of them looked. It must be nice, Kai thought, to have the kind of deep voice people instinctively associate with authority. The voice wasn't the only reason they did as they were told, though. Benedict was used to being obeyed.

There were a couple of people who didn't stay put. Ackleford, for one. The police lieutenant for another, unfortunately. Kai did not like Lieutenant Jenkins.

"What's going on?" Ackleford demanded.

The cop at the next table attempted to answer. Cammy's mother spoke right over him, saying pretty much what she'd already said. And the heat in Kai's veins turned searing. She gasped at the pain and gasped again at the sudden dazzlement of color washing over the room. Dell was finished—and her Gift was back, full-force.

Hastily she dialed it down. That seemed to work like it was supposed to. She checked quickly with Dell, who sent a complicated wave of nonverbal information that meant Dell had fixed the problem with the eye drops. The burn in Kai's veins eased to a gentle warmth. Dell released her hands . . .

which were unblemished. They didn't itch, either. She didn't itch anywhere, thank all the Powers.

She did feel the weight of her familiar's exhaustion and the edginess of her hunger. That had been a major amount of work. Kai sent her gratitude, along with an apologetic *eat soon. Not yet, but soon.* Dell leaned back in her chair, looking very bland. That wasn't at all how she felt. It was hard to be around all that lovely blood when hunger bit deep, but the chameleon was nothing if not practical. She accepted the need to delay her meal.

Nathan leaned down and spoke near her ear. "If Dell's finished—"

A startled wail cut through all the voices.

"Cammy!" The redhead stooped, then shot upright again holding a bawling toddler in navy blue shorts and a white shirt. "She's okay," the woman assured everyone, though she didn't sound convinced. "You're okay, sweetheart, it's all right, there now, love . . ." While she murmured reassurances to her daughter, she ran a hand over the little girl's arms and legs to reassure herself. "She's okay," the woman repeated, this time with real relief.

Naturally everyone started talking again, with those closest telling the others that the little girl had been found, looked like she hadn't been missing after all, she'd been right there all along.

"She wasn't, though," Nathan said softly. "She was gone. Now she isn't."

What in the world was going on? Flowers that turned into bloodsucking butterflies. Toddlers who vanished then reappeared.

"You're okay now?" he asked.

"What? Oh, shit, I forgot. I mean yes, I'm fine, but I'm not sure about everyone else." Fine, but blithering. Sometimes it took a while for her brain to come fully online after she'd tranced deeply. She looked around. "Where's Cullen? You said he was coming with you."

Benedict said, "Headed this way." He gave a jerk of his chin to indicate the direction.

Kai stood and peered through the crowd until she spotted

a cinnamon-colored head moving toward them, or maybe for the table next to theirs, where Ackleford was talking to the mother newly reunited with her child and Lieutenant Jenkins was talking into her lapel mic.

Cullen Seabourne was unlikely in several ways, but the most obvious was his appearance. Beauty isn't all that rare. Sunsets achieve it all the time. But if Cullen Seabourne were a sunset, he'd be the one that slowed rush hour traffic because drivers kept wanting to look. The people he was moving through wanted to look, too. That might have bogged him down if he hadn't applied liberal doses of his personal antidote to beauty: sheer rudeness.

Nathan said, "Kai, I need you to go to the Ladies'."

"Now?" She turned to him, surprised. "Why?"

"Because if I do it's likely to upset people."

"Yes, but—" She stopped. Her spine prickled, raising the hairs on the back of her neck. Even without the return of her Gift, she'd know what Nathan's expression meant. He was utterly calm. Utterly focused. And his thoughts swam in an amethyst sea.

Nathan was on a Hunt.

Oh, this was going to be interesting. "Can it wait? I need to tell Cullen what Dell did. Others may be in danger."

Dell shoved her chair back. "I go."

Accustomed to translating for her familiar, Kai explained that Dell meant she'd check out the ladies' room while Kai spoke to Cullen.

"Good." Nathan nodded at Dell. "I need to know if someone is in there."

Dell headed for the door with the skirted icon. Nathan went with her, though he stopped on this side of the door. Now, where was Cullen? Oh, there he was, next to Ackleford. Before Kai could head his way, someone else stopped her with a hand on her arm.

This time it was Benedict. "Hunter's right. The little girl was gone. I didn't see her return, but I smelled it when she did."

"I imagine Nathan did, too."

"Something changed with him just now."

She tipped her head, curious. "Does he smell different?"

"I don't know what's different, but something is. I want to know what."

"You do realize he can hear you, don't you?" Not that Nathan seemed to be paying any attention to them. He was leaning against the wall beside the restroom door that had closed behind Dell. "Benedict, I need to talk to Cullen. It's important."

He frowned but released her, his gaze fixed on Nathan. Benedict's colors were calm enough, but a deep reddish violet was spiking through the wary pewter that dominated at the moment.

Oh, yeah, this would be interesting. Kai shook her head and started again for Cullen. Arjenie followed her, so Benedict did, too.

"What just happened?" Cullen demanded of Ackleford.

"Hell. I was hoping you could tell me."

Cullen shook his head. "Something happened. I know that, but it was over too fast. All I saw was a flash of power. The little girl's okay?"

"Seems fine. There's some confusion about whether she really disappeared or not. The officer here says—"

Kai broke in. "She really disappeared. Cullen, you need to check her for magical contamination. The others who were bitten, too."

Piercing blue eyes zeroed in on her. One more unlikely thing about Cullen—when all his shields were up, she couldn't see his thoughts. Kai had only met four beings who could completely shield their thoughts from her, and three of them needed a few thousand candles on their birthday cakes. It made no sense that Cullen would have shields on a par with the Eldest and the two Queens, but he did. All Kai had to go on with him were the things everyone else could see and hear.

Right now, he looked and sounded irritated. "Why?"

"Dell had to remake my blood. That's why it took so long. I couldn't tell what she was worried about, and she was in too much of a hurry to wait until I sensed it, too, but there was something in my blood she considered dangerous. That same something might be in the others' blood, too."

"Dammit." Cullen turned his frown toward Cammy's mother, who wasn't paying attention to anything but her little girl. One of her friends was arguing with the police officer, insisting Cammy had truly disappeared. The officer now seemed to think Cammy had been there all along. Amazing how people could remake their memories to fit what they thought must be true.

Cullen studied mother and daughter for a moment, then sighed. "I can't tell without a closer look. If I find something, I'm going to have to look at all of them, and that is going to take time. Time I ought to be spending studying the residue, dammit. How many people were bitten?"

Ackleford answered. "Lieutenant Jenkins tells me nineteen have reported being bitten, but that may not be a complete count. There were forty-four people on the patio."

"Are they all still here?"

Lieutenant Jenkins didn't like being left out. "Damn straight they are. My orders were clear."

The next voice was Nathan's. He'd joined them so quietly Kai hadn't noticed. "Some orders can't be followed. At least one person is missing. Someone was in the ladies' room ten minutes ago. It's empty now."

The lieutenant curled her lip at him. "People *do* leave the restroom."

"There's only one exit. She didn't use it."

They didn't believe him, of course. No one here had any idea what a Hound could do, and it didn't look like Nathan meant to tell them.

How could he be positive there'd been two people in the ladies' room if he hadn't seen them enter?

He heard them.

Benedict accepted that. Kai's fellow humans looked skeptical. Even if Nathan was right about what he'd heard, he hadn't been watching the ladies' room the whole time, had he?

He hadn't been looking directly at it, no.

Then he couldn't be sure both occupants hadn't both left the usual way.

Yes, he could. He'd been guarding Kai and Dell.

Naturally they didn't consider that proof of anything. They had no idea what it meant when a Hound set himself to guard. At least Ackleford decided to check out Nathan's claim instead of dismissing it altogether. He raised his voice. "Anyone here aware of someone who isn't accounted for?"

That generated a lot of uneasy looks and an uneasy silence. Kai opened her Gift up a bit . . . she couldn't be sure, not with so many people whose colors all crowded each other, most of them agitated, but . . .

—hungry!

Kai glanced at Dell, who stood next to the ladies' room door. The chameleon's hunger was becoming a problem if she made the effort to send a word. The crowded conditions were bugging her, too. Crowds were never Dell's favorite thing, but when she was hungry they were more of a strain. If she'd been in her other form, her tail would've been lashing. *Okay*, Kai sent, along with a wave of reassurance. She spoke quickly to Ackleford. "See that dark-haired young man in the blue shirt standing near the serving counter? I think he's missing someone."

Ackleford's brows drew down. "I thought you didn't really read minds."

"I don't. I'm interpreting what I see. When you asked about someone being missing, first he was alarmed, then this big, gray doubt oozed over the alarm, trying to smother it. He doesn't want to think what he's thinking."

"What's he thinking?"

"I don't know. Talk to him, okay?" She looked around for Nathan—ah, there he was, talking to Benedict. Kai moved closer so she could keep her voice down. Arjenie was sitting next to the two men, but she had her laptop out and was working away at something. "Nathan, Dell's getting seriously hungry."

"Eh." He glanced around. "It's crowded here. That doesn't help. I guess we can use the men's room."

"Wait a minute," Arjenie said, looking up. "*You're* going to feed her? Is that safe?"

"Sure. She won't take more blood than I can afford. It won't make a full meal for her, but it should help her settle."

Benedict rubbed his chin thoughtfully. "She's got good control, then, if she's that hungry."

"Nathan has given her blood before," Kai explained. "Once Dell accepts blood-gift from someone, he or she isn't prey. Ever."

"I make blood pretty fast," Benedict said. "I could donate some. My men could, too."

"That's, um, generous, but . . ." Kai dwindled to an embarrassed halt.

Nathan rescued her. "What Kai's uncomfortable saying is that Dell prefers not to permanently shrink her possibilities for prey if she doesn't have to. It's not that she intends to hunt you or the others—just that she prefers to keep her options open."

Benedict nodded. "Makes sense." He looked over at Dell, who still stood next to the ladies' room, as far from everyone else as she could manage. He raised his voice slightly. "Keep it in mind, though, if the need arises."

Dell's face didn't show any reaction, but Kai felt her heightened interest and what felt like . . . utility? Pragmatism, maybe. "She's thinking about it. She's, ah, she's been curious about you lupi."

Benedict's eyebrows lifted a fraction. "Wonders what our blood tastes like?"

"Well, yes."

Benedict just nodded. It was not the reaction she'd expected from either his human side or the wolf. Predators don't usually like being seen as prey. "Something you should know," she went on. "I would've told you before you made your offer, but I didn't know you were going to. Blood-gift goes both ways. Neither of you can be prey to the other, so you have to taste her blood, too."

Benedict slid an amused look at Nathan. "Tastes like chicken?'

"Not in the slightest."

"Benedict," Dell said clearly. "I accept offer of you. Not men of you. You."

When Dell made the effort to form full sentences, she was being formal. Benedict seemed to recognize this. He gave her a small bow, then looked at Kai. "Anything else I should know?"

"She'll want to change back to her original form. Give her—" Kai interrupted herself when the chameleon started to go in the ladies room. "Use the men's room!"

Dell looked back at her, affronted. Females were very much at the top of the chameleon hierarchy. They were rarer than their male counterparts. Larger, too, and—according to

Dell—smarter, stronger, faster, and better in every way. She did not like being mistaken for a male. "I know, but the cops might need to check out the ladies' room. You don't want to be interrupted." She looked back at Benedict. "She'll need a few minutes. I'll let you know when she's done."

Arjenie's brow was furrowed. "Benedict, are you sure this is a good idea? You're not getting into some kind of macho I-can-do-it-if-he-can game, are you?"

"Probably to the first," Benedict said, "no to the second." That's all he said, but it satisfied Arjenie, who went back to whatever absorbed her on her laptop. He frowned at Nathan. "Hunter. You have any idea what's going on? I don't see what the Great Bitch gets out of this."

Nathan looked faintly astonished. "You're still thinking it was your Great Enemy behind this?"

"Who else? Whatever the motive, it took a helluva lot of power to transform flowers to butterflies."

"Which attacked *Kai*. Who is not a target for your enemy."

"Kai and thirty or more other people." Benedict was impatient. "Look, we've been through this sort of thing before. The opening salvo in one of *her* attacks often seems pointless, but who else has that kind of power to lob around?"

"Itzpapalotl, for one," Arjenie said.

Benedict blinked. "What?"

"The Aztec warrior goddess. That is, she's the goddess of childbirth, but the Aztecs considered that the female equivalent of a warrior." She turned her laptop so the screen faced them. It held the image of a being with a skeletal head, butterfly wings, and the clawed feet of a big cat. "It's the butterflies. I've done a lot of research on the Great Bitch, and she's never been associated with butterflies, not under any of her goddess names. Itzpapalotl has. Her name means obsidian butterfly, or possibly clawed butterfly. She's particularly associated with the Rothschildia orizaba moth, which doesn't look anything like the butterflies that attacked us, so we should keep other possibilities in mind, like Xochiquetzal, the Aztec goddess of pleasure and beauty, whose retinue is birds and butterflies, only the way these butterflies bit people doesn't really fit. She was one of the few peaceable sorts in the Aztec pantheon. There aren't many butterfly associations with any of the Western pantheon. There's Psyche, of course, but even if she is still able to manifest—which doesn't seem likely—her only association with butterflies is the wings she was sometimes depicted with."

The expression on Benedict's face suggested he was about to get himself in trouble. "You don't think we've had enough deities messing with us, you have to go looking for more?"

"What I think," she said tartly, "is that transformation on this scale means either an Old One or a deity is involved. Not necessarily an Aztec deity, but that's a place to start."

Benedict's expression darkened further. Kai spoke to save him from himself. "Dell's ready."

"Okay." He ran a hand over the top of his head, muttered, "Itz-papa-what-il?" and headed for the men's room.

SIX

AS soon as the door shut behind Benedict, the one next to it opened and a female cop came out of the ladies' room. Kai hadn't noticed her go in. Either the woman had an awkwardly weak bladder, or someone wanted to find out if Nathan was right about it being unoccupied.

"Hunter!" Ackleford called. "Come here a minute."

Kai glanced that way. Ackleford stood next to the man she'd suggested he talk to. He hadn't asked Kai to come, though, had he? He wanted Nathan—who frowned, but started that way. Kai huffed out an impatient breath. She'd been told that Ackleford had a bias against women. Looked like she'd heard right. Should she elbow her way into that discussion, or would it be better to—

Outside, someone screamed.

Dammit! She didn't have any kind of weapon with her. Others headed for the front door—Ackleford, and of course Nathan, and even Lieutenant Jenkins—

"Wait up," Cullen called out. "It's just Sam. He must have startled someone when he landed."

Kai sent reassurance to Dell, who'd just started to feed when the scream put her on alert. "Who's Sam?"

"Also known as Sun Mzao." Cullen paused, grimaced. "Sarcastic bastard. He isn't talking to the rest of you?"

"The black dragon," Kai said flatly. "You call him Sam?"

"Right," the lieutenant said. "Out." She touched her lapel mic to disconnect and announced, "The dragon has parked himself on the roof of the building next door. It upset people." She looked tense, which was a more appropriate reaction, Kai thought, than Cullen's. "I don't—hang on." She touched her mic again. "No, Phillips, you don't do a damn thing about the dragon, except make sure that no idiots bother him! Got that?"

Everyone in the room was listening avidly. Two men stood up, and two more were already headed for the front door.

"Sit down!" Ackleford barked. "No one's going out to look at the pretty dragon. I mean you," he said, pointing at a young man with blue-streaked blond hair and a nose ring who was still edging toward the front. "Sit your ass down and stay put."

Kai wasn't surprised when the man did as he was told.

"You can do that?" Cullen asked the empty air in front of him. "Okay, dumb question, but I want . . . yeah, yeah, okay."

"You're talking to Sun Mzao?" Nathan asked.

Cullen nodded, clearly listening to something the rest of them couldn't hear. "Deal," he said crisply. Then, to the rest of them: "Sam wants a closer look. He's in a bit of a hurry, so he's going to borrow my Sight so he doesn't have to take out a wall." Apparently thinking he'd explained things adequately, he turned and headed for one of the wrought iron gates that led to the patio.

Nathan turned to Ackleford, who was a few paces away. "You wanted me for something, Special Agent?"

Ackleford stared at Cullen's departing back, then shook his head hard, like a horse shaking off biting flies. "Yeah. How did you know there's only one exit from the restroom?"

"Aside from where it's located, you mean? Dell checked."

Ackleford cast a glance out at the patio where Cullen was doing whatever it was the dragon wanted him to do. "You think he's okay? I mean . . . hell. Will whatever he's doing take long?"

"It's hard to say how long a dragon in a bit of a hurry will take," Nathan said, "when we don't know what he's interested in. You might want to arrange for that private space Cullen wanted to use to check out those who've been bitten."

Ackleford heaved a sigh. Kai didn't hear what he muttered—the level of babble in the room was rising again, as people got over their shock at having a dragon right outside. She decided to have a word with Arjenie and headed back to where Arjenie was still sitting with her laptop. Kai took the chair next to hers. "You checking out more deities to annoy Benedict with?"

Arjenie grinned. "He does hate having gods messing with us. I can't say that I blame him." She cast a quick glance at the restrooms. "How long does Dell usually take to feed?"

"She doesn't know Benedict's tolerance for blood loss, so she's taking it slow, stopping to check with him. Um . . . I thought you should know that deities aren't the only ones who can pull off transformational magic."

"I've heard that sidhe lords can, but surely only on their own terrain?"

"A few could do it elsewhere, but you're right—it would be a lot harder. Still possible for some, though. But also, we don't know for sure that we're looking at real transformation. It could be illusion."

Arjenie looked dubious. "They weren't really butterflies?"

"No, they probably were. But we don't know that they started out as flowers. They might have been bloodsucking bugs all along, but we saw flowers. That would be an easy illusion for an elf whose talents ran that way."

Arjenie's brow puckered. "Okay, I can see that. It wouldn't explain where the creatures came from, though, or why some elf wanted them to bite us."

"True. No doubt I've got elves on the brain after dealing with them so much." Kind of like the way Benedict assumed the lupi's enemy was behind this—he'd been dealing with *her* way too much. Kai suspected that her own response wasn't as reasonable as his. Benedict knew for certain that an Old One was actively seeking to destroy his people. Kai had no reason to think there was an elf anywhere in this realm, much less one who'd send butterflies to suck her blood. She shrugged. "I thought we should keep the possibility in mind."

"Sure. Until we have more data, we can't—"

Pay attention. I won't be here long.

The mental voice that cut through Arjenie's physical voice was as cold and crystalline clear as ice. *Sun Mzao*, Kai thought, her heart jumping once, hard, in her chest. The black dragon. One of the four beings whose thoughts were utterly hidden from her, though the reverse was emphatically not true. She had shields, but nothing that would keep out the Eldest.

Glancing hurriedly around, she could tell by their expressions who else had heard him. Arjenie, yes. Nathan. Also Ackleford, who looked like he'd been hit in the head. But the lieutenant was talking to one of her officers, oblivious.

Nathan Hunter is correct that today's event almost certainly did not involve the being we do not name. He is also, obliquely, the cause of the event, which created considerable disruption in the probabilities. Those took me some time to trace, although I was reasonably certain of their origin. I have now confirmed that origin. Kai Tallman Michalski.

"Yes?" Had she squeaked like a mouse? She felt like one, with the weight of that mind pressing on her.

Did you see any sign of intention in the thought patterns surrounding you at the time of the event?

"I had my Gift turned off. Looped, actually, not turned off, but the effect's the same. The eye drops the doctor used messed it up. My Gift, I mean. I was afraid I'd go into fugue."

You have been taught to loop your Gift?

Was it scorn or incredulity flavoring that icy voice? "Um. Yes."

Your instructor is either incompetent or has little regard for your welfare, the Eldest observed dispassionately. *You are far from ready for such a technique. It is unfortunate that you chose to employ it at that particular time. I can say definitely that the event was caused by an outbreak of chaos energy. I cannot say whether this outbreak was directed or random.*

"The knife." Nathan's voice rang with sudden understanding. "Nam Anthessa. You're saying that its power didn't return to its maker when I killed it."

That is both clear and puzzling. I can theorize about why the power remained here, but I do not know, nor do I have time to speculate. I have delayed longer than I like already, but since you are in this realm at my request, I chose to discharge my obligation before leaving. I do so now.

I see two possibilities, both of which will entail additional outbreaks. In the first possibility, the chaos energy was undirected, in which case it will continue to break out randomly until it has been exhausted. In the second, the chaos energy was directed. If so, it is unlikely that Dyffaya áv Eni achieved his goal—whatever that may be—with a singular outbreak, so you may expect more.

"Wait a minute," Kai said, her stomach going tight and unhappy. "Wait one minute. Dyffaya is the sidhe god we just—well, not killed, because he was already partly dead. Defeated, I suppose. But his knife is truly dead. Nathan killed it. That was supposed to destroy his link to our realm."

So we believed. But while Nam Anthessa is gone, its energy is not. If that energy is being directed, who better to do so than the god of chaos? This is why I owed Nathan Hunter a warning before departing. Dyffaya is best known as the god of chaos, compulsion, and madness. He was also, at one time, the god of revenge.

SEVEN

"YES, but it was a very long time ago," Nathan said.

Kai straightened from extended triangle back to mountain pose. "How long?'

"Dyffaya hasn't been the god of revenge for . . . eh. I'm not sure of the years, but he hadn't yet been killed when he lost that particular domain, and his body-death took place during the Great War. A very long time ago." He tossed several pairs of socks on the bed, where a small pile of underwear and two pairs of jeans waited.

Kai inhaled and bent to the left. When they got back to the lupi Clanhome, she'd traded her glasses for extended wear contacts. She didn't even have to take them out at night, which she loved; waking up unable to see clearly had been a problem on one of her quests. "So you don't think he's keen on getting revenge on you for killing his knife?"

"I expect he'd like that very much. I'd better have the new suit along, don't you think? Just in case." He went to the closet.

Now to the right. "You don't seem upset at the idea."

"I don't much care for suits, but—oh. You meant about Dyffaya. I've made enemies before. I expect I will again."

"You have any other enemies who are gods?"

"I don't think so. Should I take one dress shirt or two?"

Exasperated, she stopped to look at him. He was studying the clothes on the bed, his eyebrows pulled together in thought. His colors were as thoughtful as his expression—blues and greens, mostly, with traces of the amethyst she always saw in the Wild Sidhe.

Even at times like this, when she was ready to knock some sense into him, the sight of him pleased her eyes. Not that he was extravagantly gorgeous like Cullen Seabourne. Nathan was more Jimmy Stewart than Brad Pitt—tall and lanky, with the kind of face that made people feel welcome instead of making them swoon. A Hispanic Jimmy Stewart, that is, or Native American, or some other nationality with warm brown skin and hair as black as the space between stars. Hair as black as a hellhound's, in fact. At the moment, it was much shaggier than those sleek beasts. Nathan didn't let his hair grow long, as that gave an opponent something to grab in a fight, but he hated haircuts and put them off as long as possible.

He must have felt her looking at him, because he looked up and smiled. A soft, pleased pink washed through his thoughts.

When she first met him, Nathan hadn't smiled often. He smiled more now, but each one still arrived like a discovery, created on the spot for just this moment. This particular smile said, *there you are*, with as much pleasure as if he'd been looking for her for hours instead of sorting through socks and underwear. She smiled back. She couldn't help it. "I think it doesn't matter about the shirts. You don't even know for sure you'll be going anywhere, much less when or where."

"The when and where depend on when and where the next chaos outbreak occurs, don't they? Maybe it will happen nearby, maybe it won't. Best be ready to travel if I need to." He gave a single nod. "You're right. It doesn't matter about the shirt, easy as it is here to buy almost anything. I'll just take the one." He set his backpack on the foot of the bed.

It was a queen-size bed, which was nice. Neither she nor Nathan was bulky, but they were tall enough to find a double cramped. It was a nice bedroom, too, with a comfy reading chair, the dresser where her chain with its collection of charms waited, and enough space for yoga. The room used to be reserved for the heir to the clan. When Isen offered it to them three weeks ago he'd said, "Rule and Lily have their own place now, and in any event they'll be leaving soon for their honeymoon. I understand that humans need more privacy than my people, so I won't be offended if you decide a hotel would suit you better—but I hope you don't. Dell would be happier here than in the city, I think, and we can provide pasturage and care for any livestock you need to feed her. And," he'd added, his eyes merry, "I can promise that your food will be delicious, too."

He'd been right about Dell and about the food. Right, too, that Kai's first impulse had been to opt for the purchased hospitality of a hotel, where guests owed nothing more than money and a certain level of courtesy. She suspected Isen Turner was right about people a great deal of the time.

"Did you get hold of your grandfather?" Nathan asked.

"No, but I got hold of his neighbor. Calvin had a message for me. Grandfather's gone up the mountain. He wasn't sure how long he'd be."

"Odd time for it, with him expecting us to arrive soon."

"When the mountain calls, he goes." Finished with the extended triangle, she set her feet about seven inches apart and bent forward for the big toe pose. Funny how she'd had to leave Earth to learn to love yoga. She'd always been athletic, but yoga had struck her as a trendy way to avoid a real workout.

Kai rolled her eyes at her previous self and exhaled as she lengthened her torso and pulled on her toes, deepening the bend.

Turned out yoga was anything but easy. During their travels, Nathan had offered to teach her some basic poses—he was on board with the Eastern concept of chi and he liked the way yoga combined fitness with the smooth flow of energy through the body. At first she'd felt challenged to prove she could do it, but gradually she'd fallen in love with the practice.

Kai released her toes, put her hands on her hips, inhaled, and swung back upright.

Best be ready to travel if I need to, Nathan had said. Not we. I.

Of course she'd go with him. He hadn't asked her, hadn't said she needed to pack, too, but he probably just assumed she would. They were a team. They'd been a good team, too, on all three parts of her quest . . . which was over now, wasn't it?

Maybe she was the one doing the assume thing. She'd been part of Nathan's hunts while they were in the realms, but those hunts had been connected to her quest. This one wasn't.

She should just ask him. But what if she didn't like his answer? Kai sighed, unhappy with herself. Where were all these doubts coming from, anyway?

Done with the standing poses, she lowered herself to the floor. First a gentle twist—bend her knees, swing her legs to the side, left ankle resting in the arch of her right foot . . . "Only elves would think a god of revenge was a good idea."

"I don't know about that. It was the Dirushi, not the elves, who elevated revenge to an art form."

"You're kidding."

"*P'tuth*, it's called. You might think of it as a type of performance art."

Revenge as performance art. Kai shook her head and dragged her wandering mind back to her routine.

Nathan planned to go up against a god.

Hush, she told her mind, and *eleven, twelve, thirteen . . .*

The relationship rules might be slightly different when you were involved with a man who used to be a hellhound, but most of them still applied. Like the one that you do not interfere when your beloved is doing what he was born to do. Nathan was born to hunt.

From cobra she shifted into downward dog. Knees below hips, hands in front of shoulders, toes turned under, and exhale and lift . . .

But he was hunting a *god* this time.

No, she told herself firmly. She didn't know that. Even the Eldest didn't know if chaos had erupted at Fagioli because the god was directing it, or if the power freed by the knife's destruction was breaking out randomly. If only Kai had left her Gift open! She might have seen the orderly thought-remnants left by the intentional working of magic. But if she'd left her Gift open, she'd probably be trapped in fugue still and unable to report on anything she'd seen or not seen.

Enough with the might-have-beens. The point was, if the black dragon didn't know if today's chaos outbreak involved a semidead deity, who could?

She lowered herself into prone position. She'd been so

busy arguing with herself she'd failed to pay attention to downward dog, which was a favorite of hers. She needed to do better with the next pose. The upward bow or wheel was basically a very tight backbend, and it required both strength and focus. So: roll over onto her back. Bend her knees, tuck her heels up against the ischium bones . . . the sit bones, many yoga instructors called them, but Kai had been a physical therapist until the collision of a starving chameleon, a Hound, and a queen sent her off to Faerie. She called the donut-shaped bottom of the pelvic bone by its proper name. Bend her elbows and flatten her palms on the floor by her head, fingers pointing toward her shoulders . . .

Nathan was on a *Hunt.*

The Eldest might not know, but Nathan did. He was on a Hunt; therefore, there was someone or something to be hunted. His instincts wouldn't have been triggered by some random outbreak of chaos.

"If you're too tired for the wheel," Nathan offered helpfully, "you could substitute—"

"No." She said that through gritted teeth. "Lack of focus is slowing me down, not lack of energy." And she forced her mind back on track, and got through the wheel and the next two poses without injuring herself. She skipped Sukhasan, being not at all in the mood for quiet reflection, and stood.

Nathan was leaning against the wall, arms crossed, head cocked. "You want to tell me what's got you all wound up?"

"I'm going with you," she told him fiercely. "I ought to ask if that's what you want, but I won't, because it doesn't matter what you want. I'm not letting you go hunting a god by yourself. I don't know how much help I'll be, but you are not going without me."

His eyebrows flew up. He uncrossed his arms and came to her and laid his hands on her shoulders. "Kai." He looked at her intently, his storm-cloud eyes grave. "Have you been reading women's magazines?"

Well, there went that nice head of steam she'd worked up, dissipated in pure bewilderment. "Uh . . . have you heard the phrase non sequitur?"

"This is relevant. You were at the doctor's office today. Doctors always have magazines lying around, and there are dozens of those infernal women's magazines. Maybe hundreds," he added darkly. "And they are all crammed with advice. Mostly about losing weight, but about men and children and sex and cooking and exercise, too. And relationships. A great deal of the advice is about relationships, and a lot of women must read them, or they'd all go out of business." He shook his head. "I don't understand why every woman in this country isn't hopelessly confused. How can so much advice do anything but muddle your mind?"

"My mind seems muddled to you?"

He stroked her cheek. "You thought I might not want you with me. That's muddled and mazed."

It was. It was, and she knew it. She might not understand why Nathan felt the way he did, but she *knew* he loved her, and he was incapable of loving halfway. Kai put her arms around him. He accepted her as easily as he always did, and the warmth and delight of his body smoothed her out. She sighed. "I got to muddled all by myself, without any help from infernal magazines."

"Did you, now?" He paused, giving her a chance to speak. Since she lacked any explanations, she didn't offer one. After a moment he went on, "I maybe ought to make a push to get you to stay behind, only I can't seem to persuade myself you'd be safer that way. *Nathveta* on Dell for urging me to hurry today, even if she couldn't explain why."

A prick of confusion told Kai that the magical translator in her head didn't have an English word for the elvish one he'd used. She leaned back, keeping her hands at his waist, and dug into the rather fuzzy options the translator offered. "*Nathveta* means blessings?" Her brow furrowed. "Or maybe fulcrum. And something about debt?"

"Eh, that's nothing English deals with, is it? Blessings, yes, offered to one who acted as a fulcrum or lever, altering events in a way that creates . . . I wouldn't call it debt, though elves might. More like a strong desire to favor the one who acted."

Her mouth twitched. Her lover and her familiar had a good deal of respect for each other, but they did not always get along. "You strongly desire to favor Dell?"

"I do. My suspicion is you were his target today."

"His . . . you mean the god? Dyffaya?"

"You were bitten twice as much as anyone else."

Cold gripped the base of Kai's spine and walked up it with clammy fingers. It pissed her off. Did she have to be scared for everyone now? "It wasn't enough that I was frightened for you. Now I have to be afraid for me, too, and maybe for Dell, in case this Dyffaya decides he's pissed that she messed up his plan for me, whatever that might be. If he really does have a plan. I can't see why he'd be after me."

He shrugged. "Could be he wants to use you against me. Could be he wants to use you, period."

"I somehow doubt he's desperate for mindhealing."

"He's too mad to know he needs it," Nathan agreed. "But you're a power, Kai. You don't see it, and I don't see what shape your Gift will take as you're trained up into it. But my Queen does. So, too, might Dyffaya."

He was right about one thing. Kai couldn't see herself as any kind of power. She had a Gift, yes, and a powerful one, made even more so by her tie to Dell. But she doubted that helping others heal from trauma was high on the chaos god's list of priorities. "Maybe he's mistaken about me. Even Winter thought I was a binder at first."

He frowned. "I hadn't thought of that. I should have. I've grown accustomed to thinking of you as you are, not as my Queen once feared you to be, but if your magic still looks a great deal like a binder's, then that is possible. Though I would expect even a half-dead deity to be able to tell the difference."

"What do you mean, *if* my magic still looks like a binder's? Why wouldn't it look the same as it used to? *Kish* is supposed to be unalterable."

"Your ground doesn't change, but the magic that flows through it is shaped by the ground and by you—your thoughts, actions, habits, beliefs. As you grow and change, so does your magic, within the parameters established by your *kish*." His brows drew down. "Hasn't Eharin explained this?"

"Eharin presents definitions and theory and tells me what to do. She observes my efforts. She doesn't answer questions—unless you consider it an answer to say that I'm not ready for that knowledge yet. Or that it touches on an area not covered by our agreement."

He muttered something she didn't catch, except for one significant word. She grinned. "If that was some version of 'a pox on her house,' I agree. It would be so satisfying to blame these stupid doubts on her, but—"

His eyebrows flew up. He said encouragingly, "Doubts?"

She used one hand to wave that away. "Never mind."

"Kai." He tugged on her braid. "If there's something I've done or not done, you need to tell me."

"No, no. I didn't want to talk about it because I don't understand it, but I guess it's okay if you know. Lately—not all the time, but sometimes—I get hit by all these doubts. About me, you, anything, or everything." She scowled in frustration. "I can tell I'm not being reasonable, but that doesn't make it *stop.*"

"Ah." He ran a hand down her back soothingly.

"What kind of 'ah' is that?" she asked, rearing back to look at him suspiciously.

"Now, there's a question I don't know how to answer."

"It sounded like a knowing *ah.*"

"That's a bit strong. I wouldn't say that I *know* what's bothering you."

"Don't stop there."

"Maybe I've a notion, but I'm not going to be like those women's magazines, handing out advice at the drop of a—"

"Nathan." She gripped his shoulders but refrained from shaking him. "Tell me your notion."

He sighed. "Your problem is that you don't know what you want."

That was just silly. "Of course I do. I want to help others with my Gift. And you. I know I want you."

"And I'm glad of it, but I'm talking about larger wants, the framework everything else grows from—the *kith* of your identity, you might say. It's why the Queen's offer troubles you, why you haven't told her yes or no."

"Maybe I haven't given the Queen an answer because it takes time to make a decision like that! We're talking about the entire rest of my life. She recognized that. She doesn't need an answer right away."

"You wouldn't have to hunt an answer if you truly knew what you wanted. You'd have to think to see how her offer fit or didn't fit, but you'd have a way of deciding. Instead you've got a big smear of uncertainty that's leaking out over everything, making doubts spring up like weeds. And look there." His mouth took a wry twist. "There's why I should've kept my mouth shut. You're working your way around to being mad."

She was, and that was stupid and unfair. She'd asked, hadn't she? Insisted he tell her, and now he had, and it made her mad. And it just made her madder that he'd noticed she was being stupid and unfair. "I don't—"

There was a rap on the door, then Benedict's voice: "My Rho would appreciate it if you'd join him in the great room. He's got a problem you might be able to help with."

EIGHT

THE great room was a long, inviting room at the back of the house. A big fireplace held down one end; an oversize dining table, the other. In between were couches and chairs that made up three seating groups and a wall of windows that looked out on the back deck. Kai liked the room's colors—rich browns and several shades of green with splashes of yellow, like sunshine breaking through forest branches. Personally, she'd add a few touches of sky blue . . . but she was always mentally altering or adding to the colors in other people's spaces.

Color was important. The colors people surrounded themselves with mattered, yet too many people settled for bland. Ask a hundred people what their favorite color was, and not one would say "beige." Yet that's what half or more of them lived with.

Tonight she didn't pay much attention to the room's colors, however, or to the colorful thoughts of the people in it. She was too busy wishing they'd stayed in a hotel in spite of the excellent food here. She and Nathan hadn't been loud, but they didn't have to be. Not around lupi. Benedict didn't give any indication of having overheard their argument, but Benedict wouldn't give any indication of having caught on fire, either—other than briskly and efficiently putting it out.

"Can I get you something to eat or drink?" Benedict asked.

"Nothing for me," Nathan said.

Kai shook her head. Why was Benedict here, anyway? It was after eight. Shouldn't he be home with Arjenie?

Hospitality taken care of, Benedict moved to one of the couches. The coffee table in front of it held a disassembled gun of some kind. It was large and military-looking. Benedict picked up one of the pieces and a white cloth and began wiping it down.

Their host and the Rho of Nokolai Clan stood near the fireplace. He wore jeans and a plain green shirt and looked not at all wolfish. If Puck had decided to masquerade as a village blacksmith, Kai thought he would have looked just like Isen Turner—burly and bearded, with arms that could swing a hammer all day and a spark of amusement burning bright in his eyes.

The cell phone in his hand seemed an anachronism. "Yes, I know you do . . . hold on a moment, please." He smiled at Nathan and Kai. His thought-colors went well with the room—lots of greens with swirls of midnight blue and a few yellow crinkles, but a worried sludge-colored snake wound through them at the moment. "I'm speaking with my pig-headed son and my lovely new daughter—who is, if anything, even more stubborn than her husband. They don't trust the rest of us to handle the situation. You might be able to talk some sense into them."

"I don't know that words can put sense into someone who lacks it," Nathan said, "but I don't think your son lacks sense."

"Many times I'd agree with you. Tonight, sadly, I cannot."

Nathan's phone dinged from back in their room. "I'll be back," he said, and headed quickly for the hall.

"Very few people have that number," Kai explained. "It's probably important. Not that your request isn't, but—"

"But it may be less urgent? Of course. Would you object to answering some questions?"

"No, though Nathan could do that better than—"

"Thank you." With that, he handed her his phone.

She looked at the phone in her hand, unsure why she'd accepted it. With a sigh she held it up. "This is Kai. You have some questions I can help with?"

"Don't be too upset with Isen," a cool soprano voice told her. It sounded like she was on speakerphone. "It's hard on him, being unable to order us around."

That was Lily Yu, the Special Agent who'd stopped a god from destroying Earth. Dyffaya had come all too damn close to unbalancing the world's time-stream in an effort to gain entry. Lily sounded pretty wide awake for someone who couldn't have been up long. Kai had only a sketchy notion of international time zones, but she thought it was pretty much dark-thirty in France. "I see why Isen can't give you orders," she said, "since you're FBI, but Rule is his heir, right? He can give his heir orders."

This time a male voice spoke. "I am also Rho of Leidolf. Isen can expect obedience from his Lu Nuncio. He can't give orders to another Rho."

Kai had been told Rule was heir or Lu Nuncio to his own clan and Rho of another. She didn't understand how he could be both, but she didn't need to figure out lupi politics right this minute. "Listen, I feel like I've been thrust into the middle of a family spat, but if I understand right, the two of you intend to cut short your honeymoon and return here?"

"Of course," Rule said.

"Don't."

"I beg your pardon?"

He sounded like an English nobleman confronted by unexpected insolence—ever so politely astonished. It made Kai grin. "The thing is, we—Nathan and I—are convinced Dyffaya is behind today's chaos outbreak. I know the, uh, the black dragon—" For some reason the Eldest didn't use his title here, so she wouldn't, either—"couldn't say for sure, but Nathan can. His certainty is based on instinct, but when it comes to a Hunt, his instinct is more reliable than gravity." Gravity could be fooled, given the right spell. Nathan couldn't. Not about a Hunt.

"And for some reason," Lily Yu said, "you think that means we should stay away."

"Did Isen tell you that Dyffaya used to be the god of revenge?"

"Yes, but he isn't the god of revenge now, so whatever spiritual stuff is associated with being god of that, he can't tap into it."

"No, but he's got a high opinion of revenge and plenty of other powers to tap into. He's going to put a priority on payback. At the moment we figure Nathan is his primary target, but I'd bet you're high on his to-do list. If you show up here, he might put his revenge on Nathan on hold long enough to deal with you."

"Nadia," Kai heard Rule say, then the voices went faint and muffled. Someone had put a thumb over the phone's mic. After a moment, Lily Yu came back on. "You seem to be assuming that he won't come after me in France."

"He can't. At the moment, he's strictly a local deity."

"You want to explain that?"

"I'll try. I had something of a crash course in godheads right before I left Winter's court. Um . . . this applies to godheads occupied by a former mortal like Dyffaya, not to Old Ones like your Great Enemy. Most godheads start as local accumulations tied to a particular place. Mountains are popular. Look at how many mountains all over the world are held to be the home of a god or powerful spirit. This is because of the way spiritual power grows, building up like rainwater, with little eddies trickling into larger ones, until there's enough for it to either become or attract a godhead."

"Okay," Lily said slowly. "But all that building-up happened with the chaos god a few millennia ago. He's obviously broken free of whatever place generated him. Why would he be stuck in San Diego now?"

"That would be easier to explain if I understood it myself." It had been a hurried lesson, and in elvish. Some of the words hadn't translated well. "But what I did understand is that Dyffaya is not of our realm. He's never been worshiped here, so even though he's been a god a long time, it's like he's starting over. He doesn't have a way to act in our realm except through the chaos energy from the knife Nathan killed. That energy is a mix of spirit and magic, and while spirit is unpredictable, magic isn't. You know that spells lose coherence over running water, right?"

"They do?"

"Oh, yes. Unless a spell is bound in specific ways, like in a potion, amulet, or artifact, running water separates intention from action. Think of it as a spell coming unraveled. The more water a spell crosses, the stronger the effect, and the ocean is really big. Nam Anthessa could have crossed the ocean. The unbound energy released by its death can't. Which means that unless Dyffaya has somehow come up with a lot of French worshipers, he can't get there from here."

"Are you sure this chaos energy is unbound? If the magic part of it is tangled up with the spiritual part, doesn't that mean they're bound up together?"

"No, but—oh, Nathan's back," she said with relief as she saw him emerge from the hall. "That explanation is above my pay grade, so I'll let him handle it." She raised her eyebrows, asking Nathan what the call had been about. He gave her a reassuring nod, but she wasn't sure whether that meant, "no big deal" or "I'll tell you later." She held out the phone. "I've been telling Lily that Dyffaya can't cross the ocean. She wants to know why chaos energy isn't the same as the bound energy of a spell."

"Ah," he said, and took the phone from her, then stood a moment, rubbing the side of his nose. Then he touched the face of the phone. "Hello, Lily," he said. "I've put you on speaker. Your question takes a fair amount of background to answer. Now, I'm no expert on magical theory, but—"

"No theory," Lily said firmly. "Please."

Amusement flickered over Nathan's face. "A simile, then. The magic in a spell has been put in order, like a ball of yarn. In chaos energy, the yarn isn't neatly ordered. It's tangled all up with itself and with snarls of thread, with all of that wrapped around a tiny kernel of true chaos. The thread," he added helpfully, "being *arguai*, or spirit."

"I can picture that."

"Good. I should add that spirit is geographically sticky. It can and does move, but it tends to move in relation to itself."

"Is that supposed to explain anything? Because I can tell you right now it doesn't. But never mind—I'll take your word for it. The chaos stuff can't get to France, and without it, Dyffaya can't, either. But that doesn't matter, because we'll be on the next flight back."

"You and Rule both, I suppose?"

"Of course."

"Hmm." Nathan considered a moment. "That's your decision,

of course, but you should keep in mind that Dyffaya was born an elf. Elves don't consider humans as worthy targets for truly elegant revenge. You don't live long enough. He'll likely settle for something more pedestrian, but just killing you wouldn't please him. He'll be after making you hurt, which means his first target is likely to be your Rule . . . just as he's already taken a swipe at my Kai." Nathan looked at Kai as he said that. Something dark and burning hid at the back of his eyes, and red splashed through his colors like spilled blood.

Lily said, "My family."

"They're here?"

"In the city, not at Clanhome."

"He's more likely to target them if you're nearby so he can see you suffer."

Three heartbeats of silence. "Can he watch us from wherever he is, then?"

"He's a god, so he has some degree of clairvoyance. It's likely limited, and we don't know how much or by what factors—but location will be one of them."

"You think my family is safer if I hide out over here."

"No guarantees, and it's not a matter of hiding. But that's my best guess."

"Toby," Rule said, his voice taut. "He's in North Carolina. How far can Dyffaya reach?"

Toby was Rule's son, a hard-charging charmer maybe ten years old. When Rule and Lily went on their honeymoon, he'd stayed with Isen, but the day before yesterday he'd left to visit his grandmother on the other side of his family.

"I don't know," Nathan told Rule. "I believe it would be somewhere between extremely hard and impossible for the god to reach that far, especially with the Mississippi in between. But I can't guarantee that he won't."

"Can you hold a moment?" The call went mute again, but only briefly. Lily Yu came back on. "Tell Isen we'll be flying Toby to France. His grandmother, too, if she'll come."

"He'll be safest there with you."

"He'll be in France. Whether I am or not is still undetermined. You need a Unit agent. Regular FBI can't handle this. I haven't talked to Ruben yet, but—"

"No worries there." Nathan's voice was soothing, but amusement shot hot pink through his thoughts. "He'll be calling you any time now to let you know he's found a Unit agent. The fellow he's given the job to is an outsider who will have to use borrowed authority, but I think he can do the job."

Kai's eyebrows shot up. She didn't ask. She knew.

So did Lily Yu. "He's made *you* a Unit agent?"

"More or less. Seems he had one of his feelings. Ah," he added, turning toward the front of the house. Kai hadn't heard anything, but he probably had. "I think some of my borrowed authority has arrived."

NATHAN'S borrowed authority scowled at him across the big dining room table. "Let's get one thing clear. You may be able to tell me what to do, but you are not in charge of my people."

Nathan nodded seriously. "I understand the distinction."

Special Agent Derwin Ackleford was not happy. He probably wouldn't have been happy about following any hunch handed down from on high, but one that took him away from his regular caseload and put him at the disposal of someone who wasn't even Bureau set a whole new record in asininity, in his opinion. Kai knew this because he'd told them so.

He wasn't seriously angry, though. The amount and shade of red-orange winding through his thoughts suggested aggravation, not rage, and the patterns his colors formed spoke of an orderly mind. "If it makes you feel any better, Special Agent," she said, "Nathan does have law enforcement experience."

Ackleford snorted. "Yeah, as some kind of legal hit man for his queen."

"Here on Earth, actually. He was a deputy when I met him."

Ackleford gave Nathan a level look. "Where?"

"Texas. The Bureau has a dossier on me," he added helpfully. "They pulled it together when State was figuring out how to get me a visa. I imagine you can have a look at it, if you ask."

"Huh. I'm betting it's not complete."

"Not very, no."

Ackleford scowled and reached inside his suit jacket. "Mind if I smoke?" he asked Isen.

"Not as long as you do so outside."

Ackleford sighed and withdrew his empty hand.

The door at the front of the house slammed. A moment later a beautiful man stomped into the room. "I'm here. I don't know why, but apparently this is more important than my doing delightful things with and to Cynna—who falls asleep pretty damn early these days, so I hope this won't take too long."

"Cullen," Isen rumbled, "complain about your sex life later. You're needed."

"There's nothing wrong with my sex life, except that it keeps getting postponed." But the grumbling was more pro forma than heartfelt, and Cullen's eyes took quick note of the others at the table as he joined them.

A couple more people had arrived right after Ackleford. Altogether, there were six people present—seven if you counted Dell, who'd fed again after they got back to Clanhome and was impersonating an oversize house cat, sleeping off her meal in front of the fireplace. Isen sat at the head of the table, flanked by Benedict and Arjenie, with Nettie Two Horses next to Arjenie. Nettie was a physician, a healer, and a shaman of the Diné. The People, that meant, that being how those called Navajo traditionally named themselves. Nettie had been out of the hospital about a month after being shot by someone taken over by Dyffaya. Kai had been told that Nettie's hair used to be very long, but they'd had to shave part of her head at the hospital, so she'd chopped it all off. What remained was a feathery pixie-cut.

And now, of course, there was Cullen Seabourne. "Does anyone have any idea why I'm here?" he asked plaintively.

"Ruben Brooks gave me permission to assemble what I'd call a hunting pack," Nathan said. "The Special Agent here would likely call us a task force. Your Rho wants you to be part of it."

Cullen glanced at Isen. "That's all right, then."

"I'm pleased you think so," Isen said dryly. "I'm concerned that this Dyffaya might wish revenge on Nokolai in general. Even if he doesn't, he wants to harm Lily. We can't allow that."

"I get that." Cullen looked at Nathan. "But I'm not sure why you need me. You know ten times more about magic than I do."

Nathan made the *tch* sound that could mean anything from disgust to amusement. "I know things you don't, true, but you can likely perform ten times as many spells as I could. Think about it. When I lived in the sidhe realms, I was a hellhound. How many spells do you suppose a hellhound learns?"

"Ah . . . not many?"

"No. Plus I lack the Sight. If chaos erupts nearby, you'll see it. That could be more than a bit handy. Now, what I want to do first is get each of us caught up on what the others know. We'll start with what you discovered when you checked out those who'd been bitten by the butterflies."

"That took for-freaking-ever." Cullen pulled out a chair and sat. "I checked the toddler first, but didn't find anything. Then I sorted them roughly by number of bites, starting with those who'd been bitten the most. The first guy I checked did have a trace of noninherent magic, just barely enough for me to see without my magnify spell. I confirmed that it was worked magic—a spell—that was tied to his blood, and that's about all I can tell you about it, other than the color, which didn't make sense. It vanished while I was studying it. None of the others had any trace of externally imposed magic."

"What color was it?" Arjenie asked.

"Purple. That color is usually associated with those of the Blood, and specifically with whatever magic is their heritage—the Change for us, illusion and body magic for elves, all things rock-related for gnomes. Which is why it doesn't make sense."

"Why not?" Kai asked."

"I'm oversimplifying now," Cullen warned. "But generally speaking, while spells often retain some of the color of the caster's innate magic, that's intermingled with the colors of the elements and other sources a spell draws on. This was worked magic, yet it was uniformly the color of one type of innate magic."

Nathan nodded. "Likely that's the color of magic generated by chaos energy."

"Maybe." Cullen spread his hands. "Only that still doesn't

make sense. It was *worked* magic. It should've taken on some color from its components or the elements."

"Hmm. We'll come back to that later, but likely there weren't any components. Do you have any ideas about why the purple magic vanished?"

"Most likely, the spell simply expired. There wasn't much power left in it by the time I spotted it. But it's possible the caster yanked it. Maybe he didn't want to leave something for us to study. Maybe he'd gotten what he wanted with that one woman and didn't need the others who'd been bitten."

"That poor woman," Arjenie said. "I just don't see what he wanted with her."

"That's the question, isn't it?" Nathan said. "Something he couldn't get from the little girl, it seems, since he sent her back. Your turn, Special Agent. What happened today ended with one person missing. What can you tell us about her?"

Ackleford looked sour, but opened one of the folders he'd brought. "Britta Valenzuela went to Fagioli with Henry Lester, who didn't initially respond to my question about people being missing due to him being an idiot. Valenzuela and Lester work at Littleman-Hughes, a legal firm a couple blocks from Fagioli that specializes in maritime law. She's a paralegal. He's fresh from law school. They've been on two previous dates. She's wearing an orange shirt and brown slacks."

He went on to tell them about Britta Valenzuela. She was twenty-eight, five-six, weight around one-thirty. She drove a ten-year-old Fiat that spent a lot of time in the shop and lived in a tiny studio apartment in Clairemont with two cats. Her father had died when she was eleven; her mother never remarried. Her mother said she was a good girl. Her older sister said, "Britta likes men and they like her right back."

No arrests. Two speeding violations. Catholic, but didn't attend mass regularly. Two previous jobs: one at a fast food place when she was in high school, followed by a stint as a receptionist at a posh salon while pursuing paralegal training. She'd graduated with decent grades, gone to work for Littleman-Hughes, and had been there ever since. Well-liked by most of her coworkers and received good evaluations from her boss. Her neighbors didn't know much about her except for one old woman, who broke down in tears when she learned

Britta was missing. Britta had been doing the old woman's grocery shopping for the past year. Every Saturday, Britta would get Mrs. Cruz's list before heading to the store for her own groceries.

Britta's mom was right, Kai thought, rubbing the back of her neck even though that wasn't what ached. Britta was a good girl . . . or had been. No way of knowing if she was still alive. She glanced at Ackleford and wondered if she understood his scowls and sourness better now. He'd been dealing with this kind of ache for a lot of years, hadn't he? Not that anything in his voice, his words, or his expression gave a hint of anything more profound than irritation. But she saw the deep, sad blue at the base of his thoughts as he spoke about Britta Valenzuela. He kept it shoved down, but it was there.

". . . Mrs. Valenzuela would like to know what the hell happened to her daughter," Ackleford finished. "So would I. You have any goddamned ideas about that?"

Nathan looked at Cullen. "You didn't find any traces of death magic."

Cullen shook his head. "None. And I ran the test three times."

Ackleford said, "People are killed all the damn time without creating death magic."

"There's no body," Kai pointed out.

Nathan leaned back in his chair. "And that suggests she was transported elsewhere. We can't say if she's still alive, but that toddler came back unharmed."

"Hell." Cullen grimaced. "Teleportation? You're the expert on what sidhe can do, and if you're right about this Dyffaya being behind it, he started out an elf. But teleportation? That ought to be impossible for anyone, elf or not! Unless he used spiritual power, which breaks the rules, but you told me earlier you don't think he's got much of that right now, but—"

"Wait a minute," Ackleford said. "I want to hear about that. It's this spiritual power shit that lets him possess people, right?"

"He doesn't possess people in the sense that demons do," Nathan said, "but I understand what you mean. We'll come back to that later, since the answer's not clearly a yes or no. About Britta's apparent transportation—"

Cullen broke in. "Don't tell me this Dyffaya used a gate. I know what a gate looks like, and I didn't see one."

Arjenie frowned at Cullen. "But you said the power flash was gone too quickly for you to see what happened."

"Gates leaves traces," Cullen insisted. "This didn't. Maybe where Nathan comes from gods teleport random people every other Thursday, but I'm not buying that it happened here. Aside from the fact that it ought to be impossible, it would take a godawful amount of power. He needed a boost from a version of his death magic before, so where's that power coming from now? And for what? What could he get out of it?"

"That we don't know," Nathan said. "Yet. As to the business of traveling without a gate—that's unusual, but hardly unheard of. I do it, and I take Kai and Dell with me. Well, technically Kai takes Dell with her, but I do the moving."

Benedict frowned. "How?"

Nathan's eyebrows lifted. "How do you Change?"

Cullen leaned forward impatiently. "It's an innate skill, right, we get it. Are you saying this god transported the toddler and the woman the same way you'd travel between realms?'

"I think it's possible. Likely, even."

"Even though he wasn't here to grab them? Can *you* grab someone from a realm you aren't in?"

"No, but under some circumstances my Queen can."

Cullen sat back in his chair. "Remind me not to piss off your Queen. All right. It's reasonable to assume that if the Queen of Winter can do it, a god might be able to pull it off, too. But from what I understand, Dyffaya isn't in a realm, and living people can't go where he is. Not physically. So where's Britta?"

"Wait a minute," Ackleford said. "If he's not in a realm, where is he?"

Nathan rubbed his nose. "He's in his godhead."

"What the hell does that mean?"

"It's a locus."

"Which is what?"

"Well . . . not exactly a place. Not exactly not a place, either." Nathan shrugged. "Maybe you can think of it like in the movie *Tron.*"

Ackleford scowled. "This nonplace is like cyberspace?"

"Only made with spiritual energy instead of computers."

"I hate this magic shit."

Everyone was silent a moment, perhaps in sympathy with the sentiment. Then Isen spoke. "You're saying you think Dyffaya took this woman into his godhead, which is not a physical place. Wouldn't that mean her body was destroyed?"

"Hmm." Nathan rubbed his nose. "I can't say I've ever studied on this, but I know of at least one immaterial locus that can support a physical intrusion. The toddler—"

"What locus is that?" Cullen asked quickly.

"I won't speak of it. As I was saying, the toddler didn't die, so I'm thinking the godhead will sustain physicality, at least for a time."

"Why would he do such a thing?"

"I don't know."

"And where," Cullen put in, "did he get the power?"

Nathan thought that over for a few heartbeats, then nodded. "That I do know. Best tell you, I think. You've got the shields to safeguard such knowledge. However . . ." He glanced around apologetically. "I'll need to speak with Cullen privately. I can't justify telling the whole lot of you. I'll be asking for his pledge not to reveal it to anyone."

"Cynna," Cullen said promptly. "You'd think I would enjoy keeping some juicy bit of magical knowledge from her, given how much she keeps from me, but . . ." he shrugged. "Somehow it doesn't appeal."

"I'm sorry," Nathan said. "You cannot share it with your Cynna."

Cullen's frown looked more uneasy than upset. "How important is it that I know this?"

"Important enough that I risk my Queen's anger telling you."

Cullen looked at the bearded Puck at the head of the table.

Nathan did, too. "Isen, this type of information transfer is considered a loan among my people. This means Cullen will have the use of what I tell him, but it isn't his to share, not as gift or in trade or sale, and he must safeguard it zealously. Yet I know he has to obey you. I'd like your word that you won't ask or require him to reveal what I tell him."

Kai's eyebrows lifted. She'd been told that lupi took vows as seriously as any elf. Apparently Nathan accepted that.

Isen thought it over a moment. "I'd need a caveat that he must be free to tell me if he judges that I truly need to know."

"Need can mean many things, especially for a people at war."

"Then let us say, 'only in profound need,' and to underline that, I will agree that my clan incurs a debt burden to your Queen if Cullen shares this information with me, with that burden being proportionate to the extremity of the need."

Nathan nodded. "That's well thought of. You understand debt burdens?"

"We have an example of such an obligation in our history."

"Very well. I must ask for one more condition. I hope it's not offensive, but it's one any sidhe negotiating at this level would require. Cullen must drop his shields when giving his vow so Kai can confirm his intent."

Isen's eyebrows lifted. "That is unnecessary, but I choose not to take offense. Whether or not Cullen is offended is up to him."

"Are we agreed, then?"

"You have my word not to ask or require Cullen to reveal what you tell him under a vow of secrecy, if that vow has the exception as stated."

"Agreed," Nathan said, and stood. "We'll go outside, I think."

NINE

KAI, Nathan, and Cullen went out back for the big reveal. Nathan led them to the middle of the upper deck, where he stopped, glanced around absently, then moved slightly to his left. Kai knew what that meant. Nathan had taught her a spell to do what he did instinctively: find true north, a necessity for casting a circle.

"The two of you stand still for a moment, please." He then walked around them, humming. He circled them three times, nodded once, and stepped inside the circle he'd set. He gave Cullen a quick, amused look. "That's to keep anyone from accidentally overhearing us."

The sorcerer was staring at what, to Kai's eyes, was empty air. "That is a very handy type of ward. How does it work? What would you take to teach me how to do that? I've got a couple spells—original ones, so you won't know them—that are pretty useful. You might want to consider a trade."

"We can discuss such things later. Please drop your shields."

Cullen grimaced, but an instant later Kai saw his colors for the first time. The orange was no surprise. Cullen Seabourne was confident enough for five normal men. The mossy green lacing it seemed to be common to his people; she'd never seen that exact shade in the thoughts of anyone who wasn't lupi. The annoyed red-orange wasn't unexpected, either. But those purple threads were.

Surely that couldn't be what it looked like? Lupi were of the Blood, after all, so she expected to see purple in their thoughts. But not that shade of purple.

Nathan spoke formally. "The promise I need from you, Cullen Seabourne, is that you will zealously guard and protect from revelation the information I am about to give you; that you will not reveal or attempt to reveal it to anyone save your Rho; that you will only reveal it to your Rho if you are convinced the need to do so is profound; and that such revelation will place your clan under debt burden to the Queen of Winter, with that burden inversely proportional to the level of need."

Cullen's scowl didn't abate as he repeated, word for word, the promise Nathan asked, ending with, "I so swear." His colors held no trace of the pus green of a deliberate lie. In fact, the purple threads flared briefly—a clear sign of deeply felt conviction. And those threads sure as hell looked like the same amethyst she often saw in Nathan's thoughts, or in others of the Wild Sidhe. Or in those descended from one of the Wild Sidhe. Such descendants were rare, and how one could have ended up on Earth . . .

She looked from Cullen to Nathan, drawing more strongly on her Gift as she compared their colors. Well. Now she knew why Cullen was the only Gifted lupus. Did he know? "He considers himself fully bound by his vow," she told Nathan.

"Thank you," Nathan said gravely. "I apologize for any perceived insult, Cullen. If my Queen were here to safeguard the loan of her information, she could have verified your integrity in ways I can't. Since she isn't, I must in all honor do what I'm able to."

Cullen's shields must have come back up, because his colors winked out. He leaned forward. "*Her* information?"

"Winter wanted to be sure I understood who and what I'd be dealing with when she sent me to kill the artifact Nam Anthessa, so she explained some things in depth. Some of it I already knew, but . . . eh." He rubbed his nose. "I'm starting this backward. Best begin with what you know. Where does magic come from?"

"There are a dozen theories about that, but none that

I—wait a minute." His eyes narrowed. "That's what this is about? It can't be. The source of magic has been debated for centuries, but from what I can tell, even the adepts gave up on finding real proof for any of the theories."

"Are you not prepared to believe what I tell you, then?"

Cullen stared at him intently. "It truly comes from the Queen of Winter?"

"It truly does."

"Then . . ." Cullen took a deep breath, as if readying himself to leap from a very high place. "I will believe you."

Nathan nodded once. "Magic is the product of the friction between chaos and order. Specifically, it is the friction between the realms, which are ordered, and that which lies between the realms, which is chaos."

Cullen stood absolutely still. She wasn't altogether certain he was breathing.

Kai looked at Nathan. "I don't get it. That's the big secret?"

His mouth quirked. "I should have asked for your silence, too."

"Okay. But why?"

"There are those who would torture you for that information if they so much as suspected you possessed it."

"That's a great reason for me to keep quiet, but I still don't get why it's such a big deal."

"Because the information comes from Winter. As Cullen said, there are myriad theories about the source of magic, yet only a very small number of beings in all the realms suspect the full truth. Even fewer are certain. You don't see what it means. I'm not sure I do, either. But he does."

"Son of a bitch," Cullen breathed.

"I'm afraid he's precisely the sort of person my Queen would prefer to keep that information away from," Nathan went on. "Seeing that—"

"Addler's Theorem of Two Spaces," Cullen muttered. "And gates. By God, gates must be a way of dodging the chaos altogether, not just bridging it, which means—"

"—he can grasp the ramifications and put them to use."

"—they *can't* be a product of temporal displacement, the way Perez insisted. Son of a bitch!" Cullen repeated with great satisfaction. "*That's* what happened when the realms shifted!"

Nathan nodded. "Yes, that's why you've more magic here now. Chaos is once more pressing against the order in your realm. The point I want you to think about is what this says about Dyffaya. A god of chaos, you see, has a great deal of power available to him."

Cullen's eyebrows snapped down. "He ought to be bloody unstoppable."

"He very nearly was, I understand, before he was killed."

"Wait a minute," Kai said. "I'm not following. Why does being the god of chaos mean he's got mega-oomphs of power?"

Cullen looked at her as if just then remembering she existed. "Because a god of chaos must have some *access* to chaos. If he can bring even the smallest mote of it through to our realm—" He looked at Nathan. "Is there any way to quantify what would happen then?"

"There may be, but I don't know it." Nathan met Kai's puzzled eyes. "Likely friction doesn't sound very powerful to you. Think of bringing order and chaos together as similar to what happens when matter and antimatter touch."

Kai did think about that for a couple scary seconds. "That would be mega-oomphs, all right."

"However, Dyffaya has a problem bringing in that mote of chaos because he can't enter a realm himself. His body was killed and he can't enter any of the realms without a body."

Cullen's eyebrows climbed. "And yet he planned to do just that."

"Not exactly. He was trying to disrupt the time-stream so severely it would allow him to pull his original body into the present."

"You're joking," Kai said. Only clearly he wasn't. "But if he yanked his still-living body out of the past, wouldn't he be bringing his former self along with it? And then his body wouldn't have been around when whoever-it-was killed him, so he wouldn't have died after all, so—"

"I don't pretend to understand it. I'm telling you what Winter told me. He needed Nam Anthessa to do that. Without the knife, he's limited to acting from outside this realm. Cullen? Are you listening?"

With a visible effort, Cullen dragged himself back from

whatever fresh thought had held him enraptured. "Sure. Go ahead."

"Just as chaos disrupts order, so order destroys chaos. This is why the chaos energy set loose by Nam Anthessa's death is not pure chaos, but an amalgam of chaos, *arguai*, and magic. When the knife was whole, it held chaos bound up in spirit to protect it from the order in our realms. When the knife shattered, that chaos came into greater contact with order, which means—"

"Of course. Of course. Freshly minted magic, and tons of it." Cullen paced three quick steps, stopped, and turned. "Think of what this tells us about nodes! Node magic is the most powerful because it's freshly created, and so is the least ordered. Do you see what that means?" That was more demand than question.

"Not as clearly as you, I suspect, but—"

"That's why it's so much harder to work with node energy, slightly easier to work with ley lines—not that you can't blow yourself up that way, too. It's why plant-based magic is the safest and the weakest. Living things are complex, which means they're highly ordered, so their magic is, too. Although that doesn't explain why living things like you and me can possess a great deal of magic—"

"Because of our *kiths,*" Kai put in, getting into the spirit of discovery. "Somehow our grounds filter the magic in a way that doesn't order it as completely as a plant would."

"That makes sense. And the ramifications go on and on. Intent is a key component to every spell and the hardest to master, but I think . . . yes, by all the gods, that's why Gifts are so much stronger than spells! It must be! A Gift lets us impose intent on magic without any other components, which means no power is lost through the additional ordering those other components impose. My God, this is huge!" Cullen's eyes glowed with a zealot's joy. "Then there's the so-called lunar limit on charms—not that I see how exactly that ties in, but it must. When I think of—"

"Don't," Nathan said firmly. "Not right now."

"—the implications for the way we classify magic—"

"Cullen."

"Take mind magic, for one. That has to be highly ordered, doesn't it? While fire is closer to chaos, so it—"

"Cullen! There's a god who wants to dabble in your realm, and while he's at it, he'd like very much to kill Rule Turner and harm or kill Lily Yu. I'd like you to pay attention to that particular ramification for a moment."

"Right." Cullen drew in a slow breath. "I see that this Dyffaya has beaucoup power to sling around because the chaos energy creates it for him. He didn't before because that power was bound up in Nam Anthessa, but he does now. Yet he can't enter our realm, so he's limited to the power generated by the bits of chaos energy set free by the knife's destruction. Or so we think." He frowned thoughtfully. "Eventually those bits will be used up, won't they?"

"I'd think so, but how long is 'eventually'? A week, a century, several centuries? I have no idea, and no idea how we could find out. Then there's the *arguai*, the spiritual energy. Dyffaya is a god. He can use that."

Kai said, "But no one here worships him."

"Not him, no, but chaos is important here as it is everywhere. Anarchists celebrate it, the mad are trapped in it, and artists and creators of all sorts draw upon it. As does everyone who works with magic."

Cullen blinked. "Shit."

"None of those ties to chaos means that those people actively worship Dyffaya, but their connection to chaos matters to the spiritual side of things." Nathan paused and frowned. "Not that I know how, exactly."

They all fell silent, contemplating the possible resources of a god tied to magic in such a fundamental way. After a moment, Kai spoke slowly. "There's something I don't understand."

Cullen's eyebrows lifted again. "Only one thing?"

She ignored that. "He's the god of chaos, so that's what he draws on. But if intention supplies order, then isn't he acting antichaos every time he uses his power intentionally?"

Nathan beamed at her. "That is very much what Winter told me. Yes, he is, and that's an important limitation. Every time he acts toward a goal it imposes order, which drains some of his spiritual power. He's done a lot of that, so I think he must be spiritually depleted. He's more likely to use magic against us than spiritual attacks. Kai and I can't be compelled, but—"

Cullen broke in. "Listen, I need to get a look at chaos energy."

"We can try to arrange that," Nathan said. "But first I have to stress that you are not to try to touch it or use it yourself."

"I'm not an idiot. It would be as hard to control as node energy, so only as a last resort—"

"Not as a last resort. Not under any circumstances. Three components to chaos energy, Cullen: magic, spirit, and chaos. And basically, the spiritual part *is* Dyffaya."

"You think he would take over my mind if I tried to handle chaos energy."

"You can't use it without touching it, can you? And if you touch it, he'd have you. Your shields won't work against a spiritual assault. Unless you've the sort of soul-deep faith that might allow you to resist . . ? I didn't think so. Then there's that kernel of chaos at the core. Try to bring it under your control and you expose it to order."

"And—boom." Cullen huffed out an impatient breath. "I get it, okay? No messing with the chaos energy."

"Good. Now that we're clear on that, I'd like you to figure out how to destroy it without destroying half the state."

Cullen stared at him. "You just finished explaining why I can't. Pretty damn convincingly, too."

"Destroying it wouldn't be the same as trying to use it, now, would it?"

"In the sense that destroying it may be possible without connecting with it, which would let Dyffaya take me over? Nope, not the same. In the sense that destroying it will release a catastrophic amount of power? That part's pretty much the same."

"That's how it looks to me, too. Which is one reason I told you what I have. Cullen, when I told you about the source of magic, ideas began fizzing and popping around in your head. You saw what it meant in all sorts of ways that had to be explained to me. You've got a chance of figuring out how to destroy the chaos energy released by Nam Anthessa's death. I don't. And we need to destroy it. We can't get to Dyffaya, so we have to make it impossible for him to get to us."

Cullen's eyes went unfocused. He shook his head, muttered something Kai didn't catch, then suddenly paced right up to the edge of the circle, stopped, and glared at it. "I can't even figure out how you did this." He waved at the invisible ward. "And you want me to come up with a way to safely dispose of chaos energy?"

"Well, hell," Kai said. "You're doing it, too. Even you."

He turned the glare on her. "What the hell does that mean?"

"It's what I saw in almost all the humans in the Queens' realms—this damnable assumption that elves know more, can do more, than anyone else, so the only way to get ahead is to get hold of *their* knowledge." She shook her head. "Elves do not like change. Their whole system works against it. What they know now is pretty much what they've known for centuries. When you offered to trade Nathan a spell or two in exchange for learning how to set a silence ward, you said they were spells you'd come up with yourself. You do that a lot? Come up with new spells?"

"Sometimes, sure, but there's a wee bit of difference between coming up with a magnification spell and safely disposing of the most volatile energy in existence."

"The point is that we don't need someone who already thinks they know everything worth knowing. We need someone who's used to banging his head up against all that he doesn't know in order to come up with something *new*."

Cullen was silent for a long moment. When he spoke again, his voice was mild. "Nathan is not an elf."

"What?"

"You thought I was coming over all insecure because of exposure to Nathan, but your argument was about elves. Nathan isn't an elf."

"You pick every nit you find, do you?"

"Damn straight. All right." He faced Nathan again. "I'll do what I can, but like I said, I need to see chaos energy. We'll have to figure out a way for me to do that. Also, you're going to have to ante up information when I ask for it."

"Blank check?" Nathan said dryly.

"You have my word that I won't ask unless I believe the information is relevant to my finding a way to destroy chaos energy."

"Very well. If it's something I know and am not honor-bound to withhold, I will answer you."

"Good. We can—no." He shook his head, then stood frowning off into space. "I need to think. I need time to think. Is there more you need to tell me under my vow of secrecy?"

"Not unless you've a question whose answer might need to be included in that vow."

"I need to digest awhile before I know what to ask."

"We may as well rejoin the others, then." Nathan stepped up to the circle Kai couldn't see and broke it with the side of his hand.

Cullen watched intently, but shook his head as if unable to figure out what, exactly, Nathan had done. "About how you set that ward—"

"Not now."

Unexpectedly, Cullen grinned. "I'm going to ask again, you know."

Nathan's voice was very dry. "I had guessed you might."

Cullen turned away. Paused. "Oh. You need to ask Lily about the godhead. She was there, after all. Not physically, but her experience might offer some information." He gave Nathan a nod and headed for the house.

Kai started to follow, then stopped when she realized Nathan hadn't moved. He was watching Cullen, his expression bemused. "What?" she asked.

"Just wondering what I've turned loose on this world. I'm thinking he's going to be the first full mage your realm has seen since the Purge. Maybe even the first full adept."

A mage wielded a lot of power. An adept, though . . . "You really think he could go that far?"

Nathan shrugged. "He hasn't found his true name, but if he does, then yes. He's brilliant, fascinated by magic, and obsessed with learning more and more—the three qualities all human adepts require."

"Only the human adepts?"

"Well, all adepts are all fascinated by magic, but elves have longer to spend on the learning. Humans need to get there in a hurry if they're to arrive at all, so there's more need for obsession."

And elves, for all their faults, had evolved a system of

checks on the power of their adepts—one largely composed of other adepts and backed up, in the end, by the two Queens. Kai thought of some of the stories about adepts that she'd heard. "It's not like I think Cullen's going to go over to the dark side, but if he did, no one here could stop him. Even if he just got careless . . ." She shivered, thinking of one story in particular, about an adept who'd made a small mistake once when opening a gate.

"You're forgetting the Eldest."

True, and that did make her feel some better. Still, dragons did not have the same priorities as humans. The black dragon might do nothing as long as Cullen didn't interfere with his own plans, regardless of what Cullen did in the human world. He might decide to kill Cullen tomorrow, just in case.

Maybe not tomorrow. He'd left, hadn't he? Taken off on some mysterious business of his own.

"It isn't Cullen we need to worry about, though, is it?"

She shook her head as if to dislodge her previous thoughts. "What?"

"Cullen will never violate his oath to Isen. Whatever power he acquires will belong to his Rho, so it looks like he will be Isen's problem. Did you know Lily Yu had been inside the godhead?"

"He yanked her there mentally when she was injured and tried to persuade her she was dead. Apparently he could have trapped her there if she'd been convinced she didn't have a body to return to. She talked about it once, but I guess you weren't there. You didn't know?"

"It seems I've been insufficiently curious." He held out his hand. "Let's get back inside."

Surprised, Kai took his hand. Nathan wasn't much for holding hands in public. He loved to touch, but when out in the big, dangerous world he preferred to keep his hands free in case an assailant dropped out of the sky or burrowed up from the ground or whatever.

She tossed a mage light into being with her other hand, being unable to see in the dark the way he did, and they headed for the lower deck. It felt good to hold hands as they ambled back to the house on this cool April night, but Kai couldn't help wondering. Nathan kept doing things she didn't expect . . .

like holding hands. And arming Isen Turner with a soon-to-be mage who might even become an adept. Isen was an honorable man, but he was at war. War could bring even honorable men to make choices they'd never otherwise consider.

They started down the steps to the lower deck. "How angry will your Queen be that you shared that information with Cullen? And with me, for that matter."

"Eh!" His mouth turned up, but this wasn't one of his freshly-minted smiles, for his eyes stayed dark with trouble. "As you pointed out, we're going up against a god. I'm betting she'll understand."

TEN

SOMEONE new sat at the big table, talking to Cullen, when Kai went back inside—a tall woman with short blond hair and beautifully intricate tattoos. Cynna Weaver was Cullen's wife, a former Dizzy, former FBI agent, new mother, and a very strong Finder. She was also the Rhej of Nokolai Clan, with Rhej being a term no one could define very well for Kai, save to say that it did not mean priestess.

Kai sat down across from her. "Hi, Cynna. No Ryder?" Kai loved babies, and Cynna and Cullen's little Ryder was beyond adorable.

"She's full, happy, and fast asleep under Marianne's watchful eye. Isen called me to see if I wanted to join your task force. I do."

Nathan spoke gravely, but humor lurked at the back of his eyes. "You're welcome to join us, but I understood you were likely to be asleep by now yourself, worn out by the rigors of parenthood."

Cynna rolled her eyes. "Oh, please. I fall asleep on the couch once, and this never-needs-sleep wolf I'm married to—"

"Once?" Cullen said, his eyebrows lifting. "Once? I know math isn't your thing, but I'm pretty sure you can count above 'one.'"

"Speaking of sleeping on the couch . . ." Cynna gave Cullen one of those couples' looks, the kind that outsiders can't decipher but know carries meaning. He grinned and leaned close to whisper something that made her grin right back.

Isen spoke dryly. "Now that we have, once again, covered the topic of Cullen's sex life, perhaps we could talk about the god who's sending chaos into our world. Cullen? Was the explanation you received worth the vow?"

"Yes and hell yes. Two hundred percent worth it. A thousand percent. The ramifications . . . but I won't go there right now. Like Nathan said, Dyffaya has a helluva lot of magical power to toss around because chaos energy generates it in crazy-big lots. He probably can't use much *arguai* against us, though, for complicated reasons, so spiritual attacks are less likely than they were when Nam Anthessa was intact. The only way he can act in our realm is through the chaos energy created by the knife's destruction. That will be used up eventually, but we've no way of knowing how long that might take, so Nathan would like me to speed things up. He wants me to devise a way to safely destroy chaos energy."

Cynna frowned. "Is that even possible?"

"Not very, but what he told me makes it slightly less impossible."

She didn't look reassured. "We don't even know what this chaos energy is, so—"

"You may not, but I do."

Her frown tightened another notch. "Is that what you can't tell us?"

"In part," Nathan said, "but part of it you can know. We discussed that before you arrived. Chaos energy is a tangle of magic and *arguai*—what you call spiritual energy—with a kernel of chaos at its center."

Arjenie frowned. "I keep wondering why it stayed here after the knife was destroyed. I got the impression your Queen didn't expect it to."

"No," Kai said. "And that bothers me. She tends to be right about that sort of thing."

"It seems pretty obvious to me," Nettie Two Horses said.

Kai turned to her, surprised. "What do you mean?"

"This god must have worshipers—or people who serve him—here."

"I don't see how," Cullen said. "Or why that's so obvious, for that matter, but I'll defer to your expertise on spiritual matters. If you say having worshipers here would keep the chaos energy in our realm, fine. But how did he have time to acquire any? The only worshiper he had when Miriam and Nam Anthessa nearly yanked him into our realm was Miriam."

Nettie gave him the kind of look teachers have been giving students for generations. "The only one we know about."

"And yet," Isen said, "I think I see what Cullen means. Manifesting in our realm was hugely important to Dyffaya, yet the only worshiper he used in his attempt was poor Miriam. If he had others, why weren't they present at the rite?"

Nettie shrugged. "Maybe he doesn't have the kind of hold over them he did over her, so he couldn't count on them to be okay with all the throat slitting. That's particularly true if they serve rather than worship." She looked around the table. "You lupi should understand the distinction between service and worship."

"Service would be a bit tepid for Dyffaya," Nathan said. "He'll want to be worshiped."

Nettie nodded slowly. "If so . . . worship has to be genuine to be useful to a deity. Miriam may have started out as a true believer, but in the end she was under compulsion. That wouldn't feed or anchor him. He may have been picking up followers all along because Miriam's compelled service didn't feed him."

"Eh." Nathan drummed his fingers on the table thoughtfully. "I can't say I understand how deity functions, but worship is surely the most recognized way to link a godhead to a realm. Occupied godheads are different from the unoccupied ones, of course, but—"

"Wait a minute. Occupied and unoccupied?"

"That's a sidhe concept," Kai explained. "They believe that godheads exist whether or not there's a being connected to the quality or qualities being worshiped, and they have a cultural preference for godheads that aren't personified. Most of them worship beauty, for example, but it's considered rather déclassé to worship one of the gods or goddesses of beauty. Although some do, especially among the lower sidhe."

Nettie's snort made her opinion of that clear. "I'd like to turn Coyote loose on them. He's personified as hell."

"Actually," Cynna said, "Godheads are also a lupi concept. I can't say much—it's secret lupi stuff—but the Lady speaks of occupied godheads. She makes a distinction between those occupied by former mortals and those occupied by Old Ones. This Dyffaya isn't an Old One, so—"

Ackleford broke in impatiently, "Look, maybe all this godhead shit matters in some way I don't see right this fucking minute, but what do we do with it? What's the plan? How do we keep this Dyffaya from grabbing more people?"

"Does he need more people?" Cynna asked.

"We'd best assume so," Nathan said. "He grabbed the toddler and sent her back. He grabbed Britta and kept her. He tried to grab Kai. That failed because—"

"That's unproven," Ackleford said. "It's a strong possibility, not established fact."

Nathan looked at the special agent. "It's what happened. I *know* he tried for Kai."

Ackleford met his look with his trademark scowl. "You can be as sure as you like. Doesn't mean I am. I repeat—do we have a plan?"

"Basically, I want to cut Dyffaya off, make it so he can't act in our realm. If he has worshipers here, he's got more of an anchor than I realized—and we need to find them. Special Agent, I'd like you you to find out everything you can about the people who were present at Fagioli today. It would make sense for the god to have one or more of his worshipers present when he acted. Meanwhile, Cullen will try to come up with a way to get rid of the scattered chaos energy. Cullen says he needs to see it. I'm hoping a Finder might be able to help with that." He raised his eyebrows at Cynna.

"Yeah, well . . ." She grimaced. "The problem is getting a pattern I can use for a Find, when chaos is the opposite of pattern."

That started a discussion about patterns and Finding that quickly got too technical for Kai. She knew the basics, but what in the world did "null-sequenced pulses" mean? Nathan seemed to get it, or at least he was able to follow well enough to ask the right questions. The upshot seemed to be that Cynna needed a pattern for the particular flavor of magic chaos energy generated—which meant she needed to be present at a chaos incident or very soon after one occurred.

After that, Nathan explained why he thought Dyffaya had less spiritual power to use against them than he had before. "But," he added, "we can't assume he won't mount any spiritual attacks. Corruption's the easiest for him, but it's also the easiest to spot. It's essentially selfish—that little voice that says it's okay to have what you want, no matter what. Watch for those kind of thoughts in yourself and others. Persuasion—that's more subtle, a way of tilting your thoughts in a certain direction. It can fly under the radar, but will be harder for him to use without the knife to direct it. Still possible, though. Of course, if you actually touched chaos energy, Dyffaya could persuade you of pretty much anything. Put you under compulsion, too, though that's a magical trick, not spiritual."

"Hold on," Ackleford said. "Wasn't everyone who was bitten today touched by this chaos energy?"

Cullen answered that one. "Nope. The butterflies were created using chaos energy, but what they transmitted was a magical hook, not a spiritual one."

"You're sure about that?"

Cullen shot him an irritated look. "I can't be a hundred percent sure because I don't see spirit. I see magic. But spiritual energy causes a perturbation in magic that I can see, and I didn't see it in the hook I was able to study." He tipped his head, looking at Nathan. "Sam told us you were immune to persuasion."

Nathan rubbed his nose thoughtfully. "I can be fooled, but not that way. Persuasion is all about fooling you into accepting thoughts that aren't really your ideas at all. Dyffaya could maybe put a thought in my head. He couldn't make me think it was mine, which makes it easier to push it right back out again. But . . ." He looked vaguely embarrassed. "It's just a knowing, not something I learned, so I can't tell you how to do it. I can say that knowing your true name helps, but that's no help for most of you, is it? Having a strong faith helps, too. I'm hoping Nettie has some ideas about protection."

Nettie advised them to pray frequently, if that was part of their faith tradition. Meditation was good, too. Even if they weren't especially religious, a religious object might offer some protection if they had a strong emotional tie to it—"like your grandmother's cross or Bible," she said, "if your grandmother was a believer." The older the object, the better. She also said that Cynna was probably protected by the Lady, and Isen might be as well. The lupi all nodded. No one explained.

Kai didn't ask. Lupi weren't quite as big on secrets as elves, but they came close sometimes.

After that Cynna wanted to talk with Isen privately, Nathan wanted to talk to Nettie, Cullen wanted to argue with Benedict, Benedict wanted to go home, Arjenie wanted Cullen to stop arguing, and Ackleford wanted to talk to Kai. He asked her to walk out to his car with him because he had "a couple questions."

She could only think of one subject he was likely to ask her about. She was right.

"I need to know more about Hunter," he said as they walked out into the cool night air.

"And yet you're talking to me, not him."

"Some of my questions might piss him off. I don't mind pissing people off. Sometimes you get better answers that way. But Seabourne tells me the sidhe are touchy and hold a grudge, so I wanted to know what I shouldn't ask him about."

He was not, she noted, worried about pissing her off. People mostly didn't. Somehow she never struck anyone as scary. "I wouldn't worry about it too much. Elves are touchy, but Nathan's not an elf."

"So what the hell is he? I mean . . . he used to be some kind of dog, right? A hellhound. But his Queen did a big spell on him a long time ago, and poof." He made a circling gesture, as if stirring a cauldron. "Now he's . . . what?"

Kai's lips quirked. Calling a hellhound "some kind of dog" was accurate—in the same way that calling a dragon "some kind of lizard" would be. "He's Wild Sidhe and he's a man. He lived as a human for a long time, Special Agent. That doesn't make him one, but he's not that different from us, either. Just think of him as a man with an unusual skill set."

He snorted. "Unusual skill set. Sure. What exactly are Wild Sidhe?"

"That's a pretty large question. The short answer . . ." She thought for a moment. "They vary a lot, and some are one-offs—an individual rather than a species—but they're all nature-beings, mostly animal, though some look human or elfish, and a few resemble some kind of plant. Ents, for example."

"Ents? Like in *The Lord of the Rings*? You mean they're real?"

She grinned. "I'd never have taken you for a Tolkien fan. You have unexpected depths, Special Agent. Yes, ents are real, rare, and powerful, but you won't find any here."

"I've got a son. Two sons, but it's Brian that's the Tolkien fan. He had to see all the movies."

Two sons, yet here he was at nearly midnight . . . "It must be hard, being away from them so much."

"Divorced," he said glumly. "Their mom moved to Albuquerque and . . . shit. How did you do that? That's not what I want to talk about." They'd reached his car. He turned and leaned against it, crossing his arms. "I'm trying to get a handle on how Hunter thinks."

"I don't know how to answer that. If you want to know what I see in his thoughts, that's confidential."

"No, I'm not talking about that shit. More like . . . he talks about knowing stuff as if the knowledge arrives from outside him. Like he doesn't need any logic to reach a conclusion. Is that for real? Is he, like, a precog or something?"

"Oh, I see what you mean. No, it isn't any kind of precognition. More like instinct on steroids. Magic gives his instincts a boost, but the process isn't that different from you've experienced, I bet. You've been an agent a long time. You probably have an instinct for when something's off—when a witness is lying, or when the obvious answer doesn't quite fit."

"Sure, sometimes. But when I look back I can usually see that something was there, tipping me off, even if I couldn't see it at the time."

She nodded. "Nathan's instinct is like that, only whatever triggers it may be so small it's invisible to anyone else even when he explains. But it's accurate. When he says he *knows* Dyffaya wanted to grab me, I take that as fact."

He looked down, scowling at his feet as he thought that over. Finally he gave a nod and straightened. "I'll keep that in mind. Thanks for the explanation."

Kai wasn't sure he believed her, but it was probably enough that he wasn't dismissing Nathan's instincts completely. She told him good night, but instead of going back inside right away, she let her feet meander down the road.

She ought to go in. She needed sleep. It was the last, sticky end of a long and twisty day, one that had pivoted over and over until she wasn't sure which direction she faced, much less what lay ahead. But all that twisting about had left her mind too crowded for sleep to elbow its way in. As she moved, she began picking at the logjam of thoughts, and found them hung up on the same one that had kept intruding earlier.

Nathan was on a Hunt.

There were hunts and there were Hunts. That's how Kai thought of the difference, at least—a typographic shorthand for what she saw in his thoughts. During his long years of exile, Nathan had learned to hunt when there would be no death at the end of the chase. He'd hunted criminals and arrested them. He'd hunted children, too—lost or stolen children—and restored them to their families. Those were lowercase hunts. However satisfying he found it to recover a kidnapped child, it didn't wake his deepest instincts.

What she thought of as a Hunt, Nathan called a true hunt. A true hunt ended in his quarry's death. Always. She'd seen that this was a true hunt in the amethyst glow that sharpened every curl and swirl of his thoughts, but she would have known even without her Gift. Even Benedict had sensed the change. Nathan was on a Hunt, and his instincts were true.

But how could he Hunt and kill a god—one he couldn't even reach? One whose body had died three thousand years ago?

ELEVEN

WIND whispered through the darkness, carrying messages and mystery. Among the messages were sage and dust, the distant howl of a wolf, and the nearby sound of a car starting.

That would be Ackleford leaving, Nathan thought as another wolf answered the first one. He leaned on the railing at one end of the deck behind Isen Turner's home, absorbing the wind's messages and thinking about the mystery.

Memory was a capricious bugger, wasn't it?

Nathan had come to Earth on a Hunt. His Queen had set him to find and kill a renegade mage who'd thought to evade her justice by hiding here, outside her realms. It had been a long Hunt. By the time his quarry lay dead, the magic here had grown so weak he couldn't leave. He'd been trapped—trapped on Earth, trapped in the man's body his Queen had imposed on him for the Hunt.

For years he'd dreamed of being a hound again. In those dreams he'd run on four legs with the wind streaming past, filled with the joy and power of the body he'd been born with. For years he'd hated those dreams, hated them bitterly, for he always woke to the knowledge that never would he feel that, be that, again. But time performed its healing. Eventually he'd come to treasure such dreams for the beautiful memories they were . . . although by then, they'd come only rarely.

How long had it been since he dreamed his way into his birth form?

Long and long, he thought, though he couldn't put a number on it. Yet here was memory pressing on him as if blown in by the wind. Memory of another night, one so far in the past it should have picked up all sorts of lint and fuzz over the years.

It hadn't. On the long-ago night he'd been a hellhound—a young one, less than a century old. He'd left his first master, the Huntsman, because he knew he belonged to Winter. The Huntsman had been willing to release him, but it had taken Nathan some time to convince Winter of the obvious. In the end, she'd accepted him into her service and her household. On this night he'd lain stretched out on the warm stone floor before her hearth. He remembered the precise blend of scents in her chamber, the way the wood popped as the fire burned, and the bitter weeping of the woman with him.

Funny how often even those who should know better forgot that Winter was Queen, not just of snow and ice, but also of the blazing hearth, the heart's home during the days of darkness. The fire in Winter's chamber that night had burned hot and bright, but in the memory-moment that visited him now, it had begun to die down. She'd wept, his Queen, wept over the loss of one dear to her . . . he frowned, trying to recall the name. Gwyfellyth, that was it, and he'd been a strong and wily fellow, both friend and lover to Winter.

Who or what had killed him? Nathan couldn't remember now. He remembered his Queen's grief, though. She'd paced and wept until both wore her out, then settled beside him on the fire-warmed stone, playing with his ears. After a time, she'd begun to talk as she sometimes did, telling him things no one else would ever hear. Even as a young hound he'd known many languages, though of course he could speak none of them. Back then, he'd prized his silence for the gift that it was. It had made him safe for her in a way even his love could not.

She'd spoken of Gwyfellyth, of his life and his death, then sighed. "Ah, Nadrellian, it hurts. It hurts more because I didn't realize how much I cared until he was gone. Why did I let myself care so much? Damn him anyway for dying, and damn me for being silly enough to damn him for it. There's folly, isn't it? Winter's Queen, railing against death!" She'd laughed in a way he hadn't understood, but the pain in it had been clear enough, so he'd licked her face, trying to comfort.

Maybe it had helped. She'd curled up against him—he'd been larger than her, so his body made a comfortable backrest—and stared into the dying fire for a long time. Some internal process continued, though, because all at once she'd sat up, looked him in the eyes, and stroked both hands along his muzzle. "What I said about not letting myself care—that was the pain talking, and a false lesson. Forget I said it."

He'd cocked his head, being rather literal in his thinking at the time. Forgetting wasn't one of his gifts.

She'd smiled briefly, perhaps reading his thought—sometimes she did—and scratched behind one of his ears. "Let me tell you the true lesson, then, to supplant the false one. You will live a long time, my beautiful Nadrellian. Not as long as I, but long enough to grow weary, as many of my people do. Remember this: the only way to live is to *live*—and death is always, always, part of living. We die over and over. Oh, the big death comes but once, but a thousand deaths arrive with every turn of the seasons—the death of a day or a lover, of a friend or a dream, death piled upon death. The slow sundering of years parts us even from who we once were and from the memories which parented us. *Live anyway.*"

She'd straightened, suddenly regal, the mantle of her power falling over her—Winter in full truth. "With those thousand deaths come a thousand births. Ten thousand, if we're alive enough to notice. Drink whatever comes to you, death or life or both together, drink it down, whether the draught be sweet or bitter. If you refuse the one, you won't be able to taste the other."

With that, she'd spoken a *word*. Power washed the room with silence. True silence, lacking the thinnest hush of noise, as if even the meaning of sound had drained out of the world. Regality vanished along with sound and she'd grinned like a pixie, delighted with her own mischief, leaned forward, and whispered in his ear. Whispered a string of syllables that rolled and reverberated through him, shocking him to his core. Whispered her name. Her full, true name.

She'd sat up, dismissed the silence with a gesture, and said in quite a normal voice, "There. I've placed a burden on you, one you didn't ask for, but—oh, don't shake your head at me. You understand very well what such knowledge means, and that you'd willingly take on any burden for me doesn't make it less of one. But now you can call me to you, should your need be great, and the way I placed it in you means you needn't speak it aloud. And now . . . now I am wholly known to you." She'd sighed again, this time with relief, and smiled an easy smile with peace at its heart. "There's your last lesson for tonight, or perhaps it's my own." She'd chuckled. "Oh, yes, it's my lesson. For you already know, don't you? True connection, deep connection, is as rare as it is precious. When it happens in spite of all we can do to hide from it—you must have noticed how you terrified me at first?—when it happens anyway, hold nothing back."

Some twenty feet away and centuries later, the door onto the deck opened and Kai stepped outside. Nathan's heart lifted. So did another part of his body. He chuckled. Little Brother was ever the optimist.

No mystery after all about why that particular memory had visited him tonight. The future smelled bitter indeed. Death drew near, though he didn't know if it would be one of the many deaths any life holds or the final one. It depended, he thought, on where Dyffaya's revenge was truly aimed: at himself or at the Queen who'd sent him here . . . the Queen who, with her sister, had killed Dyffaya áv Eni over three millennia ago.

Looked at that way, the answer seemed clear. It was likely the final death Dyffaya had in mind for Nathan, for that would hurt Winter the most. Nathan was hard to kill, but a god—even a half-dead one—ought to be able to manage it. But in elvish, "Dyffaya áv Eni" meant "beautiful madness." The god was irrational on the deepest level, for that was the nature of chaos. Nathan couldn't assume he knew Dyffaya's priorities . . . and the best way for the god to hurt Nathan was to hurt Kai.

"There you are," Kai said, having spotted him in the shadows.

There you are, his heart sang back. Right here and right now, she was with him, whole and healthy, if somewhat anxious. And he smiled all over.

AMAZING what clarity a little walking and a fair dose of mad could bring. Kai felt quite clear-headed as she made for Nathan. Stars and moon provided the only light, but it was enough. "Stop smiling at me like that."

He did not obey her. "You'd like me to smile another way?"

"I'd like you to level with me. So far, you haven't."

That did the trick. His smile faded away—which, perversely, did not make her happy at all. "I don't lie to you."

"There's a difference between lying and telling the whole truth. You've got something in mind you haven't told me about." Her breath huffed out. "You're on a true hunt. Did you think I couldn't tell? And yet the only plans you've talked about involve shutting Dyffaya out of this realm, which means shutting you away from your quarry."

He rubbed a hand over his head. "I was afraid you'd notice that."

"*Can* you get to him?" she demanded. "Is that what you aren't telling me? Can you use your ability to cross realms to enter his godhead?"

"No. No, it's not enough of a place for me to get there that way."

Which didn't make a great deal of sense to her, but then, she didn't understand what a godhead was, not at all. "Then you've got some screwy plan to let him grab you."

"It's much more mushy than a plan," he assured her. "More like a possibility I'm keeping in mind."

"I want to shake you. Hard." She took a calm-me-down breath. "Killing him has been *tried.* It only halfway worked. How are you going to kill someone who doesn't have a body?"

"In my hands," he said with perfect certainty, "Claw can kill anything."

"That's assuming that your blade will go with you if he snatches you—"

"It's not precisely with me now."

No, Claw was in the little fold in reality the Queen had made to hide it. And that was beside the point. "Don't quibble. You know what I mean."

"I believe Claw will go with me. My Queen said the link could only be severed by my death. It's possible she's wrong, but I think it unlikely."

"When she said that, she wasn't considering that you might go chasing a halfway dead god into his godhead! If that's even where you'd end up. It's supposed to be impossible."

Wry humor flickered through his thoughts, the color of old gold. "I try not to assume I know what Winter has considered and what she hasn't. As for what's possible . . ." He moved close and laid his hands on her shoulders. "I know it's possible for me to kill Dyffaya. I don't know how or why, or if he will snatch me, or where I'd end up if he did. That's all guessing on my part. But I know I have a shot at killing Dyffaya." More softly he said, "You're scared, Kai. I am, too, and we've reason to be. But I won't be setting myself up as bait, if that's what's worrying you. No sticking my tongue out at Dyffaya and double-daring him to come after me. And yet he may do that, so I have to think about what my options would be."

She stared at him a moment. "You're such a damn adult." When he cocked his head, puzzled, she sighed. "You're being so reasonable. It makes me want to have a temper tantrum, and that makes me feel about five years old."

He tucked a loose strand of her hair behind her ear. "You'd rather I got mad along with you?"

"Sometimes." But maybe not this time. Maybe she didn't want to fight with him, after all. Kai tucked herself up against him and his arms went around her, easy as breathing and just as natural. They were almost of a height, and she loved that, loved the way their bodies fit. He rubbed his cheek along her hair, soothing both of them. After a moment she confessed on a wisp of breath, "I don't know how to stop being scared."

He tightened his arms to tell her that he was here with her now, that they were both okay. Then he chuckled.

"What?" She raised her head.

"Little Brother has a suggestion. I'm not sure it's a valid one, mind, but he hopes you'll consider it."

"You are such a guy." She shook her head. "I'm guessing it's the same suggestion he offers when I'm cold or bored or happy or just breathing."

"Oh, yes." He bent and nuzzled her neck. "Bit of a Johnny One Note, isn't he?"

"Sure is." Her arms tightened around him. "Just as well that it's such a good suggestion, then, isn't it?"

TWELVE

THE first time Nathan had referred to "Little Brother," Kai had laughed. Fortunately, considering the circumstances, Nathan thought sex and laughter were a natural combination—sex being, he liked to say, proof that God loved them. And that She had a sense of humor.

She'd asked him why so many men named their Tab B when she didn't know any woman who'd named her Slot A. To which he'd replied: "Have you ever taken a Great Dane for a walk on a leash?" Which hadn't seemed to answer her question, so he'd added, "Though that's an imperfect metaphor. Great Danes can be trained."

Meaning that Little Brother had a mind of his own, so why not a nickname? She'd laughed again, of course, and that led to tickling, and on to what they'd been doing to begin with.

In a sense, however, Nathan had trained his Great Dane. He could control his body in ways a Tibetan monk would envy, and that included shutting down desire. He'd done that routinely for a long time before he decided to trust Kai. To let her in. Because, he'd told her, sex was too lonely if you weren't with a friend.

Maybe that was why he took such delight in it now. Or maybe the mix of passion with play was just plain Nathan.

First he suggested a large oak tree on the west side of the deck as an appropriate spot—"being as we haven't tried that since we were in Adelsfrai." Ants, she reminded him, in case he'd forgotten what else had been in that tree. He insisted as they ambled toward the house that ants were not active at night, which she was pretty sure wasn't true, but if she was going to be picky, how about the roof? Private as could be except for that one guard, and no doubt he'd be tactful enough to stay on the other side of roof's peak.

She looked at him with raised brows. Privacy aside—and Nathan knew very well she wasn't going to put it aside that far—Isen's home was roofed in Spanish tiles. Talk about a bumpy ride. "You're in the mood to be on the bottom?"

They'd reached the lower deck, which was shadowed by the roof. "Speaking of bottoms," he murmured.

"Speaking of guards—"

"None nearby," he told her, and kissed her thoroughly, putting his hands where he'd indicated he wanted to. She found something to do with her hands, too, as heat washed through her the way it did every time he touched her, every time . . . and sometimes when he just looked at her, too. Friction, she thought, could be a most powerful force, just as he'd said, when it was the friction created by rubbing a bit of Nathan against a bit of Kai . . . "I want a bed," she told him firmly. "Just for novelty's sake." Which wasn't entirely accurate. Sure, they'd made love without one often enough on their travels, but they hadn't missed a chance to explore the possibilities beds offered, either.

The house was dark and quiet. Everyone had either departed or gone to their own beds. Even Dell was gone . . . heading back to the node, a quick check told Kai. The air held a spicy tang from the enchiladas they'd had for supper. And wasn't it lovely to eat enchiladas again? She'd missed Mexican food almost as much as coffee. Kai's heart beat strongly, desire hummed its sweet song, and Nathan was warm and solid at her side, adding thrumming bass notes to the rising tempo.

He continued to offer low-voiced suggestions—that first couch? No? What about this chair? It was roomy enough, he promised her even as they passed it by, heading into the hall. It was darker there, bumping-into-the-wall dark for her, and she let him do the steering and open the door to their room.

The drapes were open. Moonlight cast the room into shades of charcoal and pearl and reflected from the liquid surfaces of his eyes when she stopped, turned, and seized his head in both hands so she could pull his mouth to hers.

Nathan was wonderfully oral. He loved kissing, licking, pretty much anything he could do with his mouth . . . and he did know some lovely things to do with his mouth. For now they enjoyed little sips of each other, lips brushing and teasing rather than clinging. The damp touch of his tongue sent flicks of pleasure zinging up her spine. She nipped at his lower lip. He made a rumbling noise deep in his chest that meant *yes, yes, do that some more.* So she did.

When his hands went to the hem of his shirt, she brushed them aside and met his gaze as she replaced his hands with her own. Asking permission. Could she do this for him tonight?

Undressing each other held meaning for Nathan in a way that simple nudity did not. Usually they stripped with haste or humor or teasing touches, but once he'd told her—with a single whisper, with his actions, and in the unspoken colors of his thoughts—that he needed something else. Something more. He'd made a ceremony of it, a ritualistic baring that clearly mattered to him greatly. Afterward, she'd asked if that was a sidhe rite. "No," he'd whispered. "That was for me. Just for me."

She hadn't asked again, sensing that explaining would diminish it for him. Tonight she wanted to give that meaning to him again.

Or was the gift for herself?

He went still, searching her face. She looked at him steadily.

He nodded.

She pulled his shirt off over his head. He moved only enough to make it possible, his gaze fixed on her . . . and there was nothing playful in his thoughts now. They rose around him in billows of red-smeared gold sparked with amethyst flames. She wanted to touch the smooth skin of his chest, glide her hand down to his stomach, but didn't. That wasn't part of the ritual. Yet his muscles quivered once, sharply, as if she had touched him there. Slowly, as if performing one of her asanas, she reached for the button on his jeans. Then the zipper.

Still moving deliberately, she knelt in front of him and pulled off his shoes, one at a time. His socks. All the time she felt him watching. She rose again and began tugging down his jeans and underwear. She didn't touch Little Brother, though she smiled at that part of his body as it bobbed happily into view. Again, Nathan moved only enough to let her get his jeans off.

Then it was her turn.

With great care, he pulled off her shirt. He unfastened her bra and let it fall away. He touched her no more than he had to—a brush of fingers, a whisper of heat—and it was unbearably erotic. He unfastened her braid next and ran his fingers through her hair, spreading it out over her shoulders. It tickled her bare skin and she shivered. When he knelt to remove her shoes, she rested a hand on his shoulder. Nathan could stand on one foot forever without wobbling, but her balance wasn't so perfect.

When they were both naked, they stood silently in the moon-drenched room, looking into each other's eyes. Then, as he once had for her, she held out her hand. He took it.

When they came together this time, skin to skin, she felt naked from the inside out. That skin wasn't so much a barrier now as a carrier, the staging place for a thousand nerve endings to sing with need and delight. She felt him with every inch of her body, even where he wasn't touching her, as if the air itself was part of him, whispering wishes along the skin of her back and bottom and thighs. And all along her front was the tactile joy of his skin, the play of his muscles as he smoothed back her hair . . . then the damp warmth of his breath along her neck as he nuzzled her. And the quick jab of need when his hand slid between her thighs.

She jolted. And snaked her foot around behind his calf, pressing up against his touch with a low moan. And tripped him.

Good thing the bed was so close.

He let out a shout of laughter as he fell over backward onto it, and she dived in after him.

NATHAN lay in the close and quiet darkness with Kai's head on his shoulder, listening to the faint stir of her breathing and breathing her in. She smelled so good . . . all the time, really, but especially right after sex. Humans, he knew, weren't fond of the way bodies smelled. They particularly disliked the rich scents given off by genitals. It was very odd.

He didn't feel guilty at all. Should he? Or was that simply another difference between him and humans?

Kai had been right, of course. You could speak truth all day and still deceive. Nathan had learned how to do that from those who'd mastered the art—yet another thing Kai disliked about elves, their skill at deception. Earlier, Kai had tumbled to one omission on his part. She hadn't noticed that beneath it lay another, larger one.

He wasn't setting himself up as bait. That was true enough, but the hidden truth was that he didn't have to. The god would likely try to snatch him without any need for encouragement. The thing was, Dyffaya apparently needed to insert something into the blood to do his snatching. Something that didn't work immediately. There'd been quite a delay between the butterflies' attack and the disappearance of the toddler and the woman, hadn't there? Something that Dell had been able to remove from Kai's blood.

Which meant there was a physical component. If Dell could remove that component, so could Nathan. He'd have to use healing magic, not body magic, but he didn't doubt he could do it. There were things he couldn't heal, but those tended to be sudden and extremely thorough, such as chopping off his head. Anything Dell could fix, he could . . . if he let it happen.

That was the trick, the omission, the point where he deceived Kai with silence. Nathan could control his healing to a large degree. He couldn't shut it off, but he could slow it, even delay it entirely for a time. Judging by how long it had taken Dyffaya to snatch the toddler and the woman named

Britta, he'd need to refrain from healing for thirty minutes to an hour. That was well within his abilities. Then the god would grab him and take him right where he needed to be.

How else was he to get to Dyffaya, unless the god himself brought him there?

Of course, getting there was only part of the problem.

Lily Yu had been where Dyffaya lived. In the godhead. He needed to call her, ask about that. But she hadn't gone there physically, and that surely made a difference. He had no way of knowing if her experience had been a subjective projection onto some immaterial ground, or if the godhead possessed fixed referents. He might not perceive what she had.

Not that it mattered greatly, he supposed. The real question was whether he could live long enough, trapped in a godhead, to kill the being who held it . . . and what would happen to him when he did. Death wasn't the only possibility there. Just the most likely.

Kai's breathing changed as she shifted slightly without waking.

She hadn't asked him what had set him on this Hunt. Probably she assumed he didn't know, but he did. The moment he'd realized who the god was after, his instincts had awakened. Dyffaya wanted Kai. He meant to hurt her, kill her, in order to hurt Nathan. That couldn't be allowed. No matter what it took.

True connection, deep connection, is as rare as it is precious, Winter had told him one long-ago night. *When it happens, hold nothing back.*

And, as she'd also noted, that was a bit of wisdom he'd already understood, though he took no credit for it. That was the only way he knew to be. It would be hard, very hard, to leave Kai, knowing she was still Dyffaya's target, but if he stayed with her as instinct urged, sooner or later Dyffaya would succeed.

He would not allow that. No matter what. Nathan lay quietly in the darkness on this night so far removed from that one and breathed in Kai's scent. And smiled.

THIRTEEN

"MORE eggs?" Isen said politely.

Kai eyed the bowl wistfully. Isen's houseman, Carl, made incredible scrambled eggs. She couldn't figure out why they were so good. She'd watched him cook, and he didn't seem to do anything special aside from adding milk. Though he did often stir in bits of whatever he had on hand. This morning he'd added chopped up roasted red peppers and scallions, and accompanied the eggs with freshly baked biscuits and a platter of thin-cut pork chops.

That platter was empty. So were both plates of biscuits. Of the six people at the table, three were lupi, and lupi ate a lot. "I don't think I can stuff in another bite."

"I can," Nathan said, and emptied the last of it onto his plate. His phone chimed. "Whoops. That'll be Lily."

Isen's eyebrows lifted. "You're psychic now?"

Nathan managed to get one big bite of eggs in his mouth and swallowed. "I texted when I first got up and asked her to call me. Good morning," he said, speaking into the phone now. "Though it's afternoon there, isn't it?"

"If you're finished," Nettie said, "I'd like to get started."

Kai frowned. She wanted to hear what Lily told Nathan about the godhead. But what Nettie planned was going to take a while, so yes, they'd better get started. Kai pushed her chair back and stood. "Isen, I thank you—and Carl—for another delicious meal. Nettie, you said we'd have a bit of a hike. Where are we going?"

The "us" she referred to included her, Benedict, and the third lupus at the table—a small, compact man who looked about sixty, which meant he might be a hundred or more. Abe Keetso resembled his lupus father more than his Navajo mother, but he'd been raised in his mother's spiritual tradition. As had Benedict. As had Kai, for that matter.

When Kai got up this morning, Nettie was already here, drinking coffee with Isen and Carl. She'd asked for Kai's help with a protection ceremony, saying that the participants needed to be of the Diné spiritually as well as genetically. Kai had agreed, of course. Abe Weaver had joined them shortly after that.

"You and I will head for the node on Little Sister," Nettie said. "Cynna's already there with Cullen."

"What about Benedict and Abe?"

"They'll be needed at the node out back."

"You'll keep an eye on Nettie," Benedict told Kai. "She insists she's up to this, and God knows I haven't been able to talk her out of it. But I don't think hiking up a mountain when she's only halfway healed is a good idea."

Nettie snorted. "Halfway?"

"Maybe that's the wrong percentage, but you're not healed."

"I'm weaker than I like, but I can walk."

"Hiking up a mountain is not going for a walk."

"Azhé'é." Nettie went to Benedict and laid a hand on his shoulder. "I will be well, and this is not your decision."

Their eyes held briefly, then Benedict nodded unhappily. "At least drive as far as you can."

Nettie didn't roll her eyes, but she looked like she wanted to. "All right."

"We can take my car, if you like," Kai said. Though it was a rental, not really hers. Neither she nor Nathan owned a car at the moment.

Nettie nodded. Kai bent and dropped a kiss on top of Nathan's head—he'd stayed seated, still talking to Lily—and he looked up, smiling with his eyes. "Not sure how long this will take," she told him, "so I'll see you when I see you. My phone will be off."

He nodded to let her know he'd heard and asked Lily something about trees. Nettie slung a large, bulky tote on her shoulder and started for the front door. Kai followed. Nettie didn't say a word until they reached the rented Hyundai parked on a patch of scruffy grass across from the house. When she did, she sounded as testy as her colors looked. "You know where the path up Little Sister is?"

"By that pair of oaks on the other side of the day care center." Kai slid behind the steering wheel. "I've walked up it with Dell a few times."

Nettie got in on the other side. "So you know that the node isn't that far up. I may have to go more slowly than usual, but I'll be fine." She fixed Kai with a stern look. "And if I weren't, I'd know it before you did."

"You wouldn't be much of a healer if you didn't," Kai said agreeably as she put the car in gear. "And I suppose Benedict wouldn't be much of a father if he didn't worry anyway."

Nettie grimaced. "Everyone says doctors make terrible patients. I've lived up to that cliché, I suppose, but let me tell you—he's worse. The only one who can make him behave at all when he's hurt is Isen, and that's because he has to obey his Rho. And," she added on a sigh, "I sound as if I'm thirteen and bitching because he told me not to stay out late. I wish I'd quit doing that."

Kai grinned. It had been weird at first, seeing the fifty-something Nettie with her father. Benedict looked at least ten years younger than his daughter—but that was on the outside. Kai couldn't describe the difference age made in thought patterns; it varied greatly from one person to the next. But there was a difference, and Benedict's thoughts looked older than his face. That had helped her adjust her expectations. Once she did, the relationship was obvious.

She felt a nudge at the back of her mind. "Oh. Dell wants to come with us." Though it was more that she intended to go with them than as if she were asking permission. You might say that the chameleon was of the "ask forgiveness, not permission" school of thought, except that Dell wasn't much for asking for forgiveness, either.

Nettie looked around, but obviously didn't see the chameleon. Kai did, but she knew where to look. "I suppose that's all right. She can't participate, but she's female, so her presence shouldn't disrupt the rite."

"If this is a women-only party, why is Cullen waiting at the node?"

"I didn't explain much, did I?"

"You said we'd be doing a protective ceremony."

"Not at all, in other words. Sorry. You know that Dyffaya sent dworg through the node on Little Sister to attack us, right? That was before you arrived."

"I was told about it."

"We don't want that to happen again," Nettie said grimly. "Not with dworg or anything else. The node by the house is tied to the clan in a way that makes it unavailable to Dyffaya, but the one on Little Sister isn't—or hasn't been. Cynna's trying to change that."

"Cynna's doing node work?" Kai's eyebrows flew up in mingled surprise and alarm. Cynna was a capable spellcaster, but Kai had been taught that no one short of a mage should work with node energy. If someone had to, though, Kai would pick the guy who could at least see the volatile stuff he was messing with. "Why not Cullen?"

"Cullen is assisting, but she has to do the work herself. It's a Rhej thing."

"Would the answer to 'why' be a clan secret?"

"It would."

Kai wasn't entirely reassured, but at least Cullen was monitoring the node. "What's our part?"

"Cynna's working on the magical end of things, but magic isn't all that Dyffaya has available. We need to close it off spiritually as well."

"That sounds tricky." Actually, it sounded impossible, but Kai was no shaman.

"It is. We have to obtain Little Sister's permission and assistance."

Kai's eyebrows shot up. "Little Sister has a guardian spirit? But it's, uh . . ." She shut up before she offended the spirit they were supposed to contact.

"Not much of a mountain?" Nettie smiled. "It is on the small side, but yes, it has a guardian. A female guardian."

That explained why this was a females-only rite. "I take it Cullen will leave after we arrive. Why are Benedict and Abe at the other node?"

"Because that node will only respond to lupi."

Who were always male, so it made sense for them to handle that end. Except that it didn't explain why someone was needed there at all. Unless—"Tell me you're not trying to tie the nodes together."

"Good God. Is that even possible?"

"Only if you want to blow things up," Kai said dryly. "Though if you've been an adept for a millennia or two, you might pull it off."

"Then it's as well we won't be doing that. We need the second node because—well, I can't explain in detail, but we'll use talking drums at both nodes to create a path that lets me show Little Sister what we want."

"Glad to hear it." They'd reached the nearest spot on the road to the path, so Kai pulled over onto the verge and got out. Nettie did, too, after retrieving her tote from the back seat. "May I carry your bag for you?" Kai asked.

"It's not heavy, and it has my drum. I prefer to keep it close."

"Okay, but let me know if you change your mind." Kai headed for the path. "Can you tell me anything about the ceremony we'll be performing?"

"You told me that your grandfather introduced you to Doko'oosliid."

Kai nodded. Joseph Tallman was the mortal guardian for the western sacred mountain of the Navajo. Doko'oosliid—Abalone Shell Mountain—had spoken to him before he'd ever thought of being a shaman, saying he'd been chosen and would someday return to stay. Joseph had gone home, apprenticed himself to a shaman, married, and raised a daughter. After Kai's grandmother died, he'd fulfilled the rest of the mountain's prediction. He lived at its foot and took young Navajo partway up for their vision quests. Once in a while the mountain had a message for the Diné; more often, Grandfather needed to warn intruders away or rescue any who hadn't listened. Doko'oosliid was not friendly to outsiders.

"The first part of today's rite is similar to the rite of introduction." Nettie cocked her head and smiled. "Did I tell you the role your grandfather played in my becoming a shaman?"

"He did? How?" The path grew a bit more steep along here. Kai kept a surreptitious eye on Nettie's colors, but so far the older woman seemed to be doing okay.

"You may have noticed that the People don't usually have female shamans," Nettie said dryly as she started up the path. The slope was an easy incline here. "Yet that's what I was. Shamans are chosen on the other side, and that's what happened on my vision quest. But the stubborn old farts on this side didn't believe me."

Kai snorted. "Now I know you're talking about Grandfather." Who was no more stubborn than the mountain he served.

"Not exactly. Everyone knows Joseph Tallman will take no apprentice. Everyone also knows he values his privacy. So when I set up camp thirty feet from his front door, I didn't speak to him. For two and a half days he didn't speak to me, either. On the third morning, he came to my camp. I offered him coffee and fry bread. He accepted. After we ate and drank he asked why I was there. I told him I'd been sent to him by Coyote, who spoke to me in a dream. He grimaced when I mentioned Coyote," Nettie added, "but didn't argue."

"Coyote is not Grandfather's favorite Power."

"So I gathered. Anyway, I explained that I'd been chosen for a shaman, but none of the shamans would take me as apprentice because I was female. He said he would take no apprentices, male or female. I agreed that everyone knew that to be true, and he went back to his cabin. Those were the only words we spoke for the next twenty days."

"Twenty?" Kai waved a hand. "Sorry. Go on."

Nettie smiled. "Twenty days later, I was running low on supplies and beginning to worry about that, the weather, and my life in general. It was nearly September and school was about to start—I was sixteen, did I mention that?—and there I was, camped out on a mountain. I was also pretty damn bored. But I wasn't leaving.

"The next morning, your grandfather came to my camp again. Again I offered him coffee and fry bread and he accepted. After we ate he told me that I was Ahiga Brown's apprentice. I expressed surprise—Ahiga Brown was the oldest of the *hataali* back then, and very traditional. He'd turned me down flat. Joseph Tallman smiled. 'My friend Ahiga does not know this yet,' he said. 'I will explain it to him. You will remain here until I return.'

"He was gone a week and a day. When he came back I was completely out of coffee and almost out of everything else, but Ahiga Brown was with him, and he agreed to take me on as apprentice. I didn't find out until later what your grandfather's explanation consisted of." Nettie chuckled the way one does at an old joke that has never lost its savor. "He set up camp thirty feet from Ahiga's house and waited. Ahiga came almost immediately to offer hospitality to his fellow *hataali*. Your grandfather refused politely and offered him fry bread and coffee. Although impatient to find out what Joseph Tallman was up to, Ahiga had to accept. After they'd eaten, your grandfather said that Coyote had sent him to ask Ahiga why he kept refusing the apprentice he'd been sent by the Powers. Ahiga tried to be courteous, but he always had a quick temper. It was none of Joseph Tallman's business, and who ever heard of a female shaman, anyway? Everyone would think he was crazy or a dirty old man if he took a young girl as apprentice. Coyote was just stirring up trouble. Coyote loved trouble. Ahiga didn't.

"Your grandfather didn't argue. Didn't speak at all. He also didn't leave. Nor would he accept anyone's hospitality, though everyone in the village tried to house him or at least feed him. Six days later, Ahiga agreed that I was his apprentice."

Kai laughed in delight. She could just imagine how people had reacted to a visiting medicine man who wouldn't let them honor him properly. "That sounds just like Grandfather. It's like him, too, that he never told me the story."

They were maybe halfway up. It was steep here, and Nettie was beginning to look drawn. Her colors suggested she was hurting a bit and tiring a lot. "Hold up a moment," Kai said, and she bent and pretended to disentangle her jeans from an encroaching gooseberry branch.

"Be careful," Nettie said. "You don't want your vest getting hooked by those thorns. It's crazy beautiful."

"And a lot tougher than it looks." The temperature had been just nippy enough that morning for Kai to use it as an excuse to wear her long vest which, when sealed, looked much like a medieval tabard, slit at the legs for ease of movement. She'd left it open this morning. It was heavily embroidered in shades of brown and gold, and it was, as Nettie said, crazy beautiful. It was also crazy durable. "It's spelled against dirt, rips, punctures, knives, swords, fire, rain, and several types of magic. If I keep the spell renewed, the vest might outlast me."

"Is it sidhe work, then?"

Kai nodded. "It was made for me by the mother of a patient."

"That must have been a very sick patient. I can't imagine how long it would take to make something like that. Or did you mean she had it commissioned?"

Kai explained that the vest was an *adit*, an honor gift made by the giver's own hands, and yes, the young man she'd treated had been in bad shape. As a healer, Nettie was naturally curious, so as they continued up the path Kai told her about the rare type of madness that afflicted a few unfortunate half-elves. From the outside, the condition resembled autism; from the inside, it was a hellish disordering of the senses. Tastes might itch or turn yellow while the color purple shrieked or burned. It was synesthesia on steroids and randomized. "It's genetic, of course, but they don't know what triggers the—"

"Wait a minute. If it's genetic, then it's physical."

"I'm told a lot of madness is, to some degree."

"But you aren't a physical healer."

"No, but brain and mind are so intertwined—I couldn't heal one without affecting the other. Um, I should add that my teacher says that mindhealers only affect minds, but the connection between mind and brain encourages the brain to change, too. I'm not convinced that's always what happens. Some amendments take a lot of power. In those instances, I think I'm making a physical change in the brain. I can't sense physical structures myself, so I can't be sure, but that's what it feels like. Eharin doesn't agree."

Nettie's slightly lifted eyebrows expressed disapproval. "You don't have much confidence in your teacher."

Kai grinned. “Sound pretty full of myself, don’t I? I’m sure Eharin is teaching me what she was taught, what fits her experience. The thing is, well . . . she’s less powerful than I am, so she can’t do some of the things I can.” Which chapped Eharin’s ass big time, but Kai wasn’t going to go into that. “So she doesn’t have experience with the kind of amendments I’m talking about.”

“Surely she’d have heard of such things, though.”

Kai shrugged. “The sidhe don’t share knowledge much, so maybe not. Plus the Gift takes an unusual form in me. Other mindhealers experience thoughts tactilely. It’s like they have a mental hand they use to touch thoughts or move them around. What I see as color and pattern, they experience as texture and structure.”

“It sounds like the difference between the way Lily experiences magic and the way Cullen does. It’s a texture for her, but he sees it.” Nettie gave her a sharp glance. “Do you think seeing thoughts gives you more information than your teacher gets from touching them?”

“Well, yes, I’m pretty sure it does. On the other hand, my teacher’s form of the Gift gives her very fine control in crafting temporary amendments, and that’s what’s needed most of the time.”

“And these temporary amendments, as you call them, don’t change the brain, but they encourage changes in it. Sounds like the placebo effect.”

“It may be the same mechanism.” They fell into a discussion of the mind-body connection that lasted until they reached a spot where the path widened and flattened out. Just ahead was a steep stretch. Kai wasn’t surprised when Nettie heaved a sigh and dropped to the ground to sit cross-legged.

“Dammit. I need to catch my breath.”

“Okay.” Kai sat, too, to be polite.

“I thought I was doing better than this,” Nettie said. “I’ve been walking two miles along the road every day for a week with no problems.” She cocked an eyebrow at Kai. “Aren’t you going to point out this is not exactly a nice, level road? Remind me that you offered to carry my tote? Ask if I’m all right or if you should summon help?”

Kai grinned. “You’re in a little pain, but not enough to

worry me. Mostly you're annoyed because you tire so easily compared to what you're used to."

"You can see all that in my thoughts?"

"Physical pain is mostly red, sometimes with shards of orange. Other feelings are red or orange, too, like annoyance, but pain looks different. Jagged. You've got some flickers of pain-red, but not enough to worry me. Then there's those grumbly, red-orange wrinkles that tell me you're peeved about something. They don't tell me what. I was just guessing about that."

Nettie laughed. "When we first met, I was uncomfortable about what your Gift might tell you. That didn't last. You're just too easy to be with. I'll bet people end up telling you all kinds of things they hadn't—oh!" She sat up straight as Dell slipped into view about ten feet up the trail. "I could swear she wasn't here a second ago."

"Chameleon, remember?" Kai smiled at Dell, who was pleased that she'd startled the human. Not that humans were much of a challenge, but Dell took her pleasures where she found them.

"Does she get tired of being told how beautiful she is?"

"Not that I've ever noticed."

Nettie grinned and addressed Dell directly. "You are, you know. I realize I shouldn't stare at you, but you're so lovely it's hard not to. Especially when—what is it?"

In a micro-second, Dell had gone from smug to hackles-raised alert. Kai spun to face the way the big cat was looking, her hand going automatically to the sheath at her waist—and she wasn't in San Diego now. The knife was right where it was supposed to be.

Somewhere up the mountain someone yelled loudly, the words lost in the distance. Dell tipped back her head and let out her war cry—a deep-chested grunt of a roar halfway between leopard's cough and lion's bellow.

And it was answered with an identical coughing roar.

FOURTEEN

NATHAN was in the kitchen getting more coffee and talking to Ackleford on the phone when he heard Benedict's outraged bellow. He tossed the phone at Carl and took off, shooting through the open French doors a few paces behind Isen—and stopped dead.

Like some vegetative snake, a vine had thrust itself up onto the deck to wrap itself around Abe's middle. It was a damn thick vine, too, with twisted, woody cables like an old wisteria. Benedict hacked at one cable with his knife. Parted it, too, but the snake-vine was growing incredibly fast, like the one in that Disney film that swallowed Sleeping Beauty's castle. Another cable twined across the deck and shot out tendrils, green and supple, that whipped themselves around Benedict's leg and yanked him off his feet.

Isen sprang at it. Two guards rounded the corner of the house and another leaped off the roof onto the ground. Abe was down now, with a new tendril wrapped around his throat while others sprouted and began to cover him. Benedict had cut off the ones that pulled him off his feet, but more arrived, trapping his other leg and heading up his torso.

The guards and Isen had knives. Nathan left them to do what they could. It wouldn't be enough. He dodged around them at a run, headed for the end of the deck where the vine had arisen. Claw could kill anything, but it would die faster if he struck near the thing's source of power. With animate plants, that was almost always the roots. He leaped off the deck as he reached into thin air—and drew Claw.

The second he landed he swung at a cable whipping through the air at his head. But though he cut it cleanly, the damn vine didn't wither. A pair of cables snaked across the ground toward him, coming from a veritable thicket that must be the vine's origin. He got them, but missed the one whipping at him from the side—and damned if the thing didn't sprout inch-long thorns in time to rake his arm!

He was in a T-shirt, so the thorns slashed him pretty good before he sliced that stalk free from the plant. Blood dripped from his torn biceps. He felt his healing rev up.

And calmly, deliberately, slowed it as close to a dead stop as possible. This was it. This was when he found out if he was right.

Kai was going to be so pissed.

A strangled shout from behind him reminded him that the others needed the vine dead *now*. He advanced on the thicket, where tendrils writhed like Medusa's hair, but the vine didn't sprout anything new to attack him with. He'd cut it four times now with Claw. Not enough to kill the thing, but it was hurting.

Time to put an end to this.

DELL was in a rare fury. These males were in *her* territory, threatening her and her person! It was intolerable—and baffling. Males might challenge a female, but this was no challenge. They were treating her as prey! She would punish them, punish them badly, for this.

Kai felt her familiar's confusion as well as her furious determination to punish the males. But punishment wasn't going to work. She could see the lattice of *intention* laced through the two chameleons' thoughts. That intention was lovely, really—thin ribbons of silvery lavender in an elegant pattern. The damage it caused wasn't so lovely. Any place that the chameleons' thoughts threatened to escape the pattern imposed by the silvery cords, pus-colored yellow oozed up.

It was clear what was happening. She formed a thought as firmly as she could and pushed it at Dell: *They're controlled.*

Quickly she summoned her Gift and reached out to begin removing the alien intention. But the instant she touched a shimmering ribbon she recoiled, shocked by the sheer power. Then the fast-moving blur of chameleons surged closer, forcing her to dance back. The two males were darting at Dell, trying for a quick strike or to maneuver her into leaving an opening, neither daring to fully engage—for obvious reasons. Although the males were no more than a foot shorter than Dell nose-to-tail, she must have had nearly twice their mass, and all of it muscle.

A few feet behind Kai, Nettie drummed steadily. Whatever the shaman was doing left her wholly unprotected. Kai knew the outcome of this battle would be up to Dell, but she could watch Dell's back. She could stay between the chameleons and the defenseless shaman. She had Teacher's help. She just had to keep her muscles loose and the knife ready and—

One of the males either miscalculated or got tired of aborted strikes. He and Dell collided in a whirlwind of snarls and claws. That let the second male jump in, lightning-quick, while Dell was entangled with the first. Kai stiffened against the need to go to Dell's aid—she'd just get in the way, dammit!—when a dun-colored chunk of the cliff turned into a third chameleon and flung himself down at her.

That instant's stiffening nearly cost Nettie her life.

Once Teacher considered a lesson learned, the knife would not step in if Kai flunked the lesson's application. Staying loose was the first lesson, one Kai was supposed to have mastered, so she was on her own for that first critical second. And she called it wrong.

The third cat wasn't after her. He was aimed at Nettie.

The stroke Kai began was meant to protect herself, so her knife was in the wrong place as the chameleon sailed over her head. But her muscles were loose again. With smooth haste, Teacher took over. Kai's upper body twisted, her grip shifting minutely as the knife changed the arc of her strike. The sudden change made for a weak blow—but it did connect. Hot blood spattered her head as she spun into the next position the knife wanted: one leg back, knees flexed, right side forward, right arm swinging into a new strike as if she'd planned that first, awkward one merely to set herself up for this.

The chameleon's head was down. Either he'd already latched onto Nettie's throat or was about to, for she was prone now, the drum a couple feet away. No chance for a killing blow from this angle. Instead Kai's blade sliced into the beast's rump, cutting deep into muscle.

Got his attention but good—and gods, he was fast. Even as Teacher danced Kai backward, the cat flung himself around and launched himself at her. Surely even the best teaching blade couldn't stop eighty pounds of speed and fury when—

A gray blur sailed in out of nowhere and smacked into the male, knocking him aside. This time, Dell wasn't thinking of punishment. As they hit the ground she head-butted him under the chin, throwing his head up to expose his throat. Which she slit open with one swipe.

That took two seconds. It was one second too many. Both the remaining males had already launched themselves at her—and now Kai saw that Dell was wounded, with one haunch cut to the bone. She wasn't bleeding. Her body was knitting itself back together already.

Not fast enough. She couldn't heal fast enough.

Sheer terror for her familiar made Kai do instinctively what she'd recoiled from before. She tossed out caution and training and *reached* for the glowing ribbons controlling the chameleons—latched onto them and clung even as the alien power shrieked through her and burned, gods, but it burned!—and she *pulled*.

They broke.

The recoil sent her spinning in a dizzy cacophony of movement that had nothing to do with the physical. She spun and spun in a rainbow brilliant with color and pain, a silent rainbow where, after an eon or two, even sight began to fade. Darkness fluttered at the edges. And she knew, with a sudden bolt of terror, that she wasn't just spinning. Something had grabbed her the way she'd grabbed those ropes. Something was reeling her out and away, thinning her out . . . .

All at once her world held sound again. The sound of a drum.

The unseen grasp loosened. Vanished. Kāi's spinning slowed, slowed, until she was nearly steady when she blinked herself back into the regular world.

She was still standing. That surprised her. How had her body been able to—oh. Teacher, probably. The knife couldn't animate her body if she were truly unconscious, but she hadn't exactly passed out. She'd nearly been removed, but she hadn't passed out.

Dell stood beside Kai, her big, warm body pressed against her as if she meant to prop Kai up. She was purring frantically and broadcasting frustration and worry—and the certainty that the other two male chameleons were gone.

Gone?

Just gone. Dell didn't know where or how. The body of the one she'd killed was still there, but the living chameleons weren't.

Kai stroked Dell's head—*I'm here, I love you, I'm fine, are you okay?* Dell sent back impatient reassurance. Kai looked around. Turning her head made the world spin, but it wasn't the same sort of spinning and it quickly stopped.

The two males were nowhere in sight. Nettie was, though. The shaman had retrieved her drum and was sitting up and beating it again . . . the same drumbeat Kai had heard in her excursion into otherwhere. There was a long, bloody scratch along the woman's cheek, but otherwise . . . "Are you okay?" Kai croaked, then thought to add, "Dell is sure the other chameleons are gone."

Nettie drew the drumbeat to a close before she replied. "Only bumps and bruises. You got that bloodsucker off me before he got his mouth on my neck. Dell's right. The other two winked out about five minutes ago, just as you went into trance. Or whatever that was."

"I was gone for five minutes?"

"Didn't seem that long to you?"

Kai made a vague gesture. "It seemed like either a very long time or no time at all. Five minutes." She shook her head, marveling that such a finite limit existed for her time away, and noticed the knife still in her hand. She frowned at it thoughtfully, then pulled out a cloth from one of the vest's pockets and began cleaning the blade. "Your drumming went there. Wherever I was, your drumming reached me and it let go."

"Not it," Nettie said grimly. "He."

"You know what happened?"

"I know Dyffaya tried something. I don't know what."

"He tried to grab me. Did grab me," she corrected, "and was pulling me away, but you made him let go."

"Someone did. My drumming called and Someone answered."

She'd been saved by one of the Powers? A chill touched the base of Kai's spine—not fear, but awe. "I need to thank him or her. You don't know who answered your call?"

"No. We'll do that." Nettie set her drum aside and stood. "You didn't feel a presence when the Power responded?"

"I was distracted. Stretched pretty thin." Literally. She'd been pulled out, reeled out, thinner and thinner . . . would she have snapped like the cord in another moment, or just continued to unravel until she was too thin to hold together?

"How do you feel now?"

"Okay." She finished cleaning the blade and tried to sheath it. Her hand was shaking. She scowled at it and tried again. It worked this time, and she gave Nettie a twist of a smile. "Scared spitless, maybe, but okay."

"We'll need to do a cleansing ceremony."

"Why? I didn't—"

Dell butted Kai's hip with her head. Kai looked down. "Oh. Right." If that grasp had been the chaos god, he might have left something behind—some bit of his power, a hook he could use to persuade or delude her. She didn't feel anything, but even Cullen couldn't see a spiritual—"Shit!" She spun around to look up the trail.

"What?"

"There was a shout. Just before we saw the chameleons, someone shouted from up near the node. And the fight—Cullen should've heard it, shouldn't he?" And he hadn't responded. Kai did not like to think of the likely reason.

"I can't run. You can. Go!"

"I'm not leaving you to—"

"Who just saved your ass?" Nettie gave Kai's shoulder a push. "Go!"

* * *

"No."

Cullen blinked blearily up at his beloved's stubborn face. "I'm fine. Already healed. You need to go see—"

Cynna snorted. "Healed, my ass. You were unconscious. You're still so weak from blood loss you can't sit up."

"Making more," he assured her.

"Why do men and small children think that if they keep asking for the same thing over and over they'll get a different answer?" Cynna's words were a verbal eye-roll. Her hand was tender as she stroked his neck—which was, indeed, healed. "Your blood carries a lot of your magic. If you lose much of it, your healing's slowed. I don't how much that beastie stole, but somewhere in the vicinity of a whole lot. You'll be hours, maybe all day, replacing it. I'm sticking. His friends could come back to finish what he started."

The problem with being married to the Clan's Rhej, Cullen thought as he lay flat on his back, too weak—as she had so annoyingly pointed out—to sit up, much less stand, was that she knew so damn much about lupi. Sometimes that came in handy. Sometimes it was a pain in the ass. "I can keep an ear out for—shit. Help me sit."

One thing about Cynna. She knew when not to argue. She was buff, too; the arm she slid behind his shoulders propelled him up with little effort on his part. She flowed to her feet the second he was sitting and began drawing power.

He did, too—from the diamond in his earring, which was fully charged, unlike his personal power, which was sadly depleted at the moment. He might not be able to use stored power to heal, but he could for damn sure use it to throw some fire now that . . . "It's okay," he said as the scent he'd caught intensified enough for him to fully identify it. "It's Dell."

Cynna cast a dubious glance at the dead chameleon lying about a foot from his left hand—where, he assumed, she'd left it after heaving it off him after stopping the chameleon's heart with a spell that she could use, which he, frustratingly, could not. "You don't think she might object to—"

"He attacked us," Cullen said firmly, knowing Dell could hear them. Best if the chameleon thought he'd done the killing until they knew how she'd react. "I'm sure she'll understand why I had to—"

"What do you mean, why you—"

"Ah, there you are," he said to Dell, who'd paused when she reached the relatively flat area that held the node. "Kai's right behind her," he added in an aside to Cynna, whose ears wouldn't tell her that yet. Kai, but not Nettie—he knew from the sound of the footfalls. Nettie couldn't possibly run up that slope. Anxiety threw another loop around his gut and tightened.

Dell's smoky gray head tilted as she took in the scene, her nostrils flaring. She looked from the body to Cullen to Cynna and gave a little grunt. It sounded more like aggravation than any furious need for revenge, which he found heartening. "He jumped us," Cullen told her, "and at the worst moment possible, which was either a happy coincidence for him or—"

"Not so happy," Kai said as she loped into view. "Considering he's dead and you aren't. Which I'm very glad to see, by the way. What happened?"

"Where's Nettie?"

"She's okay. She'll be here soon, but she had to come at a slower pace."

The tight clutch of fear eased. "Good. That's good. Clearly you guys won, but how?"

"Dell, mostly. We were jumped by three of that fellow's buddies. At first Dell tried to discourage them without killing them, but that didn't work because they were under someone's control. The obvious suspect is Dyffaya, who nearly grabbed me—well, he did grab me, but Nettie's drumming made him let go. Or summoned Someone who made him let go." She shook her head. "I get tangled up when I talk about it. The upshot is that Dell killed one of the male chameleons and the other two winked out when whoever answered Nettie made Dyffaya go away. I heard you yell just before they attacked. You were hurt?"

"That was me who yelled," Cynna said. "Like Cullen said, the chameleons picked the worst time possible to leap out of the node."

"They gated in?"

"Yep. What I was doing to prepare the node . . . shit, it's

hard to say this in English. You might say I was patterning the node in a way that has elements of a gate, but isn't one. This patterning is inherently unstable until you reach the end, and I was nearly there—"

"Marblypouth," Cullen said, or something like that, only with more consonants.

Cynna nodded grimly. "The *marbligpot'th* configuration is the most unstable point of the progression, and that's when someone nudged the node and it flickered into being a gate. Give him credit—he did it smoothly, with minimum power, and didn't make it blow up, which by all rights it should have. Four chameleons came through and the node immediately flickered back to the unstable pattern I'd left it in. I had to keep going, finish the patterning, or the node damn sure would have exploded. Two of the chameleons took off. The other two sighted in on me. Did you ever see a cat just before it pounces on a bird? Like that. Then one of them leaped at me, but this guy"—she nodded at Cullen—"has really fast reflexes. Not much sense, trying to wrestle with a chameleon, but great reflexes."

Cullen snorted. "Like I had a choice. I couldn't throw fire, not with the two of them almost on top of a seriously unstable node. And I don't Change as fast as Rule does, so that was out."

"You don't look nearly badly enough hurt," Kai observed.

He sighed. "Probably because the damn chameleon didn't want to waste any blood by slashing me up. Once they fasten that mouth on you, you can't break 'em loose. Got one hell of a suction. I kept hitting it until I passed out, but it didn't seem to notice."

"Chameleons are very single-minded about feeding. What about the other one? You said two took off—those would be the first two who attacked us, I imagine—and two stayed. You killed one. The other one?"

Cynna answered. "Instead of attacking me, it—he—decided he needed a turn at Cullen's blood. He was growling at his buddy, trying to get at Cullen, so I got the node into a stable array as fast as I could. Then I flung a spell that . . . actually, that spell is really illegal, so I'd rather not say what I did."

Kai cocked her head, looking down at the sprawled body. "Did you touch him?"

"Uh . . . no."

"I doubt you know Sudden Death, so . . . a heart-stopper spell?"

"You know it?"

Kai shook her head. "I've heard of it, but it's demon magic, right? Not true body magic. Elves can't work demon magic. None of the sidhe can."

Cynna's grin woke. "Neither can lupi, from what I can see."

Cullen frowned at her. "I can make it work sometimes."

"Half the time. Maybe."

"Gloating is not attractive."

"That's never stopped you."

"What does that have to do with . . ." The expression on Kai's face got Cullen's attention. She looked like someone who was trying not to say something. Naturally he wanted her to go ahead and say it. "You know something."

"Umm. Yes, but this is the wrong time and place. Ask me again later. I take it from the way we're chatting all relaxed that the node is still stable. How about you? I know you heal well, but—" She stopped, frowning at Dell. "He won't do that. Yes, of course a wolf might, but—oh, all right. I'll ask." She looked at Cullen. "Dell wants to be sure you don't eat the chameleon you killed. It would be a terrible insult to treat him as meat, and she thinks he doesn't deserve that, since he wasn't making his own choices when he attacked you."

Cullen looked at Dell, who was watching him steadily. "Don't worry. I'm not going to turn furry and chow down, though God knows he did just that with me." He switched his attention to the corpse, adding a scowl, "Got plenty of my blood, too. And I suppose I'd better quit putting this off. Not that knowing is going to help." He sighed once, then quickly ran through the preparatory sequence. He'd used this spell so often it had well-worn grooves in his mind, and there were no external components, so it only took a moment. He held out both hands, thumbs and forefingers touching to shape a rough square.

"What are you doing?" Kai asked.

"That's his magnify spell," Cynna explained. "I don't know why—wait, shit, yes, I do! I wasn't thinking. That beastie blooded him, which means it could have inserted a hook into his blood, just like the butterflies did with you."

"Not that it'll do me any good if I do spot something," Cullen muttered, staring through the square his fingers and thumbs formed as he inspected one leg. "I can't tell my healing to ignore the blood loss for now and focus on getting rid of some intrusive little hook the chameleon left behind, so unless it decides to prioritize that on its own, I don't—"

"Son of a bitch," Kai breathed.

That surprised him enough to make him look up at her. She was staring off into space, her face transforming from revelation to fury. "Son of a bitch! *That's* what he was oh-so-carefully not saying! That's what he's up to! *You* may not be able to control your healing," she said as she grabbed her phone from a pocket, "but Nathan can, and if that son of a bitch doesn't answer I'm going to kill him!"

FIFTEEN

NAUSEA faded to a faint queasiness. Nathan swallowed and looked around.

He saw trees.

He stood in the center of a small clearing. All around him were trees. Not redwoods, though they were massive, towering up and up the way those giants did. But these trees bore leaves, not needles. The branching was more like an oak, he thought as he tilted his head back, trying to make out the tops, but they weren't oaks, either. The leaves were cupped like saucers and the bark was smooth, peeling away in patches like an earthly crape myrtle or the moonbeech of Faerie. No, these weren't any kind of tree he'd ever seen before, though they did remind him of the pushpulls in Angorai. Larger, and with more symmetry in the boughs . . . and that was a surprise. Wouldn't the godhead of chaos tend toward asymmetry?

The color was different from other trees, of course. These were black. Black in root, trunk, branch, and leaf. As black as the empty sky overhead, which made it hard to see exactly how tall the trees were, especially with most of the light coming from the dry, pebbly ground. That ground was as warm as if it had baked in the sun during the day and was now releasing that heat to the air . . . air utterly still and so heavy with magic it seemed to have substance, pressing in on his lungs with every breath.

He heard nothing. Not a squirrel in those impossibly tall trees. Not a rodent or a roach scurrying along the ground, where there was no litter of fallen leaves. Not the tiniest susurration of a breeze. All he heard was the faint seashell sound of his own blood pulsing in his ears. All he smelled was magic. Magic and dust.

He did not like this place.

Nathan sucked in a ragged breath. His hand tightened on the hilt still in his hand. Reminded, he looked down at Claw. At least he'd killed the monster vine before being snatched here.

But he'd been snatched much more quickly than he'd expected. Only a few minutes had passed between his getting stuck by the thorn and the god yanking him here. A much shorter time than he'd expected, based on. . . . well, a sample of two, which wasn't enough to count on, clearly. Could be Dyffaya had gotten better at his snatches. Could be other factors affected the interval between the god's creatures sampling your blood and the god snatching you up.

Now that he thought about it, he felt foolish for assuming the interval was fixed. Several of the realms weren't time-congruent. Why had he thought the godhead would be fixed in time relative to Earth?

Experimentally he tried sheathing his blade without releasing the hilt. Claw slid into the pocket of elsewhere just as it should—and, more importantly, slid back out again.

Might as well find out, he told himself. This time he let go of the hilt after sheathing the blade—and drew it out again just as easily. He sheathed it again and left it there. Very few could take Claw from his hands, but a god might manage it. No one but him could draw Claw from its pocket of elsewhere. Not even a god.

That was half of what he'd needed to go right for this to work. Or a third, maybe, depending on how he divided things, but still, a huge relief. His heartbeat was racing; he told it firmly to slow down. But the back of his neck still bristled, trying to raise hackles he hadn't had for over four hundred years. His lips wanted to pull back from his teeth.

Someone was watching. He could feel it. He began to turn in a slow circle.

"Are we where I think we are?"

At the very edge of the clearing, Benedict stood in a half-crouch, poised for attack or defense. Nathan headed for him. "If you think we're in the godhead, I'd say yes. It fits Lily Yu's description." A pang of regret squeezed his chest. "I'm sorry you were grabbed, too."

"Don't be an ass. How is it your fault?" Benedict straightened, rolled his shoulders, and looked at Nathan. "I don't feel dead."

"We're here physically. I'm experiencing breath, a heartbeat, and normal sensory input—although the smells are odd. There's so much magic that at first I thought it was masking all the other scents, but it seems more as if scent itself is diminished. I couldn't smell you until I got close."

"Same here." Benedict wrinkled his nose. "It's like I stuffed cotton up my nose. Sucks."

"I wonder if this is how humans feel with a cold."

"Something like this, though with a cold you usually get aches, cough, and fever, too."

That's right. Lupi didn't acquire their healing until they went through the Change, and that didn't happen until puberty. "I'd forgotten. Your people are like enough to me in some ways that I fall into assumption sometimes." He frowned. "The way smells are dampened here reminds me. I think we'd best not eat or drink anything here unless we're sure it smells right."

"What do you mean, smells right?"

"I'm thinking that if something lacks scent—" Nathan cut off as the big man's skin suddenly turned ashy. "What is it?"

"I reached and—there isn't—I can't—" His voice broke. He stopped. When he spoke again, his voice was entirely dispassionate. "There's no moon here."

Nathan didn't know what to say. The moon was integral to the lupi's power. What did its loss mean to Benedict? How much did he lose when there was no moon? "You won't be able to Change."

"No, but that's not . . . I've never been where I couldn't hear Her. Not since First Change." Benedict shook his head as if trying to clear it. "Do you feel like we're being watched?"

"Oh, yes."

"I know a cue when I hear one," a pleasant tenor voice said.

The god who stepped out from between two trees looked human, though he moved with the grace of an elf. He was shaped like a half-grown boy, a beautiful boy on the edge of adolescence, his limbs pure and perfect, his hair a tousled black cap. His eyes were black, too—as black as the trees around them. He wore a short pleated skirt similar to a schenti. His feet were bare.

And that was another part of what Nathan had needed to happen. Two-thirds down. Dyffaya had taken a body to deal with them. He had done that when he spoke to Lily, but Nathan hadn't known if that was his usual practice, and he needed Dyffaya embodied. Not that killing this body would hurt the god, but being in a body concentrated Dyffaya. Pulled more of him into one spot.

Or so Nathan hoped. The only noncorporal being he knew much about was the Alath. If a god was much like that odd trinity, this would work. Which was maybe a large assumption, and there was still that third element . . . the beautiful boy was too far away. The twenty feet between him and Nathan would give Dyffaya time to do all sorts of things before Nathan could strike.

The god grinned like a mischievous urchin well aware of his dimples. "Shall I introduce myself?"

Nathan offered a small, polite bow. "If you've a name you prefer to Dyffaya, I'd be happy to use it. I'm guessing you know who we are?"

"Dyffaya will do. And of course I know who you are. A good host always knows his guests—though 'tis true only one of you was invited."

"Which one?"

"Oh, come, Nathan—I believe that's the name you use these days?—you know the answer to that. But perhaps what you meant to ask was why I took both of you, if only one was invited?"

"I would like to know that, if you've no objection."

"Not at all. The answer is: because that's how it works. You must arrive in pairs. I choose one. Chaos determines the other. There, you see how helpful I can be?"

"That's quite helpful. Thank you. You returned the toddler. If you didn't invite Benedict, why not send him back?"

"The poor little mite needed her mum, of course. Besides, I didn't want her. I do want him. I was hoping for Isen Turner, but his son will do. But I'm forgetting my manners." He clasped his hands together and bowed. "You're welcome in my domain, Benedict Jones."

Be polite, Rule urged the lupus silently. *Be very polite.*

Unfortunately, Benedict was no more telepathic than Nathan. "Where's the woman?" he demanded. "The one you grabbed. Britta something."

"Sweet Britta." This time the smile was lascivious, startling on such a young face. "She's sleeping, poor dear. All worn out by her exciting day and all that fucking we did. Why do you ask?"

Benedict didn't cry out. He simply fell as the ground opened beneath him in a hole perfectly sized to swallow the lupus and leave Nathan standing on its edge.

Nathan dropped to his knees to peer into the hole—which glowed all the way down, so he could see Benedict's furious, upturned face some twenty feet below. He could also see how the hole narrowed. Benedict was pinned in placed by smooth walls of glowing dirt. "Please," Nathan said very, very softly to the angry man below, "do not speak yet. Let me deal with him."

Dyffaya sauntered up to the other side of the hole and cocked his head to one side. He clucked his tongue. "Nathan, Nathan. You really should have explained civilized behavior to Benedict instead of comparing your childhood—or puppyhood?—experiences of illness."

Nathan murmured a phrase in High Elfin which, in English, meant something along the lines of, "Who would doubt what you say?" He used the third form of the phrase, which conceded nothing while implying that the person addressed was of such high state that only the crudest of souls could find fault with his words, never mind what their relationship to reality might be. High Elfin did have its uses. It was so curlicued with courtesy that it took real determination to use it rudely—or to convey much of anything in less than a couple thousand words, which was why it was seldom used outside of court. Even the elves found it cumbersome; most Low

Sidhe never learned it. He switched back to English. "I wonder if you will bring him back up here so I may amend my omission."

"It has been a long time," Dyffaya said wistfully, "since I heard the beautiful tongue. But there's time, isn't there? Time and time and more time we'll have for that." He flashed Nathan a brilliant smile. "And of course I shall bring him back up. He'll do me little good in a hole. The question is: when? Perhaps . . ." He stopped, his expression smoothing out to a blankness as complete as a doll's. "How disappointing." The face he turned toward Nathan remained eerily blank, though his voice was light and chipper. "You'll be pleased to learn that your lover won't be joining us here, after all."

Nathan gave another little half-bow, that seeming the safest response. His heart sang. Kai was safe, safe, safe . . .

Between one second and the next, Dell was crouched in the exact spot where Nathan had first appeared, and Cullen Seabourne lay prone on the ground at the far side of the clearing. He blinked, winced, and said, "Aw, shit." The chameleon's ears flattened. Her lips drew back in a snarl as she looked around, her tail lashing. And she launched herself at Dyffaya.

"No!" Nathan threw himself at Dell. She dodged, but he managed to snag one foot, jerking her around. She hissed and nearly got him with one clawed foot before he danced back. "He'll kill you. You can't kill him. You can't hurt him. He'll kill you before you even draw blood."

She glared at him, tail lashing—but after a moment she put her back to him so she could glare at Dyffaya.

Nathan fought not to sound desperate as he turned to face the god. Three thousand years ago, most elves had still held stubbornly to the old understanding of sentience. It had caused trouble back then, but now—if the god thought that way, if he took Dell for a beast . . . Nathan offered a deep bow. "I apologize on Dell's behalf. She isn't capable of understanding the need for courtesy."

"Of course not. No one capable of creating a familiar bond could be stupid enough to impose it on a sentient—who might have a different notion of who is to be master, and who servant, in the relationship."

Nathan didn't know what Dell's relationship had been with

the mage who created the bond, but Dell was no servant, nor did she wish to be master. She and Kai had a partnership, satisfying to them both. Dyffaya would not understand that.

"Or perhaps you thought I didn't know what a chameleon is." The boy's lip curled in regal scorn. "Are you among those of your kind who believe any kind of thinking qualifies as sentience? You may rest easy. I know better. Chameleons lack the capacity for language. Clearly, they are not sentient."

"Hey!" Cullen's voice was weak, yet full of indignation. "Dell knows lots of words!"

Dyffaya turned to face the sorcerer. "How interesting. He chooses to challenge my statement."

"I haven't had a chance to instruct Cullen about courtesy yet," Nathan said quickly. Was Cullen being really smart or really dumb?

The black eyes narrowed to slits. "He should know better. Even without instruction, he should know better than to contradict Me."

"Shit. You're right." Cullen's voice dripped with contrition. "I've lost a lot of blood, but that's no excuse. I apologize, sir, uh . . . I'm afraid I don't know the proper way to address you. Or even if it's okay to address you, but I'm really sorry I spoke so disrespectfully."

Okay, he was being smart. Horribly reckless, but smart, encouraging Dyffaya's conviction that Dell was nonsentient by claiming to think the opposite. Though he was laying on the humility pretty thick.

Not that Dyffaya seemed to mind. "I suppose I shouldn't expect you to understand."

"I don't," Cullen said humbly. "I thought sentience was the product of language. Dell knows words, so . . ." He shrugged. "I made the wrong assumption?"

Dyffaya sniffed. "You barely grasp the concept of sentience yourself, so how would you know? The Hound should, however." He began to stroll in a wide circle around Dell. "The chameleon may have absorbed some understanding of some words through the familiar bond, but she lacks the ability to think in them. Therefore, she lacks the ability to think conceptually, which is the mark of sentience. Though it should be enough to know that she's a familiar to realize she can't be sentient." He paused, studying Dell, who watched him slit-eyed. "What shall I do with her?"

Politely Nathan suggested, "As you have said, even an uninvited guest may be welcome."

"Oh, Dell is here by invitation. It's the sorcerer who was dumped on me by chance. She was not, however, my first choice. That was your lover, who evaded me again. Instead, I ended up with her familiar. Do I keep her, kill her, or return her?" He slid Nathan a sly smile. "You offer no opinion?"

"I fear that expressing my desires might not have the effect I wish."

Dyffaya snorted. "You aren't stupid. I won't return her, of course. The whole point is to separate your lady from her familiar, who is far too good at body magic. No, it's either keep her or kill her, and I believe . . ." He stopped and posed, tapping one finger against his chin. "Yes, I will keep her for now. On one condition." He paused, clearly wanting to be prompted.

Nathan did. "Yes?"

"That you accept responsibility for her. If she behaves badly, I will either kill her or punish you. That will be my choice, but you must accept responsibility or I kill her now."

"I accept responsibility for Dell's actions." He looked at her and spoke firmly. "Hiding form, Dell." And prayed she'd figure out what he meant: *Pretend you're a beast. Pretend you obey me. Help me fool him.*

She gave him a long look over her shoulder. The skin on her back twitched . . . and slowly she began her transformation.

He kept his relief to himself . . . and lied. "She takes on some aspects of the form she wears. I can't control her well in her original form. When in a human shape, she obeys better."

From his hole in the ground, Benedict said, "I would speak with Dyffaya."

Cullen jolted and almost managed to sit up. "Benedict?"

Dyffaya's eyebrows rose. He sauntered back to the hole and dropped into a crouch, knees splayed like a Beduin. He lacked the Beduin's concealing robes, however, and the schenti was short. He had a boy's penis and scrotum, small and hairless. "I will hear you, Benedict. What do you have to say for yourself?"

Benedict answered slowly and carefully. "I mistook your status. I spoke to you as I might to a lone wolf of my people. This was a mistake. I should have spoken as I would to the Rho of another clan—a Rho who might be an enemy, but is accorded respect."

Dyffaya was still for several heartbeats before saying sternly, "That was not an apology." Then he bounced to his feet and dusted his hands—and Benedict began to rise. He rose more slowly than he'd fallen, but he did rise. "Still, he did acknowledge his mistake. That's a start. You will further instruct him, Nathan?"

"I will."

"I would prefer not to kill him."

"That is my preference as well."

That made the mad god giggle, then break into full-throated laughter. "Oh, yes! Yes, of course. This is going to be fun. More fun for me than for you, but then, your comfort and pleasure are not my primary goals."

The tall black tree nearest Nathan bent like it was made out of rubber. Instinctively, Nathan leaped to one side—and the branch from another tree impaled him from behind. Agony screamed hot and hoarse through his blood, though not a sound escaped his gaping mouth.

Not that he objected to screaming. He couldn't. The damn thing had got him through the lung.

Dyffaya walked up and looked Nathan in the eyes. Never mind how young the bones of that face might appear. The expression it wore was old, very old, the eyes as black as the void between stars. "Quite the opposite, in fact."

SIXTEEN

THE rear deck was a mess. Limp cables of vine thick enough to choke a horse lay everywhere. It smelled like broccoli. Kai picked her way around chunks of monster vine until she reached the end of the deck. It was obvious where the thing had been rooted. She tipped her head, studying the hacked-up thicket, then turned to look at the pieces strewn across the deck. "Nathan was chopping at it here?"

"Yes, ma'am. He raced over there right away and started hacking at it with that blade of his," Abe said. "I didn't know why at the time, but it's obvious now. He wanted to cut it off from its roots. Must've been right. It sure didn't die of what we were doing, which consisted mostly of trying to stay alive. That damn plant grew fast."

"It stopped growing all at once, you said. At the same instant that Nathan and Benedict vanished, the plant died."

"Near as I could tell. I didn't have Nathan in sight right that second, but I saw Benedict wink out. One second he was there. The next, he wasn't."

There were probably more questions she should ask. She couldn't think of them. Her stomach churned. "Thanks."

"Sure thing. Okay if we burn it now?" She must have looked baffled, because he added, "That's what Isen said to do, soon as you'd had a chance to look it over. Dig it up, haul every bit of it off, and burn it."

"It's not going to burn easily." And the man who could have crisped it to ashes with a flick of his hand was missing. Just like Nathan. And Dell. And Benedict. She rested a hand on her unhappy stomach.

"Use enough gasoline and it'll burn."

It probably would. "You might stay upwind of the smoke, just in case."

"You think the smoke might do something to us?"

"I don't know." That was the problem. She didn't know anything—what questions to ask, what kind of crazy plant had attacked them, what was happening right this moment to Nathan and the others. Most of all, she didn't know how to get them back.

Kai had called Isen when Nathan didn't answer his phone. Isen had been telling her about the monster vine when Dell and Cullen were suddenly—gone. Just gone. Kai had felt it happen, the indescribable twisting, Dell's rage and terror. Those sensations had faded as Dell was pulled farther and farther away. But the familiar bond hadn't snapped. That was the most important thing. Kai couldn't draw power from Dell, not at this distance—or whatever you wanted to call the separation—but she could sense her. Dimly. With effort, she could get a little more . . . Kai tuned out the world around her, focusing on a place that was both within her and outside her. The place where Dell was.

Anger. She picked that up clearly. Anger and frustration and . . . but the rest was so faint Kai couldn't tell what she touched. Not pain, though. Dell wasn't currently in pain. Kai grabbed hold of that reassurance and clung to it as she blinked herself back into the world, sighed, and headed for the back door.

Arjenie, Cynna, and two lupi were sitting at the big table at one end of the room. Isen was pacing as he spoke on his phone—to Rule, she guessed, from what she heard. ". . . and how does it serve Nokolai for its heir to be in danger along with its Rho when the only other potential heir has been taken?" A brief pause, then, coldly: "The Rho of Leidolf will do as he pleases, of course. But if my Lu Nuncio returns before I give permission, I will put him in chains."

Kai stopped, jarred by how much he reminded her of Winter. Isen had a bass so deep it seemed to rumble up from the bottom of a well, while Winter's voice was an alto pure enough to hurt the heart . . . but that note of implacable authority. That was the same.

For a moment her mind was taken by an image of the Winter Queen and the Nokolai Rho butting heads. Better hope that never happened, she decided. Probably best if they never met. Winter recognized that even her authority had limits, but Kai wasn't sure the Queen was prepared to encounter those limits in the person of the leader of a small clan that was part of a small, unimportant race living in a single backwater realm.

That's how the sidhe saw Earth, anyway. Kai grimaced and veered toward the group at the table. Arjenie's eyes were damp. Cynna looked ready to gut someone. And everyone's thoughts were a roiling, unhappy mess. Normally that would make her want to soothe or comfort or distract, whatever helped. Right now it made her want to turn around and head in the other direction.

She was not going to run away, dammit. That was stupid and cowardly and would not help.

". . . going to tell her," Arjenie was saying when she drew near—and stopped short of her goal. A pale chalk line circled the table and those seated at it.

The two lupi looked worried. Cynna shrugged. "I can't stop you. Kai, I haven't set the ward yet, so it's okay to cross the circle. I don't know if you've met Josh and Ridley?"

"I don't think so." She gave the two men a nod and pulled out the chair next to Nettie and planted her butt in it. There. She had officially not run away. She did dial down her Gift, though. Seeing their distress made it hard to control her own. "What is it you don't want Arjenie to tell me?"

Instead of answering, everyone exchanged one of those looks. The kind that shouts "we've got a secret." Josh spoke. "What do you mean?"

She snapped, "Oh, come on. Arjenie wants to tell me something. The rest of you don't want her to." She didn't have to put up with this. She could make them—

No. Shit, no. Where had that come from? Coercion was what binders did, not mindhealers. The two Gifts might look the same, but they weren't. She scrubbed both hands over her face. "Sorry. I'm wound tight." She wanted to keep hiding behind her hands, which bothered her enough to make her put them on the table. "I need to call that FBI agent. Ackleford. I don't know what the hell to tell him."

"Is there some reason you can't just tell him what happened?" Arjenie asked.

"That's not it. Nathan's in charge, but he's gone. Ackleford—what can he do? I don't know, but 'nothing' comes to mind. Only I don't know what I can do, either. I've done stuff like this in Faerie—well, not like this because we are dealing with a frigging god, but never mind that. I've investigated, but always with Nathan. He calls it a hunt, but his lowercase hunts *are* investigations. So I've done that with him, but not on my own. I—"

"Hush." A warm hand squeezed her shoulder firmly. Isen had put away his phone and moved up behind her without her noticing, no doubt because she'd been busy babbling. "You'll want to wait a few minutes to call so you can be nice and crisp when you talk to the special agent. Always be crisp with law enforcement. Otherwise they slot you into one of their boxes—'victim' or 'troublemaker' or 'suspect' or whatever—and never take you seriously again. And you're right. There's very little the FBI can do, so waiting a few minutes won't matter."

"Right." She drew a deep breath. "Right. I'm not in the habit of falling apart."

"That must be why you're so bad at it. You wobbled a bit. You didn't manage to fall." Isen moved away and took his usual seat at the head of the table. He had a notebook in one hand, which he put on the table.

Cynna cocked an eyebrow at him. "I take it Rule isn't coming?"

"No."

The single word was a slammed door. One Cynna ignored. "What about Lily?"

"Lily has some sense. The anti-eavesdropping ward?"

"I'll close it now." She stood and dug in her pocket, pulling out a piece of chalk.

Kai felt it when the ward closed—a subtle twanging like

the snap of a rubber band, only far fainter. That told her two things. It was a powerful ward—she wasn't sensitive enough to pick up the spillage unless there was a lot of power involved—and it wasn't as efficiently set as Nathan's. That wasn't surprising. Nathan had had a few hundred more years than Cynna to practice.

Cynna resumed her seat and Isen turned to Kai. "I have two questions about what happened on Little Sister that I need to ask right away. I understood from your account that you could see in the chameleons' thoughts that they were being controlled."

She nodded.

"Do you see something like that in anyone present now?"

"No, but . . ." But she hadn't really checked. "I'll make sure." She dialed up her Gift and looked around the table carefully. Everyone was still upset. No one showed any signs of being under control or compulsion. "Everyone looks okay. I need to warn you, though, that I might not spot an inactive intention. A compulsion, sure, since—"

"Excuse me. What's the difference between intention and compulsion?"

"Intention imposes structure. Compulsion *is* a structure. So if I see a rigid, unchanging pattern, that's a compulsion. I can tell whether a compulsion is native or imposed because an imposed compulsion is always present. Innate compulsions—hand-washing or whatever—are only visible when they've been triggered. I didn't see rigid patterns in the thoughts of anyone here, so no one is under compulsion, imposed or native."

"And intention?"

"That's my own term. It fits what I see better than the way the sidhe talk about it. I could explain their terms if you like—"

"Not at this time, I think. What does it mean?"

"It's my way of referring to the more common method of mind control." She could see that they had no idea what she was talking about. "There's two kinds, see? One—the really rare one—is what binders do. They permanently bind someone's thoughts. Binders are extremely rare, in part because they're killed the moment they're discovered."

"Harsh," Isen murmured, "but understandable. I take it what you saw in the chameleons looked like the other type of mind control?"

She nodded. "It's not a common skill, either—well, except in dragons—but some of the older sidhe develop it. It's not the same as compulsion. Compulsions either evaporate when the action is completed, or they gradually lose power and dissipate. That may take a while, depending on the amount of power involved, but compulsions are basically temporary. Mind control is different. It's an irresistible *intention.* That intention acts on the victim's thoughts, and it requires an active, ongoing link. When that link is severed, so is the control. The thing is, I don't see the link. What I see is the result. I could tell that the chameleons were being controlled because of the way the imposed intention made the other patterns bleed, but if a link was passive—if Dyffaya had a hook in someone but wasn't actively controlling them—I don't think I'd spot that."

Isen had been jotting notes down while she spoke. He looked up. "Sam told us that the knife—Nam Anthessa—could act through compulsion, corruption, or persuasion. Compulsion is magical. You can see it. Corruption and persuasion are spiritual. Am I correct in assuming that you wouldn't see them?"

"I won't spot corruption, not unless it drastically alters the patterns of a mind I know really well. I think I'd see persuasion—it's a thought, after all, even if it's inserted spiritually instead of magically. I don't know if I'd be able to identify it as persuasion. I've never encountered it, so I'm not sure what to look for."

Cynna was frowning. "Sam didn't mention mind control. He didn't warn us that Dyffaya might use that against us, too."

"The Queen didn't warn me and Nathan about it, either. I suspect that's because she didn't know it was a possibility. Dyffaya didn't have that skill before he was killed—it must be something he's developed since. God knows he's had time to learn a new trick or two. Uh . . . you're on good terms with him. With the black dragon." She could not bring herself to refer to the Eldest as casually as these people did. "If you could ask him—"

Isen shook his head. "I'm afraid not. He's off on some unstated business of his own. My other question is about Dell. I understand that the two of you can pass information back and forth. Has she shared anything we should know about?"

"No. She's alive. I know that much, but the familiar bond is really faint, as if she were a long ways off. I get some of her emotions if I concentrate, but that's all. Still, the bond is intact, so whatever the godhead is, it isn't a separate realm, and it is able to sustain life."

"If she'd been taken to another realm, that would have severed your bond?"

"So I've been told." By Winter, so it was both true and accurate, if not necessarily complete.

"Interesting. All right. I'm assuming that Dyffaya orchestrated these two attacks using a technique similar to that which he employed at the coffee shop yesterday. Does anyone have reason to think otherwise?" He glanced around the table. "No? We will proceed on that assumption. Next we need to cover immediate threats. Josh, Ridley, and I were all bloodied by the thorns. Nettie said the scratch on her face came from something on the ground, not the chameleon, so she should be free of hooks. Cynna and Kai, you weren't bloodied by the chameleons?"

Cynna shook her head. Kai said, "No. If you're wondering if you're likely to get snatched—"

"It has crossed my mind," he said dryly. "Without Cullen, we've no way of knowing if we have magical hooks swimming in our bloodstreams."

"I'd say it's unlikely, given how much time has passed. Yesterday the hooks faded after a little over an hour."

"Seventy-two minutes," Arjenie put in helpfully.

"After seventy-two minutes," Kai repeated faithfully, "and that was with humans. It's been at least half an hour since the attacks." It had taken them twenty minutes to get back to the house. It would have been longer—Nettie had been moving really slowly, making Kai worry that she'd been hurt worse than she claimed—but Isen had sent guards racing up the mountain to them. Nettie had made the last part of the descent piggyback. She'd still been so fatigued that Isen had taken one look at her and suggested that she put herself in sleep for a bit. She must have been feeling pretty bad, because she'd agreed. "If you did have a hook in your blood, your healing should have gotten rid of it by now."

"You sound confident of that."

"I think she's right," Cynna said. "Cullen thought his healing would get rid of the hook, only Dyffaya didn't give him time. But his healing was slowed by blood loss. Yours isn't."

"Hmm." Isen rubbed his chin. "Earlier, Kai, you indicated that you thought Nathan deliberately kept his healing from eradicating the hook in his blood. Even if you're right about that—"

"I'm right." She'd done more than "indicate," as Isen delicately put it. She'd been fired up and furious then. She was still angry, but not enough. Behind the anger was a big, black mass of misery. Nathan meant to return. She believed that. He thought he had a chance to kill Dyffaya, to come back to her. But when? Even if he succeeded, how long might it take? Nathan didn't think of time the way she did. To an adult, "next week" sounds like an easy wait, but to a toddler it's an impossibly long time. To Nathan, a decade might seem like an easy wait, while to her . . .

"Even if you're right," Isen repeated, "it doesn't necessarily follow that our healing can clear out these hooks. I don't know that Nathan heals the same way we do. He can control his healing. We can't. And what about Dell? Why didn't her healing clear out the hook in her blood before Dyffaya snatched her? Do you believe she, too, slowed her healing so she would be snatched?"

"No, she wouldn't risk the familiar bond that way." Kai grimaced. "I suspect she wasn't paying attention. Body magic takes conscious control. With everything that was going on she probably left things up to her healing, but it didn't prioritize clearing out the hook. She doesn't sense in the healing range," she added. "Just the body magic part. If she didn't stop and look for the hook using body magic, she wouldn't know it was there."

"I don't follow you," Isen said.

"Um. Okay, did you know that healing magic, body magic, and transformational magic are different aspects of the same kind of magic? The sidhe call it birith. It's like with the electromagnetic spectrum—all the same kind of energy, only at different frequencies. If magical healing were the visual spectrum, body magic would be more like ultraviolet—higher energy, so it has different properties than healing magic. Transformational magic would be . . . I don't know what's that high energy on the electromagnetic spectrum. Something way above ultraviolet, though."

"Gamma rays, maybe," Arjenie offered. "What Dell and the lupi do—is that transformational magic?"

"Yes for lupi, no for Dell. Dell uses body magic, not true transformation, which is why it takes her so long to change her form compared to lupi. Lupi have healing and transformational magic, but not body magic—which is supposed to be impossible, and that's one reason the sidhe are so fascinated by them. You aren't supposed to be able to have the low end and the high end of the spectrum and skip the middle one. The body magic part. But never mind that. The point is, lupi have healing and transformational magic, but you don't sense those energies, so they aren't under your conscious control."

Isen spoke patiently. "And yet the Change is under our conscious control. We spend a good deal of effort learning to make it so."

"I meant that you can't decide to Change into an eagle or a cat instead of a wolf. You can't Change into a different style of wolf, either, by varying your coat or bone structure. You can choose when to transform, but not what you transform into. Although," she added, "you're right, in a way. Having any control at all means you do sense those energies, but in a very limited way."

Arjenie nodded. "Like phytoplankton."

Isen looked as puzzled as Kai felt.

"Oh. Sorry. I meant that phytoplankton are sensitive to light, but they can't actually see. Lupi may be like that with transformational magic. They're sensitive to it, but they don't see with it."

"Good analogy," Kai said. "Nathan only has the healing portion of *birith*, but he does sense it, so he has some control over it. Only for himself, though. He's not a healer, so he can't extend that sense to others, so . . . oh." She shook her head. Stupid. Why hadn't she thought of that before? "I just realized that Nettie ought to be able to sense those hooks if they're present in anyone's blood. Anything Nathan can spot and heal in himself, she should be able to spot in others."

"We'll find out after she's recovered," Isen said. "For now, I'll accept your optimistic prognosis about whether Josh, Ridley, and I are likely to be snatched. Arjenie, you look like you want to say something."

Kai realized that she felt better. Not good, but not like she was going to fall apart any minute, either. Forcing herself to think clearly enough to explain had steadied her.

"There is something I noticed," Arjenie said.

Could Isen have done that on purpose? Asked her questions that forced her to think instead of feeling? It was the sort of thing she might do to help someone get a grip, but he didn't have her Gift. How could he have known what she needed? Probably it was a happy coincidence. Still, she was curious enough to check out Isen's colors.

"Go ahead," Isen said.

His colors were darker than usual. More of that midnight blue and no happy yellow, and there was red anger smoldering away at the base of his thoughts. But no churning. Isen's colors were calm, amazingly so, not roiling the way . . . the way everyone else's colors had been, she saw as she looked around the table. Not anymore. Like her, they'd steadied.

Maybe it hadn't been coincidence.

Arjenie was saying that so far, everyone had been snatched in pairs. ". . . two people at Fagioli, two here at the house, and two on Little Sister. I realize we're talking about a pretty small sample, so while this is suggestive, it doesn't prove anything. But maybe he has to grab people in pairs."

"Interesting," Isen said. "And reassuring in its possibilities. I don't—ah, thank you, Carl."

The houseman had apparently decided it was lunchtime, though it was still short of eleven o'clock. He'd appeared with a tray of sandwiches. Lots of sandwiches. They were passed around, with each of the lupi taking three or four. Kai ended up with one, though she wasn't sure who put it in front of her. She certainly hadn't; the thought of eating made her queasy. Carl vanished and reappeared with another tray, this one carrying lemonade and glasses. "Coffee's coming up," he said tersely.

"The ward," Cynna said, pushing back her chair.

"Ah, yes. Carl, we'll wait on the coffee so Cynna doesn't have to keep resetting the ward." As Cynna stood to take care of the ward Carl's entrance had broken, Isen went on, "I don't want to interrupt your meal, Kai—ah, I see you got one of the roast beef sandwiches. You'll have to let me know what you think of the horseradish spread. I think it needs a bit more kick, but Carl disagrees. While you're eating—"

"Give me a minute," Cynna said. She was crouched on the other side of the table, so Kai couldn't see what she was doing. She felt it when the ward sprang back into place, though.

"I need to call Ackleford," Kai said.

"You will. From what I've put together, the attack on Little Sister may have taken place a trifle ahead of the one here, but they might have been simultaneous. In both, Dyffaya appears to have used a node to bring in the attacker, which is troubling given that—"

Kai broke in. "Not exactly."

Isen tilted his head. "No?"

"He used the node on Little Sister to bring in the chameleons. Here, I think he used chaos energy to transform an existing plant."

"Hmm. I would prefer to think that he can't access this node, which ought to be closed to him. But why do you believe this?"

"Two reasons. First, from what Carl told me, Nathan didn't react until the guard out back shouted."

"That was me," Josh put in.

"Where were you?"

"On the roof. A big stalk from that vine shot out over the deck. I'd never seen anything like it. It was so fast—and it grabbed Benedict's leg."

"But the vine was rooted already when that stalk shot out."

"Yeah, I guess so. Over by the west end of the deck."

"And the node is underneath the deck right outside the French doors. That's twenty feet from where the vine rooted."

Isen spoke. "You don't think the plant could have moved away from the node after being gated in?"

"It's theoretically possible. Mobile plants are rare even in high-magic places, but this was not a normal plant. But why would it move? Why not put down roots where it came in?"

"It needed sunlight?" Arjenie suggested.

"Maybe, though mobile plants tend to depend on magic and meat for energy more than sunlight. It's the timing that wrecks that scenario, though. If the plant had been gated in and scuttled down to the end of the deck, then set roots—all that took time. Maybe only a few seconds, given how fast it grew, but those seconds mean it didn't happen that way. Um . . . you know that Nathan doesn't use gates to cross between realms, right? Well, people with that ability are sensitive to gates." They made Nathan's gut tickle. That's what he'd told her. "But he didn't react until Josh shouted, which means he didn't notice anything. There's no way Nathan would miss something like that. Therefore, no gate was used."

Isen nodded slowly. "I can accept that. And your second reason?"

"The vine looks like a giant, mutated version of one I've seen growing here. It doesn't have the purple flowers, but the leaves look the same. I don't know the name of the native vine—"

"Morning glory," Isen said dryly, "of some kind. Lily would know the exact name. They spring up on that side of the house every year. I didn't note the resemblance at the time, but I believe you're right."

"Morning glories don't have thorns," Josh said.

"This one only grew thorns where it needed them," Kai said. "Where it was attacking people."

Isen nodded. "That I did notice. All of which means that the node here is still closed to Dyffaya. This is good news. But the timing of the attacks suggests that he wants to keep us from closing the other node to him, which in turn means we need to do just that. Cynna? Nettie? How quickly can you finish what you started?"

Cynna grimaced. "Um . . . it *is* closed to him."

Both of Isen's eyebrows shot up. "Explain."

"When the chameleons attacked, the node was primed and ready for the next step. I didn't have time to undo everything, not with the chameleon draining Cullen's blood, so I finished the rite . . . only Nettie wasn't there to involve the mountain's guardian, so I couldn't do it the way we'd planned. So I, uh, tied the node to me."

"That's not possible," Kai said without thinking.

Cynna looked at her. "Actually, it is."

"But . . ." She shook her head. "I can see that you believe what you say." Cynna's colors were clear, without the snot-green of a deliberate lie. "But you may be mistaken. It's hard to believe that you did something that only an adept or sidhe lord with the land-tie is supposed to be able to do. And if you did, you wouldn't be sitting here talking to me. You'd be screaming in pain. If you were still alive, that is. Node energies are *strong*."

Cynna and Isen exchanged one of those looks—the kind that had bugged her so much when she first sat down. She resisted the urge to snap this time, but it reminded her that she still didn't know what Arjenie had wanted to tell her.

"I can't tell you how I know what I do," Cynna said finally, "or how I'm able to handle the tie, but you're right about one thing. Unlinking myself from the node will take time and a lot of prep, especially without Cullen to help, but it has to be done as soon as possible. The energies involved aren't compatible with mine."

SEVENTEEN

"SO that's what they did!" Dyffaya exclaimed. He slapped Nathan on the shoulder, friendly-like. "Clever bunch your lover's mixed up with."

Nathan didn't scream. Screaming took too much energy.

He hung upside down from one of the trees. Twin branches impaled his feet. His arms were bound tightly to his sides by a vine. A black vine, just like the trees.

The first impalement, the one through his gut, had hurt worse initially, a shock of pain so intense he hadn't been able to breathe. Benedict, Dell, and Cullen had all sprung forward to help, but that wasn't part of the god's plans. He'd opened another pit to drop them into—this one, he'd chattily explained to Nathan, with a tunnel to take them to the place where he'd left "pretty little Britta." He'd then closed off their access to the clearing.

Nathan had walked off that branch one agonizing step at a time. When he came free, Dyffaya had applauded—and immediately wrapped him up in the vine, pierced his feet, and set him to dangling. Giving him no chance to draw Claw, much less use it.

That pain kept getting worse. It was interfering with his concentration, and he needed to be able to concentrate. If he could slow his healing enough, eventually his weight would finish ripping his feet apart and he'd fall to the ground. Of course, Dyffaya likely had something else in mind to do if that happened, but at the moment Nathan didn't care.

"No comment?" Dyffaya inquired. "I thought you'd be cheered by your friends' cleverness. They've got me quite blocked from that node. Of course, the woman will probably incinerate in a day or two, so this is only a temporary setback."

Nathan's voice was breathy. "I can't . . . understand the display, I'm afraid."

A visual display of some sort hovered in the air between Dyffaya and Nathan. It consisted of swirling colors that Nathan couldn't resolve into any kinds of shapes. There was no sound, just the colors.

"You can't?" Dyffaya glanced at the display. "Silly me. I'm using the wrong setting. You're really quite human in some ways, Nathan."

The swirls suddenly resolved and Nathan was looking at a small, three-dimensional representation of Isen Turner's face. Isen was speaking, but Nathan only caught a few words; the man's beard made lip-reading difficult. Something about a sandwich, though. Then Nathan saw a plate holding a sandwich and a hand reaching for it.

Kai's hand.

He was seeing the world through Kai's eyes.

KAI found herself taking a bite of the sandwich she didn't want without knowing why she'd given in to Isen's suggestion that she finish eating. The man was uncanny.

Her stomach didn't approve. She set the sandwich down.

"Too much kick in the sauce?" Isen asked. "Not enough?"

"No. No, it's good." She laid a hand over her unhappy stomach.

"All right. We've settled that we aren't under immediate threat, either of attack via the nodes or of having more of our number snatched. Our next priority is those who've been taken."

"Nope," Nettie said, startling Kai. She twisted in her chair. Nettie was crossing the room from the wing that held most of the bedrooms. She looked rested; her color was back to normal, and the faint pain lines bracketing her mouth were gone. "Sorry to disagree, but our next priority is a cleansing. At least that's mine and Kai's priority."

Kai's stomach clenched.

Isen frowned. "I don't understand."

"I can't believe I forgot." Nettie shook her head. "I must have been more wiped out than I realized. When Kai went into that trance—"

"It wasn't a trance," Kai said, then turned to the others to explain. "Dell had just killed the chameleon who nearly killed Nettie. Dell was wounded already, and the other two attacked her. They were under Dyffaya's control, so I had to cut that, and fast. But . . ." She swallowed, remembering that terrible stretching. "I guess I shouldn't be surprised that a god is really, really powerful. I did manage to break his control, but the recoil slammed me out of my body. While I was out there"—wherever *there* was—"he grabbed me."

Isen's eyebrows lifted. "You broke a god's control?"

Put that way, it did sound kind of impressive. Or unlikely. The look on Isen's face suggested he was leaning toward the latter.

Nettie frowned. "You didn't tell me that you weren't in your body when Dyffaya grabbed you."

"I didn't?" Kai searched her memory and found she didn't have much idea what she'd said right after returning to her body.

"You mentioned being gone. I thought you meant . . . never mind what I thought. I didn't follow through. We'll do the cleansing now."

Kai shook her head. "Getting Cynna clear of her tie to the node is more important."

"Her what?" Nettie gave Cynna a look, then waved her hand. "Explain later. Come on, Kai."

The phone in Kai's rear pocket buzzed. Not her phone. Nathan's. She'd gotten it from Carl when she questioned him. She took it out. "This is Kai."

"I need to talk to Hunter."

"Is this Special Agent Ackleford?"

"Yeah."

"I was going to call you. Nathan's been taken by the god."

The curses that followed were brief but heartfelt. "Then I need the other guy. Seabourne."

"He was taken, too." Be crisp, Isen had said. Kai did her best to be crisp as she gave Ackleford a brief account of the two attacks.

"Shit." A moment's silence. "I'll let Brooks know, but he'll want to hear from you, too. You got his number?"

"I can get it."

"Good. Call him on the way. Looks like we've got another chaos event. I need someone who can help with the woo-woo end of things."

"I guess that's me." The coven that used to help the Bureau had pretty much dissolved after their high priestess's death while under the control of Nam Anthessa. Kai borrowed Isen's notebook so she could jot down the address he gave her, along with a few details. When Ackleford finished, she looked around at the others. "A historic building in Old San Diego just sprouted flowers or turned into a plant or something. Reports are garbled. I'm headed there now."

"I'll go with you," Arjenie said.

Cynna stood, too—then sat again abruptly. "Shit. I can't go. Not while I'm tied to the node."

"How's your stomach, Kai?" Nettie asked suddenly.

Kai blinked. "What?"

"You keep rubbing your stomach."

"I'm fine," she said impatiently, and when Nettie just kept looking at her, snapped, "A little queasy, okay? Nothing major. Stress. Arjenie—"

"You'll come outside for the cleansing before you leave."

Kai shook her head. "Ackleford needs someone who has some understanding of magic. I'm not Nathan or Cullen, but I'm what he's got."

"After you've been cleansed."

Anger flared. She pushed to her feet and turned her back on Nettie. "Come on, Arjenie."

"Isen," Nettie said. "I need you to stop her."

HEALING took energy. Slowing his healing did, too. Most of that energy was magical, but some was physical. Hanging upside down didn't help. The pooling of blood in his head called for continual, low-level healing, which was draining. All in all, Nathan was getting very hungry—enough that he noticed it in spite of the agony radiating from his feet. It was hard to focus on the images hovering near his head.

But he saw two of the lupi lay hands on Kai, stopping her. Why did they do that? He'd missed something. If Kai wasn't looking right at someone he couldn't read their lips. Even when she did look at them when they spoke, he was bleary with pain. Hard to concentrate . . .

"I knew that shaman was going to be a problem. Oh, well. Change of plans." Dyffaya had hunkered down in the easy squat he'd used before so he could watch along with Nathan. "Look at her fight! A little panic is a wonderful thing. Pity she didn't have time to draw the knife. A nice blade, that. Custom work?"

Nathan licked dry lips. Thirst was beginning to compete with hunger and pain for his attention. The images showed Kai being held by two lupi while Nettie walked up to her. "Yes."

"Very nice," Dyffaya repeated. "Not as fine as your blade, of course—we really must chat about that—but very nice. I'd enjoy seeing her use it some time, but that won't happen today." He snapped his fingers—and the images vanished.

"Tired of . . . watching?"

"I could have made the shaman do it, but this is more fun. If I retrieve my power myself, when they go through their little cleansing ritual they won't find a thing. They'll wonder if anything was there in the first place—or if it's still there and they simply can't find it. They won't quite trust the only one who can see my handiwork, and she will begin to doubt herself even as she resents their distrust."

Kai was free of Dyffaya's influence. As of right now. Relief made Nathan dizzy. It would be nice if he could pass out. "Didn't have . . . much of your power in her, did she?"

Dyffaya shrugged pettishly. "She's more resistant than I'd expected, but it's challenges that make life interesting, don't they? You don't answer. No doubt you're feeling slighted. I can't blame you. This"—he waved a hand, indicating the way Nathan hung—"is hardly worthy of either of us. So simplistic it scarcely counts as revenge. Don't worry. I'll do better."

"I'm . . . not entirely . . . happy to hear that."

Dyffaya gave a boyish peal of laughter. "In which case, do worry. But not right now. I've been indulging myself, playing with you while others attempted the less interesting chores, but that hasn't worked out. I'm sorry to have to abandon you, but I really must take a more direct hand." With that, he vanished.

And popped up again some fifteen feet away—in front of a table complete with white tablecloth and silver covers over dishes Nathan could smell vividly. And water. There was water in the crystal carafe. "I've been forgetting my duties as host! I'm sure you're getting hungry by now. Please help yourself. Everything will stay warm, however long it takes you to get here. Some of it is even safe to eat." He winked and vanished once more.

Nathan's thoughts were sluggish. He might not be able to pass out or go into shock, but this amount of pain made it hard to think. He worked his way through events slowly to be sure he understood.

First Kai's situation. Clearly the god had managed to sink a mote of power into her. He could see through her eyes, probably influence her, but he wasn't in full control or he would have gotten all her senses, not just vision. Now he'd retrieved that mote of power, releasing Kai . . . or had he? Had he said that outright or only implied it?

Dyffaya might be wearing a human form just now, but he was sidhe, and sidhe do not lie. They enjoy deception, they hoard truth, but they don't lie outright because it puts a crimp in their power. The more powerful they are, the worse they're affected by false speech. There were a few rare exceptions. Nathan was one himself. But Dyffaya wasn't. At least he hadn't been before his death, which admittedly was a very long time ago, but the dead don't change much. Nathan thought he could count on Dyffaya speaking some version of truth.

The god had implied that he'd released Kai by making the images go away. He'd stated what he believed the results would be . . . if he retrieved that mote before the cleansing.

If. Powerful little word, that. *If* meant Dyffaya might still have a mote of power in Kai that he believed he could hide from the Powers that Nettie would call on. Or it might mean he'd done exactly what he implied, but put that maddening *if* in place so Nathan couldn't be sure. Or it could mean he wanted Nathan to spot the deceptive phrasing and conclude that he'd removed the mote, but the deception itself was the lie and he'd really left the mote in place.

It was typical elfin circumlocution: tell the truth in a way that looks deceitful to keep your opponent off balance. Nathan's brain obviously wasn't operating at full power—he should have noticed the phrasing right off. Unfortunately, noticing it didn't keep it from working. Just as Dyffaya wanted, he couldn't be sure. He set the question aside for now.

Which meant it was time to address his own situation. Which he'd been putting off, hadn't he?

The solution was obvious.

Oh, but he did not want to do this.

Nathan squeezed his eyes closed and counted to five in his head. Then he used all his considerable strength to rip one foot free.

This time he went ahead and screamed. Then he panted and whimpered for a time. Eventually he yanked again—and screamed a second time as his other foot, left to support his entire weight, ripped open. And he fell.

THE clean, astringent scent of sage hung heavy in the air. Kai's left foot had fallen asleep, which made no sense because she was lying on her back. She felt stiff, as if she'd been lying there for hours, though she didn't see how the cleansing could've taken that long.

Not that she knew. When the lupi grabbed her, she'd fought—briefly and ineffectually, but she'd tried to get loose. So Nettie had put her in sleep. She still felt dopey, reluctant to open her eyes . . . though the latter was more because she didn't want to look at anyone. She wiggled her foot.

". . . successful?" That was Isen.

"As far as I can tell," Nettie said. Her voice came from just behind Kai. "How do you feel, Kai?"

"Groggy."

"Not angry anymore?"

"That was panic earlier, not anger. I told you that."

"True," Isen said. "You smelled of panic then. Now, however, you smell angry."

Kai made the effort, opened her eyes, and sat up. Shit. She had quite an audience. Nettie sat cross-legged nearby. Isen, Cynna, Arjenie, and a rangy lupus named Pete were stationed at the various compass points, forming a large circle around Kai. Lots of wary gray or worried purple in their thoughts as they watched her. Waiting to see if her head started spinning, no doubt.

Kai gritted her teeth against the urge to stick her tongue out at them. "How would you feel if you'd been grabbed and held and put in sleep against your will?"

"Royally pissed. Though I hope I'd get over that once I understood the necessity."

Had it been necessary? She frowned. She'd felt like herself all along . . . except for that panic. She'd never had a panic attack, but that must be what one felt like. Still, she was so raw and scared for Nathan and Dell, it wouldn't be surprising if today was her day to react badly to being grabbed. And that was the only time when . . . no. No, it wasn't. She'd thought about binding someone. Earlier, when she realized the others shared some secret they didn't want her to know about, she'd actually considered forcing someone to tell.

That really, truly wasn't like her. "Shit," she whispered.

"How's your stomach?" Nettie asked.

"Fine." She grimaced. "Really fine, not I-wish-you'd-quit-asking-that fine. I take it I'm all cleansed?"

"As far as I can tell."

"I'd rather hear a nice, solid 'yes.' "

"I'd rather be able to give you one. If you'd been possessed by a demon, I'd know for certain. Dyffaya is much harder for me to sense. I suspect I only become aware of him when he's actively influencing his host."

His host. Meaning her. Which made him a parasite, didn't it? A parasite god.

"But the cleansing was properly conducted, so you ought to be free of him." Nettie placed her hands on the small of her back and arched it in a stretch. She looked tired. "Just in case, though, pay attention to your gut."

"Ah . . . okay. Why?"

"We may think we live right behind our eyes—in our brains—but we experience our core identities in our guts. That's why we talk about gut feelings, gut instinct, or say that something disturbing was gut-wrenching. Your gut was disturbed."

"That's not exactly foolproof. Being stressed half out of my mind can mess with my stomach."

"Yes. So can the intrusion of someone else's desires in your core. You've got a strong sense of identity, Kai, or you wouldn't have reacted to Dyffaya's intrusion that way. Pay attention to what your gut tells you."

Right. Kai took a deep breath and tried not to feel like she'd been slimed from the inside. "We have to assume that Dyffaya knows everything we said."

Isen nodded. "As well as everything you know."

"What? No, it doesn't work like that."

Isen's face looked polite. His colors were angry. "He was in your head. We have to assume he browsed around while he was there."

Kai tried again. "He's sensitive to thoughts in some way, but so am I. We don't know what form his sensitivity takes, but sensitivity isn't telepathy. And even telepathy doesn't make someone able to access information the target isn't actively thinking about."

"Sam can do that. Is this god less powerful than the black dragon?"

They really had no idea what the Eldest was capable of, did they? "When it comes to mind magic? Yes."

Isen's eyebrows shot up. "You sound very sure."

Cynna spoke. "She's right, Isen. About the difference between telepathy and mind control, I mean. I may not geek out on theory the way Cullen does, but I know that much. Reading a mind is a whole different skill set from controlling one. It's like . . . I can drive a car, but I can't build one." She grimaced. "And that analogy sucks, but the point is, we've got no reason to think Dyffaya reads minds."

"Maybe," Arjenie said, "it's like with the *birith* spectrum and how Isen can turn into a wolf, but not a fox or a chicken."

"Rooster," Isen said dryly. "Surely you mean rooster, not chicken. Very well. I was making an unwarranted assumption, but neither can we afford to categorically eliminate the possibility. Dyffaya has already exhibited one skill he wasn't supposed to have."

And there was a depressing notion. Tired of sitting in the dirt, Kai stood and brushed herself off. "How long was I out? Special Agent Ackleford is expecting me."

"Us," Arjenie said. "I'm going with you, remember?"

EIGHTEEN

BENEDICT wasn't there to insist that Arjenie take guards along, so Isen did the insisting, sending a full squad with them. He wanted them to take his car, too—an armored Lincoln Town Car slightly smaller than a tank. Kai didn't argue. She couldn't help wondering how much the guards were there for protection and how much they were supposed to keep an eye on her. Just in case.

"How's your stomach?" Arjenie asked as they buckled up.

"I'll let you know if it starts acting up." She looked at the backs of the heads of the two lupi in the front seat. Four more would follow them in another car. "You and everyone else."

"Kai." Arjenie patted her hand. "I think you're doing what they call projecting. You don't trust you, so you think everyone else doesn't, either."

"Why would you?" she said bitterly. "I let that parasite in. I let him listen in as we made plans. I—"

"Didn't *let* him do anything. Really." Arjenie shook her head disapprovingly. "Is this what you'd tell a patient? 'Yes, it's all your fault. Shame on you for letting yourself be traumatized.' "

"When you put it that way . . . okay, you're right. It isn't my fault he got a hook in me. It's a lot harder to fix my own thoughts than someone else's, though."

"Other people's problems always seem so fixable compared to our own."

Reluctantly Kai's mouth turned up. "True. Isen agrees with my mistrust of me, though. That's not projecting. He's genuinely angry."

"Of course he is. He thinks it's his fault."

She stared. "How in the world could he?"

"Oh, lots of ways. I bet he thinks he shouldn't have urged Nettie to go rest and heal as soon as she got there. If he'd had her tell him what happened right away, she would have remembered that you needed to be cleansed. So if Dyffaya learned too much from our discussion, Isen figures that's on him."

"He had no way of knowing he needed her to remember something."

Arjenie shrugged. "That's how they think. All of them, really, or at least all the dominants. Isen, Benedict, Rule—they always think things are up to them. Isen's the worst because he's Rho and a lot really is up to him, but all the dominants have that 'the buck stops here' attitude. It's one reason they need a clearly defined hierarchy. They need to know where their responsibilities end." She raised her voice slightly. "Am I right, José?"

"Damn straight," their driver said.

José was a wiry fellow about an inch shorter than Kai. He was in charge of the squad, although some of the others looked like they could toss him around like an oversize football. Kai liked the look of his thoughts—crisp, yet flowing, the greens girded by on-alert pewter, with reassuring flickers of confident orange. "What does dominant mean to a lupus?"

Arjenie answered. "A dominant wants to be in charge, but he wants that so he can take care of things. Of people. He's especially protective of those under him. And by that I don't mean tucking them in at night, but making sure they have what they need to succeed—food, training, responsibilities that fit their skills. But deep down, a dominant would really like to be able to take care of everyone."

The man in the passenger seat chuckled. "She's got you pegged, José."

"She lives with Benedict," José said dryly.

"Point." That man grinned. "Benedict took great care of Sammy last week."

"Yeah. Smacked him halfway across the room."

That put both men in a good mood. As the Lincoln turned off onto the highway, leaving Clanhome, they continued to swap examples of how Benedict took care of them. It was, she realized, their way of reassuring themselves that they'd get him back. He was tough, strong, and wily, and he'd survive, and they'd get him back.

Benedict had a lot of people who'd move heaven and earth to reclaim him. A whole clan. Nathan and Dell only had her.

What was happening to them right now? What . . . no, don't go there. Nathan wasn't the god's victim, whatever Dyffaya might believe. He was there on purpose. He was on a Hunt, which meant he had a chance of killing the god, even if Kai didn't see how that was possible. He just had to stay alive and, sooner or later, he'd get that chance. And he was hard to kill.

Which made him a perfect subject for torture, because he'd live through just about anything the god did to him.

"You're fingering that big knife of yours," Arjenie observed. "I'm not going to take that personally, but it does look menacing."

Kai pulled her hand away. "Sorry. It makes a gruesome sort of security blanket, doesn't it?"

"Benedict gets all Zen when he's cleaning his weapons, so I do understand. Sort of. But the authorities aren't going to. You are going to leave it in the car, aren't you?"

"I'm not going anywhere without Teacher. Not now." She'd worn her vest for the same reason, knowing she'd stand out like a sore thumb on a warm, sunny day like this. And her amulet. And the necklace that held a number of charms she hadn't bothered with lately. Not that she expected to need to start a fire or detect poison, but better to have them and not need them than the other way around.

Arjenie's eyebrows shot up. "Your knife has a name?"

"It's more of a use-name. It's a teaching blade."

"Meaning—?"

"I thought you might have heard of them. Pretty much everyone in the Queens' realms knows about teaching blades."

"My father's idea of an education was pretty threadbare," Arjenie said dryly.

"Well, they're not commonplace. They're expensive, and there's a high demand, so it can be hard to get hold of one." Nathan never would tell her what he'd paid for this one, or even where he got it. One day he'd said he had something to check out and might be "gone a bit." When he showed up five days later, he had Teacher. "A good teaching blade speeds up how fast you learn bladework. You get the right moves into muscle memory quickly because it assumes control of your body to show them to you. The best ones give that memory a little magical push to make it stick better."

"Wait a minute. It takes over your body? And you're okay with that?"

"I can resume control at any time. And by taking over, Teacher's saved my life more than once. Like today. I couldn't have fought off a chameleon on my own. They're way faster than humans."

"So you've got a named blade that's good enough to take on a chameleon." Arjenie sighed. "That is so cool."

Kai's grin flickered. "It is, isn't it?"

"Why learn to use a knife? Couldn't you have taken a gun along if you needed a weapon?"

"Guns are an iffy proposition in Faerie."

"You'll have to explain that later. Your stomach still okay?"

"Fine. Are you going to ask that often?"

"No, but there's something I want to tell you, and it really needs to be just between us."

"Um." Kai glanced at the two men in the front seat.

Arjenie grinned. "Oh, they already know."

"Is this the thing you wanted to tell me earlier? When Cynna said she couldn't stop you? Because I can't guarantee that we aren't eavesdropped on. It's really hard to listen magically to someone who's moving as fast as we are, so we're probably okay. But I can't set a ward to make sure the way Nathan can."

"It's a risk, I guess, but a tiny one, and you really need to know this. You said that your bond with Dell would've snapped if she'd been taken to another realm."

Kai nodded.

"The mate bond doesn't work that way."

The passenger-seat guard made a strangled noise. José said, "Uh, Arjenie? Did Isen know you were going to say that?"

Arjenie leaned forward to pat him on the shoulder. "I'm sure he does. He was in the room when I said that I'd tell her. I didn't say it to him, but he was in the room."

José did not look reassured.

Arjenie looked at her. "You need to know about the mate bond because you need to know what I learn from it, and why would you believe me if you didn't know where the information came from?"

"I take it this mate bond is between you and Benedict?"

"I should've said that right off. Yes. Mate bonds are very rare, they're unbreakable, and they come from the Lady. They've got a lot of upsides, but the downside is that the bonded pair can't be too far apart physically or they pass out. Unfortunately, 'too far' can vary. Right now it's at least thirty miles for me and Benedict. I know that because he's a little over thirty miles that way." She pointed in the general direction they were going.

"Uh . . . but he isn't. He's in the godhead."

"Well, yes, but—wait. You don't get a sense of where Dell is?"

Kai shook her head. "A little if she's close, but distance thins it, just like it makes it harder to pick up detailed information, much less actual words. Right now it's as if she were a hundred miles away. I don't see how you can feel Benedict's direction when he's in the godhead."

"Apparently the godhead is sufficiently congruent with Earth to have a physical referent here."

Something clicked when Arjenie said that. "The godhead is physically congruent with Earth . . . and it's a spiritual place, not physical, yet it can support physical life. Arjenie, it sounds like the Upper World."

Arjenie cocked her head curiously. "That's from your people's origin story, right? The Holy People led your people up from the Lower Realms to the Glittering World—also called the Surface World—but they themselves went on to the Upper Worlds."

"You've heard the story?"

"My cousin is apprenticing as a shaman. Not that he talks about it much, but I did some research. Do you think the Upper Worlds are real places, then?"

She snorted. "I asked Grandfather that once. He said I sounded like a *bilagáana,* and that when I could tell him what reality was I should ask again."

Arjenie grinned. "*Bilagáana* meaning white person?"

"You speak *Diné Bizaad*?" The language of the People, that meant. Navajo to the rest of the world.

Arjenie waved one hand dismissively. "I've picked up a few words, no more. Tell me about the Upper Worlds."

"Sometimes they're referred to as plural, sometimes in the singular—the Upper World. Grandfather says they're both singular and plural, and if that makes sense to you, please explain it to me."

"Buddhists might say that everything's both singular and plural, and yet neither."

"And that means—?"

"I have no idea."

Kai grinned. "Anyway, the Upper World or Worlds—never mind. I'm going use the singular, but keep in mind that may not be accurate. The Upper World is tied to our world, but there's a barrier between them. In holy places, like the mountain where Grandfather lives, the barrier is thin, but the two worlds are linked everywhere. In other words, the Upper World and Earth are physically congruent. And according to the stories, a lot of the early heroes traveled to see one or another of the Powers and came back to share what they'd been taught. That suggests that the Upper World is capable of supporting life—and that it's possible to travel there and return."

"I like the part about returning," Arjenie said.

So did Kai.

"You think Dyffaya somehow parked his godhead in the world or worlds where the Native Powers live?"

"When you put it that way," Kai said, reaching for her phone, "I think I'd better call Nettie."

THE food had been both hot and plentiful when Nathan crawled up to the table. His host had neglected to provide a chair, so Nathan was sitting on the ground, finishing his second helping of everything except the carrots and potatoes, which look good but lacked scent, when a chameleon slunk up to the edge of the clearing. It stopped and looked at him out of unblinking yellow eyes.

Not Dell. This one was smaller, much less muscular. A male?

It had come from the direction Nathan had decided to call west. With no sun, moon, or stars, directions were difficult to fix here, but like migratory birds, Nathan had a directional sense. It seemed to work here.

When the second chameleon appeared beside the first, he put his fork on his plate and set the plate aside. He might have to draw Claw. "Hello to you both. I wonder if you understand me. I'd rather not fight you, so I hope—oh, Dell. Benedict. Good to see you."

Dell loped into the clearing. She was back in her original form, which worried him a bit. He'd thought she understood why he wanted her in human shape. Benedict strode along behind her. He scowled at Nathan. "You're pretty damn cheerful for a man I thought was being tortured."

"Nothing like having the torture stop to cheer a man up." The two smaller chameleons hadn't budged, still hanging back at the edge of the clearing. When Dell reached him she sat and looked at his feet. Then she looked at his face, her head cocked in question. "It will be another four or five hours before they're healed enough to walk on," he told her. "I'd rather not accelerate the healing. I had to do that with the chest wound, and I don't know when I'll be able to eat again. Which is why I've been stuffing myself. Why are you back in your original form?"

She looked over her shoulder at Benedict.

He recognized his cue. "When the other two chameleons showed up, she said she needed to take care of the stupid males and Changed. They obey her. Seem to understand what she wants pretty well, too, which helps. I don't know if I could have found you on my own. This place is seriously weird. You sure that food is safe?"

"I doubt anything here is truly safe, but aside from the carrots and potatoes, everything smells okay. Where's Cullen?"

"Back in the grotto. That's where we ended up, in this grotto where Dyffaya stashed Britta. She's a mess. Won't leave the grotto, but she got real scared when she understood we were going, so Cullen offered to stay with her." He glanced down at Nathan's feet. "What did he do to you?"

"His version of a crucifixion. Impaled my feet and hung me upside down while we chatted. He left about an hour ago. It took me a while to get myself down, then get the vines off my arms."

Benedict looked at Nathan's feet another moment, then grunted and pulled his knife from its sheath. He cut off a hunk of venison. "Seabourne says the god can hear us. He may or may not be paying attention at any given moment, but if he is, he'll hear us."

"Cullen's right. Everything here *is* Dyffaya, in a sense. It's all the godhead, and he's spread throughout it."

Benedict looked at the meat in his hand. "Everything?"

"Including the food, yes. It's godhead stuff that's been magically transformed. Even the air we breathe is godhead stuff. But the venison, the bread, and the apples smell right, so they should be okay."

Benedict still didn't eat. "You warned me about the smell thing, but you didn't get to explain. Why does the smell make it okay?"

"Food that lacks scent probably has some of Dyffaya in it. He doesn't have a scent—I imagine you noticed that? I think it's because he's dead. The godhead itself is alive, though, so food that's made purely from godhead stuff without any of the god mixed in smells like it ought to." He paused. "Or so I think."

Benedict sighed. "Be nice if you were sure." But he took a bite of the venison. "Damn, that's good. He gave us salad."

Nathan's eyebrows lifted. "Salad?"

"His idea of a joke. Feed the carnivores green stuff. We

get plenty of water—there's a spring—and we've been making the bar of soap last. Twice a day a roll of toilet paper and a huge bowl of salad shows up. After a couple days of that—"

"Wait. Wait a minute. A couple days?"

"Guess you lost track of time. Easy to do here. After we got to the grotto, Cullen cast a timekeeping spell. Don't ask me how it works, but it does. When I left to hunt for you, we'd been in the grotto for thirty hours. Add two hours to that to allow for the period before he got his spell going, and another ten hours that I spent looking for you. That's forty-two. Not quite two days, but close enough."

Oh, hell. "I have not been here a couple of days. Not even close to that. I'd estimate that, for me, slightly over three hours have passed."

"You must've passed out for longer than you realized."

Nathan shook his head. "I didn't pass out. I can't. I can be knocked out, either physically or magically, but not for that long. And I wasn't knocked out. Dyffaya enjoyed having me conscious and hurting."

"That does not make sense."

"Time must fluctuate here, with different parts of the godhead experiencing different time flows."

"Shit. We need to go. Now. For me it's been five hours since I left Cullen. God only knows how long it's been for him." He pulled off his shirt and began loading the remains of the meal onto it. Fortunately, Dyffaya had been generous. There was a lot left, enough for four or five humans or a couple lupi.

"Not the potatoes and carrots," Nathan reminded him, and gripped the edge of the table to help himself stand.

"Sit down, dammit. You'll ride on my back. Shouldn't take us as long to get to him as it did to find you, since we won't be casting around, so less than five hours. A lot less, I hope." He looked at Dell. "Got an estimate?"

Dell thought a moment, then tapped the ground with one paw three times.

"Three hours?" Relief shaded Benedict voice. He tied his makeshift bundle together with the sleeves. "Hope you're right."

"What is it you're afraid has happened to Cullen?"

"If Dyffaya kept up his little joke and Cullen's been fed lettuce for several days, a week, whatever it's been in his time . . . we need meat. We starve without it. Plus it's not good if we're alone too long."

Only Cullen wasn't alone. He was with Britta. "There's no moon, so his wolf can't come out."

Benedict crouched in front of Nathan. "He can't Change. Doesn't mean his wolf can't come out, and it's worse if that happens without the Change. Hop aboard and hold on. I'll be running."

NINETEEN

EVEN the fittest of werewolves gets winded after running for roughly three hours carrying a hundred and eighty pounds of Nathan on his back. The terrain wasn't flat, either. They left the impossibly tall black trees behind after the first hour, entering a rocky region where the plants were much smaller, but they remained black. Aside from the color of the vegetation, it was typical of extremely high-magic regions—emphasis on the "extreme." At one point they crossed a river. It began as a waterfall pouring out of a cleft in a rocky slope. It ended that way, too, some thirty yards away, pouring straight up into a second cleft.

Dell led. She, too, had a directional sense, one even stronger than Nathan's. The two males coursed behind, watching their back trail. According to Benedict there were creatures living here—furry things, he said, with the size, build, and temperament of badgers, but with more teeth. The male chameleons had been living off the blood of those creatures; Dell had dined on Benedict's blood.

"My feet are healed enough to support me now," Nathan told the man carrying him as he loped along a dry stream bed at the base of an arroyo. The rocky walls on either side were all shades of black and gray.

"We're about there," Benedict said. Or huffed. And a few paces later he slowed as they rounded a curve in the rocky stream bed . . . slowed, and then stopped. "Cullen." He spoke the name as if it were a command, adding very softly: "Dropping you now. Don't move or speak."

Nathan caught no more than a glimpse of Cullen hunkered down by a campfire before Benedict suited actions to words and dumped him. He let himself go limp, rolling as he hit the ground and coming up onto his knees rather than his feet. He might have exaggerated a bit about how healed they were.

He had a clear view of Cullen now. And everything else.

The grotto itself was a surprise. Shaped roughly like a triangle with walls of black stone striated with white and gray, its floor was the usual pale, glowing sand. A spring tucked into one corner burbled quietly to itself. As usual, there was no grass . . . but there were flowers. Brilliantly colored flowers. Red, fuchsia, yellow, blue, pink, purple—they sprouted from crevices in the rocks, from the dead sand, from the skinny black twigs of small bushes.

In the center of the grotto a campfire burned merrily, though it lacked any wood to consume. Cullen crouched on one side of the fire. He wore shoes and a wedding ring, nothing else. On the other side of the fire a young woman lay on her back, her long black hair bound in a single braid. Beneath her head was a bit of cloth—Cullen's underwear, posing as a thoroughly inadequate pillow. His jeans and shirt had been tucked carefully around her, improvised covers. She was utterly still except for the slight rise and fall of her chest. Nathan could hear her breathing—the crescendo-diminuendo of Cheyne-Stokes.

Britta Valenzuela was dying.

Cullen was looking straight at Benedict. His eyes were the same startling blue as ever . . . and entirely different. The being who looked out of those eyes was intelligent, but he was not a man. "Not meat," he said hoarsely. Paused, and added, "Yet."

"No," Benedict said. "She isn't. I brought meat."

Cullen rose with his usual fluid grace—which was remarkable, given how he looked. Every rib stood out. "I need meat."

Benedict held out a hand in Nathan's direction and waggled his fingers.

Nathan had tucked the shirt-bag of provisions inside his own shirt. He pulled it out and tossed it to Benedict, who caught it and spoke firmly. "You'll submit first."

Cullen growled.

"Don't test me." Benedict kept his eyes fixed on Cullen.

The starving man-shaped wolf dropped his gaze and went to his knees, head down. When Benedict bit into the venison, a tremor passed through Cullen's emaciated body. Benedict tossed him a piece of venison. Cullen snatched it from the air and devoured it.

Nathan knew enough about wolves to understand why Benedict handled it that way. He needed to control the starving wolf until the man reemerged, so he'd used language the wolf understood: a dominant wolf eats first.

Benedict tossed another piece of meat at Cullen. Softly he said to Nathan, "Check on Britta, but circle wide. Your scent's likely to bother him."

Nathan nodded and pushed to his feet. It hurt. He moved slowly. Cullen paused, growling.

"He's mine, too," Benedict told him. He began walking toward Cullen. "He won't take your meat."

Nathan didn't argue about whether he was Benedict's. It worked to let Cullen go back to the important business of filling his belly, which was what counted. Right now, the lupus was operating on pure instinct. It was a tribute to his training that they hadn't arrived to find a pile of gnawed-on bones on the other side of that fire, but training can only go so far. It was even more of a tribute to whatever core the man shared with the wolf.

Benedict kept Cullen's attention on him, moving steadily closer while Nathan circled around. When Benedict reached Cullen he signaled Nathan to wait, squatted, and gripped Cullen's shoulder. "You're going to be okay." Cullen made a sound, half sigh, half whimper, and did something the man would never have done. He leaned against the big man's solid bulk. Benedict didn't hug him. That human expression of comfort wouldn't have the same meaning to a wolf. He simply braced and let Cullen lean into him. "There's more meat, but it's for later. Too much too fast isn't good for you. I want you to go get a drink now."

Cullen twisted to look at Benedict. After a moment he

nodded—a thoroughly human gesture Nathan found encouraging—and stood. When he headed for the spring, Nathan started moving again.

Benedict looked up at him. "You said your feet were healed. They aren't."

"The skin and tendons are. The bones aren't quite baked." He knelt beside Britta, bent low and sniffed, then listened to her heartbeat. He straightened with a sigh and clasped her too-cool hand. Those in coma sometimes recognize touch even when their other senses are lost. "She's almost gone."

Benedict made a low, angry sound. "What's wrong with her? There's no blood."

"It's magic sickness. Humans can't tolerate areas of extremely high magic. At first they're just weak, tired. They chill easily, get disoriented. I heard a man who'd been a victim of magic sickness talk about it. He said it was like he didn't fit in his body or his brain, as if the magic was pushing him out. Eventually victims lapse into coma and the body's organs start shutting down. If you can get them out of the high-magic area before the coma hits, they usually make it, although their children may . . . but that's another issue. Once they're in coma, it's too late."

Benedict glanced over his shoulder. Cullen had knelt at the spring and was drinking thirstily. "What about. . . ." He indicated Cullen with a jerk of his head.

"You and Cullen should be okay. Most of those of the Blood are affected eventually, but it takes a long time—usually a matter of years, not days. Gifted humans have some resistance, too, but those without a Gift, like Britta, are entirely vulnerable." Nathan frowned. "It hit her awfully fast. Based on Cullen's condition, can you tell how much time passed for them?"

Benedict shrugged. "Assuming he didn't get any meat, maybe a week to ten days."

"There's one hell of a lot of magic in this place, and individual tolerances vary, but still—that's too fast."

"She wouldn't get up." Cullen spoke abruptly, his voice ragged. He stood beside the small spring, swaying as if there were a strong wind. "I tried and tried, but after a while she wouldn't get up."

Benedict looked up. "You back already?"

"Some." He swayed a bit. "The man's better with words, so we . . . but the wolf doesn't want to let go."

"Your wolf did a good job of watching over things, but he needs to sleep now. I'll take care of you and Britta. He can let go and sleep."

Cullen looked at him out of not-quite-human eyes for a long moment. "Okay." He took three steps, folded gracefully at the knees as if he'd planned it, and sank onto the sand, where he curled up in a ball the way a small child might . . . or a wolf who lacked the proper form, but was making do. Within moments, he was out cold.

So was the campfire. Cullen had been keeping it going. How long had he gone without sleep so he could keep the fire burning, trying to keep Britta warm?

Benedict nodded once in satisfaction. "He won't sleep long. Too hungry. But when he wakes up, the man should be back in charge."

Nathan settled more comfortably next to the dying woman, keeping hold of her hand. "Good. I have some questions for him. I don't see the magical timekeeper you mentioned."

"Probably his wolf either forgot to maintain it or didn't see the point."

Britta's breathing paused. For a painfully long moment, she didn't inhale. Nathan and Benedict both watched, waited . . . and her chest lifted again. Nathan continued to watch her as he spoke. "What he said about getting her up made me think he recognized the symptoms of magic sickness. Movement delays the progression. Hard to see where he might have learned about it, though."

Benedict grunted. "He picks up all sorts of shit from his scraps of old documents. Then there was the time he spent in Edge. No telling what he heard about there."

Was Britta's hand growing colder? Hard to be sure, but he could add his shirt to Cullen's. He wasn't sure she'd notice, but it was something he could do. He tugged it off over his head. "Likely someone in Edge warned him. Edge has—"

"What the *hell*?"

Nathan looked up. An enormous version of the display he'd watched earlier hung in the air halfway between him and the spring. Dead center of the visual field were the crosshairs of a telescopic scope. They rested on Special Agent Derwin Ackleford. "Shit. We're looking through the eyes of someone on Earth."

Enlarged so greatly, the fuzziness outside the direct line of view was obvious, fading into the blur of peripheral vision. Nathan could make out the rifle the sniper was using and part of his hand . . . no, her hand. Dyffaya was using a woman's eyes for this. The sniper was on a roof. A red-tiled roof. Nathan could barely make that out; it was at the very edge of the sniper's peripheral vision. Ackleford was at street level and maybe a block away with several other people—uniformed cops, men in suits, and one of the other FBI agents. The woman.

"I do like those big-screen TVs, don't you?" a mellow tenor said from overhead. Nathan looked up.

Dyffaya stood at the edge of one of the black cliffs surrounding the grotto. He'd chosen a different form this time, this one ostentatiously godlike—around seven feet of nude male with a face and form copied from Michelangelo's David, right down to the cupid-bow lips. Though Dyffaya had altered one thing: he was better hung than the statue.

He'd stayed with a human shape, though, hadn't he? Not elf. Interesting.

The god stepped off the cliff and began floating down. "Does the sniper's view worry you? No one need die right away. If the two of you behave—oh, by that I mean Nathan and Benedict. I may invite Dell and the sorcerer to play later, but for now it will be just you two. I do hope you've finished healing, Nathan."

"Not quite."

"Pity. You'd enjoy the next part more if—*no*!"

The last word emerged as a wail. The god forgot his posing and his grand entrance. He disappeared and, in the same instant, reappeared next to Nathan. One arm swept out, shoving Nathan aside. It felt like being smacked by the statue Dyffaya had copied. Nathan fell over on his back and skidded a couple feet—rolled, and came up ready to fight.

Dyffaya seemed to have forgotten about him. He was cradling the dying woman. "There now," he said tenderly, and stroked her face. "There now. Wake up for me, sweetheart."

Nathan froze, listening intently. Maybe Dyffaya could heal her. He was a god. Surely he could . . .

Britta's heartbeat steadied. Her breathing grew more even, but it was still shallow. Terribly shallow. Her eyes fluttered open. "You came," she whispered.

"Of course. I am sorry I was slow." He smiled down at her.

"You're here now." She sighed happily. For a few moments she lay quietly in the god's arms while he stroked her hair. When she spoke again her words were clear, but her voice was faint. So faint. "I was scared, but then I got tired. So tired. There's something wrong with me."

"Yes."

"You can't fix it?"

He shook his head. His eyes glistened. "I can keep you from suffering. I can hold you. I can't . . . keep you." The tears spilled over. "You'll leave me soon. Very soon."

"I don't . . ." Her voice had grown so soft Nathan doubted a human could have heard it. ". . . want to."

"It's not your fault. You've been loving and loyal." His voice deepened, the resonance turning compelling as the air grew thick with the scent of beguilement, a sweet-tart smell Nathan knew well. "I have loved thee, Britta, well, but too briefly. Fare thee well." He bent and kissed her lips.

Because Nathan was listening so carefully, he heard it when her heart stuttered. And stopped.

She vanished.

Dyffaya lowered his empty arms. Slowly he looked up—not at Nathan or Benedict. Not at anything in particular. His cheeks were wet. "They die," he said, his voice terribly level. "Sooner or later, they all die."

He, too, vanished.

So did the enormous display with the crosshairs . . . just as Kai and Arjenie came into view.

TWENTY

OLD Town, San Diego, was a tourist magnet, but locals enjoyed it, too. There were over thirty restaurants, plus all kinds of shops, galleries, museums, historical sites, and activity centers where you could make bricks or pan for gold. Not to mention the ghost tours, which featured, "the number one most haunted house in America," according to America's Most Haunted. Today being Friday, they wouldn't catch thc artisan's market, but there were strolling mariachis and presentations from both the Quilt Guild and the Blacksmith's Guild.

Kai knew all this and more—so much more—because facts were Arjenie's security blanket. She knew a lot of them, too. They clung to her mind like burrs to a collie's fur, and they clung with remarkable specificity. Most people couldn't say how many miles lay between the East Coast and the West. A lot, surely, but how many? A few would vaguely recall or guess it was around three thousand. Arjenie could—and would—tell you that the shortest coast-to-coast transit in America lay between San Diego, California, and Jacksonville, Florida, which were 2,092 miles apart.

It wasn't that she had an eidetic memory. Arjenie was quite firm about that. Scientists, she said, weren't convinced that true eidetic memory existed, and she certainly didn't log every conversation, every meal, every face she saw into her personal data bank. Nor did she consider it a particularly useful skill. Between Google and smart phones, she said, anyone could find almost any information quickly and easily.

That was true, but Google couldn't make sense of the facts and fact-like objects it offered, nor could it put them together in a helpful theory or narrative. Sometimes Arjenie couldn't, either, of course. That proved true on the drive into the city. She told Kai what she knew about Old Town, but neither of them could build any kind of theory from it.

The drive had also been punctuated by phone calls. Nettie did not dismiss Kai's theory about the Upper World. Far from it. She thought it all too likely, and deeply worrying. Kai had called the FBI special agent, too. While she'd been in sleep, Cynna had let Ackleford know Kai would be delayed—"getting treated for psychic trauma from the attack," was how she'd put it. So Kai called to let him know she was on her way and warn him she was bringing a magical knife she needed to do her work. Which was true enough, in an elfish sort of way. She couldn't get much work done if she was dead.

The moment she'd disconnected from that call, Ruben Brooks had called her.

Brooks reminded her of Nathan in the way he listened and in the questions he asked. Sometimes those questions helped her put her thoughts in order. Others, they suggested his mind had moved off on surprising tangents. Like when he asked her to confirm her conviction that Nathan had expected to be grabbed by the god. Assured that she did, indeed, believe that, he'd said, "Strange that he agreed to take charge of the investigation, then. It seems out of character for him to accept a responsibility he knew he wouldn't follow through with. Do you think he expected leadership to devolve onto you?"

"I . . . I don't know." It hadn't occurred to her that it could.

"I don't know the nature of your partnership," he'd said apologetically, "so I may be presuming too much. It simply occurred to me that he might believe you could, in all honor, act on his behalf."

Shit. He might at that. "I don't have any law enforcement experience."

"True." Brooks had fallen silent, then sighed. "Chaos does make a mess of the possibilities. I'm not getting anything helpful now. Earlier it was clear that you were essential, but everything's jumbled at the moment."

Essential? What did that mean? "I'm not in charge, though," she'd said quickly, wanting to be clear on that before he disconnected. "Not of your investigation."

"Not just now."

Kai was thinking of that ominous "not just now" as they headed for the scene of the transformation on foot, having parked the car several blocks away. She wanted her hands free in case she needed to draw Teacher, so she carried the essentials in her pockets: phone, wallet, charms, eye drops, and glasses, in case the drops didn't do the job. Arjenie was toting a backpack that held her tablet and a number of spellcasting components.

The weather was San Diego gorgeous, balmy and bright. Plenty of tourists and locals had been enjoying Old Town when the chaos event hit, and they were all trying to leave at once. The mayor had decided the entire area needed to be evacuated. The guards, Arjenie, and Kai had to swim upstream against a tide of people going the other way. A news copter hovered overhead, but Kai didn't see any reporters among the crowd.

They were bound to be around, though. Kai hoped to avoid them. She didn't have any official role, so she had no obligation to talk to them. And if Ruben Brooks wanted to change that—if he was crazy enough to try to put her in charge—she would simply say no. She wasn't qualified. She was a mind-healer, not any kind of cop, and while her Gift could be helpful in an investigation, it didn't do a damn thing to tell her how to conduct one. Besides, she wasn't dominant in the way the lupi used the word. She didn't need to be in charge. She wanted to get Nathan and Dell back. And Benedict and Cullen. Britta Valenzuela, too.

But *could* she say no? If the strongest precognitive in the nation, maybe in the world, thought he needed her to be in charge . . . *that's tomorrow's battle*, she told herself, shorthand for something her grandfather often said: when you fight tomorrow's battle, you fight an enemy that doesn't exist and miss the one standing in front of you.

"Police cordon up ahead," José said.

"They should be expecting us," Kai said. She had her ID ready. "Can you see the transformed building?"

"Not yet. It's in the middle of the next block, past where the street turns."

Their goal was Whaley House—the place billed as "the most haunted house in America." Naturally.

The cops manning the cordon were, indeed, expecting her and Arjenie. They knew about Kai's knife, too. Or so she assumed, because all three of them frowned at the scabbard at her waist but didn't comment on it.

They were not expecting six armed lupi. "My fault," Kai said. "I should have let Special Agent Ackleford know we had an escort. I need them to come in with us. If you need his okay for that, then call him, please."

One of the cops did that. He was fortyish, with dark skin, glasses, and a receding hairline. His uniform sleeves had chevrons on them. Did that mean he was a sergeant? Maybe a corporal. Did police have corporals? If she was going to work with cops she needed to learn that sort of thing.

Arjenie spoke low-voiced. "Do you have any idea what we're going to do when we get there?"

"Other than having Doug sniff around, you mean?" Doug was one of the guards who'd been at Fagioli, and Isen had made sure he got a good sniff of the vine before it was burned. He'd detected a scent common to both sites, so they wanted to know if he smelled it here, too. "I'll check for intention. Beyond that, I'm open to suggestions."

"Lily always says it's a matter of asking the right questions."

"I'm stuffed with questions, but how do I know which are the right ones?"

"Ask them all?"

The older cop gestured at them. "You're all to be admitted. Sign in, please."

Kai thought it was pointless to keep a record of who entered a scene that had probably held hundreds of people before being evacuated, but she signed dutifully. While the others did the same, her mind returned to the call from Ruben Brooks—who might or might not decide she was the one to take charge of things officially.

Did Nathan really expect her to do that? To take over the investigation?

How could he? Even if she were willing and able, it wasn't up to her! And he had no right to expect her to step in when he hadn't even discussed his plans. No, he'd gone out of his way to keep her from guessing what he meant to do. If he'd expected her to take on his responsibilities, he should have—

Whoa. When she started diving into shoulds and shouldn'ts, it meant she'd stopped looking for answers. All she'd find in that pool were reasons to be mad, and she didn't need more of those.

"Thank you," the cop with the clipboard said when the last of the guards had signed his sheet of paper. The one with the chevrons on his sleeve said, "Akins, escort these people to the special agent."

In other words, don't let the weird, armed civilians wander just any-old-where. The third cop told them to follow him, please. The guards formed up around Kai and Arjenie and they set off down the middle of the street. It looked like everyone but the official types had left the cordoned-off area.

What did Nathan expect?

Put that way, the question almost answered itself. He expected her to have his back. To be his partner on this Hunt.

He hadn't treated her like a partner. He'd hidden his plans from her. He must know she'd be mad about that, but he'd expect her to set that aside and . . . shit. Trust him. Oh, yeah, that's exactly what he expected. For her to trust him to do his part of the job. To stop Dyffaya, and then to do everything possible to get himself and the others home safely.

But that was his job. Not hers. She couldn't get to the god, and even if she could, she couldn't stop him. No, her job lay in this world, and never mind what Nathan expected, because thinking about that just made her mad and miserable.

What did she expect of herself? What was up to her?

The answer came a bit more slowly this time, but it came. If she couldn't stop the god, maybe she could distract him. Slow him down. To do that, she needed to figure out what he was after, then make it really hard for him to get it.

"All right," she whispered. "I'll do my part, but you'd damn well better come back."

Arjenie tipped her head. “What?”

“Oh.” Kai felt her face heat. “I was talking to Nathan. He’s not here, but . . .” She shrugged.

“I know what you mean. I’ve been holding conversations with Benedict.”

“But not out loud,” Kai said dryly. “I’d have noticed. Um . . . where is he now?”

Arjenie nodded toward the west.

It had to be reassuring, that sense of where her lover was. Frustrating, too, she supposed. Presumably Arjenie could stand in the precise spot where her bond told her Benedict was, but they’d still be separated by the barrier that lay between the godhead and what people liked to think of as reality.

“How’s Dell?’ Arjenie asked just as softly.

Kai took a moment to focus. Faint, so faint, but . . . “She’s anxious about something or someone. Tired. That’s all I can—wow.”

They’d rounded the curve in the road. Ahead of them was a cluster of people in and out of uniform in front of what used to be Whaley House.

“It’s a hobbit house!” Arjenie exclaimed.

What had been a two-story Greek Revival house was now a single story—the upper one. It looked as if half the house had sunk into the ground, then someone had drawn a blanket of grassy sod up over the remaining above-ground part, tucking it in. Wildflowers grew cheerily amid the tall grass. The second-story porch—now the first story—still boasted a white picket railing, but the rest of it . . . “It’s supposed to be brick, right? You said it was brick.”

“From the Whaleys’ own brickyard. Yes.”

The walls were a mass of vines. Blooming vines. Yellow, orange, purple, pink, blue . . . if there were still bricks beneath the flowers and the twisted mass of vegetation, Kai couldn’t see them. The vines avoided the windows, though, leaving their blank glass faces staring out at the street unimpeded. Three floor-length windows opened onto the porch.

“Ackleford said everyone got out, right?” Arjenie asked.

“Yes.” There’d been a tour group in the house when it transformed, but no one had been hurt. “Maybe they got out through the windows." And it was time to get to work. Kai dialed up her Gift and looked for any lingering traces of intent. There were plenty of thought-remnants on and around the newly transformed structure, but so far she didn't see any that . . .

"Michalski, are you here to work or do you want to play tourist a while longer?"

That, of course, was Special Agent Ackleford. He stood in the center of the knot of officialdom clotted up in the middle of the street facing what used to be the Whaley House. In addition to Ackleford, Kai counted three uniformed cops, four men in bad suits who were either cops or FBI agents, one man in a good suit, and one lone woman—the female FBI agent who'd been at Fagioli yesterday.

"I am working," she told him, but started toward him anyway.

José must possess some kind of radar. He didn't glance at them for an instant, but the second they started moving again, so did he. "José, I don't think you need to guard us from all the nice cops."

"No, ma'am," he said politely. And stayed in front of the two of them until they reached the law enforcement types, only then stepping aside.

"You get your psychic trauma fixed?" Ackleford asked.

"Yes. I need to finish checking the site, but first I have a question. Did you get names and pictures of everyone who's been evacuated?"

Ackleford snorted. "Not with the rush the mayor was in. Got his panties in a twist, scared to death a tourist might get hurt."

One of the others spoke—the one in a good suit. He was a tall, hefty man, with sandy hair quietly going gray and no-nonsense glasses. "Wouldn't have made much difference if we'd tried to take names, and it would've been a huge job. Too easy for someone to slip away without my people spotting him or her. My name's Franklin Boyd." He gave Kai and Arjenie each a nod. "Assistant chief of police. I believe you're the experts we've been waiting for?"

Reminded, Ackleford introduced Arjenie, calling her "an FBI researcher with a strong background in Wiccan spells." When he got to Kai he frowned. "What the hell do I call you?"

Her mouth twisted wryly. "I'm the closest thing you've got to an expert on sidhe magic and religion—specifically, one pissed-off chaos god. I'm also a mindhealer," she added to the assistant chief. "My Gift lets me see the colors and patterns of thoughts, which is why I need to look over the transformed building carefully. Intent is a component in spells, and it often leaves traces—remnants—I'm able to see. We don't know if that will be true with chaos-fueled transformations like this one, but it bears checking out. I understand there haven't been any injuries this time? Not so much as a scratch?"

Franklin Boyd shook his head. "We've had the paramedics check everyone who was in the building at the time of the incident. No broken skin on anyone."

"And no one's missing."

"Not that we can determine."

Was this a snatch that hadn't worked? Kai frowned. "I'd like to send Doug over to sniff out the transformed building. He—"

A load of bricks smashed into her. Training took over; she went limp as the bricks followed her down, flattening her, and she heard someone shouting, "Sniper!" even as the loud *crack*! of a high-powered rifle sounded. Someone cried out. A second shot came almost on top of the first and Arjenie joined her on the pavement, her eyes wide and startled, flattened beneath a blond-haired lupus. Doug. Doug had tackled Arjenie.

More shots, crazy loud, each one jerking her heart rate higher, coming from close by—cops or feds or maybe those of their guards not currently pretending to be body armor. She couldn't see, didn't know what the hell was happening.

"We need to get to cover!" the bricks on top of her shouted in José's voice. "Doug, carry Arjenie. Everyone else form up—"

"No!" Kai tugged her left arm free. "Thirty seconds. Give me thirty seconds." She'd practiced this one, practiced it over and over and over—surely she could make it work now. "*Arenthyla-en-ná-abreesh*—" She rushed through the syllables, the images that went with each rolling through her mind automatically as she pressed her thumb to the palm of her hand and drew hard. Power rose within her, shooting down her arm—"*makabaj*: *ta'vo!*" She flung out her arm, fingers and thumb spread wide. Felt power rush out with the snap of a spell well-wrought.

Someone cursed.

"Now we can take cover without being shot at," Kai said. "The spell won't last long, though. I had to cast it too wide."

"What did you do?" José asked urgently.

"Gun control, sidhe-style."

TWENTY-ONE

JOSÉ chivvied Kai and Arjenie under cover quickly—the wide, shaded patio between the two buildings occupied by Café Coyote, across the street from the hobbit house.

"That was you who shouted sniper, right?" Kai asked him as they stopped beside a table where two people had been eating tacos before being evacuated. "What did you see?"

"Gun barrel. Pure luck I saw it in time." He was grim.

"That's not luck. That's good training and practice. If you hadn't been looking everywhere—not just at ground level—you wouldn't have seen it. Thank you. But I thought I explained earlier about my vest."

"You said it's probably bulletproof. Probably isn't enough."

"It's more bulletproof than you are."

"And I heal better than you do. You're bleeding."

"I am?" Only then did she notice the stinging. She raised a hand to her cheek. "It's nothing. I scraped it on the pavement. Is everyone okay? Arjenie, you weren't hit, right? But you got knocked down. Did—"

"I'm fine." Arjenie cut her off in an abrupt way that wasn't like her. She looked shaken, but she'd scooped up her backpack from where it fell when Doug tackled her and held it in one hand now. "He was aiming at you."

Kai's eyebrows shot up. "You saw him?"

"No, but the policeman who was shot—you were between him and the sniper. If José hadn't knocked you out of the way—"

"A policemen was shot?" Her heart jumped back into alarm-mode.

Doug spoke. "I don't think it's too bad. Look, here they come with him now."

Two of the men in suits had made a chair with their arms to carry one of the uniformed cops. They were accompanied by Boyd, Ackleford—who was talking on the phone, unfazed by being in the middle of a fire fight—and the female FBI agent. Blood covered one side of the wounded man's face and turned the shoulder of his crisp blue uniform dark and shiny. A head wound? Yes—his black hair was soaked with it. But he was conscious, even able to hold on to the shoulders of the men carrying him. They lowered him carefully into a chair. "EMTs will be here in a snap," Boyd told the man. "We'll have you taken care of real quick, Ruiz. You're going to be fine."

Boyd looked around in that assess-the-room way most cops had. It reminded her of Nathan. His gaze latched onto Kai. He strode toward her. "What the hell did you do?"

"Made everyone's guns stop working. It'll wear off soon."

"When?" he demanded.

"Another five or ten minutes?" She paused, considering. She had put a lot of power into the spell. Too much, considering she didn't have Dell to draw on. She'd panicked. Kai grimaced, acknowledging that. "Maybe more like fifteen or twenty."

"I need to know when my people's weapons will be operational again, damn it!"

Kai matched him scowl for scowl. "I gave you my best guess. I haven't field-tested the spell under these conditions."

Ackleford walked up, shaking his head. "Funniest damn thing I ever saw." One corner of his mouth crooked up. "Like we were all kids playing cops and robbers." He held out a hand, shaping it like he was holding a gun. "Bang. Bang." He shook his head again. Now both sides of his mouth crooked up—his version of a belly laugh. "Like a bunch of kids. Funniest damn thing I ever saw."

Boyd stared at him. "Are you nuts? One of my men is wounded, and that—"

"You need to get a goddamn sense of humor, Boyd. Your man's okay. Bullet barely grazed him. Didn't even knock him out."

"She kept us from nailing that perp!"

Ackleford snorted. "Which of your men is good enough to nail a perp from nearly two hundred yards away with a handgun? That's assuming he could even see the bastard. I sure as hell didn't." He cocked his imaginary gun, sited. "Bang." Grinned—at least that twitch of his lips might be taken for a grin—and holstered the nonexistent weapon. "We'd have more people hurt or dead if she hadn't put the woo-woo on that bastard's rifle. He could've picked off another three or four of us, easy, before hightailing it."

Boyd gave a grudging nod. "Maybe so. Maybe so. How far does this damn spell extend?" He directed that question at Kai. "My people are going after him. It would be good to have some idea of when and where their weapons will work. Or the sniper's."

"I'm not sure. I understand why you need to know, but—well, I meant to cover a quarter-mile radius, but I think I overshot."

Another uniformed officer came up to him, this one with a gold bar on his collar. Lieutenant? Captain? He and Boyd started talking, Ackleford answered his phone's urgent chirping, and a pair of EMTs came in from the other end of the mall-like patio with a gurney.

"You know," Kai said, "I'd like to sit down." Her body had used up its adrenaline and was suddenly in the shaky stage. Really shaky. Dammit.

"Over here," José said, gesturing to the building on their left. "We'll be out of the way."

Feeling foolish—it was such a beginner's mistake to overspend power!—Kai followed him inside the café proper. She plunked herself down at the nearest table and looked around. The place was deserted. "I wish there was someone I could order coffee from."

"I can get you some," a young-looking guard said cheerfully. He had gorgeous dark eyes and tawny skin . . . Kennedy, that was his name. Kennedy Garcia. "If it's okay with José, that is. My sister used to work here. The owners are good folks. They won't mind."

"You can't just go grab whatever you want."

"We'll leave money to cover it," José assured her. "Arjenie?"

She shook her head. "I'm wired already."

José studied Kai's face. "You do look wiped. You should probably eat something. Kennedy—"

"No," she said quickly, before he appropriated a three-course meal for her. "I used too much power too fast, but food won't help me recover the way it would you."

Arjenie sat next to Kai. "Who knew Ackleford had a sense of humor? A weird one, sure, but I had no idea he found anything funny."

"Surprised me, too. People do have unexpected nooks and crannies." Kai felt disconnected. One moment she was getting shot at. The next she was sitting in a deserted restaurant while someone fetched her coffee. "You're acting like the danger's over," she said to José. "Is it?"

"Of course not, but the sniper's probably gone. His rifle isn't working." A quick grin. "He won't know what happened or why, so it's bound to make him want to be elsewhere. They might even catch him. It will take some luck, but either the cops Boyd sent after him or the copter Ackleford diverted might—"

"Ackleford diverted a helicopter?"

"The one those TV types had hovering over the scene. I heard him arranging it while we were headed for cover. The man does know how to multitask." His eyes stayed busy checking out their surroundings. José might think the sniper was gone, but he wasn't assuming anything. "I should report in while I have the chance. Isen will want to know what happened. Justin, you've got the patrol for now." He made one of those hand signs the guards used. A dark-haired man nodded, and José stepped back and took out his phone.

"That is one amazing spell," Arjenie said. "You look drained, though."

Kai made a face. "It's a power hog even when done right, but I pumped more into it than I should have. Beginner's mistake."

"Is that spell why you didn't take a gun when you went

questing with Nathan? Because people in Faerie can make guns not work?"

"That's right. The spell's widely known, though not everyone who knows it can cast it. Like most spells that are primarily oral, it takes a ton of practice, and not everyone wants to invest the time. Not everyone has the power needed, either, but enough people can cast it to make guns unpopular."

Doug looked surprised. "They've got guns in Faerie? I thought they were all about swords and knives."

"They are. A few hundred years ago, though, guns started showing up. Probably a gnomish invention—at least, the elves blame the gnomes for it. The elves were seriously unhappy. Guns offend their aesthetic sensibilities, plus they were destabilizing the power balance, and elves are almost as big on stability as they are on beauty. The Queens came up with a special ward that can be set over a large area, like a city. It targets gunpowder, turns it inflammable. The ward was only partly effective, though. Some of the—oh, thank you, Kennedy." She accepted the mug of coffee gratefully and sipped. Good and strong, just what she needed. Maybe it would do something about the headache knocking on her door.

"So what went wrong with the ward?" Arjenie asked.

"The ward works great, but not every place could be warded, plus not all the lords accepted the Queens' terms for the spell to set the ward. Maybe the Queens would have ended up adding guns to their thou-shalt-not list. Opinions vary about that, and the Queens aren't saying. In the end, it didn't matter. There was this one lord—an adept, a real top-drawer, A-list kind of guy—and he really, really hated guns. He developed the spell I just used. And he *gave* it away."

Arjenie looked suitably shocked. Doug looked puzzled. "That's unusual?"

"Elves give away lots of things casually—food, clothes, art, even gems. Not spells. Their economy is partly knowledge-based. They hoard knowledge in general, but magical knowledge especially, because it's dangerous. Giving it away would be like—oh, like giving away guns to anyone who wanted them. This adept broke that taboo, and it worked. His spell spread throughout the realms. Now no one can depend on guns to work, so no one uses them. Almost no one," she added conscientiously. "There's still a few around, so it pays to know the spell."

José must have been listening even as he spoke with Isen, because when he put his phone away he asked, "How does this spell work? It doesn't change the gunpowder. You said our guns would start working again, and they wouldn't if the gunpowder had been rendered inflammable."

"It tells guns not to fire. And no, I don't know what that means, except that it's the sort of thing adepts can do. That's the remarkable thing about this spell. It isn't adept-level, but it ought to be."

Arjenie's forehead pleated. "We ran into an elf lord once," she said. "Me and Benedict and Cullen and Lily and Rule. He wanted to make Rule and Benedict slaves. He didn't use that spell when Lily started shooting him. The bullets couldn't hit him, but her gun worked."

Kai shrugged. "Either he wanted to show off—you know, see the tough guy, bullets just bounce off me—or he was conserving his power for some reason. Even when you cast it properly, this one's a power hog."

"That makes sense. He'd just finished opening and modifying a gate, so he must've been lower on power than he liked. He was here on Earth, you see, so he couldn't draw on the land-tie."

Which was interesting, but beside the point, as was her own explanation of the sidhe history with guns. She needed to focus, dammit. Which was hard with her head pounding. Kai rubbed the back of her neck with one hand.

"Headache?" Arjenie said sympathetically. "That's a common reaction to depletion. You sure eating won't help?"

"Nothing helps but time. Ibuprofen wouldn't hurt, though, if anyone has some."

"Sure, in my purse." Arjenie grimaced. "Which I left in the car because I had the backpack to carry. Sorry." Her gaze shifted. "I wonder what's got him worked up?"

Kai followed her gaze. Franklin Boyd was headed their way. His lips were tight and he was scowling, but his colors didn't look angry so much as frustrated.

"He got away," the assistant chief said abruptly when he reached them. "He did leave us a couple cartridges. Highly unprofessional of him. Either he was panicked or he isn't a pro."

"Why are you saying 'he'?" Kai asked.

"Playing the odds. A female sniper is possible, but highly unlikely."

"Well, if he or she is gone, we need to get busy. I need to give the building a thorough survey while Doug does it his way. And maybe . . ." Kai looked at José. "Can one of your men Change and check out the spot the sniper was? See if he can pick up the sniper's scent?"

José considered that briefly. "I'd like to keep as many men with you and Arjenie as possible, but Doug's got to Change, anyway. He can check out the sniper's perch as well as the transformed building."

"Okay. If you could have one of your men go with him, Assistant Chief—"

"Hold on. I haven't agreed to let any of you go anywhere."

Kai huffed out a breath. "Do I need to get Ackleford? Because this is the sort of thing he brought us here to do. If nothing else, Doug can tell us for sure if the shooter's a human."

That startled him. "What else could it be?"

"A team of brownies. An elf. A gnome. Various kinds of halflings. A lupus from another clan. None of those is likely, but it's good to be sure."

Boyd called someone over—the man with a gold bar on his collar, who started toward them. José motioned to Doug, who stepped slightly apart. And Changed.

Kai loved watching lupi Change. She'd seen it several times now, and she couldn't have said why she loved watching it, no more than she could say what she saw, which literally made no sense—as in, it didn't register properly on her senses. Not sight or hearing, smell or touch. And yet it moved her. Everything about Doug slid sideways into an elsewhere she couldn't perceive, yet somehow knew. Even his thoughts were both here and not-here as they froze for an instant in a pattern of great pain—then broke free.

An enormous black-and-tan wolf stood atop the pile of clothes that Doug had been wearing a moment ago. He grinned at them, tongue lolling.

"Son of a bitch." Boyd sounded almost reverent.

"That's an expression we don't care for," José said, "but I understand you meant no offense. Doug, you know what you need to find out. Remember—no heroics. If anything sprouts thorns or seems likely to attack, you get out of there fast."

Doug nodded.

"He understands you." Boyd must have known that four-footed lupi understood language, but it was obvious from his patterns that he was having trouble processing what he'd seen.

"Of course," José said, and nodded at the man Boyd had summoned. "Lieutenant Calverone? I don't know if you recall, but we met a few months ago. I'm—"

"José Alvarez. You helped two of my officers nab a rapist. I'm not likely to forget that." Calverone held out a hand for José to shake. "Good to see you again. I take it this is . . . I was going to say one of your men, but that's not the right word at the moment." He gave a wry smile. "One of your people?"

"Doug McMillan," José said. "He needs to check out the transformed building and the sniper's perch on top of that church."

Calverone glanced at his superior, who nodded. "I'm to be his escort? Good enough. Shall we go, Doug?"

"Um—hang on a minute," Kai said. She looked at Arjenie. "It might be good to know if any wards have been set around the hobbit house."

"Oh? Oh! I see what you mean. Maybe that's the reason no one's been hurt or snatched. There could be some kind of trigger that didn't get pulled, but it's still there, waiting."

"It seems possible." A side effect of Arjenie's Gift was her sensitivity to wards. "Do you think you can do it without, uh . . ." Kai made a vague gesture. Arjenie's ability to slip into stealth mode was supposed to be a secret. She'd used it at Fagioli, but in all the confusion, no one seemed to have noticed.

"I only have to be slightly unobtrusive in order to sense wards."

In other words, she'd use her Gift so marginally that she'd still be seen, though people might forget she was there. Kai nodded and looked at José. He'd put his body between her and the bullets. She understood the logic. Lupi healed better by far than she, faster and more completely. But logic be damned. They could be killed, and she did not want him playing shield again.

Asking about the risk to him and his men wouldn't get her a straight answer, though. Asking about the risk to Arjenie might. "I need your professional opinion. Is it safe for Arjenie and me to go out there?"

"If I thought the risk was unacceptably high, I'd let you know. You do what you need to do."

Kai wasn't happy with her choices, but that was often the case. "Okay. Let's go."

TWENTY-TWO

"I vote we go." Cullen still looked emaciated, but Benedict had been right. There was a man in the driver's seat again, not a wolf.

Nathan and Benedict had waited hours for Cullen to wake up. Those hours had passed slowly, but Nathan's initial terror had faded as it became obvious the sniper had not shot Kai. If Kai had been seriously injured, Dell would have known; if Kai had been killed, Dell would either be dead or unconscious. So Kai was all right, and Benedict was sure Arjenie had survived, too. He wouldn't explain how he knew, but his certainty was persuasive.

"It's worth trying," Benedict said. "If we're wrong about the way time works here, might as well find out."

"Dell?" Nathan said.

The chameleon nodded firmly.

"We're agreed, then." Nathan wasn't surprised. None of them wanted to stay in the grotto, and if their reasons were a mix of the practical and the emotional, there was nothing wrong with that. On the practical side, they hoped to find a more stable time zone, which is why they would head for the clearing where they'd first appeared. Dyffaya had used it twice to bring people here, so it was probably highly congruent with the physical world. They could hope that meant it was time-congruent as well.

Clearly, even if location was a factor in how time flowed within the godhead, it wasn't the only one. The magical displays proved that Dyffaya could control the flow of time here when he wanted to. The enormous one that had appeared just before Britta died had shown Earth in lockstep with time here. So maybe they'd improve their time-flow, maybe they wouldn't. Why not try? Britta had died here. Cullen had suffered here. Those were reasons enough to leave.

It was easy to do, with nothing to pack. A moment to settle their marching order and they were off, with Dell and her two-member harem ranging out ahead and Benedict serving as rear-guard. Cullen walked beside Nathan. They'd no need to run this time, which was just as well. Cullen wasn't up to it.

As they moved out down the dry ravine Cullen returned to a subject they'd touched on briefly. "Why did her body poof?"

It was obvious who he meant. He'd been grimly amused when he learned that the meat his wolf had waited for so painfully wouldn't have been available to him, after all.

Benedict said, "Maybe Dyffaya sent it back."

Cullen nodded. "Could be. Could also be that the godhead itself doesn't keep dead things around. We haven't seen so much as a dead leaf, have we?"

Now that was an interesting notion. Was it the god or the godhead that didn't want dead things around? "Dyffaya isn't exactly alive himself."

"Not exactly dead, either. But his body is. Do you know what happened to it?"

"Mage fire. That's not what killed him, mind, but that's what they did with his body. Burned every trace of it."

"Hmm." Thoughtfully Cullen sprouted a tiny flame on one fingertip. Black flame.

Nathan stopped dead. "Don't do that!"

The tiny flame winked out. "Needed to see if I could. If things work here the way I'm used to."

"Try asking," Nathan said dryly. "Mage fire is chancy under the best circumstances, and this is an extremely high-magic place."

"I can see that." Cullen spoke with exaggerated patience. "It's damn distracting at times."

"Then maybe you didn't realize that using mage fire in a high-magic area is like playing with matches while floating in a swimming pool filled with kerosene."

Cullen glanced at his hand, then back at Nathan. "Anything else I should know?"

"Undoubtedly, but I'm not sure where to start."

Benedict was amused. "Start with the assumption that he doesn't have the sense not to play with matches when floating in a pool of kerosene."

So as they walked, Nathan talked about the properties of high-magic places. He went into more detail on magic sickness, touched on the kinds of spells that might function differently here, and warned them about changes they might notice—loss of appetite being one symptom, but not everyone developed that. Looked like lupi were among those who didn't. Sleep problems were common, with some people sleeping too much and others finding it difficult to fall asleep at all. The latter was common with elves, some of whom stopped sleeping altogether.

He also warned them again that they had to assume Dyffaya overheard everything they said. He doubted that the god was listening at all times, but they'd have no way of knowing when he was. No way, either, to know which Earth languages Dyffaya knew. Nathan doubted the god could absorb a new language the way dragons did, mind-to-mind, but there was an adept-level spell that was almost as good. It could capture an entire language from only a few sentences. They couldn't try writing in the dirt, either. The god might not be observing them every moment, but Nathan suspected he'd set up magical triggers. Certain actions would probably draw his attention. Writing in the dirt was likely one of those triggers.

The telling took an hour or so. Answering Cullen's questions took longer. He was—surprise!—intensely curious about this strange place in which they found themselves, and he had information of his own to offer. He'd run a few basic experiments on the materials at hand, with interesting results. "Leaves, rocks, bark, dirt—it's all elementally balanced."

"Leaves with Fire attributes?" Nathan said, startled.

"And rocks with Air. Everything partakes equally of North, South, East, and West, too. I think it's all the same substance."

"It's all spirit, of course, but . . ." But Nathan had assumed that what looked like a leaf was a leaf, regardless of what stuff had been used to make it. "It's not created," he said slowly. "Nothing here was created. It's shaped. Shaped at a very fine level, or it wouldn't matter if you ate lettuce or meat. But shaped."

"You say that like it matters," Benedict said.

"Of course it matters," Cullen said. "We may not know why yet, but it matters."

"Yeah, well, here's something that I know matters. Why aren't we all under compulsion?"

That startled Cullen into silence, but it didn't last. "Good question. Can we be sure we aren't?"

"I'm not," Nathan said. He didn't know why compulsion didn't work on him, but it didn't. The Eldest himself had confirmed that when he and Winter were negotiating for Nathan's assistance on Earth. "Oil on water," his Queen had murmured, as if that made sense to her. Probably it did. "Of course, I could be under compulsion to tell you that I'm not, so my saying so proves nothing."

"Reassuring," Benedict said, bone-dry.

"He's probably telling the truth." Cullen sounded gloomy. "Hellhounds are supposed to be immune to compulsion. Doesn't help the rest of us."

Nathan couldn't help smiling. Cullen chose the oddest things to be troubled by. "Maybe it will help to know that I haven't smelled beguilement except for that once, when Dyffaya was soothing Britta."

"That's supposed to help?"

"Eh. I keep thinking you know things you don't." Cullen was amazingly good for someone who was basically self-taught, but there were gaps. "Beguilement is a form of compulsion. It has a strong, distinctive odor when it's laid. I think Dyffaya renewed it, there at the end."

"What does it smell like?" That was Benedict.

"Somewhat like a mixture of cooked peas and spoiled apricots."

Benedict's voice sharpened. "With a metallic undertone? Hot metal, not cold."

"That's it."

"Huh. I smelled it, too. Didn't know what it was. I didn't smell it on Britta before that."

"The scent doesn't linger—at least, not to my nose. I've only smelled it when someone was actively laying or refreshing a beguilement. Other compulsions have a similar scent, with different notes." Which got him thinking . . . why had Dyffaya beguiled Britta so completely?

They all die. That's what Dyffaya had said, and his pain had been real and deep at that moment. Sooner or later, they all died. Who were "they"?

And why had he not beguiled anyone else? Nathan was immune. Cullen might be—his shields were amazing—but the god might be able to overwhelm them. Benedict was obviously vulnerable. Nathan wasn't sure about Dell. The familiar bond should confer a good deal of resistance, but resistance was not immunity.

And yet none of them had been beguiled. Other types of compulsion could be difficult to spot, but beguilement was easy. For Nathan, anyway. A lot of elves could use it, so he'd learned to spot the signs ages ago.

Why hadn't Dyffaya beguiled any of them?

Maybe he could guess.

Or maybe he was making a connection where none existed. There was a word for that, though he couldn't recall it at the moment. Might be a dragon word. He never could hold onto much of their speech, constructed as it was out of thought-engrams. But minds love connections and were prone to creating them on the spot whether they were accurate or not. That was one thing every sentient he'd ever met had in common. But this connection . . . this felt right.

Nathan returned from his reverie and realized that the other two had fallen silent, too. Following their own connections, maybe, or hunting for them. Or thinking about the lovers they'd been so abruptly parted from . . . .

Kai. Her name went through him like a blade made of longing instead of steel. *Stay well. I'll come back to you somehow.* "He wants to keep us."

"What do you mean?"

Without looking over his shoulder, Nathan couldn't see Benedict's scowl. But he heard it. "Dyffaya. That's what I'm thinking, anyway. He's feeding us. Not properly, in your case, but there's every chance he didn't know what happens to lupi who go without meat. Your people are new to him. He's provided the basics for sustaining life; therefore, he wants us to live. He wants to keep us."

It was Benedict who saw the connection Nathan had spotted. " 'They all die.' That's what he said. He wants people around who won't die on him anytime soon. But why us? We're his enemies."

"Because his followers die." This was Cullen. "Followers or lovers—I'm not sure he sees a difference, and that's what he meant, isn't it? Those who love him die."

"Or those who've been beguiled into loving him."

"Hmm." Cullen thought that over. "I've never heard of beguilement shortening anyone's life expectancy, and it's not one of the things you said operated differently in a high-magic zone."

"I haven't heard of it doing so," Nathan said, "but we shouldn't rule that out. I'm thinking, though, that maybe something about Dyffaya himself makes it work out badly for anyone he beguiles here. Here in the godhead."

"Which maybe doesn't tolerate dead things," Cullen said slowly.

Nathan nodded. "And Dyffaya himself isn't exactly alive, is he?"

EVERYTHING *is relative,* Kai thought as she knelt on the ground near the hobbit house. No one had shot at her for over an hour, and she'd recharged enough for her headache to subside. Enough to do little stuff like this, too, though it didn't look like she'd get much from it. *Come on,* she told the pretty lavender fragment hiding in the vines. *Come on out where I can . . .*

"What in the world are you doing?"

The voice made her jump. And lose the fragment. She huffed out an annoyed breath and looked up. Franklin Boyd stood a few paces away, frowning at her. José stood just behind him, looking apologetic.

Kai heaved a sigh. "Do you ever talk to Special Agent Ackleford? Because he could tell you what I'm doing. He might also mention that it's painstaking, tedious work and I hate being interrupted."

"Didn't mean to startle you."

"You know that I see thoughts, right? As colored patterns."

"That's what you said."

"Lies are snot green."

His discomfort was more obvious in his colors than his expression. "I'll keep that in mind. I'd still like to know what you're doing."

Kai reminded herself that it was usually best to get along with local law enforcement. "I told you that when magic is used intentionally, it usually leaves fragments of that intention behind. Fragments I can see. I'm collecting them."

His eyebrows lifted. "That's pretty amazing, but what do you do plan to do with them?"

"Reconstruct as much of the original intention as possible."

"And what will that tell you?"

"I don't know. Maybe nothing. It's like crime scene people vacuuming up everything. You don't know what will be useful, so you get everything you can. Look, I explained this to the special agent earlier. Why don't you . . . hey, there," she said as Arjenie rounded the corner of the hobbit house, followed by the three guards who'd been with her. "That is not your 'tired but triumphant' face."

"No, this is my 'curses, foiled again' face. I'm not going to be able undo it. Cullen might, but I can't. It's strong, I can tell that much. And it's not a—what did you call it? A lockdown ward. I checked that by pushing a piece of paper through it. Nothing happened, so it's probably keyed to living things, but I don't know what it does to living things. I'm pretty sure I could cross it without triggering it, but if it isn't triggered it won't dissipate, so the guys couldn't go with me. Which really bugged them, so I didn't. I thought I'd see what you think."

"Is there a compelling reason to check out the first floor?"

"Other than the fact that it's warded?"

"There is that."

Arjenie had found two wards. The external one seemed to be a simple alarm that covered the entire house, but it had already been triggered. Some wards evaporate after being triggered; this one hadn't, but neither had it been reset. Arjenie thought it was safe to cross, so she'd gone inside to check out the house. She'd found the second ward stretched across the stairs that led to what used to be the first floor.

"I'm not following you," Boyd said. "I know you found a ward on the outside of the house. That's why no one's supposed to touch the house, though apparently it's okay for you to do that. Now you're saying there's another one?"

Arjenie nodded. "Inside, on the staircase."

"Which you'd know," Kai said, "if you talked to Special Agent Ackleford. Arjenie told him about it."

Boyd ignored her. "And you were considering crossing it? Don't."

Arjenie's eyebrows lifted. "Oh? And you're in charge here now, not the special agent?"

He had put Arjenie's back up, hadn't he? Kai decided to let her handle it while she went back to coaxing out the fragment of intention Boyd's appearance had startled her into letting go of. This one was badly faded, but it had a lot of silver threads, which suggested it might be an important part of the overall pattern.

She'd stabilized the fragment already so it wouldn't fade any further. That wisp of power would answer her call. She held out a hand and lightly brushed the sliver of lavender she could see. "Come on," she whispered. It did, but grudgingly. It wanted to stay stuck to the vines. So had most of the others she'd found. Maybe the vines were imbued with a type of magic that attracted them. She fed a smidgeon more power into the coating she'd used to stabilize it . . . careful, careful, too much and it would simply burst.

Here it came.

She reached out with her left hand and picked it up. Not that her hand really did anything, but it made a great trigger for her Gift. She *knew* her hands could pick things up, so her mind automatically followed their lead.

Yes, lots of silver on this one. Maybe that would help. She tugged on the thin power cord where she'd hung her collection of fragments—a tattered collection of small lavender and silver blobs fixed to the cord like fish on a stringer. A dab of "sticky" power added the new fragment to the rest.

"That is the damnedest thing," Boyd said. "Like watching a mime. I take it you've got your, uh, fragment?"

Kai nodded and stood, then twisted. Her back was stiff.

"So you found plenty of intention stuff here. That means someone did this on purpose."

"Yes. We suspected that, of course, but until I found evidence of intention, the possibility remained that this was a random occurrence. We're dealing with chaos, after all. Randomness must be part of the package."

"Funny how different today's incident was from the one at Fagioli. The attack here wasn't magical. Any idea why someone would shoot at you?"

His colors were nowhere near as casual as his voice. Did he think he was asking a trick question? "I've certainly wondered about that. Why me? That's what everyone asks when random badness strikes, but this wasn't random."

Arjenie spoke. "Just because he was aiming for you, that doesn't eliminate the 'random badness' explanation. Maybe you were a random target. We're talking about a god of chaos, so maybe he just wanted to stir things up. He tried to snatch you before, so why would he be trying to kill you now?"

"He didn't kill her, though, did he?" Boyd observed. "Maybe the shot would have missed even if Mr. Alvarez hadn't tackled her." He looked at Kai. "Could be someone wanted you scared, not dead."

"I wouldn't bet on that," José said from behind Boyd.

Boyd snorted. "What, you saw the bullet whizz past?"

"I saw where the cop was hit." José tapped his head just behind the temple. "He's the same height as Kai. If the sniper just wanted to scare her, he's an idiot. An intentional near-miss on a head shot . . ." He shook his head. "If she moves even a little when he's pulling the trigger, she doesn't end up scared. She ends up dead."

Arjenie frowned. "I'm wondering why there was a target at all. Why would anyone be shooting at anyone?"

Kai's mouth twitched. "Oddly put, but it's a good question. Why a sniper? Why switch from magical hijinks to material mayhem? Who does that benefit? And why wasn't anyone snatched this time?"

"All good questions," Boyd said dryly. "Got any answers?"

"No, but . . ." She sighed. "I probably ought to tell you something, though I don't see how it fits. Or if it fits, for that matter. Ruben Brooks thinks I'm somehow key."

Boyd frowned. "Brooks. The head of Unit Twelve. He's some kind of precog."

"Yes. And I don't know why he thinks that. He doesn't know why he thinks it. He also said that the probabilities are all messed up because of the introduction of chaos," she added, "so he might be wrong."

Arjenie tossed up her hands. "I can't make sense of any of it. But this has to be another chaos incident. Transforming a building that way has to mean chaos energy was involved, so it's still all about this chaos god and what he wants."

The obvious reached up and smacked Kai in the face. "Oh. Shit. Yeah." When the others looked puzzled, she explained. "He's already got Nathan, but he's not finished, is he? Revenge isn't all he wants. Maybe that isn't even his primary goal."

"What he wanted before," Arjenie said slowly, "was to enter our realm. To get a living body so he'd be fully alive again."

They looked at each other. "I don't see how—"

"Doug's back," José said. The big wolf trotted into view, trailed by his temporary official partner. Doug sat next to José and made a low, whining noise. "Can't Change back yet?"

Doug shook his head and pawed the ground once with his right foot.

"He thinks it'll be another hour," José explained. "Doug's got a great nose, but he can't Change too often, not without a boost from his Rho or Lu Nuncio. But we've got a few signals he can use to tell me some basic stuff." He looked at the wolf. "Tell me what you smelled."

Doug sniffed loudly and nodded firmly. He tilted his head to the left, flattened his ears and lifted them, then raised his right rear foot and held it in the air briefly.

José spoke. "Doug got a solid scent. The smell is new to

him, female, and . . . our designation is 'other,' meaning not animal, lupus, or human."

"Female?" Boyd said sharply, at the same moment Kai and Arjenie repeated, "Not human?"

Doug nodded vigorously.

"He didn't recognize the scent," José said, "so we can't get much more information from him until he can Change and tell us more about—"

"Michalski!" Ackleford yelled from across the street. "Fox! Get over here."

Kai rolled her eyes. "I'm not your subordinate!" she called back.

"Get your butts over here anyway."

Kai scowled and glanced at Arjenie, who shrugged. "It must be important."

So they headed for Ackleford, who was talking into his phone, though he did put it up when they reached him. "We've got another chaos incident. This one with casualties. Someone's taking credit, and they want to talk to you."

TWENTY-THREE

"IT'S beautiful," Arjenie said quietly. "Vicious, but beautiful."

Kai nodded as she looked out at the beach.

Out on the clean white sand was a monster. Inanimate now, but monstrous. And, yes, beautiful. It looked like a serpent, that long, glittering strand, like a serpent made from gems and light. But it was glass, not jewels, thrusting up from the sand. Thousands of shards of colored glass made up that long, undulating shape. Big ones, little ones, glass in every color of the rainbow.

Sharp, sharp glass.

From here on the boardwalk, Kai could see two large red splotches on the sand. There were more, she knew, but she couldn't see the others, perhaps because of all the thought bubbles—hundreds of them, it seemed, remnants of horror ripped from the minds of those who'd been here.

"You see any of that intention stuff?" Ackleford asked.

"I can't tell from here. There're a lot of remnants to sort through." She didn't darc dial her Gift down as much as usual. Someone had tried to kill her once today. People who claimed they were connected to this chaos event insisted that she be brought here to talk to them. It didn't take a genius to wonder if the idea was to give the shooter another chance. Her Gift might give her a bit of warning. Not that there was a pattern for, "I am about to kill you," but she could watch for compulsions.

Something tugged at her consciousness. She turned, frowning.

They'd followed Ackleford here, parking the big Lincoln and the guards' Toyota amid all the official cars. Their eventual goal was the main lifeguard tower farther down the beach, but Kai and Arjenie had wanted to see the scene first. To reach the boardwalk they'd passed through a parking lot crowded with people who'd been present or nearby when the chaos event hit. They'd drawn some stares. Doug was still a wolf.

A whole slew of police officers were on the scene, many of them busy interviewing the witnesses, one-on-one. One of those witnesses suddenly had Kai's complete attention.

". . . chased us! I never saw anything like it. Then that piece, that blue piece, it just pushed right up. You can see it, right next to the part that looks like a grape popsicle, only sharp. Phil didn't have a chance. It was just *there*, pushing into him, and . . . will he be all right?"

The speaker was young. Sixteen or seventeen. Tanned and fit, he sat hunched over on the low wall that separated the boardwalk from the sand. He was shirtless and barefoot, with khaki shorts of the saggy, baggy sort young men his age were so fond of. Heavy blood spatter decorated one side of the shorts.

"He's at the ER by now," the uniformed officer with him said soothingly. She was young, too. Not as young as her witness, but not that much older. Her hair was blond and shiny. "They'll take care of him. I need your name and address."

"Mark. Mark Weinerman. 4322 Harrow Drive. I should've gone with him. In the ambulance."

"They'll call his folks from the ER. Does he live here?"

"Yeah, yeah. We all do. Penny." He sat up straight. "Shit, poor Penny. She and Phil, they're a thing. I need to find her." He stood. "I need to find Penny."

Out on the white sand, one coil of the glass monster looped around an abandoned volleyball net. Of the ten young people who'd been playing beach volleyball, seven had been taken to the ER. So had twenty more people of varying ages. No deaths, not yet, but at least two were in critical condition.

Two more had vanished. One of them was named Penny.

"Come on, Michalski," Ackleford said impatiently. "The people you need to talk to are up at the lifeguard tower."

"I . . . just a minute." The young man's colors were dark, but so were those of most people here. But something was wrong with him, something that wasn't wrong with the others. "I need to see his patterns better," she said abruptly, and turned.

"Hold on. Is he possessed or something?"

"No. It's not that. He needs me."

"Damn it—"

She didn't stay to see what else he had to say. Her Gift was pulling too hard.

The young blond officer was trying to calm Mark down, telling him again that Phil was at the hospital, that the doctors were taking care of him, and he could call his friend Penny in just a minute.

It wasn't working. He'd started jittering from foot to foot. "I need to go. Where's Phil? Where's Penny? I need to find them."

"Mark," Kai said. She moved in front of him and stopped. "My name is Kai. I'm a mindhealer. I'd like to help you. May I?"

He looked at her, but not as if he saw her. His eyes were glassy. His colors were dark, dark, but it was the pattern she saw overtaking them that worried her—a turbulent, disruptive pattern. "I should've gone in the ambulance."

"Miss," the officer began.

"I can help him," Kai said, "if he gives permission. Mark?"

"All that blood. They took his leg, too. In the ambulance. It wasn't on him anymore, so they took it with them. I didn't want to sit next to his leg. I should have gone."

"Look," the cop said, "I don't know what you think you're doing, but—"

"Mark." Kai put her hands on either side of his head and sent a tiny pulse of shaped power through them: *calm*. Not enough to interfere with his thoughts permanently, or make this any less his choice, his decision. Just a brief respite. "I can help you, but only if you say it's okay."

Someone seized her arm. “Hey,” the officer said. “I’m talking to you.”

Vaguely Kai heard Ackleford’s voice. She tuned it out. The hand on her arm fell away, and at last Mark’s eyes focused on her. Drowning eyes. “Help Phil,” he whispered.

“Phil has other people helping him now. I want to help you.”

“I didn’t get hurt. Everyone else did. I ran away.”

“You’re hurt. Will you let me help?”

Mutely he nodded.

She hated to trance in public, especially without Dell or Nathan to watch over her. Half the time she couldn’t do it with strangers around, but that wouldn’t be a problem this time. Not with her Gift pulling so hard. “We need to sit down.” She took his arm, guiding him to sit on the wall again. She sat beside him and took both his hands in hers.

The smallest intervention possible—that was always the goal. Eharin had told her so over and over, often accompanied by a disparaging glance or a comment about how powerhouses like Kai seldom developed any delicacy. It was too easy for her to hammer in her amendments.

There’d be no hammering today. Her headache might be gone, but she was still depleted. Kai reminded herself of that as she took a slow breath and slid into healing trance.

NATHAN reached for the next handhold. When he, Benedict, and Dell came this way before, they’d followed a narrow valley that ran between the two impossibly high peaks on either side. That valley was gone now, filled in by a mini-mountain. Much lower than the peaks on either side, it had still presented them with a challenge: Dell couldn’t climb it. Not this part. She’d indicated that she wanted them to take this route, however, and after a bit of discussion they’d agreed. Once they started the climb, she’d led her little harem away to find another route.

Nathan hoped she knew what she was doing. He was getting increasingly frustrated by the inability to communicate with her. No doubt Dell was frustrated, too—but not enough to change forms. Not so far.

From what they could tell about the passage of time, they were overdue for a load of salad, or whatever other meal their host might offer. The lupi were feeling it, too. "Maybe he wants to see which of us turns cannibal first," Benedict said. "His kind of bastard might be amused by that."

"Too easy," Cullen said. He was winded and trying to hide it. "Where's the drama when the answer's obvious?"

The first part of their trek had been easy enough. Even this stretch wasn't bad . . . for Nathan and Benedict. Benedict had taken the rear position so he could keep an eye on Cullen, help out if necessary. Not that anyone said this out loud. Instead, the two lupi had been alternatively speculating and bickering since they began the climb.

"My control's better," Benedict agreed. "I don't know about Nathan, though."

Cullen snorted. "Not what I meant. You'd be first to chow down."

"You've got a damn poor idea of my control."

"You'd eat me with plenty of control," Cullen assured him. "But if the god stops feeding us, obviously I'll die first, given how underfed I already am. Therefore, I'd get eaten first. Not by Dell, who needs blood, not flesh. Not by Nathan, because I'm pretty sure he can't starve to death."

"Is that true?" Benedict demanded. "You can't starve?"

"I'm unlikely to die of it." Especially in a place this rich in magic. He'd lose weight, he'd get very, very hungry, but his healing wouldn't let him actually starve to death. "Your healing doesn't keep you alive if you go without food?"

"I don't think so," Benedict said slowly. "Now that I think about it, though, I've never heard of a lupus dying of starvation. That's not to say it's never happened, but I haven't heard about it. What about you, Cullen?"

"Never heard of it happening, no, but that doesn't mean we can't starve. We're very capable predators, though we may eat things we shouldn't if we get too hungry."

"I always figured we'd starve faster than a human would. Healing itself makes us hungry. How could it cure what it makes worse?"

Nathan spoke curtly. "Healing keeps you from starving, but it doesn't cure hunger. At least, my healing kept me alive.

I don't know what yours does or doesn't do." He reached for the next hold, wanting to climb faster, as if he could escape what he carried with him. Foolishness, but he did not like those memories.

"You've experienced it," Cullen said quietly from below him. "Not simple hunger. Starvation."

"Yes. The rock's not as stable here as I'd like," he warned them as he moved the toes of his right foot off an outcropping that felt a bit crumbly. Almost at the top now. "Whatever it's made of, it acts like sandstone. If you . . . eh." The smell was faint, but it stood out in air so nearly dead. "I guess we won't have to find out who eats who just yet."

"What do you mean?"

"I smell chicken. Barbequed chicken."

AS the world dimmed and faded, Mark's color's sharpened into a glowing darkness, a writhing forest of murky grays, browns, and purple. Flickers of his natural green and yellow showed, but they were being overwhelmed by the tangled pattern of wrongness.

Kai's thoughts faded, too. All was instinct, the imperative of her Gift pressing on her. Showing her what to do. She squeezed off a nubbin of power. It hung in the air in front of her, an iridescent soap bubble the size of her thumbnail. Yes. Yes, that should do.

Now she had to watch, to study the turbulence, waiting for the prompt of her Gift. There. She pushed her thought-bubble forward . . . and it entered Mark's thoughts, drawn into the churning mass, yet still separate from it. Wait, wait . . . *now*. She popped the bubble and the iridescence flowed out, coating his thoughts.

Time to do the real work. That iridescence was hers to order, and she did, using it to slow the turbulence, then to amend it . . . just a nudge, the tiniest of nudges here, and over there, now breathe a momentary calm and see how that settled—yes, a hint of green reappeared. Not hers. His. That's right, that's what she wanted, for his thoughts to form their own links, the patterns native to him. The turbulence was less now, especially at the center, and oh yes, there was the weak part, the spot she had to brace. The pattern there, deep at the base of his thoughts, was so thin it was almost gone. That's what her Gift had dragged her here for.

Everything she'd done so far was temporary. Most of her work was. Minds usually healed on their own, given time. She helped them heal faster and more completely by encouraging some thought patterns and blunting the effects of others, but her amendments were usually temporary.

Not this one. What she did next would be permanent. No one but another mindhealer or a dragon would be able to change it. Mark would live with what she did now for the rest of his life, so it had to be right.

Kai created another thought bubble, this one milky, not transparent. She studied it and the place it would go, the thin place that needed reinforcing. Something still didn't feel right. She watched his thoughts arise, watched them filter through the weak place deep in his mind . . . oh, there it was. A thread had broken entirely. Such a tiny thing, but without it, he'd never be whole.

She'd need more power. She fed the bubble carefully, forcing it to stay small. When it gleamed hard and bright like a pearl, she moved it into place. Careful, careful . . . stretch it out and anchor it here and here. Leave the base free to complete this portion of the pattern while wrapping the top part around this delicate arc. Now breathe motion into it. Motion meant resilience, room for growth and decisions and changes . . .

Yes. Done. With an effort, Kai pulled herself back. All the way back. "There," she whispered, and withdrew her hands along with her Gift. "Mark. How do you feel?"

His eyes were wide and startled. Abruptly he burst into tears.

She sighed in relief.

"What did you do to him?" the female cop demanded.

"He's good. Tears are good. You might get a paramedic over here, though. No, wait." A girl about Mark's age had broken free of the officer interviewing her and was hurrying their way. "A friend is even better." Kai started to stand—and nearly toppled.

An arm slid around her waist and hauled her upright. "Damn fool," Ackleford muttered. "You okay?"

"More or less." Her headache was back and had shot into *ohshit* territory, but she was okay. And so was Mark. Hurting, shocked, scared, but okay.

"People who are okay can stand up all by themselves."

"I can do that." When he withdrew his support, she hardly wobbled at all.

Kai lingered long enough to see the girl and Mark make a teary connection, complete with hugs and questions. The girl was one of the volleyball players. She needed Mark's support as much as he needed hers, and that was perfect. They'd help each other.

Time to see if she could walk. She took a few steps and nothing fell off. "A couple ibuprofen would be welcome," she admitted. "Speaking of which, where's Arjenie?"

"Getting you some water. She figured you'd need it when you, uh, came to."

"How long was I tranced?"

"Twelve minutes," José said.

Ackleford snorted. "Twelve freaky as hell minutes. The two of you just sat there. Didn't move, speak, didn't do a damn thing but stare at each other. Listen up, Michalski." He stopped and looked at her with his usual scowl . . . but while his words remained caustic, his voice wasn't. "I need you to focus on those four goddamn persons of interest we're sitting on. They know something about this, or so they claim. They sure as hell knew your name. Don't go haring off fixing people. You can't fix everyone."

"I know that." She was pretty sure she wasn't going to throw up, but oh, her head. . . "Almost everyone here is traumatized to some extent. Several of them could use help getting over that trauma, but it doesn't necessarily have to come from me. Except for Mark. He would have kept getting worse, not better."

"How the hell do you know that?"

"My Gift. It doesn't insist often. When it does, I'm needed."

Arjenie came hurrying up, trailing three of the guards—two of them on two legs and one in fur. One of the two-legged lupi held three paper sacks like the one in Arjenie's hand. She also held two bottles of water. She handed one of them to Kai.

"You didn't eat at Clanhome, and ibuprofen on an empty stomach is not a good idea."

True. Kai took the sack and found several fish tacos inside. They smelled wonderful.

The guard with the other sacks started passing out tacos. Arjenie dug in her tote, retrieved the ibuprofen, and shook two of the capsules onto the palm of her hand. "What was wrong with that young man?"

"It's hard to put in words." Kai took the capsules and washed them down with a healthy slug of water. That felt good, so she drank some more, then stuck the bottle in one pocket of her vest so she could unwrap one of the tacos. "I know what I saw, but what kind of diagnosis would a psychiatrist use? Extreme PTSD? Psychotic break?" She shook her head, winced, and reminded herself not to do that. She took a big bite of the taco. Her taste buds rejoiced.

Ackleford shook his head. "You don't know what was wrong with him, but you tried to fix him anyway."

"What's the word for that particular shade of blue in your tie, Special Agent?"

His scowl looked more confused than anything else. "I have no goddamn idea."

She nodded. "And I don't know the psychiatric term for what I found, but I know what was wrong. There was a weak place in Mark's patterns, something innate. Maybe something in his brain chemistry." She'd had to use more power than she'd intended to; that and the location of the fix suggested she'd made a physical change. "Whatever it was, it left him unable to deal with what happened. People say that sort of thing all the time—that we're falling apart, going nuts, coming unglued. However true that might feel, it usually isn't, not in a permanent way. But Mark . . . Mark really was coming apart."

"And you fixed it." Arjenie gave a firm nod and accepted a taco from the guard named Casey. "That's a wonderful Gift you have. Eat now. I'm going to."

Casey held out a paper-wrapped taco to the special agent. He scowled.

"You might as well," José said. "We are."

Ackleford looked disgusted, but he took the taco. "Multitask.

Walk while you eat. Michalski. You can tell when people are lying, right?"

Kai swallowed quickly. "Yes."

"These assholes aren't talking. Can you make them?"

"It depends on why they aren't talking. If they're compelled to silence, I can remove the compulsion. Not quickly," she warned him, "and with me so low on power, not at all until I recharge. But eventually I can remove it. If they've decided on their own not to talk, though, I can't make them."

"Can't or won't?"

"Both. I'm a mindhealer. Technically, the ability to force someone to talk may be within my skills, but I can't describe how repugnant the idea is. I won't do it. However, there's a way to get around someone's self-imposed silence. People react mentally when you mention something they're trying to hide. They might be able to control everything else—expression, body language, even blood pressure. Elves with good body magic can do all that and more, but their minds still react."

"But you can't read their minds."

"No, but I see the reaction. I may not know what they're thinking, but I know they reacted. That kind of interrogation is like playing a game of hot and cold—one that can go on a long time," she admitted, "because people react to lots of things, not just their secrets. But if I keep talking, asking questions, and watching their thoughts, eventually I'll find the spot they most want to hide."

"Huh." Ackleford stuffed a last bite of taco in his mouth, chewed. "So you can learn something from these people, even if they don't say a word."

"Oh, yes." She felt a grim sort of optimism. "We wanted to find the god's followers. Now four of them have delivered themselves to us."

"Which means either the god has made a big mistake, or that we are. Guess we'll find out which." He looked at the guard with the white sack. "You got any more tacos?"

TWENTY-FOUR

DYFFAYA was waiting about thirty feet away from the cliff's edge when Nathan reached the top. He sat in a bright red recliner that was elevated, throne-like, by the large, flat rock it rested upon. He was gnawing on a chicken wing. A trio of green recliners faced his, their backs to Nathan, with a large open space between his chair and the others. Next to each green recliner was a TV tray; each tray held a big bag of Fritos and what looked like a bowl of salsa.

There were twenty feet between the green recliners and the red one. Dyffaya seemed to like that distance. How damnably sensible of him.

The god was using a different body again. This one reminded Nathan of Dell's hiding form. It was hardly inconspicuous, but it mixed several racial types. The skin was dusky, the hair long and black, the features an arresting, androgynous blend—full lips, strong nose, sharp cheekbones. The eyes were dark and large, with a slight epicanthic fold. He wore jeans and a bright red ball cap. Hard to judge height accurately with him in that recliner, but his build was lean and supple, almost elfin.

He had two young people with him, one male, one female. And Dell.

The blond—she was quite young, a teen, he thought—wore a bikini top and shorts. She sat on the ground at Dyffaya's feet, leaning against his denim-clad leg. The young man was Asian and bore a startling resemblance to Lily Yu, one that went beyond simple ethnicity. Aside from the sexual differences, he was built much like Lily, and was probably a similar height. Same face shape. The young man's nose was subtly different, his eyes more deeply set, but his mouth was much like Lily's. He sat in Dyffaya's lap.

But it was Dell the god stroked with his free hand, not the young man snuggled up to him. The chameleon sat beside the recliner, haughty as ever, her eyes heavy-lidded. Dyffaya smiled at Nathan, showing teeth. "You arrive at a good time. We're all set up for the big game."

"Trying out some of the local customs, are you?" Nathan asked, stalling for time. What was Dell up to? Was she beguiled?

"My new people are very fond of games. It's a passion I share, although I admit I find football baffling." He tossed the picked-clean bones from his snack on the ground . . . where they slowly sank, as if the sand were consuming them. "It's a gladiatorial sport, and yet the rules seem designed to keep the players from injuring each other. Odd. Perhaps you'll explain the game to me later." He smiled and stroked Dell's head. "I wonder why I never thought of having a pet before?"

Nathan waited for Dell to rip his throat out. When she didn't, he had to conclude she was heavily beguiled. "Perhaps because few would be as long-lived as a chameleon."

"True. Allow me to introduce you to Penny and Liu."

"My pleasure," Nathan said politely. "Liu, you bear a strong resemblance to an acquaintance of mine. Lily Yu. Even your names are similar. Any relation?"

Dyffaya chuckled. "That would be telling. I'll admit, however, that I rechristened Liu, who was given a less interesting name at birth." He stroked the young man's thigh. "I fear I'm easily amused at times. Ah, here come your compatriots."

Cullen clambered up over the edge, his breathing audible. He looked like a walking scarecrow. Benedict was right behind him. He looked more like granite—impassive and unyielding.

Dyffaya greeted them affably and introduced Penny and

Liu—"here to enjoy the game with us. There will be more guests, but they haven't received their invitations yet."

Nathan spoke before the other two could respond. "Dell, I don't see your harem."

The chameleon yawned.

Dyffaya chuckled. "I haven't decided if she's more afraid I'll take them from her, or that they might be competition for my attention. Quite jealous of my attention, she is. Chased them off." Dyffaya smiled slyly. "You seemed surprised that your pet and I get on so well now."

"Nonsentients are relatively easy to beguile, I'm told."

"Familiars aren't, however." There was an edge to Dyffaya's voice. "Do come over and have a seat. We have plenty of wings. Liu, be a good boy and get them, will you?" The young man sighed, but did as he'd been told, sliding off Dyffaya's lap and moving to the other side of the recliner. He bent and picked up a large platter piled high with chicken wings. "They're quite tasty. Oh, I nearly forgot." Abruptly a cooler appeared next to one of the green recliners, complete with ice and dark brown bottles. "Beer is traditional, I understand."

"Thank you," Nathan said, glancing at Benedict and Cullen to remind them of the need for an outward show of courtesy. "Is any of it poisoned?"

"I did admit to being easily amused, didn't I? I'm not quite that easy, however. And I have something in mind that poison would interfere with." Dyffaya's voice hardened. "Come sit down."

"Thank you." Cullen offered a small bow, exquisitely polite. "I'm starved. I mean that literally, of course."

Something flashed across Dyffaya's face, some emotion too fleeting for Nathan to interpret. "Ah, yes. I hadn't wanted to comment, but you don't look at all well."

"Something I didn't eat didn't agree with me, I fear."

That amused Dyffaya. He and Cullen continued to exchange barbs cloaked as courtesies while Nathan, Cullen, and Benedict headed for the recliners as instructed. Nathan held himself ready to intervene should Cullen slip from amusing to offensive, but Cullen might have been an experienced elfin courtier—graceful, deferent in every word and gesture, with just enough of an edge for wit. Cullen was, in fact, better at this sort of thing than he was.

Once they were all sitting down, Benedict passed them each a bottle of what the label claimed was Bud. Perhaps it was. If the god could import people, a couple of six packs shouldn't be beyond him. When Nathan twisted off the cap the smell was right. Liu approached with the platter of wings. "They smell delicious," Nathan said, wanting to remind the others to sniff before biting.

It was true, though. Fritos, salsa, beer, barbequed chicken wings—everything smelled good. Just the way it should.

"So," Cullen said, taking two wings from the platter Liu held out, "what do you think of those Chargers?"

THE main lifeguard tower was well up the beach from the place where a glass serpent had chewed into people. Kai had time to finish both tacos while they walked, but not enough time for the ibuprofen to kick in. The sun felt hot on her poor, aching head. The rest of her was hot, too. "Why did they take these, uh, persons of interest to this lifeguard tower?"

"To get them away from the crowd." Ackleford's tone made it clear he considered that obvious.

She supposed it was. The police couldn't know what part their persons of interest had played in raising glass from the sand. Maybe they'd do it again, or something just as bad. "Is that it?" Dead ahead was a two-story stucco building with a small third story perched on top like an undersize cap. It didn't look like a lifeguard tower to her, but it had a red cross on top. "I hope it's air conditioned."

Ackleford snorted. "If you're hot, take off the damn vest."

"Not a good idea." Though she really wished she dared unseal it. Kai rubbed her neck with one hand.

"I give a pretty decent neck rub," José offered.

"No, I . . . no, thanks." Nathan gave the best neck rubs. So many times when she'd been tired and sore for whatever reason, he'd sat behind her and used his big, magical hands to take away the pain and tension. She did not want anyone else's hands on her. She . . . oh, shit, her eyes were filling.

"I cry, you know," Arjenie said matter-of-factly.

"What?"

"When I hurt, I cry. I used to try so hard to hold it back. I wanted to be strong and stoic—and to have people see me that way. That was part of it, because people *react* to crying. It took me forever to figure out that the two don't always go together. I am strong. I'm just not stoic."

Kai's eyes were still brimming. Her head still hurt and she was still hot. But she was smiling. She reached out and squeezed Arjenie's hand. "Arjenie, I think I love you."

Arjenie looked pleased and a little flustered. "Did you know that women cry roughly four times as much as men? People think that's because of social conditioning, but it may also be due to how much prolactin the female body produces and its effect on the endocrine system."

"I didn't know that."

"Also, their tear ducts are smaller than ours."

She was not going to laugh. Arjenie might not understand. But she was grinning as they drew near the lifeguard tower.

DYFFAYA had apparently been serious about learning more about football. While they ate, he asked questions. A lot of questions. Nathan made his answers as detailed as possible, wanting to draw this out since he doubted he'd like whatever came next. Cullen and Benedict seemed to share that goal, both of them contributing to the discussion, but Cullen's knowledge of the game was limited. Fortunately, Benedict could have discussed strategy as it related to football all day.

Eventually, however, Dyffaya tired of the subject. "Enough!" he said, interrupting Benedict. "I am as stuffed with first downs and passing attacks as you are with wings." He snapped his fingers and the empty platter disappeared while the salsa bowls and chip bags refilled themselves. "I'd like to introduce my own game. There's a bit more at stake with it than with football."

Once again a giant display sprung into being. It hung in the air ten feet off the ground between the red recliner and the three green ones. What they saw, though, was odd. Blurry, and the colors were wrong—everything was gray, green, or yellow. They were looking at some kind of broad walkway, currently empty of people, but from almost ground level . . .

"The boardwalk," Cullen murmured. "As seen from a dog's eyes, I think?"

"Very good, Cullen. Liu, Penny, it's time you made our guests comfortable," Dyffaya said. The young man reluctantly climbed out of Dyffaya's lap. Penny stood up. Each of them held out an arm—and each arm was suddenly draped with a steaming towel.

Uh-oh. Nathan spoke quickly. "Benedict, Cullen, I need to explain another aspect of courtesy among the sidhe. Dyffaya is sending Penny and Liu to us as body servants. It would be rude to refuse them, but we can specify which services we wish without giving offense."

Dyffaya smiled sweetly. "You worry needlessly, Nathan. Liu will serve you, since you can have no cultural bias about a male attendant. Penny will serve both the lupi. I don't know if they partake of the monosexuality so rampant in the human culture of their world, so we will err on the side of caution. I wouldn't want to make them uncomfortable."

Cullen smiled. "Benedict, did I ever tell you that elves consider monosexuality perverse?"

"I don't believe you did."

"By monosexual, our host means anyone who limits himself to a single sex. Same sex or opposite sex, it doesn't matter—if you aren't bi, you're a bit of a freak."

"Now, now, I wouldn't dream of calling monosexuals freaks," Dyffaya assured them. "Odd, surely, but not freaks."

Penny stopped in front of Cullen and smiled at him. "May I clean your hands?"

Liu reached Nathan. He was smiling, too. "Allow me to clean your hands, sir."

All that smiling was beginning to get to Nathan. What was Dyffaya up to? He was behaving as a host, which ought to mean that they could refuse any service they didn't want. Politely, of course. "That would be pleasant. Thank you."

Liu knelt in front of Nathan and took his left hand first, wiping it carefully. The towel was hot, but not enough to injure. Good. Someone beguiled as heavily as these two were might not be aware of pain. He'd worried that Liu and Penny could be burned and not notice.

Dell looked from Dyffaya to Benedict to Nathan, then lay down on her stomach, looking bored and sleepy.

Cullen spoke gently to Penny, giving permission for her to clean his hands. He added in a different voice, "Elves are not as monolithic on the subject of monogamy as they are about monosexuality, but it's a rarity with them. Still, they do understand vows."

Dyffaya's eyebrows lifted. "You aren't referring to marriage, surely, as it is practiced on Earth? Even if you took such vows seriously—and the majority of humans don't seem to—your people don't marry."

At the edge of the display a black object edged into sight. It was badly blurred, but the location and general shape told Nathan he was looking at a man's shoe. It moved slowly. Very slowly.

Cullen held up his left hand, the one with a ring. "I'm such a rule-breaker."

"Do you wish to avoid intercourse? Don't worry. Penny's no artiste, but fellatio is pleasant even without that level of expertise. I assure you her skills go well with the beer and Fritos."

"There's a reason they call it oral sex," Cullen said. "That would be because it's sex. I've made vows. I won't break them."

Dyffaya sighed. "You aren't much fun, sorcerer. Penny, you have another guest to attend."

Penny heaved a disappointed sigh and stood, crossing in front of Nathan on her way to Benedict. On the display, the foot was fully in view, along with part of a leg.

Liu laid the towel down. He was still smiling as he reached for the snap on Nathan's jeans." No," Nathan said, stopping his hand. "I don't want that service from you. Dyffaya, we seem to be out of sync, time-wise, with Earth. That will make for a very slow game."

"It's a dramatic device, to build tension. Are you experiencing tension?"

"I can help with that," Liu said softly. His tongue darted out, licking his upper lip. He reached out with his other hand. Nathan caught it, too. "Please. I want to. Please let me."

"No," Benedict said. Nathan looked at him. Penny had apparently forgotten about the hand-washing and gone straight for Benedict's zipper. He pushed her hands away. "I don't want that."

"Don't be shy," Dyffaya said.

Benedict held both of Penny's hands in one of his. She squirmed, trying to get free. He looked at Nathan. "Do elves not consider rape discourteous?"

"Raping a guest would be wrong. Raping your host would be, too."

"Rape, rape, rape," Dyffaya said testily. "Why do you talk about rape? Penny and Liu will enjoy it every bit as much as you. Possibly more."

Benedict looked at the god. "They have no choice but to enjoy it. You've taken choice away from them. If I allow Penny to do what she wants, I'll be raping her."

"What if I said her life depended on sucking you off? Would you still refuse?"

"I notice," Nathan said, "that you framed that as a question, not as a statement of fact." He couldn't figure out what Dyffaya was up to. Surely he wasn't simply trying to force them to have sex with the poor people he'd beguiled. That would be cruel and demeaning, both of which Dyffaya might enjoy, but it was crude. Obvious. The former god of revenge—any god of the sidhe—should be planning something complex that would, in the end, lead them to destroy themselves.

So far, though, nothing he'd done was subtle, was it? He'd apologized for that when he tortured Nathan. He'd spoken of himself as easily amused.

Was he testing them? Dyffaya didn't know much about lupi. Maybe he wanted to learn more about where their buttons were.

"Please," Liu whispered, staring at Nathan's crotch, his expression avid. Aroused. "I want to so much."

"That's José," Benedict said abruptly. "Those shoes. They're José's."

"Is José one of the men who've been, ah, *escorting* your lady and Nathan's while you're away?" Dyffaya's delicate emphasis turned "escort" into a synonym for "fuck." "If so, you may be right."

The shoe was so blurry Nathan didn't see how Benedict could have identified it, but if Benedict said it was José's, it probably was.

"In a few moments," Dyffaya said, "two of you will be able to see your ladies. I apologize, Cullen, that you won't have that pleasure, but your lady didn't accompany the other two. I thought you might enjoy looking at them while you climaxed, but if not . . ." He shrugged. Liu went still, then he and Penny both stood and headed back to Dyffaya. "No, my dears, sit at my feet now, both of you. That's good. And now," he said, his voice like the crack of a whip, "we will proceed to the next part of the game."

Abruptly the display changed. No longer were they looking through a dog's eyes. This view was sharp and clear, the colors normal . . . and the crosshairs were back.

This time, they were centered on Arjenie's forehead.

They moved, trailing away from Arjenie—who was walking, Nathan realized. Walking at a normal speed. Time here must have popped back in sync with Earth.

The crosshairs settled on another forehead. Kai's.

"Now," Dyffaya said in a silky voice, "let's talk about what I want from the two of you."

TWENTY-FIVE

KAI stopped suddenly. Dell was trying to reach her.

"What is it?" Arjenie asked.

She waved for silence and dropped into the lightest stage of trance, focusing on the tie to her familiar . . . "Down!" she shouted. And dropped.

NATHAN watched Kai drop out of sight. By the time the shooter reacted, trying to follow her down, the lupi had closed in around her—five men and one wolf, blocking the line-of-fire.

Dyffaya clucked his tongue. "How annoying. I assure you, however, the safety of your ladies is entirely temporary. Benedict, I know your lady has sidhe blood, but I'm not sure what abilities that has given her. What, exactly, is her Gift?"

Benedict growled. It was a genuine growl, rumbling deep in the big man's chest.

Nathan's heart pounded. His mouth was dry. But fear could be managed. Harder to control was the rage building deep inside, the need for Dyffaya's blood . . . especially since the god didn't have blood. None of that showed in his voice.

That much control he did have. "I don't think Benedict is able to respond. He may be too much wolf at the moment for speech. Why do you ask?"

"I wondered if she might be a precog. It's not an uncommon Gift for one with a bit of sidhe blood."

"You may assume that to be true."

"Or I may assume that she or someone else saw the weapon. Or that someone with them has a trace of precognition. I might assume any number of things, but for now, I won't. Instead, let me show you why your ladies' safety is so precarious."

"WHAT is it?" José asked urgently. He and the other guards had not obeyed her order to get down. They were crouching in a circle around her and Arjenie, their weapons out. Ackleford had his gun out, too.

"Dell told me to get down."

"Dell isn't here."

"I know that."

DYFFAYA snapped his fingers. The display changed. Now they were looking at the sidewalk—then at a tree. A blurry view again, and bumpy. Lower to the ground than a man's eyes . . . a dog again? Trotting along a sidewalk.

The dog stopped. Looked up and to his left at the man beside him—a middle-aged man in jogging shorts and gray T-shirt. He wore glasses. His hairline was receding.

He burst into flame.

JOSÉ spoke without turning around. "I don't see a threat. Did Dell tell you why you needed to get down?"

"No." The chameleon hadn't sent words, just a strong burst of warning and the sensation of dropping to the ground.

Ackleford snorted. "How the hell could she know what's going on here?" He slid his gun back in its holster beneath his jacket. "Whatever you picked up, either it wasn't from her or it wasn't about you."

* * *

ONCE more Dyffaya snapped his fingers and the display changed. Back to the little dog's eyes, judging by the blurriness and closeness to the ground. Back to Kai and Arjenie, who were still surrounded by the lupi guards.

"I could do the same here," Dyffaya said. "Shall I?"

Nathan looked at him, scowling to hide his puzzlement. "Assassin's fire," he said to be sure.

"Give the doggie a cookie. He recognizes the obvious." Another snap of the fingers.

Now the display had them looking down at an intersection. The colors were rich but weird, with a lot of purple mixed in where Nathan didn't expect to see purple. Details were unnaturally crisp. They had a bird's eye view, he realized. Literally. Birds saw into the ultraviolet, which his eyes didn't have receptors for, so he saw those hues as shades of purple. It must be perched on a power line.

Below the bird, several cars were stopped on one street, while those on the other one hurried through the intersection. A blue pickup and a Volvo were passing each other, going opposite ways.

The Volvo's driver burst into flames. A second later, a huge fireball exploded, engulfing the entire car.

"I CAN tell the difference between something Dell sends and something she's experiencing," Kai said. "This was meant for me."

"There's that dog again," José said.

"What dog?"

SNAP.

Another dog, judging by the colors and blurriness of the display. This one was bigger than the one near Kai and Arjenie and the others. It was running down a sidewalk, the view bouncing with his motion. He ran up to—oh, God. A school bus, with children lined up, boarding it. Young children. Seven or eight years old.

"NO!" Benedict pushed to his feet.

"Fooled you!" Dyffaya laughed and laughed. He snapped his fingers. Another bird's eye view, this one of an old woman digging in a flower bed. He was still laughing when the old woman burst into flame.

Snap.

Back to the little dog who was watching Kai and Arjenie.

". . . BACK about fifteen feet. He's been following us. Doesn't get too close, but it's unusual."

Yes, it was. Dogs didn't tag along after wolves. Kai sat up. "Move aside. I need to see him."

José hesitated, but stepped aside just enough for her to see the little dog he was talking about. Cute little thing. Mixed breed, she thought. His thoughts were as simple as most animals', with very little patterning compared to human thoughts. Except for that little bubble at the base of—

"Shit!"

SNAP.

A man's-eye-view this time. Or a woman's. Impossible to say in the few seconds it took him or her to turn and look out a window—an office window. He or she was in an office. Nathan had glimpsed a desk and computer before the view shifted to the window. He or she walked up to the glass and looked out and down, three stories down, at people walking purposefully this way and that across a concrete expanse punctuated by a raised bed that held a couple small trees and—

One of the people down there burst into flame.

"GRAB him!" Kai cried. "He's got a compulsion—if I can study it—"

José made a gesture. One of the men—Nick, that was his name—took off running. "We're getting inside," José said. "Now."

SNAP.

The display returned to the crosshairs, not the dog. They

tracked various parts of Kai, whatever showed, as she and the lupi bunched up around her and Arjenie hurried into a stucco building.

Then the display vanished.

Dyffaya lounged in his recliner. He was smiling. The two young people at his feet were smiling, too. Nathan thought he could grow to hate smiles. "You see how easily I could kill your ladies. One or both of them."

Nathan held himself still. The god was half right. That gun could kill Kai. Assassin's fire could not . . . and Dyffaya seemed not to realize that. He seemed not to recognize the amulet for what it was, and he should have. Dyffaya should have been able to See the spell on the amulet and figure out what it did. Either he hadn't tried . . . or he couldn't.

If it was the first, Dyffaya was incredibly careless. Nathan was betting on the latter. The god's display didn't allow him to use the Sight on what he watched.

It was a small chink in his armor, but it was the only one Nathan had found so far. He held himself very still and didn't look at Cullen, though he wanted badly to know if Cullen had noticed the lapse. If Cullen, too, was unable to use his Sight on the images in the display.

He didn't look at Benedict, either, but for a different reason. Arjenie didn't have such an amulet.

Dyffaya let the silence go on for several moments before continuing. "No doubt you're wondering what I want. I think you won't have any trouble agreeing, given the stakes. I want to watch a more personal game, one between you . . ." He trailed his gaze from Benedict to Nathan. "And you."

Dyffaya changed. Not his body, which remained the mixed-race form he'd chosen this time around. His presence. The air—so nearly dead, devoid as it was of scent—suddenly filled with the god's power, so that Nathan breathed him in. The recliner under his butt was Dyffaya. *Everything* was Dyffaya. Nathan had known that, but for the first time, he felt it. For the first time, he felt himself in the presence of a god.

It wasn't beguilement. It was sheer power.

Dell must have felt something, too. Her skin twitched. She sat up and stared at the god beside her.

When Dyffaya spoke this time, his voice reverberated like

a deep bell. "The wolf and the Queen's Hound will fight. You may have up to five matches to kill your opponent, and you will both try very hard to win—because the loser's lady will die with him."

As suddenly as it had appeared, the power was withdrawn. Dyffaya giggled like a schoolgirl. "No cheating, now. That means you, Nathan, can't use that fancy blade of yours, and the sorcerer isn't allowed to help Benedict. Also, no holding back. If you're both still alive at the end of the fifth bout, both of your ladies will die."

TWENTY-SIX

THERE were four of them. Four healthy, pretty young people, two men and two women, none of them over the age of twenty-five, Kai thought. They sat on the floor on the second story of the lifeguard tower with their hands cuffed behind them. The two women were of European heritage; one of the men had African ancestors; another was Hispanic. All four wore jeans, running shoes, and white T-shirts printed with hanji or kanji in broad brush strokes. Under the Asian script were English words: "Before the beginning of great brilliance, there must be chaos."

They were on the second floor of the lifeguard tower. It was a bit crowded. In addition to the persons of interest, it held three police officers, Ackleford, Kai, Arjenie, and two lupi—José and Casey. The other three guards had stayed on the first floor. Nick hadn't returned yet.

Two of the police officers kept their weapons trained on the pretty young people who'd asked for Kai by name. The third one handed Ackleford back his ID after scrutinizing it carefully. "What happened out there?" he asked. "I was told not to leave these people for an instant, no matter what. I didn't, but I covered you from the window. Only I didn't see anything."

"May have been a false alarm," Ackleford said, slipping his ID back inside his jacket. "Or not. Someone else should be along shortly. Tall guy, African American, red shirt. Name's . . ." He glanced at José.

"Nick. Nick Mathews."

"He might be carrying a small brown dog. Let him in."

The officer told him "yessir" without a second's hesitation. No doubt he'd seen a lot weirder things than a man with a dog today. Kai turned to study the persons of interest sitting in a row on the floor. It took only a moment to confirm her initial impression. "They're asleep. Their minds are, anyway. There's a heavy overlay, very intricate, a combination of beguilement and compulsion, that's suppressing their thoughts."

"What the hell's beguilement?" Ackleford demanded.

"Infatuation on steroids," Arjenie said. "It's an elf trick."

None of the four reacted in any way. "It's possible Dyffaya can hear us," Kai warned the others. "They aren't aware of their surroundings, but he might be. I don't know how that kind of mind tap works, so we have to act as if he's able to overhear us."

"Got it," Ackleford said. José just nodded. Arjenie frowned. The police officers didn't react outwardly, but the acrid yellow of fear swirled through their thoughts.

A sensible reaction under the circumstances, but she'd best keep an eye on them. If the guys with guns went from fear to panic, bad things could happen. Kai moved closer to the beguiled young people, stopping just out of reach. "I'm Kai. You said you wanted to talk to me."

The thoughts of the young man nearest Kai stirred sluggishly. A thought bubble arose, heavily laced with lavender. He blinked and looked up at her. His hair was buzzed very short; his skin was unusually dark. "May I see some ID?" He spoke politely in what sounded like a New York accent.

Kai reached into her pocket for her wallet. When she started to step forward to hand it to him, José stopped her. He took her wallet and crouched, holding it out so the handcuffed young man could see it.

"What's your name?" Kai asked.

No response. Not in his face, voice, or his thoughts.

"Is she Kai Tallman Michalski?" asked the pretty blonde next to him. She wore blue-framed glasses and pink lipstick.

"Yes."

The young woman on the other end of the row of beguiled people—short brown hair, a scattering of freckles on an up-tipped nose—spoke suddenly. "The convenience store at the corner of Browning and Moran."

The young man next to her said, "The Fowler Building."

"Tuttle Park in El Cahon," said the blonde.

"The airport." That was the first young man.

"What about those places?" Kai asked. All of them were generating thoughts now, but sluggishly, as if each thought had to push its way through the lavender smothering them.

The New Yorker spoke first this time. "Our lord gives warning. These places will be his."

"Chaos gives birth to great beauty," the blonde said.

"And great terror," added the young Hispanic man.

"Blood," whispered the girl at the end, the one with freckles. "So much blood." Her thoughts were more active than the others, as if they were struggling against the overlay—but it didn't last. Her thoughts quieted, and she spoke. "He is the bringer of dreams—"

"Of fire and change—"

"Of the known made new—"

"And lovely and strange." The four-part recitation ended with the New Yorker, who smiled beatifically.

So did the other three, all at the exact same instant. It was creepy as hell.

Kai crouched to get at their level and spoke in her best healer-to-patient voice. "When is your lord going to act?" They sat there, not moving, and smiled. Their thoughts were smoothing out, receding, as they fell back into the weird waking-sleep they'd been in before. No, wait—the girl on the end. Her thoughts had stirred slightly. Not much, and they were quiet again, but on some level she'd heard Kai.

Behind her, Ackleford was on the phone, telling someone they had to evacuate the four places mentioned. Kai stood. "This is going to take time. The combination of beguilement and compulsion isn't like anything I've seen before, and it's really complex. I can't just yank out the part that keeps their minds asleep. It's woven into everything else."

"And you're already depleted."

Kai grimaced and nodded. She recharged fast, but not this fast.

"They wouldn't talk before, either," said the cop who'd checked Ackleford's ID.

She looked at him. "They can't. It might help if I had their names." People responded to their names on a deep level.

"None of them have given their names, and they don't have any ID. We've taken prints, but who knows if any of 'em are in the database?"

"Facebook," Arjenie said. "They're probably on it."

"Good point. I'll tell the lieutenant, make sure he has someone check that."

"No need. I can do that." Arjenie took out her phone and started taking pictures.

Kai spoke to the helpful officer. "They were here when it happened, right? Here at the beach, I mean, not here at the lifeguard tower."

"Yeah. The first patrol unit to arrive found them standing together near that damn glass sea serpent, holding hands. Not a scratch on them. They were just standing there, calm as could be, and—well, like they are now. The guy on the end, he told the patrol officers their lord had made the glass bloom. He said that they had a message, but they would only give it to Kai Tallman Michalski. Then he shut up. None of the others spoke until just now."

Ackleford cursed and disconnected, immediately punching in another number. After a brief wait he said, "I need the airport evacuated."

Kai turned her attention back to the four young people, absently rubbing her aching head. They'd learned so little, and that little wasn't adding up. Four people, presumably Dyffaya's followers, wanted them to know where the god would strike next. Why? And why ask for Kai? And who had shot at her back at the hobbit house? Someone female who was not human. In the realms that would leave it pretty wide open. Not so much here. She turned to José. "Can Doug Change yet?"

"We'd better give him another ten, fifteen minutes."

"I've got three out of four," Arjenie announced. "The guy on the end doesn't seem to be on Facebook."

"That was quick. The Bureau must have excellent facial recognition software."

"No, but Facebook does. It's their new DeepFace system."

"That," Kai observed, "sounds creepy as hell. DeepFace?"

"Hell you say!" Ackleford exclaimed. "Where?"

"What is it?" Arjenie asked.

He waved at her to be quiet, listened intently, then told whoever it was to "send it so I can have my experts take a look." He disconnected and turned his scowl on her and Arjenie. "Either of you ever deal with spontaneous human combustion?"

"No," Arjenie said.

"Yes," Kai said.

"Good, 'cause I sure as hell haven't. This guy was walking his dog. The dog's special—a rare breed or something—so this woman who was walking her dog decided to take a picture. That's why we've got a shot of the man bursting into flames." He held out his phone.

Kai took it reluctantly.

The image was every bit as horrible as she'd feared. She made herself study it anyway, using the phone's features to zoom in on key spots. "The fire started in his gut. There's not much of him left there—it's all flames." Bright red flames, too. She handed the phone back.

Ackleford studied the grisly close-up. "Yeah, his stomach seems to be gone. Does that mean he swallowed some of that chaos stuff and it exploded inside him?"

"If a chaos mote discharged on its own, the resulting explosion would take out several blocks at least. Probably a lot more. No, this was done on purpose, by someone with a lot of power who's good with fire and with body magic. That sure fits Dyffaya."

"Why good with body magic?" Arjenie asked.

"Because someone turned that man's guts into flames."

"Oh, eck."

Ackleford was unconvinced. "Maybe it's that damn chaos god, maybe not. Must be other ways for magic to burn someone."

"Lots of them, but this was assassin's fire. That deep red at the base of the flames—that's the tip-off. You have to have line-of-sight to use assassin's fire, and, like I said, you need lots of power and top-rate skills with body magic."

"Is that what your cuff is for?" Arjenie asked.

"Among other things." She'd told Arjenie the story that went with that gift. Part of it, anyway. "It repels all kinds of magical fire. Turns it back on whoever is trying to use it on me. Special Agent, you said—José? What is it?"

José had answered his phone while she was talking. His expression said he hadn't gotten good news. He put the phone up as he answered. "That was Nick. The little dog is dead. He ran right under the wheels of a car."

"Shit," she said, feeling sick. And turned to look at the four pretty, healthy young people as a terrible thought bloomed. "Put away your guns," she said urgently. "If Dyffaya decides he doesn't need those people anymore, or that they're a liability—"

"Suicide by cop," Ackleford said. "Got it. Sergeant, tell your men to holster 'em."

"I was ordered—"

"And I'm changing that order."

DYFFAYA left again. As gone as he ever was, that is. He said he was off to, "get the rest of the audience."

Nathan felt cold. He didn't see a way out of this. That tiny chink he'd spotted—thought he'd spotted—in Dyffaya's armor gave him nothing that helped with this. He had Claw. He could stab the ground with it. The ground was godhead, like everything else here. But all Dyffaya had to do was pull his consciousness away from the area Nathan stabbed and the death Claw sowed wouldn't touch him. Nathan still needed that third element. He needed a chance at one of those bodies Dyffaya wore, which concentrated more of the god in one spot.

Dyffaya, damn him, knew that. Nathan rubbed his face with both hands as if he could scrub a solution into his head.

"I could've sworn he meant to keep you, Nathan," Cullen said. "He wants company, even if you are an enemy. Long-lived company."

Nathan dropped his hands and grimaced. "I'm the stakes, I think. The risk of losing me will make the game interesting to him." Dyffaya would consider it a small risk. That was, in part, the usual elfin arrogance that aggravated Kai so much. Nathan was no elf, but he was sidhe. Dyffaya wouldn't believe a lupus could kill him.

Arrogant or not, Dyffaya was right . . . if Nathan fought to kill. Benedict was the best fighter he'd ever sparred with, save for that old elf. But if Nathan fought to kill, he would. His Gift was the same now as it had been when he was four-footed, the same Gift every hellhound possessed. And it was a singular Gift, in spite of what Cullen's Sight suggested, though it encompassed a range of skills.

The Gift of killing.

"Do it now," Benedict said.

"What?" Nathan looked up, startled.

Benedict's face was stony. "Do it now, not as part of his damn game. If he doesn't get his game, there's no loser. No one dies but me."

He meant it. "No."

Benedict's lip lifted in a snarl. "You're the one with a chance of stopping him, not me. If I win—and I'll fight to win if it comes down to that—it won't be the end. He can just keep using Arjenie to make me do what he wants. There's no end to her risk that way. If I'm dead before the game starts, Arjenie's out of danger."

Benedict's conclusion was logical. Beautifully brave. And wrong. "Benedict, you just saw him kill four people to make a point. What makes you think he won't kill Arjenie out of spite if you deprive him of his game?"

Benedict's expression didn't change—but he spun and slammed his fist into the back of the recliner. It toppled over. "I need to kill that bastard." His voice was tight, throbbing with fury. "I need to Change. And *I can't do either one.*"

Benedict was right. If Nathan won and Kai was allowed to live, it would be the most temporary of reprieves. Dyffaya had every intention of using her against Nathan. Unless . . .

"Your face says you thought of something," Cullen said. "What?"

"Hold on. Let me think a moment." He did that, considering

the wording, looking for some angle he might be missing. It was far from perfect, but . . . "We have to refuse to fight unless he promises not to harm or kill or allow his people to harm or kill Kai and Arjenie before or during our fights, and not to kill the winner's lady after."

Benedict gave him a hard look. "He needs to swear not to kill them at all."

"We can't get that. He's bound himself to kill the loser's lady."

"Bound himself?" Cullen's eyebrows lifted. "What does that mean?"

"You must have noticed the way his power filled the godhead when he announced the bouts. The Queens and a few of the great sidhe lords can do that, binding themselves by drawing on their full power when they speak. Dyffaya literally can't break his word when it's given in such a way. His own power will stop him."

"Why would he bind himself?"

Nathan grimaced. "I suspect he's making the bouts more interesting by ensuring he can't tinker with the outcome."

"You think you can get him to agree," Cullen said.

"It won't be easy, but yes, I do. We have one advantage. He's bored."

Benedict's eyebrows expressed his opinion of that as a bargaining chip.

"No, Nathan's right about that," Cullen said as if Benedict had spoken out loud. "Elves will do the damnedest things if they're sufficiently bored. Remember that sidhe lord I met who'd gone walkabout? He gave up his land-tie to travel here even though Earth was still interdicted at the time. He did it out of sheer boredom."

Nathan nodded. "Some of the older ones are like that. Not all, but for some, a malaise sets in. Still, Dyffaya won't give in easily. He'll try to get us to back down, and his methods of persuasion are apt to be rough. We can expect him to hurt us. He can't use body magic on us, or anything we agree to is null and void. Technically, he can't use torture, either, but there are ways around that which I can explain later. He can also threaten others. Can you watch him send assassin's fire onto some poor innocent on Earth without giving in?"

Benedict's voice was flat. "I don't give my word unless I know I can keep it. I need to think. I won't go far." Abruptly he launched into a run.

"He thinks better when he's moving," Cullen explained.

The land here at the top of the cliff was fairly flat, sloping down gradually until it met the forest of impossibly tall black trees. Nathan watched Benedict lope toward the distant trees. "We need to have this settled before Dyffaya returns, and we don't know when that will be."

"Benedict knows that. He said he wouldn't go far. I've been thinking about what Dyffaya said while his power was flooding everything . . . and what he said after he'd pulled it back."

Cullen had spotted that, had he? Nathan gave him a quick, sharp nod. "It makes some difference because he isn't bound by the latter terms. That doesn't mean he won't abide by them."

"True. Still, it's something to keep in mind."

Which part, Nathan wondered, was Cullen keeping in mind? The part where Dyffaya said that Cullen wasn't to help Benedict? Or the part where he said that both women would die if neither Nathan nor Benedict killed the other? "I'm wondering what it looked like to you when Dyffaya drew on his full power."

"Lavender. Blinding, blazingly lavender."

"Is his power always lavender, then? What did it look like when he threw assassin's fire?"

"The same color, not as bright."

"You saw that in the display?"

Cullen glanced at him, frowning. "Yes."

"Ah." Briefly he considered not drawing Cullen's attention to that small chink he'd spotted in the god's armor, in case the sorcerer was minded to try using it to help Benedict. But only briefly. He continued carefully, mindful of the possibility the god was listening. "I've reason to believe that Dyffaya didn't see what you did in the display."

Cullen's gaze turned questioning, then sharp. Nathan could almost see the gears turning in that keen mind. "Ah," he said—and idly rubbed his wrist. His left wrist. Kai wore the amulet on her left wrist. "They do say no two people see exactly the same thing. A god might see something quite different than I do when I look at the color lavender."

"I imagine he does." Nathan paused just long enough to emphasize that. "Especially in the display. The first time he showed it to me, he had to adjust something for it to work for my kind of sight. It makes me wonder about his vision. Does whatever body he's using give him the same kind of vision I have?" Vision like Nathan's would be keen . . . and lack the Sight.

Cullen's smile was tight and feral. He was following Nathan's meaning nicely—and leaping ahead. "His vision should be very much like yours, even though the bodies he uses aren't made of the same stuff."

"You think so?" Could Dyffaya have lost the Sight when he died? It was a wild notion. Why would a god lose his Sight just because he lost his body? There were disembodied beings who possessed the Sight. "Of course, some beings don't need bodies to see."

"So I've heard. It would be interesting to find out how Dyffaya's vision differs when he's using a body compared to when he's disembodied."

Was Cullen suggesting that Dyffaya only lacked the Sight when he was using a body? "I'm not sure how we could find out."

"Ah, well. It's hardly the most pressing question before us."

By which, Nathan assumed, he meant the opposite. "I have to agree." He paused. "Benedict's on his way back."

Neither of them spoke again as they waited. A few moments later, Benedict reached them. He stopped in front of Nathan. He held Nathan's eyes with his. "I'm in. Do it."

TWENTY-SEVEN

THEY got the four persons of interest to the police station without anyone dying. Kai's headache dissipated along the way. She was still low on power, but she had enough to make a start. Untangling the complex weave of beguilement and compulsion gripping the minds of their witnesses was going to be a slow process.

By the time they arrived, however, two more reports of human spontaneous combustion had come in. Possibly three, but one was iffy. An entire car had gone up in flames, and assassin's fire didn't work on inanimate things. Kai had suggested the investigators try to determine if the fire started with the driver.

One of the burnings happened just outside the Fowler Building—the place named by the young Hispanic man. That had occurred before Ackleford ordered the building evacuated. The convenience store had been easy to empty of people, and Tuttle Park was small enough that the police in El Cahon had gotten everyone out. There'd been a problem at the airport. The guy in charge had argued about whether Ackleford had the authority to order an evacuation. It was underway now, but would take a while.

None of them had any idea why Dyffaya was burning

up random people from the inside out. Of those two assumptions—that the victims were truly random and that Dyffaya was doing it—Kai was sure of the latter. The Bureau and the SDPD would be digging into the former, looking for anything that linked the victims.

The four followers of Dyffaya were mobile, fortunately, as long as someone tugged them along. They'd just been taken off to some kind of detention room when yet another report came in.

Turned out that the Fowler Building had been scheduled for two events, not just a single burning.

"How many?" Ackleford asked his phone. A long pause. "We have to find out if anyone's missing." He scowled impartially at everyone—Kai, Arjenie, and the nearby cops who'd been listening every bit as intently as the civilians. "Right. We'll be there in fifteen."

"Well?" Kai demanded.

"Spiders," he said tersely. "Big green spiders the size of a tarantula. They started pouring out of the vents in the Fowler Building along with the air conditioning about twenty minutes ago. Lots of people bitten. They don't have a firm count, but maybe thirty or forty. No obvious symptoms other than some redness at the bite."

"All spiders have venom," Arjenie told him, "but very few have enough to be dangerous to humans."

"I'll keep that in mind. Dupree, keep a suicide watch on my witnesses."

Kai frowned. "I thought the Fowler building had been evacuated."

"They'd started. A lot of people didn't see much need to hurry. Let's go."

"I need to stay here," Kai said.

"And I need you with me. I don't know shit about magic or chaos gods or any of this shit."

"There are two of us experts, you know," Arjenie said.

"Arjenie," José said, worried. "I don't like splitting up."

"I understand," Arjenie told him sympathetically. "But the special agent needs someone to advise him, and Kai needs to help those poor people so they can tell us things."

Kai really hated asking Arjenie to go out there when Kai

was the one with the antifire amulet, but Arjenie couldn't use the amulet. She didn't see what else to do. "I hope you aren't an arachnophobe."

"Oh, no. Did you know that only about a hundred people in this country died from spider bites in the entire twentieth century? That's a lot less than are killed by pet dogs or bees. Bees kill fifty or more people every year. Spiders are pretty interesting, actually. They—well, you don't want to hear all that right now. Special Agent, I'll go with you and do what I can."

Kai spoke to José. "Leave one man with me, so I'll have someone I'm sure isn't linked to the god. Take the rest to guard Arjenie. She'll be a lot more exposed. Arjenie, you'll be, uh, hard to spot as much as possible, won't you?"

"When I can," Arjenie assured her.

"You do remember who's in charge, don't you?" Ackleford said, heavy on the sarcasm.

Kai looked at him. "We need to get the silence lifted from those four. There are so many questions they could answer. How did they hear about the god? Where? Are there more followers? Who's doing the recruiting or preaching or whatever?"

"How about, why did their asshole god hand them over to us? Because that's a damned odd thing for him to do. I may not know shit about magic, but I know about perps. I'm wondering if they've been booby-trapped somehow."

"Um. Right. I'll keep that in mind."

Ackleford sighed heavily. Ran a hand over the top of his head. "All right. Do what you can with them, but be careful. Come on, Fox—and however many of you feel obliged to tag along," he added with an irritated glance at José and his men—all of them two-legged again. Doug had Changed on the way here. "Dupree, give Michalski what she needs to deal with my wits, on my authority."

Dupree was the police officer in charge at this station. Kai could not for the life of her remember his rank. Captain, maybe? He was over fifty, thin, and dark-skinned. Also annoyed. Ackleford had that effect on people. "Within reason," he said.

Ackleford snorted. "Yeah, yeah, you don't like me coming in and telling you what to do. Call them your wits if it makes you feel better, but give Michalski what she needs. She's the only one who can get them to talk—and by that I mean that they won't speak at all until she does her woo-woo thing. Mindhealing, she calls it. The way it works is, she sees everyone's thoughts like we were scribbling in the air with colored pens. We're not writing our thoughts out in English for her to read—she just sees scribbles. But she can . . ."

While Ackleford explained mindhealing to Dupree in his own fashion—it was pretty entertaining, actually—José moved closer to Kai. "I'm leaving Nick with you. Don't leave the building until we come back for you, okay?"

"I can agree to that, barring a real emergency. Arjenie, you should take some of the charms." The truth charms wouldn't do Arjenie any good; her Gift burned them out. But the one that detected poison might be useful, and the fire charm. If you used it with the wind charm, you could spray fire for several feet. The one that detected spells? No, it was tricky to use, and Arjenie didn't have time to practice invoking and reading it. Quickly Kai explained what was what and how to use them.

"I hope you won't be offended, Special Agent," Arjenie was saying as they headed for the big security door, "but I'm going to call Ruben. We need real Unit agents here. I'm a researcher, not a field agent, which means I know a lot of facts and how to find more, but I don't . . ." Her voice cut off as the door closed behind them.

Kai looked at Dupree. "Basically, all I need from you is a room where Nick and I can be private with one of the prisoners."

"Persons of interest," Dupree corrected her firmly. "Or witnesses. They haven't been charged with anything. I can have one of them escorted to an interrogation room, but one of my officers will remain with you."

"By 'private' I mean that no one has a line-of-sight on the prisoner or me. Are your interrogation rooms set up for that? The chaos god needs to be able to see someone to light them on fire. It's unlikely he's planted a link in any of your people which he could use for that, but not impossible."

Dupree didn't say anything for a long moment. "That is a

very unsettling stipulation. If the Big A weren't so sure . . . he's an asshole, but he's not stupid. All right."

NO one else burned that day. Turned out the god was too busy with other things—at the zoo, the airport, a park in El Cahon, the mall, a convenience store, and the Federal Building in downtown San Diego.

"The Federal Building?" Kai repeated as she clicked her seatbelt into place. "What do you mean, it sealed itself up?"

"All the exits were sealed with this hard gray stuff," Arjenie said. "Every duct, too. The whole building became airtight. They had to bring out construction equipment to cut their way in."

"Good Lord. I can't believe no one told me about that." It was ten at night, and she and Arjenie were in the armored Town Car once more. José had just picked Kai up—but not from the police station. From the mall. "I was in trance all afternoon, but when I broke for supper you'd think they would have mentioned a chaos event at the IRS." She'd barely managed to finish eating before the police asked for her help at the mall. Arjenie had still been tied up at the zoo.

"What about the other sites? Did they tell you about them?" Arjenie asked.

"I heard about the airport and the convenience store—and thank God no one was nearby when that went up. The gas pumps made quite a fireball. And Tuttle Park. I heard what happened there. Did they ever find all the toads?"

Arjenie shook her head. "I don't know. I do know that two people have been reported missing in El Cahon. They're assuming the toads bit them."

"So what happened at the Federal Building? Casualties? People missing?"

"No one's reported missing, and last I heard no one had died. But there were a lot of injuries, some of them pretty serious. After the building sealed itself shut, this pink vapor came out of the ducts and people went all sorts of crazy. A bunch of them held a party with dancing and sex. Most of it was consensual, but not all. Others went fighting mad. A lot of people were hurt that way. The other injuries were more random. One man ate pencils, which doesn't sound so bad, but the splinters cut him up inside. Another started a fire at his desk. He wasn't hurt, but two others got burned trying to play with the flames. A woman ran into a wall over and over until she knocked herself out."

"Ugly." Kai frowned and counted. "So as far as we know, no one's missing from the Federal Building, the convenience store, or the hobbit house. He snatched two people each from the airport, the Fowler Building, and the mall, plus five at the zoo. That's eleven. Add in Britta Valenzuela from yesterday and our people from this morning, and he's got sixteen hostages." Had that been only this morning? Gods. Kai rubbed the back of her neck.

"What happened at the mall, anyway? All I heard was that people had been bitten."

"The chaos event hit a pet store. All the cages vanished and all their occupants were transformed, except for the bunnies. Scaled puppies with vampire teeth, flying snakes, oversize lizards running around on legs like a dog's, birds with teeth . . . and they were all terrified. Their bodies were horribly altered, and all around them people were screaming. Of course the animals ran, which made people think they were chasing them."

"They weren't?"

Kai shook her head. "The poor things just wanted to get away. There was this one puppy . . . half puppy, half lizard, I guess, but his head and legs were all puppy, and so were his thoughts. They—the cops—when I arrived, they wanted me to find the transformed creatures. I told them sure, I could do that, and I could tell which ones were under compulsion, too, and if they weren't being compelled I could control them so we could get them caged safely."

"You can do that? Control animals?"

"Most of the time, if it's just one at a time. It's not compulsion, mind—I just soothe them, make them comfortable with me. I can't do anything with insects," she added, thinking of the butterflies. "They don't have enough in the way of thoughts. I can't even put them to sleep."

"I didn't know you could do that, either."

"It's not always useful. It takes a lot of power to send sleep, and it wears off unless I trance and anchor the instruction, and that's too much like interfering. Even with animals, I don't like to interfere that much with free will unless I absolutely have to. Mostly it's easier to use a sleep charm."

"You didn't put the chameleons to sleep."

"They were already under someone else's control. I would've had to put Dyffaya to sleep for that to work."

"That makes sense. So you found the transformed animals?"

"Oh, yes," Kai said grimly. "This puppy was the first one. He was terrified. I sent a lot of soothing and called him to me. He crept out from under a table—we were in the food court—all bewildered, but wagging his tail. It was a lizard's tail, heavy and scaled, and he had bigger teeth than puppies are supposed to, so I guess he looked scary. But he was whimpering and so hopeful that we'd fix things." Her mouth tightened. "One of the cops shot him."

"Oh, no!"

Kai blinked back tears. Stupid to cry over a puppy when so many people had been hurt or killed today, but she kept seeing that scared, hopeful puppy-face . . . "That puppy was not a danger to anyone. I had him calm, and he had no intention—imposed or native—of biting anyone, no compulsion . . . and I know the cop couldn't see that, but I'd *told* them. But no one was listening to me yet."

Arjenie's eyebrows shot up. "Yet?"

Kai grimaced. "I lost my temper. Set off a flash-bang."

Nick spoke from the front seat. "She doesn't mean the military kind."

"Flash-bang is Nathan's word for the spell," Kai explained. "The sidhe call it something else, but Nathan taught it to me, so I use his word. It's very Shakespearian—all 'sound and fury, signifying nothing.' "

"But with plenty of that sound and fury," Nick said dryly. "I was impressed. The cops were, too."

"At least," Kai said, vaguely embarrassed, "they did start listening to me after that. And it mattered that they listen. Not just because I didn't want to see helpless animals killed, but because I needed to *see* the animals. I'd spent hours studying Dyffaya's work in the compulsions laid on his followers and in the scraps of intention I salvaged from the hobbit house. I knew I'd recognize the patterns of his intent, and I was sure I could sort out scraps of general intent left behind from the general chaos event from compulsions laid on individual animals. I figured Dyffaya's blood-hooks would be carried by animals under compulsion, you see. And it worked. I could spot the animals with the tags easily."

"That's going to be useful. Had he tagged many of them?"

"Just the bunnies. Not the puppies or the lizards or the toothed birds. None of the scary creatures. The bunnies, because people weren't scared of them. They'd pet one or pick it up—and get bitten." Kai sighed. "Two people are missing."

"Were there a lot of injuries? To people, I mean."

"Yes, but most were minor. Bites, of course. A broken leg when someone got shoved off the escalator in the panic. The worst injured were the ones who were shot."

Arjenie's eyes went big. "Shot?"

"Yeah. A civilian idiot decided to go hunting. He wasn't the ace shot he liked to think—hit a man by accident, but that didn't discourage him. He kept shooting at this lizard thing and put a bullet in a woman's chest. She was still in surgery, last I heard. He was under arrest and screaming about his Second Amendment rights." Kai sighed again and leaned back against the seat. "Tell me how it went at the zoo."

"There's five missing."

"Five? But that's more than twice as many as he's grabbed at other chaos events! And it's an odd number. I guess we were wrong about him grabbing people in pairs."

"No, he still grabbed in pairs—he just grabbed more pairs. Originally there were six missing, but one was a little boy and Dyffaya sent him back, just like he did that toddler at Fagioli."

Kai thought about that. "It sounds like children won't work for whatever he wants with these people—but he isn't killing them. He's returning them. Do you think he's reluctant to hurt kids?"

"Maybe. It's possible that the godhead itself kicks them out for some reason, not the god."

"Thinking about the godhead makes me dizzy. Could there have been more than one chaos event at the zoo, and that's how he grabbed so many people there?"

"I don't know how to tell. There were two transformations—the wasps and some of the trees. The trees didn't do anything, though. They didn't sprout thorns or poke people with their branches, though they look weird enough to behave that way. Gorgeous, but weird. I'm pretty sure the wasps were the only things delivering hooks. Everyone who vanished had been stung. A few hundred people were stung who didn't vanish, of course. There were a lot of wasps."

"How much of a lot do you mean?"

"Thousands, maybe. Your fire charm plus the wind charm worked on the swarms, but then they stopped swarming. I had no idea how to find them all. I was really glad when that Unit agent showed up."

Arjenie had called Ruben Brooks to say they needed help. Brooks had responded by sending a Unit agent to take charge of the investigation. Kai knew that much from talking to José earlier, but that's all. "So who is this agent? What do you think of him or her?"

"Her. Special Agent Karin Stockman. She's over forty and very confident, very experienced. She's not Wiccan by faith—she told me that right off the bat—but some of her training is Wiccan. That was obvious when I watched her cast. She has an excellent vermin spell, different from any I've seen before. It's designed to repel flying bugs, which isn't unusual, only it isn't a ward. I've never seen a vermin spell that wasn't a ward, have you? She modified it on the spot to attract instead of repelling. That kind of inversion can be tricky, but she handled it beautifully. It gathered the wasps so she could deal with them. She's a Fire Gifted," Arjenie added, "so once she got them together, she burned them."

Kai frowned. "They must have been just wasps by then."

"What do you mean?"

"I don't think even an excellent vermin spell could collect creatures that were being directed by Dyffaya. Which means that by the time this Karin Stockman showed up, the god wasn't actively directing the wasps. That doesn't mean they didn't need to be disposed of. Aside from saving a lot of people from being stung—they were pretty aggressive, I understand?"

"Very."

"And just because the god wasn't directing the wasps

doesn't mean they weren't delivering hooks. They had to be destroyed. Why don't you know that vermin spell?"

"Well, it isn't part of my family's lore, so—"

"No, I mean, why haven't Unit people pooled their spells?" Kai sat up again. "Maybe not every spell, but Unit agents should do more sharing than they are. There should be some kind of common pool of spells that all Unit agents can learn."

Arjenie shrugged. "I don't see how that could work. Most of the spells I know aren't mine to give away—they're the coven's, so I'd have to ask my aunt's permission. I'm sure I'm not the only one in that situation. And anyway, I'm not an agent. I'm just a researcher."

A researcher who could call the head of Unit 12 and get him to send an agent. "Still," Kai said, "hoarding knowledge is the way the sidhe do things. We probably caught it from them, this idea that spells should all be kept secret instead of sharing the knowledge." She brooded on that a moment. "And that's enough about my hobbyhorse for now. You didn't really tell me what you thought about Karin Stockman."

"She was a police officer in Connecticut for twenty years before the Unit recruited her."

Kai's eyebrows lifted. "You don't like her."

"I didn't say that."

"No, but you're being so careful with what you do say. Come on, Arjenie. If she's going to be a problem—"

"She really is good at her job. And she really didn't pat me on the head and tell me to run along home. It just felt that way."

"One of those, huh? Is it the law enforcement background?"

"Oh, yes. She and Ackleford seemed to hit it off, by which I mean they were both rude and neither of them minded. It was funny to watch them sneer at each other. I think she discounted me mostly because I'm a civilian—"

"You work for the FBI."

"I'm an info geek, not an agent, plus I'm too girly. Some of the older female agents are like that. They had to out-guy the guys when they started out in the Bureau to get any respect. I bet Special Agent Stockman learned to cuss and spit early on. Well, not literally, but you know what I mean."

"I do." Kai had met women like that, who'd come up in a

profession back when they had to claw their way into the boys' club. Most of them were great people. A few, though, had learned to despise their own sex. "I wonder why she hasn't called me."

"She's only been here a couple hours."

"And she's been busy since she arrived," Kai conceded. "But she flew in, didn't she? She could have called me from the plane or the airport. Seems like she'd want to talk to the one person who knows something about the god."

"Give her time. I'm sure she will."

"Hmm." Kai had not wanted to be in charge. She had no right to complain if the person who'd been put in charge didn't do things the way Kai thought she should. But dammit, the woman ought to call her. Maybe it was okay if she didn't call right away, though. With a sigh Kai leaned back again. This time her eyelids drifted down. "I won't say this was the longest day ever, but it ranks way up there."

"Mmm." Arjenie sounded as beat as Kai felt. "We did learn a few things. Dyffaya doesn't grab people at every chaos event, and he doesn't have to grab just two at a time."

"True. And so far he's used a living agent, plant or animal, to deliver his hooks."

"That's something, I guess. I'm not sure what, but . . . did you learn anything more from studying the god's followers?"

That made Kai smile grimly. "Two things. First, they're linked in some weird way. I've never seen anything like it. Second, Ackleford was right. They've been booby-trapped."

"What?" Arjenie sat up. "How?"

"There's a trigger. It's so subtle, so carefully planted . . . I nearly missed it. If I'd been at full strength I probably would have missed it because I would've been trying to fix things instead of studying them. The trigger's tied to the most obvious place to start lifting the compulsions," she added. "Not that 'obvious' is a good word for it. 'Only' fits better, as in, the only place I've found so far."

"What does the trigger do? Could you tell?"

"If it's tripped, it sets off a cascade that destroys their minds. All their minds, I think, even if I only tripped it in one of them."

"That's hideous. Horrible."

Kai nodded. "All of that. There's something odd about that trigger."

"What do you mean?"

"I don't know. I feel like I'm still missing something."

"Maybe you'll figure out what tomorrow, when you're rested."

Kai nodded again without lifting her head. She'd rest her eyes a moment, she decided. Just a moment . . .

She woke when the car stopped, disoriented. Blinked herself into something resembling awareness. "Guess no one tried to kill us on the way here. I didn't . . . that truck." A 1979 Ford truck in the original orange and tan, faded and peeling, sat in front of Isen's house. "I know that truck."

She threw open the door and bolted out of the Town Car. The front door of the house opened. A short, square-built man with long white braids and skin burned dark from a life spent outdoors stood in the lighted doorway. *"Yázhi Atsa!"* he called in his gravelly voice—Little Eagle. Only one person in all the realms called her that.

Seconds later, Kai was held tight in her grandfather's arms.

TWENTY-EIGHT

THEY were back in the clearing where they'd first arrived, though it looked different now. The same impossibly tall, black trees surrounded it; the same glowing ground cast an eerie, upward radiance. But the clearing was larger now. And populated.

Eleven humans, a werewolf, and a chameleon sat in a circle some fifty feet in diameter, waiting for a god. No recliners this time. The land itself rose in tidy mounds to form their seating, with the tallest hump reserved for the absent god. The humans and the lupus ate fruit and cake and drank wine as they waited. The chameleon appeared to be napping.

Those mounds had sprouted a profusion of exotic and improbable flowers. Very festive. So were the garments Dyffaya had chosen for his imported audience—short silk tunics in bright colors. Cullen's was spring green. That was no more his choice than was his seat for this show, but that was how Dyffaya wanted it. At the moment, Cullen was chatting with the dark-haired woman on his right.

Nathan and Benedict's garb had been chosen for them as well. They wore the *liarda* that were traditional for slaves condemned to fight in the pits of Kakkar, a particularly nasty portion of an unpleasant realm. *Liarda* were basically leather jockstraps, and not particularly comfortable.

Nathan waited, too, but outside that festive circle. As did Benedict . . . but not with Nathan. Opposite him, opposing him in space as he soon would be in fact.

They'd gotten most of what they wanted. Most, not all. The negotiations had cost Nathan and Benedict some pain, but nothing they couldn't heal. The god hadn't wanted them too damaged to fight, and Benedict's healing was slower than Nathan's. What Nathan did not understand was why Dyffaya hadn't threatened to burn a school or some more random strangers. Nor had he threatened Cullen's life. Maybe he didn't believe the sorcerer was important enough to them to make it worthwhile. Maybe he had some use for Cullen that required him to be uninjured.

Or maybe he'd been in too much of a tearing hurry to bother. The bargaining had taken place at well more than arms-length—Dyffaya continued to be careful about letting Nathan get close—and in a ridiculously short time. Only three hours. When Nathan acquired Kai's knife it had taken two full days, and that had been a friendly negotiation. He'd expected this negotiation to take several days, and had hoped to draw it out for a week or more.

Dyffaya had accepted the not-killing part of the bargain almost too easily. It was the not-harming part he refused to consider. "Don't be absurd," he'd said. "I've already bound myself to a situation that may result in your death. I assume your lady would consider your death a grievous harm." Nathan had suggested they define "harm" in such a way that grief was omitted. Dyffaya had said loftily, "The binding doesn't work that way. You'll excuse me if I do not explain precisely how it does work."

In the end, Dyffaya had agreed not to kill or allow his people to kill Kai or Arjenie except in fulfillment of the terms he'd already bound himself to; not to compel or beguile them; and not to strike at their families. In return, Nathan and Benedict would fight as the god directed. They hadn't sworn to kill on his order, but that's what it would come to.

Not right away, Nathan promised himself as he began his asanas to limber up for the coming trial, while the people inside that circle ate and talked and laughed. He had decided that at the start. He didn't have to kill Benedict until the last bout.

A collective gasp of awe went up as Dyffaya suddenly appeared, standing in front of his throne-mound. He wore flowers and his mixed-race body for the occasion. It was every bit as well-endowed as his statue-of-David body. He told them to continue eating, sat, and snapped his fingers. A large goblet of wine appeared in his hand. He toasted his puppet people with it, and they cheered.

Grimly, Nathan continued his asanas. There was one problem with his decision to drag this out, hoping quite irrationally that he wouldn't have to kill Benedict. Benedict couldn't afford to return the favor. He might not know the true nature of Nathan's Gift, but he knew some of Nathan's skills. He knew, too, that Nathan healed much faster than he did.

No, Benedict would try to kill Nathan as quickly as possible, while Nathan would be trying not to kill. That meant he wouldn't have the full benefit of his Gift. It would be like those bouts they'd fought back at Clanhome . . . and this first combat would be unarmed. Just like the first bout he'd fought with Benedict. The one he'd lost.

Dyffaya set down his empty goblet and called Dell to him. She woke, yawned, and sauntered to his side. He rubbed her behind the ears.

Nathan would have given a great deal to know how deeply beguiled the chameleon was, but Dell was avoiding him. The chameleon's forced defection hurt more than he'd expected, perhaps because she was a tie to Kai. Or maybe he'd grown accustomed to not being alone anymore. The only unbeguiled person he could speak with was Cullen, and Cullen spent most of his time with Benedict.

Dyffaya had not liked being told he must bind himself to their agreement. He'd agreed, but he'd thrown a hissy fit first. That hissy fit involved taking away their clothes and insisting they wear the *liarda* from that moment on. He'd also insisted that Benedict and Nathan swear to avoid all contact with each other, save for their fights. And he'd broken both of Nathan's legs.

Fortunately, Nathan's bones knit quickly. Five days was

ample time. Nathan knew it had been five days because Cullen had recast his clock spell.

Those five days corresponded to only half a day on Earth. Nathan knew that because he'd spoken with all the people Dyffaya snatched over that five-day period, and they'd all been taken on the same day. All eleven of them. Eleven people Dyffaya had snatched and beguiled and bedded, and who now sat on those flowery mounds chattering, eager to watch Nathan and Benedict try to kill each other.

Why bed them all? Why beguile them? Why bring them here in the first place? Nathan could think of many possible answers to those questions, none of which were convincing. There was a point to this lavish importation of forced worshipers. He hadn't a clue what it was, but the god had spent a great deal of power stealing these people. He had a use for them, something more than a simple craving for adoration.

Though he liked that well enough. "My beloved ones," Dyffaya said in a rich, mellow voice that carried beautifully. Everyone fell silent, even Cullen, though that was likely common sense, not adoration. "I am happy today." That brought applause. They were so glad their lord was happy. "I am happy to have you all with me, and pleased I can offer you such fine entertainment, something never before seen in any of the realms. Nathan, Benedict—enter the circle!"

Nathan walked forward silently. So did Benedict. The crowd oohed at them. Some were betting—men, mostly. The odds, he noted, were on Benedict.

Benedict met Nathan's eyes as they came together in the center of the circle. He nodded gravely. Nathan did the same. Together they turned to face the god.

Dyffaya flung up one hand—and a ball of eerie blue fire appeared in the very center of the circle, some twenty feet above the ground. "This," he announced, "is a fight to the death—but between fighters so superbly honed and skilled, such a trial may require more than one round. Today's round ends when one of our fighters kills the other, or when the balefire touches the ground. If both combatants are still alive at the end of the round, we will hold another bout tomorrow."

Nathan did not want to kill Benedict. He liked and respected the man, and Benedict's death would hurt so many people . . . but Nathan had been a weapon in someone else's hand before. As had Benedict, he was sure. They'd been willing weapons, their loyalty freely given—his to his Queen, Benedict's to his Rho. Now they were wholly unwilling, but they understood each other's choice. Benedict would kill to save Arjenie. Nathan would kill to save Kai.

He hoped hard that he wouldn't have to. Irrational, yes, but he wasn't simply hoping for a miracle. A little luck, maybe.

The third element. That was all he lacked. He'd sworn to fight Benedict. He hadn't sworn that Benedict would be his only target.

TWENTY-NINE

KAI stared at her grandfather in dismay. "The gods need *our* help?"

"They always do, little though most see this. More help than usual this time."

They were sitting at Isen's big wooden table. Plates, forks, coffee mugs, and crumbs from the chocolate cake Carl had provided were strewn about. Isen was in his usual chair, with Nettie and Cynna on his right. On his left were Pete—the tall, rangy man in charge of security with Benedict missing—Arjenie, and Kai.

Joseph Tallman sat directly across from Kai. Even people who couldn't tell a Native American from a Mexican American took one look at Kai's grandfather and thought "Navajo." That was partly the braids, but it was also his face, so much like the mountains he loved . . . desert mountains, where time stripped rather than softening, exposing bones both strong and severe. Today he wore his usual jeans, hiking boots, and blue cotton shirt, but he'd dressed up for the occasion. He'd added his silver conch-style belt.

He'd driven into Clanhome right at suppertime and hadn't wanted Isen to call her. Nor would he say why he was here until he heard from her, so she'd brought everyone up to date on the day's events over coffee and cake.

Then he'd said he was sent here, that the Upper World needed their help. Since she'd been hoping for the opposite—a little help from the gods against Dyffaya—she was taken aback. "I was . . . when I first saw you, I thought you here to deal with the god. Dyffaya."

"This is what you call the elf god? You were right."

"But—"

"Listen, *Yázhi Atsa*. Three nights past, my dreams sent me to the mountain. I climbed to where the veil is thin and prepared myself for a vision quest, that Doko'oosliid might speak clearly to me. Ha!" He set his mug down with a snap. "No quest needed. I was awake in the normal way when Coyote came strolling up to my camp."

"Coyote? In person?"

"He was being a man at the time, but I knew him. Anyone who meets that troublemaker knows him. What he told me, though . . ." He shook his head. "Trouble for sure, and not of his making for once. Unlike the other Powers, he spends much time walking our world. He was here when this elf god usurped those portions of the Upper Worlds which connect to this part of our world. Not," he added, "that this is truly what happened. It is a way to think of it, like seeing the letters c-a-t make you think of a cat."

"Yes, well, if you've never seen a cat, those letters just confuse you."

He grinned. "True."

"Your grandfather," Isen said politely, "has summoned the Diné to Clanhome. All the Diné."

Kai's mouth opened. And closed without her saying a thing.

"I have begun spreading the word," Joseph Tallman said. "So have the other *hataali*. Several of them have been troubled by dreams, which they understood when I told them what Coyote told me. I have also spoken to our president."

By "our president," Kai knew he meant the president of the Navajo Nation. The country's leader was always "the president." "And?"

Joseph shook his head. "Gary is a stubborn man." This was said with more admiration than resentment. Grandfather had a great appreciation for stubbornness, that being one of the chief virtues of a mountain. "But he agreed to send an email to those of the Diné on his list, which he claims is very complete, telling them I call them to me here. He will do this once he hears from our friend Isen that they are permitted on his land."

"You didn't ask? You started summoning people here without asking Isen?"

"Tch." Grandfather shook his head sadly. "Coyote has a bad effect on me."

Kai had wondered sometimes if Grandfather disliked Coyote because he'd been a little too much like him in his youth. Now she thought his inner Coyote wasn't all that inner, or all that much in the past. She glanced at Isen apologetically. Nokolai and the Navajo people had long and close ties, but you didn't invite thousands of people to your friend's territory without asking. "How many people are we talking about? I don't know how many Diné there are."

It was—surprise—Arjenie who had that information. "I don't remember the exact number, but around three hundred thousand are enrolled in the tribe. Three-fourths of them live in Arizona and New Mexico."

Kai's eyes widened.

"Not all will come," Grandfather said. "Some will not be able to. Money troubles, jobs, age, sickness, or family matters will keep them home. Others have drifted too far from our traditions to answer such a call."

"If even a tenth of them do . . ." She stared at him, appalled. "Grandfather, Nokolai doesn't have room for thirty thousand people!"

"They will camp, of course. Here or maybe at that state park, or in the national forest nearby. There are campsites there."

"Not enough! Not nearly enough. Even if they bring their own food and tents or campers or whatever, they'll need water. And sanitation. Sanitation is a huge issue for so many people."

Grandfather nodded. "Arranging such things will be a great task. We are lucky that Isen is good at organizing."

Isen made a small noise. It might have been a smothered laugh or a curse.

"But why? Why do you need all these people? What will you do with them?"

"Coyote didn't know why they are needed, just that they are."

Kai closed her eyes. "You want to invite thousands—tens of thousands—of people to descend on Clanhome based on Coyote's word, and he doesn't know what he's doing."

"He seldom does. But I did not yet tell you one thing." The craggy face softened. "My campfire was also visited briefly by another. *She* told me to do as Coyote says and call the People together. Coyote's word is not so reliable. Hers, I trust."

She? Who did he mean? "Changing Woman? Abalone Shell Woman?'

"Kai." He clucked his tongue. "Your grandmother."

Her grandmother had been dead nearly thirty years. "That shouldn't seem more unbelievable than you chatting with Coyote over your campfire," she said after a moment, "but it does."

"You are wise." He nodded and pushed back his chair. "And now I will go take a shower so Isen can ask if I am sane. He needs to know this before he gives permission."

"I'm sure I haven't said that," Isen murmured.

Grandfather chuckled, appreciating the joke, then turned and headed for the hall.

"I will borrow some of Joseph's directness," Isen said to Kai. "Is he sane? Did he really talk with Coyote and your grandmother?"

"I . . . his colors are clear." She'd seen the same white-streaked blend of turquoise and lapis, yellow ochre and granite that she always saw in his thoughts. Though maybe there'd been more of that pearly white than usual. "I saw nothing to suggest confusion or any mental problem I'm familiar with."

Isen sighed. "I was afraid of that. You haven't spoken with him since all this began?"

"I tried calling him yesterday. He'd already gone up on the mountain. I left a message, but just that I'd called, no details."

"There's been no mention of a chaos god in the news, but Joseph knew about Dyffaya. Not by name, but he knew a sidhe god had intruded on our world and was causing problems in both the Ordinary and the Upper Worlds. He told me Dyffaya uses up the space there that belongs to Changing Woman and that which should be Coyote's, if Coyote were ever to spend time in the Upper Worlds, 'the way he should.' Which apparently he can't do now, because his path to the Upper Worlds is cut off."

"It would be," Nettie said. "Coyote partakes of chaos pretty directly, so Dyffaya is a serious problem for him. Dyffaya must be siphoning off some of the spiritual energy that would normally go to Coyote. But Changing Woman, too, is tied to chaos. She's about transformation, giving birth to new possibilities—but the new either arises from chaos or causes it."

Isen glanced briefly at her. "Nettie wants me to agree to allow the Diné to assemble here. She believes this is necessary. She also believes that a great many people will answer Joseph's summons, either from respect or out of sheer curiosity. She declines to speculate on how many that might be. Neither she nor Joseph seem to understand how impossible it is to suddenly house—even in camps—what might turn out to be tens of thousands of people."

"The government should help," Cynna said suddenly. "No, listen—I know you aren't used to thinking of the government as helpful, given the way it's treated lupi in the past, but this time we can use them. If huge numbers of the Navajo are needed to deal with the disasters that this chaos god keeps springing on us, that's something the government ought to get behind. I'm thinking disaster relief. FEMA. They know how to set up sanitation and supplies for large numbers of people, right? The Red Cross, too, maybe—and that isn't a government deal, but if the president declares this a disaster area, that brings them in, doesn't it?"

"Perhaps," Isen said dryly, "but I don't have the president's private phone number."

"Ruben does."

KAI stayed up long enough to learn the results of two phone calls. Isen called one president, giving his permission for the Diné to gather here. Cynna called Ruben, who would speak with another president—one whose constituency was a thousand times larger.

It was eleven o'clock California time by then, two in the

morning on the East Coast. Ruben Brooks was lupus, though that was being kept secret for now; he didn't need the usual amount of sleep. The president, however, was a hundred percent human, and Ruben didn't plan to disturb her sleep, so they wouldn't find out the results of that call until tomorrow. But it just might work.

According to Cynna, Ruben's Gift had kicked in the moment she told him about Joseph Tallman's summons. He'd agreed that gathering the People was important, although he had no more idea than Coyote why. "He says he can't guarantee anything," Cynna had reported, "but people are getting spooked, and there's pressure on the president to do something. This is something."

After that, Isen, Pete, and Arjenie fell into a discussion of what to do about any of the Diné who showed up before the hypothetical federal assistance arrived. Grandfather began talking to Nettie and Cynna about Cynna's tie to the node, which he thought he could help with.

Kai felt like a selfish wimp for abandoning everyone, but she was too brain-dead to contribute. She told Arjenie she planned to put herself in sleep. In-sleep was a healing state that would rest her more completely than regular sleep, recharging her both physically and magically, but it was harder to wake from. If she were needed in the next couple hours, someone would have to come in her room and shake her.

Arjenie assured her that exhaustion was a predictable response to expending so much power. That was true, but it wasn't all the truth.

Kai hugged Grandfather one more time and headed first for the bathroom, then to the room she'd shared with Nathan. She went in, closed the bedroom door behind her, leaned up against it, and closed her eyes. Discounting the stalls of assorted ladies' rooms, this was the first moment she'd been alone all day. She needed to be alone . . . just her and her grief and her fear.

How could she need something so much when it felt so awful?

She pushed away from the door and began stripping. Her body felt heavy, her mind dull and dazed, but that didn't fool her. Being stupid with exhaustion often made it even easier for her mind to hop on its hamster wheel and go round and round, and she did not want to listen to herself tonight. Putting herself in-sleep would sidestep all those thoughts she did not want to think.

She opened the closet door and tossed the day's clothes in the hamper—which was empty, dammit. She'd forgotten that. Nathan had washed everything yesterday. She grabbed the tote he'd packed. The one he wasn't going to use after all, since the god hadn't allowed him to bring any luggage along.

The dark green T-shirt she pulled out was soft and familiar. He'd worn it in four realms—five if you counted Edge. He'd worn it back in Midland, Texas, when he was still a deputy sheriff, a friend, and a mystery to her, long before they left on her quests. There was a small singed spot on the right sleeve and a blackberry stain. The singed spot was a bad memory, but the blackberry stain made her smile. She pulled it on. If she'd had Nathan's nose, she might have been able to smell him. All she smelled was Tide.

The sheets hadn't been laundered, though. She shut off the light and climbed into bed. She slid over onto Nathan's side and put her head on his pillow and breathed in deeply. She'd trance in a moment, in just a moment . . .

KAI woke to darkness, her heart pounding. Dell wanted her. Needed her. Dell needed her to *come*.

She blinked, confused. Why would Dell send such a message? She knew Kai couldn't come to her. But oh, the loneliness—it was like when Kai first found Dell. The chameleon had been desperately alone then and . . . oh. Dell must have been dreaming. A nightmare. Dell had those sometimes, and they usually involved that terrible time when she'd lost her mage and been hurled to Earth, alone. Maybe the nightmare had been stirred into life by their separation.

Kai sat up, circling her up-drawn knees with her arms, and laid her head on her forearms. She ached still with the echoes of her familiar's loneliness. And with her own. She told herself she wasn't alone. Grandfather was here, and she had friends, people who cared . . . it didn't help. Her mind had jumped onto the story wheel and was spinning tales of disaster. Those that had already occurred. Those that might be happening now, because she didn't know what was going on with Nathan, did she? And those likely to happen soon because she didn't know what to do, how to stop a god. The vastness of her inadequacy swamped her along with all those tomorrows stretching into the bleak ever-after.

She turned her head to check out the time and grimaced. Four-thirty in the morning, the traditional time for despair. She ought to trance and put herself in-sleep, as she'd failed to do earlier, but she didn't think she could. Not without help. She threw back the covers and got up.

Long ago, when she'd had little control over her Gift and that little was lost entirely during thunderstorms, her grandfather had made her an herbal concoction that helped her put herself in sleep. She never used it anymore, but she still had some. She dug the little baggie out of her backpack, then pulled on yesterday's jeans because she needed boiling water and a cup.

The house was dark and quiet. Too dark for her eyes, so once she reached the great room and it wouldn't disturb anyone, she tossed a mage light into the air. It bobbed along behind her, dimmer than a flashlight, but ample for avoiding bumping into couches and chairs.

The kitchen was dark, too. It wasn't empty. Kai stopped on the threshold.

"I guess you can't sleep, either." Arjenie said. She wore a loose, belted robe and was holding a steaming mug of something. "Isen suggested I sleep here, and that sounded like a good idea, since I wasn't looking forward to climbing into the bed that's supposed to have Benedict in it. Want some tea? There's water in the kettle."

Kai lifted the baggie. "I brought my own mix. It helps me put myself in sleep when my damned mind doesn't want to let go."

Arjenie nodded in understanding. "It was bad dreams for me. You?"

Kai moved to the stove. A cheery yellow teakettle sat on one burner. She checked, decided there was enough water, and turned the burner on. "I don't know what I dreamed, but Dell had a nightmare."

"Um . . . you're sure she was asleep?"

"No, but it felt like other nightmares she's had. They don't come often, fortunately." She took a mug out of the cupboard and emptied the herbal mixture into it.

"Do you often share her dreams? And vice versa?"

"Not often. Now and then one of us accidentally draws the other one in, which is confusing to the one who didn't originate the dream. Chameleon dreams are very different from ours. But the nightmare . . . when that hits, she calls for me." Normally Kai was close enough to wake Dell when that happened. Not now. Dell would have to deal with her nightmare loneliness when she really was alone. Was Nathan with her? She hoped so. Surely they could bring each other a little comfort. "Would it help to tell me about your dream?"

"I don't think so. I don't want to talk about it."

Kai nodded, understanding that very well.

"Isen believes we'll get him back. Benedict, I mean." Her sigh was long and wistful. "It would be more reassuring if that wasn't what he's trained himself to believe."

"Trained himself?"

Arjenie nodded. "That's his coping mechanism. A long time ago he decided that the only way he could deal with putting his sons in danger—which he needs to do sometimes, you know, as Rho—was by believing they weren't going to die. No matter what, he believes they'll be okay. A while back I asked him how to do that, thinking it sounded better than my way of coping. He smiled as if he were horribly sad, yet amused at himself, too. 'Practice,' he told me. 'I have had ample practice. And after all, I have been right every time except one.' "

Cold fingers walked up Kai's spine. "What do you mean? Benedict and Rule are alive."

"I guess you wouldn't know. Isen used to have three sons."

Oh, shit. Shit. Kai turned away, feeling as if she might start crying over a tragedy she knew nothing about . . . except that Isen had experienced it. He knew what it was like when the worst happened.

The teakettle was humming urgently the way it did just before the water reached a full boil. She turned off the burner before it could start shrieking and poured the hot water into the mug. She rested her hand over the mug and murmured a few words in *Diné Bizaad*, using her breath to empower the words and her flesh to direct them.

Then she set a small plate on top of the mug to hold the heat in. It needed to steep awhile. "Your coping mechanism seems pretty effective." Arjenie had been so bright and pulled-together all day. "I wish facts did for me what they do for you."

"Oh, I wasn't talking about that. When things get really bad, I cope by falling apart."

"I haven't seen you do that!"

She cocked her head. "Now that you mention it, I guess I only did it once when you were around, and that was when Benedict was first taken. You were busy not falling apart, so you might not have noticed that I did. You're very bolstering, you know."

Kai snorted. "Not today. Aside from that young man my Gift insisted on, I haven't helped anyone."

"I didn't mean on-purpose bolstering from using your Gift. It's just the way you are, I think, though maybe you are that way because of your Gift. You don't go around expecting things from people based on what you think they are or ought to be. A person is always a person to you, not a type. It's very refreshing. Anyway, I fell apart three times today. No, three-and-a-half. The first time was when Benedict went missing, like I said. Then I just dissolved when they were carrying the injured people out of the federal building. The special agent did not know what to do, but José told him to give me a few minutes and I'd be okay. And I was, enough to keep going, anyway. Then when I went to bed tonight, I collapsed into tears like a popped balloon."

Kai had to know. "What was the half-fall-apart?"

"That was at the zoo. I was too busy to come completely unglued, so I sniffled a lot and kept going. The point is, I can do it over and over. Lots of falling apart and getting back up again, because what else can you do but get up? Sometimes sooner, sometimes later, but unless you slit your throat, you're going to end up on your feet again at some point. I figured that out after my mom died," she said matter-of-factly.

And that was the final thing—maybe the biggest thing—she and Arjenie had in common. They'd lost their mothers at about the same age. Kai had lost both parents in a car wreck and gone to live with her grandfather afterward. Arjenie's father—a part-elf sidhe—was still living, but he'd never been part of her life. She'd ended up with her aunt and uncle.

Kai could tell Arjenie things she didn't normally speak of. "Usually seeing Grandfather strengthens me. He's my rock. He's also the proof that I can be okay even if the worst happens. Only this time," she said very low, "seeing him reminded me that the worst can happen."

"It can, but it hasn't. You're doing that peering into the future thing. I can tell because that's what I've been doing, too, even though I know better. My four-in-the-morning glasses distort things every bit as much as my Pollyanna glasses. Maybe more. I don't suppose you need to hear that," Arjenie said with an apologetic smile, "but I can't help pouring words all over everything. I mean well."

"I know that," Kai said, and found she could smile again. "I wouldn't call you bolstering. You're . . . clear. All the way down. If I—shit." Her phone was chiming back in the bedroom. That couldn't be good news, not at this hour.

It wasn't.

THIRTY

MORGUES are quiet places at 5:10 in the morning. Kai's athletic shoes made no sound on the stairs. Neither did José's. The rest of the guards that Isen had insisted on sending waited in the public area on the first floor, but José refused to let her go anywhere without him. When she asked if he was going to start following her into the Ladies', he hadn't even smiled. After a pause he'd said, "Lily was attacked once in a public restroom."

"Don't even think about it," she'd told him.

She didn't mind his company here, though. Kai had never been to a morgue. The issue hadn't arisen in her previous life, and the sidhe handled such things differently. She was glad she'd persuaded Arjenie not to come. Dyffaya might have stopped tossing around assassin's fire for the moment, but he could start up again. Plus, Arjenie was still low on power after using it so much yesterday, while Kai was pretty much back at full strength. Kai's ability to recharge so much faster than normal had come as a surprise after Dell used body magic on her the first time. She'd remade Kai's torso according to the pattern she had—which was the one she'd used on herself. Inadvertently, Dell had changed Kai's cells so that they sopped up magic much like the chameleon herself did.

The attendant hadn't come with them, but he had given directions: "At the foot of the stairs go left. Dr. Wilson's office is two doors down." When she and José reached the foot of the stairs, there was no left. She could go straight or turn right. She glanced at him, eyebrows lifted—and heard voices from the hall on the right.

"Damned if I see the point in this," the woman said. "There's plenty of magic on her, but it's not death magic. It's not even a spell. You think I can't handle a simple spell to detect magic?"

"How the hell would I know?" That was Ackleford, irritated as usual. "You're supposed to be good. Probably you are. I sure as hell can't tell."

"Then why are we waiting around for some lying civilian—one who has some damn close ties to the case—"

"Because I want my goddamn sidhe expert to have a look before Wilson starts cutting. You don't have to wait. Go get your beauty sleep."

"You are one sexist son of a bitch, you know that?"

"True," Kai said coolly from the doorway. The office was small enough to be pretty full already, though it only held three people and the usual office stuff. Both special agents turned to look at her. "But he's not stupid. That's what people keep telling me, anyway, and I'm inclined to agree. You're Special Agent Stockman?"

The Unit agent was gaunt. Not just thin, but bony. Her hair was a dark, tidy cap threaded with a few strands of gray. Her thoughts were all sharp edges with a lot of crisp blues and greens, though a sullen red smoldered at their base. Resentment, maybe, or some other form of anger, but it was not a fresh emotion. Both the color and the place it originated suggested it came from some old wounding.

Her face showed none of that. Sharp gray eyes lingered a moment on the dagger sheathed at Kai's waist. "I am. And you're the sidhe expert. Dressed for the part, didn't you?"

Kai smiled in a way that showed her teeth. "My name is Kai Tallman Michalski. The vest and dagger aren't a costume." She looked at the third person in the little office, who was sitting behind the desk. He wore scrubs and a name tag.

"Dr. Wilson?" She moved forward and held out a hand. "You're going to do the autopsy?"

"So I was told." He was sour, perhaps about the time, but he stood to shake her hand. "I can't start until you do whatever it is you need to do, so I'd appreciate it if you could make it quick."

"I'll do my best."

Dr. Wilson came out from behind his desk. "We've got her in Room B. I'll show you."

As they left the little office, Karin Stockman saw José for the first time. "Who are you?"

"José Alvarez. I'm guarding Ms. Michalski."

"Arjenie Fox had bodyguards at the zoo. They were all lupi."

"Yes, ma'am. So am I."

"Huh. I met one of your people down in Texas. He was okay." With that, she headed down the hall after the doctor. Apparently she didn't have a problem with having a lupus at her back.

The surprising thing about the autopsy room was how much it looked like ones she'd seen on TV. She supposed television couldn't get everything wrong. Kai started for the woman laid out on the shiny metal table.

"Gloves!" the doctor called.

She stopped. "I can't. The charm I'll use needs skin contact with both me and the body. Is that a problem?"

"It's a health hazard. No open wounds, so perhaps HIV isn't an issue, but she could carry other toxins. I understand she vanished in a most mysterious way."

"I'll take my chances." Kai glanced at Ackleford for permission—which made Stockman's lips tighten.

"Go ahead," Ackleford told her.

Kai walked up to the table.

Britta Valenzuela did not look like she was sleeping. Kai had yet to see a dead person who did. She was still wearing the clothes she'd been abducted in—chocolate trousers and an orange tuxedo-style shirt. No visible wounds, but the whites of her eyes looked a bit yellow.

Her body had been found yesterday afternoon nearly fifty

miles away. Pure luck, that; a man hiking in Corral Canyon, part of the Cleveland National Forest, had spotted it. At first no one realized that she was the missing person from Fagioli. A morgue attendant made the connection a couple hours ago and called the Bureau's local office, which had passed the word to Ackleford. He'd called the Unit agent—it was her case now—and then he'd called Kai, asking her to meet them here.

Which Special Agent Stockman did not appreciate, apparently.

Kai dialed up her Gift and studied the body. There, yes. The faintest smudge of lavender clung to one temple, so faded and transparent she could barely see it even with her Gift on high. She dialed her Gift back to a normal level and dug in her pocket.

The charm she pulled out looked like an ornate silver brooch with a large, clear crystal, cabochon-cut. She laid it on Britta's forehead, keeping her fingers pressed to it while she whispered the phrase that woke it, then pulled her hand away.

The crystal glowed brightly, then faded. It pulsed five more times before the glow died entirely. "I'm sorry," Kai told the dead woman. "I have to lay this over your heart next." She unbuttoned the orange shirt, opened it, and was glad to see that Britta's bra was cut low enough that she wouldn't have to take it off. Kai didn't like touching the dead. It felt like an intrusion when they weren't present to give permission.

She laid the crystal between Britta's breasts, activated it with a different phrase, and withdrew her hand. This time the crystal changed color, shifting to a warm brown threaded with thin red veins that formed two runes, the top one simple, the lower one complex. Kai bent, frowning. The simple rune she knew. The complex one was unfamiliar. She took her phone out of another pocket and took a close-up shot of it.

When she straightened, she slipped both charm and phone back in their pockets and turned to Ackleford. "Britta had been beguiled or compelled prior to death. I can't tell which—the beguilement or compulsion was broken when she died, and there's only a tiny scrap still clinging to her flesh. That there's any remaining at all suggests a lot of power was involved. There's a lot of undifferentiated magic on her body, as Special Agent Stockman was saying when I arrived. In addition to that, someone has used body magic on her."

"I didn't find any hint of a spell," Stockman said sharply.

"Body magic is more like a Gift than a spell. All elves possess it to some degree. They can't all use it on others, but Dyffaya can." At least he could three thousand years ago.

Ackleford's eyebrows snapped down. "Can body magic be used to kill?"

"Oh, yes, but it probably didn't this time. I don't know what this body magic did, but according to my charm, it didn't kill her." The charm's brown color indicated body magic had been used in the past week or so, while the two red runes indicated whether it was a fatal alteration—no, according to the simple rune—and what had been magically altered. That was covered by the complex rune, the one Kai didn't know. "I may know what did, though it shouldn't have, not this fast. Magic sickness."

"What in the world is that?" Dr. Wilson asked. "I've never heard of it."

"You wouldn't have. In extremely high-magic realms or high-magic areas with a realm, the level of ambient magic can be so high it makes some people deathly ill. Humans without a Gift are the most susceptible. The amount of undifferentiated magic on Britta and the yellowing of her eyes are typical of magic sickness. The problem is, I'm pretty sure she shouldn't have died of it this fast." Nathan had warned Kai about magic sickness, but she thought he'd said it took three or four weeks to kill. Was she remembering wrong? Maybe there were exceptions.

The round little doctor was looking downright perky. "What would I look for that might confirm or disprove this?"

"If it was magic sickness, she would have experienced sudden multiple organ failure at the end. I don't know how you test for that."

Dr. Wilson chuckled. "Don't worry. I do."

Hearing about magic sickness had certainly improved the doctor's mood. Kai looked at the woman with the sullen red still simmering down low in her thoughts. "Why do you think I'm a liar?"

"I'd apologize for that, but you'd know I'm lying. Or so you claim."

Kai just looked at her. And waited.

Stockman tilted her chin up. "The Gift you claim to have doesn't exist—not in humans. I'll admit I don't know what's possible in other races. Either you're lying about your Gift or you're lying about your race."

"I've a trace of sidhe blood, but that's all it is—a trace. Although the sidhe are happy to use that as an explanation for my Gift. They like to take credit for things. They aren't always right, however. I ran into several sidhe in Faerie who don't think lupi exist. They've never seen one, so how can they be real?"

"You think I'm too stupid to accept the possibility of things I haven't personally encountered?"

"I don't know. You had your mind made up about me before we met. I'm wondering why. You can't be an idiot, or Ruben Brooks wouldn't have you in the Unit."

"We'll file that under 'none of your business.' "

"It's her ex," Ackleford said. "Bastard claimed to be some kind of special with the magic shit. Turned out he was a con man. A fake. Duped a lot of people."

Stockman rounded on him. Anger blazed high in her thoughts, but Kai could see the way she clamped down, controlling it. "You son of a bitch. That is not in my file."

"I've been in the Bureau a long time, know a lot of people. They don't all like me, but they'll talk to me. I've earned that." He held her eyes with his. "I heard you were bright, hard-working. Also heard you've got buttons, and the biggest one is about charlatans. But no one said you thought you were the only one who gets to decide who's a charlatan. I vouched for Michalski. You decided I was—what? Gullible? Hot for her? Stupid?"

Nothing showed on Stockman's face, but her thoughts roiled. She wants this man's respect, Kai realized. She wants it badly, and she blew it, and she knows that. "You're right," Stockman said, her voice low and tight. "I disrespected you. I'm sorry for it."

Ackleford's eyebrows shot up. He hadn't expected that. "I'm not the only one you disrespected."

Stockman's reluctance would have been obvious even if Kai hadn't been able to see her thoughts. "Oh, the hell with it," she said suddenly, and turned to face Kai. "I'm still dubious about you and I don't think civilians belong in an investigation. But I had no call to assume you were lying. It was unprofessional, and I apologize."

"Good enough."

"If you could take these personnel matters elsewhere," Dr. Wilson said disapprovingly, "I could get started."

Personnel matters? Kai's lips twitched. She told the doctor—pathologist?—she really needed to learn some of this stuff—that it had been good to meet him, and to call if he had any questions. She might not know the answer, but he could call. Then she had to write down her number for him.

Ackleford waited impatiently. As soon as she started for the door, he headed out it. Stockman, however, lingered to walk beside Kai. "That charm you used," she said as they left the autopsy room. "That's sidhe work?"

"It is. Depending on how it's used, it can detect magic on almost anything, but it's specifically geared for detecting magic on living things or people, and it works almost as well on the newly dead."

"It's not as accurate when used on a dead body?"

"It's accurate, but can't provide as much detail about the dead. For example, if there'd been a spell on Britta it would have signaled that, but it couldn't have told me what kind of spell. If I placed it on a living, enspelled person—or dog or cat, for that matter—it could tell me what type of spell was involved."

"Huh. Handy. I've got spells I can use to learn those things, but they take time and prep. Is it a one-shot?"

"No, I can reuse it, but priming and charging it takes a while." They'd reached the stairs. Kai started up first. "I'd wondered why you hadn't called me. Was that why? Because you thought I was lying?"

"You going to bring that up a lot?"

"I'm curious. You could have called me from the plane."

"I slept on the fucking plane. First sleep I'd gotten in forty hours." Unexpectedly she chuckled. "When Ruben pulled me into this case, I asked Ida to book me the longest flight she could find. She did, too."

Kai grinned as she reached the top of the stairs. There was a short hall and a big metal door that led to the waiting room where the rest of her escort was. "You're a Fire-Gifted, right?"

"You see that in my thoughts?"

"No, Arjenie told me." She might have guessed anyway. Karin Stockman had the mercurial temperament typical of those whose Gift was Fire. It wasn't a trait that made her an easy or obvious fit for law enforcement. "She said you'd been a city cop before the Unit recruited you. What drew you to it?"

"It's a family deal. My dad, my older brother, my grandad, they're all on the job. Or were. Granddad's retired, but my dad . . . hey. How'd you do that?" Suspicion ripened in her voice.

"What?"

"Get me talking about personal stuff. I don't do that on the job."

"It wasn't magic," Kai said dryly. "Promise." Why were people always surprised that someone wanted to get to know them? She pushed open the metal door.

"You weren't looking at me, so I guess you didn't see my thoughts. Or did you? It's not your eyes you use, so maybe your magical seeing works all the way around."

"That's something I've wondered about myself. Why don't I—or sorcerers, for that matter—'see' all 360 degrees instead of where we direct our eyes? Because you're right. My eyes shouldn't be involved, except that they seem to be. Maybe the vision center in my brain can't process the information my Gift brings me unless my eyes are involved."

Karin Stockman had stopped short. She was eying the three lupi who formed up around Kai. "Who the hell are all these people?"

"My escort."

"I thought Alvarez was your bodyguard."

"Three of them does seem like a lot, doesn't it? Isen insisted." Only a half-squad with her this time—José, Doug, and a man she hadn't met before named Kevin. "Looks like Ackleford has already left," she said as José moved to the glass doors at the front of the building. He flashed the palm of his hand in a "halt" signal and went out. "Why does he want us to stop?"

"We're to wait while he checks things out," Doug said. "He'll signal if things look okay."

"What's your connection to these lupi that they guard you?" Stockman asked.

"I guess they don't want me snatched or shot, both of which Dyffaya has tried. Isen's son was one of those snatched, you know, so they're probably hoping I can—oh, looks like we're clear to go." José had reappeared in front of the glass doors, flashing a thumbs-up.

"I am so ready for breakfast," Kai said as she pushed open the door. "Any of you know where we could go that's nearby? My treat." She glanced at the woman beside her. "What about you, Special Agent? Want to join us?" Stockman shot her a suspicious look, which made her grin. "I'm not planning any civilian onslaughts on—well, on whatever it is you think civilians imperil. You do eat, don't you?"

"I could use some coffee." Stockman's gaze shifted. "Ackleford's still here. We'll get him to join us. We can discuss the plan for today."

Something in the shape of the woman's thoughts made Kai suspect Karin Stockman had an unprofessional interest in Special Agent Derwin Ackleford. How interesting. "By all means."

The sun wasn't up yet, but the parking lot was well-lit. She could see Ackleford in his car. He'd lit a cigarette. Maybe that's why he'd been in such a hurry to leave the building. There were a handful of other cars in the lot, no doubt belonging to morgue employees. Funny how many thought-remnants lingered here . . . maybe not so funny. Strong emotions tended to peel off remnants, and visiting the morgue was . . .

She stopped. *That* wasn't a remnant. Remnants don't shift and change. "José. That dark car at the edge of the lot. It looks empty, but it isn't."

"Down!" he snapped—and took off.

Kai dropped before anyone could tackle her.

Two loud shots split the air, one right after the other.

José was running flat-out, so fast her eyes didn't quite believe what she saw. Someone leaped over Kai—Stockman, running toward the shooter just like that idiot José! The dark car at the edge of the lot suddenly shot forward, ignoring the exit to thump down from the curb onto the street.

So did Ackleford's car. He must have floored it. His dingy white Ford peeled out after the other car. First one squealed around the curve in the road, then the other. In moments they were both out of sight.

"Son of a bitch!" That was Stockman. She'd stopped and stood there with her gun out and no one to shoot.

Kai supposed that, theoretically, there could be multiple shooters, but it seemed unlikely. She pushed up onto her knees, looked around—"Doug!"

He lay flat on his back. His chest was covered in blood.

THIRTY-ONE

HE missed night.

Nathan lay on his stomach, his head pillowed on his arms, his face pressed into his forearm to make as much darkness as he could. The gash on his thigh had long since healed. He should force himself to sleep. He could do that, though he wouldn't sleep long. He was one of those who didn't sleep much in high-magic areas, and by his personal clock, he'd been here sixteen days now. Sixteen days and no nights.

It didn't help that, when he did finally sleep, the god whispered to him in his dreams. Dyffaya had made no attempts to persuade or corrupt Nathan when he was awake, but when he slept, the god whispered at him.

He could hear Benedict's breathing, each shallow, pained inhalation. Each careful exhalation. If he tried, he could hear the much quieter breath of the friend who sat with him. Cullen couldn't do much for Benedict other than be there, but Nathan remembered what it was to have a pack, and how much it helped to have your packmates' warmth when you hurt.

The clearing where Dyffaya had decreed his gladiators would stay was fifty feet long and about half that wide. A stream ran down the middle, ending in a small pond where they could bathe. Dividing Nathan from the man he was supposed to kill. The man he nearly had killed today.

Nathan's mind replayed the stroke again—the parry, his own riposte, Benedict's quick counter, beautifully executed.

The wrong counter. Nathan's blade had taken him in the lung.

Benedict might be Nathan's equal in unarmed combat. He was not Nathan's equal with swords. Not even close. Nathan had thought he'd gauged his opponent's skill level fairly well, but the man's speed and reflexes, combined with an instinctive knack for grasping the dimensions of a fight, had fooled him. Nathan had employed a trick that it was clear, in retrospect, Benedict had never heard of. It had been all Nathan could do to keep from skewering the man's heart.

Could a lupus heal from a heart wound? It was taking him so terribly long to heal the lung.

Nathan had known that lupi didn't heal as quickly as he. He hadn't realized how hard it would be to spend hours and hours listening to his victim—his friend—fight for breath. Benedict healed so *slowly*. Nathan lay motionless and listened, his hidden eyes wet. He'd thought he knew himself so well. Now he wasn't sure he could kill the man even if he had to.

A fine state of affairs when a hellhound didn't know if he could kill.

Dyffaya hadn't really minded when Nathan refused to follow through with a death-stroke after piercing Benedict's lung. He was enjoying himself too much to end the games early, and there was still one bout to go. The god had gone through the motions, calling a penalty on Nathan for "insufficient roughness," but Nathan's only punishment had been to receive a foul-smelling glop instead of the usual meal. The glop tasted as bad as it smelled, but it was high-calorie nastiness. Dyffaya wanted him fueled for the next bout.

The onc Nathan desperately didn't want to fight. At least it wouldn't take place right away. Dyffaya had agreed that it would be no challenge—and therefore not fun for him—if Nathan and Benedict fought before the lupus finished healing.

Benedict's breath hitched. Nathan heard Cullen's low murmur—an offer of water—and the other's grunted assent.

It was insane to wish himself in Benedict's place, punctured lung, slow healing, and all, just because that man wasn't alone. There was another lesson for him. Seemed he'd lost the knack of being alone. Isolated. Cut off from everyone and everything that mattered.

Cut off from Kai.

If only he could see her one more time. Hear her voice. Touch her. Oh, gods, yes, that's what he wanted. Needed. If only . . .

And there was foolishness, wandering among the if-onlys. He had survived the original sundering, he reminded himself, when he'd been parted from his Queen and trapped on Earth for so long. If he failed to survive this one, it wouldn't be loneliness that ended him. If he—

Some soft sound had him rolling from prone to crouched. Dell stood at the very edge of the clearing, halfway into the trees. She met his eyes, gave her head a single jerk—*come!*—and turned.

Nathan rose soundlessly and followed.

If he'd had to say why he heeded the call from one who'd become so thoroughly Dyffaya's creature, he might have pointed out that she was still Dell. That he owed her loyalty, and if she couldn't return it just now, that wasn't her fault. He might have shrugged and said, why not? He wasn't going to sleep anyway. He might even have admitted how ready he was for any excuse to leave that little clearing, and the slow, raspy breaths of the man he hadn't quite killed.

Dell's large, padded paws made it easy for her to move swiftly, yet in silence. Even he could move quickly without making a sound in this place, with no twigs or dried leaves on the glowing ground. It felt good to move instead of thinking. For a time he gave himself up to that simple pleasure, following the gray shape of the big cat through the black trunks.

In their shared silence, it was easy to know when they drew near what she wanted him to hear. She stopped, looking back to see if he heard what she did.

He did. The fleshy slap of sex was unmistakable, even at a distance. The participants weren't trying to be quiet about it. He raised his eyebrows at Dell.

She nodded once and melted off into the trees, heading

away from the unknown pair. Apparently she didn't want to be seen escorting him. What did Dell want him to see? Most likely one of those he heard was Dyffaya; the god spent a good deal of time at sex. He continued forward in careful silence.

Climax was observed with groans and gasps, followed by murmuring—and yes, one of them was Dyffaya. He recognized the voice that went with the god's statue-of-David form, though he couldn't make out the words. He continued to work his way closer, and the next time the god spoke, heard him clearly.

He was not speaking English. "Remind me why I don't bring you here more often."

A low chuckle, then: "Something to do with the amount of power involved . . . though you seem to have plenty to spare. I must be glowing, and not simply from your sexual skills, my lord, remarkable as they are."

Nathan froze—first in shock, then because if he moved at all, it would be to kill. He knew that voice, oh yes.

"I believe that was it. Still, it's lovely to be with one who's received the proper training. My girls and boys do their best, and I do believe that sincere effort should be rewarded, don't you? But even with my guidance they have much to learn. I fear my new people are terrible prudes."

"You'll woo them away from that."

"Sooner rather than later, I think."

"You mean—"

"You're going to need as much power as I can cram into you, my lovely one. It is time for my worshipers to, as they say here, come out of the closet. Rather a nice phrase, don't you think?"

A brief silence, then Dyffaya's lover said, "It will be as you wish, of course, but that vow you gave your pet hellhound complicates matters for me. If you could just make one more effort to snatch her—"

"I will, of course, but not before making my bow to the public. That will take a good deal of power, and I don't care to spend it on less important matters."

"Of course."

The god chuckled. "Don't look so glum. Surely your

ingenuity is not so impoverished that her death is the only solution you can come up with?"

"I—oh! Yes, that feels lovely. I suppose I can . . . of course I can. I . . . mmm, yes. Is there time for another round?"

"Time," Dyffaya said, "is one thing I never run out of."

THE next "day"—an interval marked by Cullen's time-telling spell—Nathan waited by the stream that divided their camp.

He'd run for hours last night. Running was the one boon of this captivity. Because they couldn't escape the godhead or the god's awareness—because every direction took them nowhere—they were free to run. The one place that was banned was the site where Dyffaya kept his other guests. The ones who served as audience.

The combination of running and anger had cleared his head wonderfully. He'd come to several conclusions. First, while it was possible he'd been lured there on purpose and allowed to observe for some inscrutable reason, he didn't think so. He was beginning to think there was something wrong with the god—something more than chaos-wrought insanity, that is. Elves grew more devious and subtle over the years, yet Dyffaya seemed to have shed subtlety . . . or lost the capacity for it.

If so, Dell wasn't as beguiled as she seemed, and Nathan had been able to eavesdrop without Dyffaya's knowledge. Maybe when the god was engaged in sex, he didn't pay attention to other things.

He'd also realized how badly he was handling isolation. His long sundering during the years when he was cut off from Faerie and his Queen had been lonely. Desperately so, at first. He'd had it easy before that, hadn't he? As a hellhound, he'd had his pack, the Huntsman, and later, his Queen. He hadn't had to work at finding connections to others. But he'd learned. If he hadn't found the heart-deep connection he longed for, not until Kai, he'd learned to make other connections. He'd found people who mattered even though they weren't his.

Now he wasn't allowed to speak with anyone except Cullen. And Cullen was not happy with him.

That had to change. Not simply because he needed it, but because Dyffaya had so carefully arranged Nathan's isolation. He'd pitted Benedict and Nathan against each other because it entertained him, certainly, but also because he wanted their tiny group divided. If Dyffaya wanted them divided, they needed to unite. To do so, they had to be able to communicate without the god knowing. However risky it might be.

Nathan waited by the stream for two hours before Cullen approached with two cups. Dyffaya had provided them each a cup and a blanket when he sent them to this clearing. His little joke was the size of the cups—each one held only a few ounces, so they had to be refilled from the stream frequently. After not-quite-killing Benedict, Nathan had given Cullen his cup so Cullen wouldn't have to make as many trips to the stream. Dyffaya had promptly vanished it. Didn't want his joke spoiled.

Nathan didn't know how Benedict felt about him now, but Cullen's feelings were clear. The sorcerer might understand intellectually why Nathan fought. He might realize that Nathan hadn't intended to wound Benedict so grievously. But the intellect often makes a poor bridle for emotions. Cullen eyed Nathan coolly and didn't speak as he knelt to fill the cups.

"How's he doing?" Nathan asked. The moment Cullen looked up, Nathan sent his fingers flying through a trade-tongue phrase. Cullen wouldn't know it, but maybe he'd get the idea . . .

"He hurts," Cullen said shortly. But he watched Nathan's hands, then shook his head.

"I guess he can't speak yet, but he seems able to let you know what he needs." Nathan's fingers formed another phrase.

"More or less." This time Cullen's hand made a couple of signs.

Which, of course, Nathan didn't recognize, but his heart lifted. It seemed Cullen understood what Nathan was carefully not saying. He shook his head again—*no, I don't understand you, either.* "I don't know how long your people take to heal. What are the *ABC's*—" delicate stress on that—"of lupi healing?"

Cullen frowned, then said slowly. "Not *all* of us heal at the same rate." As he spoke, his right hand formed a fist with the thumb up.

Nathan mimicked the sign, which he hoped stood for the letter A. Cullen was bright, very bright . . . "*Attitude* makes a difference, of course."

"Of course. *But* . . ." Cullen held four fingers up and together with his thumb tucked into his palm. "*Benedict* could tell you more than I can about how fast he'll heal."

Surely Cullen meant that was the letter B. Nathan copied it and spoke with the same slight emphasis. "*Benedict* can't talk at the moment."

"Then I *can't* tell you much." His hand shaped a semi-circle, clearly a C.

Elated, Nathan repeated it. "You *could* make a guess."

"At least a *dozen days*." Index finger extended, thumb touching the other fingers.

They made it halfway through the alphabet before Cullen stood, admonishing Nathan obliquely to practice. Nathan was delighted to do as he'd been told, silently rehearsing the letters he'd learned while he worked through his asanas.

He was taking a chance, yes. One he thought justified, though he couldn't explain why to Cullen, not yet, not with only half the alphabet available to him. But if Dyffaya acquired languages the same way Nathan's Queen did, he did so through a spell only an adept could master. It was a complex and difficult spell, and Nathan knew little about it, but he'd always heard it needed only that a few sentences be spoken in the adept's hearing for the spell to capture a new language.

"Spoken" being the key. As far as Nathan knew, the spell did not work on sign languages.

He had one example to base that on. Despite its name, trade-tongue didn't involve the tongue at all. It was perhaps too crude to be considered a true language, consisting as it did of only sixty-five signs. Those who traveled between realms often learned those signs in case they needed to communicate with someone who spoke a language they didn't know and for which they lacked a translation charm or spell. Many of the lower classes learned it, too, since they usually couldn't afford the charms.

The point was, they did have to *learn* trade-tongue. No one had ever been able to devise a spell or charm to acquire it without effort.

Teaching Cullen trade-tongue had been out. It hadn't changed much in millennia, so Dyffaya probably knew it. And Nathan didn't know American Sign Language—but Benedict did. Nathan had seen him training Nokolai fighters, using sign to direct them. What he hadn't known was whether Cullen knew ASL, too.

Thank God he did. At least, he knew the alphabet, which was all Nathan wanted to use. That was a way of hedging his bets. They'd be signing English words, so, effectively, they'd be using a new alphabet, not an entire new language. The god might well have a trigger to alert him if they started speaking a different language. Nathan didn't know if it was possible for a trigger to detect an unspoken language like ASL, but better safe than sorry. Besides, it would be easier and faster to learn just the alphabet.

He wished he'd thought of this sooner. He hoped it hadn't occurred to Dyffaya, that the god wasn't even aware of the ASL alphabet. He hoped even harder that Dyffaya hadn't been watching them just now. That was the biggest risk—that while Nathan learned the ASL alphabet, the god would learn it right along with him.

Nathan had an idea for how to lessen that risk. It was time to find Dell, who was by Dyffaya's side so much of the time. Who would know when the god was engaged in sex, and hopefully preoccupied.

THIRTY-TWO

KEVIN called for José. Kai knelt beside Doug and ripped open his shirt. She couldn't clearly see the entry hole, but she saw where blood pumped up with each heartbeat—not the chest, she realized, but just below, and dead center. No telltale air bubbles, so probably the lung wasn't involved.

Her hands knew bodies better than her mind. She used one to trace musculature and bone and narrow down the possibilities. "Probable damage to the diaphragm, possible damage to the liver, possible damage to the spine. Depends on what the bullet did after it entered. Internal bleeding—"

"That won't last," Kevin said quickly. "Bleeding's the first thing our healing deals with."

"That will help."

Doug groaned. His eyelids fluttered as his thoughts shifted to a new pattern—one she'd seen several times now. "I think he's trying to Change. Should I stop him?"

"What?" Kevin looked at her in alarm. "You can do that?"

"I can make him sleep."

"Do it," José said as he skidded to a stop beside her.

Kai reached out in a way that had nothing to do with the hand still resting on Doug's chest, yet required that contact.

Doug's face eased as he fell into sleep. "It's regular sleep," she warned the others, "not the healing sort that Nettie uses."

"Will he wake if we talk?" José asked.

"No."

"How long can you keep him asleep?"

"Hours, if I stay in contact."

"Good. That will help. Kevin, call Isen and report." With that, José faced out once more. He'd drawn his gun at some point and held it loosely now, his eyes scanning the area.

"I've called it in," Karin Stockman said. She was slightly winded. "Ambulance on the way. How is he? Can we move him? We're not secure out here."

"No. There may be spinal damage." Kai repeated her earlier guesses about what might have been damaged.

"Huh. You sure? You're not a doctor."

"Physical therapist. I know where the parts are and how they fit together." Plus, she'd had some hands-on experience with wounds in the past eighteen months, her own and others'. "José, did you see anyone in that car?"

"No," he answered without turning around. "It was pretty damn weird, too. Even when I got close and the car took off, I could have sworn there was no one in it to steer."

"Shit. Well, that explains why Doug said the shooter wasn't human. Looks like my biases nailed it, after all."

"What is that supposed to mean?" Stockman demanded.

"There's an elf right here on Earth who's trying to kill me."

HOSPITALS did not all look the same. The one in Aléri was planted in a huge tree. Literally planted. While elves sometimes built homes in trees, those were considered temporary fancies—something that might last no more than fifty or a hundred years. They liked to grow more permanent structures out of the tree. Kai had also seen a hospital that looked like a lumpy meadow, the "rooms" nothing more than dips in the ground. She'd stayed in one that had been carved from rock by gnomes, deep underground.

This wasn't the first time some elf had decided he preferred her dead. Fortunately, this one kept missing. Thanks to the lupi. "That's twice."

"Hmm?" They were in the ER. She stood on one side of Doug's narrow bed. José stood on the other. For once he wasn't faced out, looking for threats. Instead his gaze stayed on his friend's face.

"Twice you've saved my life."

He snorted. "I didn't spot the shooter. I didn't have a clue she was there. You did. I didn't stop her, either. She got away clean."

Touch of bitterness there. Understandable. "When you ran straight at her *like a damned idiot*, you spooked her into firing at you instead of me." Which was why Doug lay in that bed, sleeping soundly, with her holding his hand to make sure he stayed that way. The two shots Kai had heard had been snapped off more to dissuade José than truly aimed. It was pure luck one of them had hit anyone.

Bad luck, for Doug. The bullet had taken out a chunk of his spine. If he'd been human, he'd be paralyzed for life. As it was, if he made it through the surgery he'd probably do fine. "It's a debt I can't repay, not to any of you, but I won't forget it."

"There's no debt."

"You may see it that way. I don't."

He shook his head, looking at her the way her sixth grade teacher used to when she got conjunctions and prepositions mixed up. "Is Pete indebted to you for the help you've been giving him? How about the others messed up by Miriam and that damn knife—do they owe you for your help?"

"That's different. Mindhealers don't ask for or accept payment."

"You did what you could because it was needed. So have we."

"Listen to José," a deep voice rumbled from out in the hall. A second later Isen strode into the tiny room, leaving some of his men in the hall. The Rho would, of course, be guarded. "He's right. You're *ospi*, you and Nathan. Clan-friends. Which means Nokolai is allowed to help you. It's very elfin of you, you know, all this talk of debt."

She smiled in spite of herself. Isen knew exactly where to aim. "Maybe the elves aren't wrong about everything."

"A remarkable concession. So." Isen moved up and José stepped back, allowing his Rho to look down at his wounded man. Isen laid a hand on Doug's shoulder and spoke to the sleeping man. "I'm here now. You've done well, very well. You're needing surgery, they tell me. Nettie is discussing it now with the surgeon. You'll do well with that, too, and I'll stay by you to be sure of it."

"Wow."

Isen glanced at her. "You observed something?"

"His thoughts calmed down so much. Our minds don't shut down when we sleep, but sleeping thoughts look different from waking thoughts. His have had a lot of pain and agitation, and he kept trying to wake up. Only now he isn't."

It was, she gathered, a big deal for Isen to leave Clanhome. Normally his heir had hospital duty when that was needed, but Rule was on another continent. José had assured her Doug would do much better once his Rho arrived. She hadn't understood why. Nettie, yes—clearly Doug needed her skills, both as physician and as healer. Anesthetics didn't work on lupi, and they had a habit of attacking people who cut them open. Sometimes Nettie operated herself, but more often she took the place of the anesthesiologist, holding her patient in sleep, advising the surgeon on the quirks of operating on someone whose body would try to heal the incision during the surgery.

But Kai would keep Doug asleep until Nettie took over, so how could Isen's presence help? Doug wouldn't even know he was there.

Except that he did. Sound asleep, he'd responded to his Rho's voice by relaxing like a babe held close in his mother's arms. "I don't suppose you're going to tell me what you did."

"Sometimes the best thing we can do is show up."

"I didn't think so."

"They'll be coming to prep Doug for surgery shortly. Before they do, I'm hoping you'll explain why you're convinced the shooter is an elf. Kevin's account lacked some details."

Change of subject. Okay. "Because the shooter was invisible. That's an illusion only elves and a few half-elves can cast."

"You believe it was an illusion, not what Arjenie does?"

"If it had been someone with Arjenie's Gift in that car, I'd never have noticed her thoughts. When Arjenie's using her

Gift I can see her thoughts if I put enough effort into it, but I have to be looking for them. I noticed the shooter's thoughts without trying, so it wasn't some version of don't-notice-me."

He nodded. "You refer to the shooter as 'she.' Can you distinguish male from female from the way their thoughts look?"

"No. Doug said the shooter on the church roof was female and not human. It's possible we have more than one elf shooting at me, but the simpler explanation usually fits. Which would be one shooter. A female elf."

"It's an assumption, then, but one with solid footing. If we—" He broke off, frowning. "Let him pass, Rick."

A moment later, Derwin Ackleford strode into the room. "My apologies, Special Agent," Isen said. "The usual rule when I'm away from Clanhome is to discourage those who aren't clan from getting too close."

"Never mind that shit." Ackleford scowled at Kai. "The city cops have arrested Stockman. I don't know who gave that damn order, and it won't stick, but untangling it will take time we don't have. Not when there's a warrant being issued for you, too."

"What?"

"The four wits, the ones that damn god's got compelled and beguiled and whatever the hell else. They're gone. Some asshole is blaming Stockman. I don't know what they think they have on you. Come on. We need to be gone thirty minutes ago."

"I can't leave yet. As soon as Nettie can take over—"

"Artie, bring me the sleep charm," Isen said, then to Kai, "Cynna provided one, just in case."

"I didn't think lupi could use spells or charms. Except for Cullen, that is."

One of the men squeezed into the little room and handed Isen a flat silver disk the size of a half-dollar. "Cullen makes these so non-spellcasters can use them. Go," he told her—and licked the charm and set it on Doug's forehead, leaving his hand over it.

A spit-activated charm? That was . . . ingenious, she decided. Cullen kept having to reinvent the wheel because there weren't any elves around for him to learn from and copy. The results were intriguing. She wanted to ask him how—

"Come on," Ackleford said impatiently.

Right. She did not want to be arrested. "Where are we going?" she asked as they hurried from the room. "Should I—wow. Six of you?" she said to one of the men who were obviously Isen's guards. They took up a lot of room in the hall.

"Twelve," he said laconically. "The other squad's patrolling."

How did you patrol in the emergency department? She didn't ask. No time. As they left the cluster of men behind, however, one stayed with them. "José, what are you doing?"

He didn't answer out loud, but his expression managed to convey entire sentences. He was assigned to protect her. She was leaving, so he was, too. What part of that was hard to understand?

She huffed out a breath.

"Turn off your phones," Ackleford ordered. "Both of you."

"I've read," José said, "that they can track a cell phone even when it's turned off."

"Those assholes at the NSA, maybe, if they've inserted a Trojan. SDPD can't."

They'd reached the double doors where ambulances unloaded their patients. Fortunately, since Ackleford didn't seem likely to slow down, no one was being brought in at the moment. "Car's over here," he said, veering right.

"Isn't it illegal to park in the ambulance zone?"

He ignored that. "How come just one of you?" he asked José.

"Kevin's not good in small, closed spaces."

"I'm not crazy about jail, either."

"He's *really* not good in them."

"Might not come to that. Michalski isn't a fugitive yet." He clicked the locks on his car.

José climbed in back. Kai got in the front. The car smelled like an ashtray. "You haven't said where we're going. I'll need some privacy. I have to trance lightly to set the charm. A restroom would work."

"What charm?"

"The Find charm, of course. I'm not Cynna. I can't just Find someone." Ackleford hadn't come and whisked her away because he was worried about her. He wanted her to Find the missing witnesses. "Not that you've asked if I can do it, but if you had, I'd say that yes, I probably can, but it may take a lot of driving around. The charm only reaches about three miles."

One corner of his mouth kicked up a fraction of an inch in an Ackleford-style grin as he pulled out of the illegal parking spot. "I'm beginning to like you, Michalski."

THIRTY-THREE

ACKLEFORD lit a cigarette as soon as they were on the way, heading for a nearby McDonald's.

"I'd rather you didn't smoke," José said.

"Ask me if I give a fuck." He drew smoke deep in his lungs like a drowning man coming up for air. "Could this elf who keeps shooting at you have made herself look like Stockman?"

"It depends on her skill level and on other variables, such as whether she was able to get hold of some of Karin's hair or skin. Would she need to look exactly like Karin?"

"Probably not exactly. Far as I know, no one at the station has ever met Stockman."

"Then yes, she could probably make it work. The features would have been only an approximation. She wouldn't have had Karin's walk or mannerisms, and it's unlikely she'd have had Karin's voice. Aural illusions have to be cast separately, and voice-matching is supposed to be tricky. But if no one there knew what Karin was supposed to sound like, that wouldn't matter. I'm assuming everyone at the station was human?"

"Far as I know."

"Then the problem with scent wouldn't arise."

"What problem with scent?"

"Illusions don't include scent. Well, I'm told the Queen of Summer can cast a scented illusion, but no one else can, not even her sister. But that wouldn't be a problem unless there were lupi around." Or Nathan. She tucked that thought away in a private place. He was alive. He hadn't been Dyffaya's prisoner long, after all, and she had to believe he was okay, or she wouldn't be able to do what she needed to so.

Ackleford stubbed out his cigarette and promptly pulled out another one. "What about the ID? Could she have illusioned that up, too?"

"It depends on . . . never mind. You don't want details. Yes, that's possible, again depending on a number of variables, but most of the older elves can carry two illusions simultaneously. If she's good enough to cast invisibility, she can probably carry two illusions." Kai frowned, thinking it over. "There's another possibility that doesn't involve her. One or more cops could have been corrupted or persuaded by Dyffaya into letting the witnesses go and lying about it."

"I don't see how it could be done with just one guy. Probably have to be several."

"What happened, anyway? I need to know what you know."

"Not much." After the shooting at the morgue, he said, he and Stockman had gone to the local FBI office. They'd barely gotten the coffee brewed when four cops showed up with a warrant for Stockman's arrest. He couldn't get anything out of the arresting officers, but after they left he made some phone calls.

"That's when I found out that my wits are missing. Funny how no one let me know about that. Supposedly, Stockman released them on her authority as a Unit agent. The timing's tight but possible. Barely. Stockman's supposed to have been at the station around 4 A.M. I met her at the morgue at 4:45."

"What was she charged with?"

"Interfering with an investigation."

"Since it's her investigation, that would be hard to do."

He grunted. "When I called Brooks, he hadn't heard from her yet. That bothered me. I made a couple more calls, found out about the warrant in the works for you. Sounds like someone's trying to clear the decks of you woo-woo folks. Just to be clear, though—could Stockman have done like they claim because she was under some kind of compulsion shit? Maybe not remember it?"

"A compulsion might have evaporated after she acted, but . . ." Kai consulted her memory of Stockman's thoughts at the morgue to be sure. "No. I'm sure she hadn't been under compulsion recently when I saw her at the morgue. Compulsions do damage. I would've seen that in her patterns, especially if it tampered with her memory. I'm pretty sure the same goes for mind control, but—"

"What the hell do you mean? Isn't mind control what we've been talking about?"

Kai explained the difference between mind control and compulsion.

Ackleford pulled into the parking lot at Mickey-D's. "I hate this magic shit."

THERE was a brief argument about her vest before they went in. Ackleford said she stuck out like "a goddamn sore thumb in that thing," which was true, but Kai didn't want to take it off. José agreed—and pulled off his T-shirt. He ripped off the sleeves, put it back on, and used what was left in an almost-empty soda can he found to dampen his hair and slick it back. Then he borrowed a pen from Ackleford and asked Kai to draw some kind of design on his face. "Tribal stuff, if you can. Or runes. Something weird."

"Uh—okay. Why?"

"So you and I look like we're together. That makes Ackleford the odd one out, especially in this neighborhood. People notice the thing that doesn't belong. They'll remember him more than you."

She looked as if she fit with a guy wearing a wife-beater with a pretend-tat on his face? Kai shrugged and drew a sidhe rune for good luck on his cheek. Just for the hell of it, she fed a trickle of power into it. Luck was the province of patterners, not mindhealers—or anyone else, for that matter. Patterners could read and sometimes manipulate the probabilities, which were not going to be affected by a simple rune.

But it couldn't hurt. God knew they needed some luck.

Maybe it worked—the costume, not the rune. They drew some glances when they went in, but the gazes that lingered were on the man in the rumpled suit. Only suit in the place, she noticed, and most of the faces here were as dark as hers or José's. Ackleford stood out.

Most people used the drive-through at this hour, so the place wasn't crowded. There was a pair of moms accompanied by five little ones, an old man sitting alone, a trio of teens, a few men in various versions of work clothes. And most of them were anxious. Kai saw that clearly in their thoughts. Some cloaked fear with anger, like the two men who came in while she and the others were waiting on their food. One man blamed the chaos events on, "all this gay marriage shit. Upset the natural order and this is what happens."

The other one told him not to be an asshole. That didn't make his companion happy, but it cheered Kai up a bit.

Say what you might about Mickey-D's, they were quick. Kai ate fast, washing down fat and carbs with surprisingly decent coffee. Nothing like Fagioli, of course, but . . . "Shit. I need to warn Arjenie. If someone's trying to get rid of everyone who can help with the magical end of things—"

"I'll call Isen," José said. "He'll take care of it."

"Keep your damn phone turned off," Ackleford said.

"It's a prepaid," José said. "Not my regular phone. Bought with cash. It's policy now for the leader of an outside squad to have one."

"Why the hell would that be policy?"

José just smiled and tapped in a number.

Ackleford scowled and looked at Kai. "What do you know about—hell." His phone was dinging. He took it out.

She frowned. "Why haven't you turned off your phone?"

"Because they aren't looking for me."

"You can't be sure of that."

"Yes, I can. I know a lot of people. Shut up now."

While José filled Isen in, Ackleford identified himself to whoever had called him; listened, scowled, asked a couple questions that didn't tell Kai a thing, then said, "Good job. Stay on it, and find out more about that fire." A pause. "How the hell do I know? Maybe nothing. Find out anyway." He disconnected. "Nieman found out who's after you and Stockman.

Assistant Chief Franklin Boyd." His scowl deepened. "Boyd's a good guy. Territorial as hell, but a good guy. I don't get it. Something convinced him that you put a compulsion on Stockman. That's how he got the warrant for her—by claiming she's under outside control and is therefore dangerous."

"That's a handy circular argument. Stockman's guilty because I am. I'm guilty because Stockman is."

"Yeah, but they've got at least one wit for what Stockman's alleged to have done. Nothing ties you in except that you're weird, and judges like to have more than that to issue a warrant. Boyd's having trouble getting one, but he's put out an APB to pick you up for questioning. We need to move. Go do your thing with that charm."

"In a minute. What was that about a fire?"

"Nieman heard gossip about a fire at Boyd's house last night. Small one. He had it out by the time the fire department got there. Probably doesn't mean anything, but the timing makes me itchy."

"Dyffaya's good with fire, but . . . no one's missing, I take it?"

"Not that anyone's heard."

A small fire didn't sound like a chaos event. The amount of power a chaos mote generated made for big, splashy fires. "If Boyd's doing what Dyffaya wants . . . Compulsions and mind control need some kind of contact. Normally that means face-to-face, but we're dealing with a god, so. . . . but I don't see how he could set compulsions long-distance. Mind control, maybe. The chaos motes carry enough of Dyffaya that he can probably use one to take over someone. Or maybe he can out-source that—place a bit of himself in one of his followers, who transfers it to the person he wants to control. But mind control requires him to stay in contact with the subject, which limits the attention he can give to other things, so it seems like he'd prefer to use compulsions—only I don't see *how*." But he had, somehow, hadn't he? He'd beguiled and compelled the hell out of the four young people who were missing.

Kai rubbed her face. Shit just kept *happening*. Her brain felt like a worker bee—busy-busy-busy, but it was all buzz, no honey. "There's always corruption and persuasion. Those aren't face-to-face deals. Dyffaya may be low on spiritual power. He isn't out of it. He could've persuaded or corrupted Boyd."

"Whatever he's done to Boyd, we need to find those missing wits. And I need to call Brooks, update him. Go get that charm working. "

"Right." She stood—then frowned when José did, too. "You've got to be kidding." They'd taken the table closest to the restrooms. José could guard her just fine from here.

"If I wait at the door, it might discourage others from going in and interrupting you. How long does it take?"

"Setting the charm only takes a minute. Getting myself into trance may take five or ten." She was good at trance normally, but in a public place, without Nathan or Dell to stand guard, and with the way her brain was buzzing . . . "Make it fifteen."

THE ladies' room was a two-staller. Kai went into the one with the wheelchair emblem, which was roomy enough for her to sit on the floor. José's wife-beater and pretend tat might discourage some people, but a woman with a small child who needed to go *right now* was going to push right on past him.

Her Find charm was fairly sophisticated. You could set it in three ways: use a piece of what you sought to Find the rest, such as a hair from the person you wanted to Find; use one thing to Find more of the same; or, if you were good at patterns, you could mentally supply the pattern you needed the charm to hunt for. Kai wasn't particularly good at patterns, but there was one she knew really well—the trigger designed to blow up the minds of Dyffaya's beguiled followers.

Some people could set a pattern into the charm without trancing. Kai couldn't. She spared a second to thank someone, somewhere, for the relative cleanliness of the floor, then sat on it tailor-style, took the charm off her necklace, and held it in one palm. She whispered the words that, along with a trickle of power, woke it. Then she paid attention to her breath . . for about three breaths, then her mind was off and running.

So much kept happening so fast . . . sure, Dyffaya was a god, but he was a little-g god. He wasn't omnipotent. Not even close. How was he orchestrating everything? What did he *want?*

Maybe he was just stirring things up. God of chaos, after all.

Back to her breath, dammit. In, nice and slow. Out . . .

First he wanted to grab Kai. Then to kill her. Now he just wanted her arrested. How did that make sense? And why Stockman? Was her arrest a device for trapping Kai? Maybe he'd decided to get Kai put in jail so she'd stay put until he could send someone to kill her. And that was just crazy, which Dyffaya was supposed to be, but why take such a roundabout path to his goal?

Maybe that wasn't his goal. Maybe he'd achieved exactly what he wanted when Boyd had the Unit agent arrested. What did that do for him?

What did any of it do for him?

Look at what else he'd done. Grabbed people, yes, and aside from Nathan she had no idea what he meant to do with them, but look at how he'd done it—in the most flamboyant way possible. Scattered chaos far and wide . . . in ways that really got everyone's attention. In ways that scared people. Hadn't she seen that in everyone's thoughts? No one had a clue how to stop him, and maybe that, too, was the point. He was making it clear that he could do whatever he wished—and that the people who were supposed to protect the country were helpless to stop him. Helpless, clueless, out of their league.

Over and over she'd circled back to the fact that they were going up against a god, and yet she'd missed the obvious.

What do gods want?

Worship.

Nowadays you heard a lot more about the love of God than the fear of God, but that hadn't always been true. Love was one approach to worship, but fear worked, too. Dyffaya wanted—needed—people to worship him, and fear was faster and easier to evoke than love. He'd arranged Stockman's arrest because she made a great symbol. Unit agents had one hell of a lot of authority. They'd been given it right after the Turning, when everyone was scared shitless, and Congress had gone overboard. Rumor said that a single Unit agent could call in the Army if necessary. As far as Kai knew none of them ever had, so maybe that wasn't true, but everyone knew they had tremendous authority. Plus everyone knew that Unit agents were Gifted. They knew how to use magic in a world where, up until the Turning, some people had decided magic didn't exist.

Stockman stood for everything the government was doing or could do to oppose Dyffaya. And depending on which story you believed, he'd either corrupted her or he'd swept her out of his way. Either way, he'd proved his power.

What she needed to do was serve Dyffaya up with a big, public defeat. Maybe the way to do that was to stop him from using his followers for . . . well, whatever he had in mind. She might not know what that was, but he'd needed them out of jail for it, hadn't he? Which meant she needed to get them back in jail, which meant she'd damn well better Find them.

Kai took a slow, careful breath. Another . . . This time she slid into trance easily. Moments later, she'd imprinted the charm with the pattern. It didn't light up. That would be too easy. They'd have to get within three miles for it to start cueing her which direction to take. But it was warm, which meant it was active.

When she left the restroom, José was leaning against the wall. Grinning.

She looked at him, eyebrows raised. "What?"

"I'll let him tell you," he said, straightening.

Ackleford wasn't grinning. For once he wasn't scowling, either. He looked . . . horrified.

"What is it?"

"That bastard. He's batshit nuts, you know that?"

"Dyffaya?"

He gave her a disgusted look. "Ruben Brooks. The man's insane. I don't know how the hell he talked me into it."

"Talked you into what?"

"He had this feeling. A strong feeling, he said. If Dyffaya wants his Unit agent where she can't act, then it's real important for Brooks to have another Unit agent in place who can."

"That makes sense. In fact, I was just thinking a lot the same thing."

He glowered at her and shoved to his feet.

"The special agent is having trouble saying it out loud,"

José said. "I'll help. Brooks just made Ackleford a Unit Twelve agent."

"Temporarily," Ackleford said, looking like the world had come to an end. "It's just temporary. Goddamn it. I *hate* this magic shit."

THIRTY-FOUR

BOREDOM is a prisoner's biggest enemy. Boredom added to the profound loss of control from imprisonment can lead to lethargy and depression. Or it can propel someone in the opposite direction—to action for action's sake, anything to break the monotony, however pointless or rash.

Nathan knew this. He was patient by nature, and he'd been on long hunts before. This one had only lasted twenty-five days, according to his personal time. It would either be over soon, or it would last a very long time.

That's why he was running.

He'd explored everything within ten miles of their clearing in the days spent waiting for Benedict to heal. He wasn't doing anything so productive now. He'd run for miles and was heading back now, following a dry creek bed with high banks through the black pillars of the trees, running for the sake of motion. Running because he couldn't be still. Pointless, maybe, but not rash. He hadn't been driven to that, though he might have been, had his isolation continued. Being able to sign with Cullen had made a huge difference.

Until today. Today, when Dyffaya had popped in right after "breakfast"—one of the two meals that appeared every day—his mood manic, his comments teasing and elliptical.

Nathan gathered the god had something big planned for Earth very soon. Some kind of chaos event, yes—Dyffaya said more guests would be arriving soon—but bigger somehow. Grander. Something that mattered greatly to the god, that moved him closer to some dearly held goal. And Nathan couldn't do a damn thing about it.

But it was tomorrow, not today, that had driven him away from their camp. Tomorrow, when he and Benedict would fight again . . . for the last time.

The problem with running away was that you still had to return. Nathan was on his way back now, uneased and uncertain. He saw three possible outcomes to tomorrow's battle. His own death. Benedict's. Or Dyffaya's.

This time he had to get close. Dyffaya had been damnably careful, but they had to make him forget care this time. Nathan had to get close enough to use Claw—

Something leaped down from the top of the bank right ahead of him. His hand flashed—but he stayed the impulse in time, leaving Claw sheathed in its pocket of elsewhere. "Do you know how close you came to decapitation?" he demanded.

"Edgy, are we?" Cullen Seabourne said. The sorcerer was completely recovered from his near-starvation, though still a few pounds under his original weight. He held a rock in one hand. It was the size of two fists and fairly round. Nathan had found it on one of his explorations of the area.

Nathan took a slow breath, calming himself. "One of us is."

"Getting yourself pumped up to kill Benedict, or practicing running away?" Cullen said that with a fine sneer—while his hand flashed through another message: *Dyf fucking magic not working.*

Spelling everything did make for short, sometimes odd messages. Nathan understood this one well enough, though. "I don't want to hurt him. You know that." While he spoke he signed, *more magic sick?*

Two bad, Cullen signed back. *Three more sick.* "Yeah, right. I just imagined that was your blade that went through his lung."

"Did you come out just to give me a hard time?" *Mary?* he signed.

"I was bored. Don't be so bloody sensitive." Cullen signed a quick *no* and tossed the rock at him. "You up for a game?"

Nathan caught it. "I suppose." He tossed it back, then signed, *Dyf planning big event. More guests soon.* He was slower than Cullen; it took a while to get all that spelled. While he did, Cullen tossed the rock from hand to hand, offering ludicrous bets on the outcome of their upcoming game. Giving a reason for the pause.

"You can go first." Cullen tossed the rock back.

Nathan caught it. "Let's go, then."

They headed down the creek bed toward the clearing, exchanging a comment now and then, but not signing. Too hard to watch each other one's hands when they were walking.

For the past two weeks, over Nathan's and Benedict's objections, Cullen had been sneaking off to watch Dyffaya play with his beguiled "guests." He'd gotten it into his head that the god was spending too much of his time at sex, that it had to be a cover for or a means to something else. He'd been convinced that the god lacked the Sight and wouldn't spot him.

He'd been right. It remained a crazy, dangerous thing to do, but he'd been right. The god hadn't spotted Cullen, and Cullen had clearly Seen that Dyffaya was performing some kind of body magic during sex.

Sex magic had been around for thousands of years, but for pretty basic stuff—as a way to generate, share, or occasionally steal power. It could be combined with other types of magic, but this was the first Nathan had heard of using it in conjunction with body magic. According to Cullen, Dyffaya was using copulation to make complex and delicate changes in his sexual partners' bodies. Subsequent spying had convinced Cullen that Dyffaya was trying to keep his beguiled guests from succumbing to magic sickness. He'd tried to explain why he thought this, but the subject was too technical and complicated to be conveyed well through short, spelled-out conversations.

If that was the god's goal, he was failing. One of the beguiled people had already died; seven of the others had been showing symptoms. Now Cullen said two of them were in bad shape and three more were sick . . . which meant all of them had magic sickness.

All but the last one to arrive, that is. That woman had showed up the night Nathan learned who Dyffaya's ally was. The god had to grab people in pairs, and she'd been the unfortunate extra person snatched so Dyffaya could bring his confederate here for a little sex and planning.

Dyffaya didn't allow them to speak with their audience between fights, and this woman was slotted to be part of the audience, whether she liked it or not. But Cullen had seen her on his spying trips. She was a tall woman in her mid-fifties, with short brown hair. He'd overheard her telling one of the others her name. Mary. Mary Boyd.

The interesting thing about Mary was that Dyffaya hadn't beguiled her. Cullen thought, based on overheard conversations, that he hadn't fucked her, either. Maybe she was the control. While the god experimented on the others, he could observe her and see if she sickened faster or slower.

Or maybe he just wasn't sexually interested in her. Who could say?

When they reached the clearing, Benedict was running through a series of exercises. He spared them a quick glance, but didn't speak. Even if he only addressed Cullen it might be construed as communicating with Nathan, and they were scrupulous about appearing to observe the restriction. Appearances matter when you're trying to deceive a god.

Cullen and Nathan went to the far end of the clearing, where their makeshift pins waited. The pins were eight lengths of wood jammed in the ground. On one of his exploration trips, Nathan had found a long, narrow limb from one of the black trees. Breaking it into pieces had been difficult, but they'd managed.

"You can go first," Cullen said, confirming what Nathan had suspected when he caught the rock. Cullen had more to say and wanted his hands free. They often used the game to disguise a signed conversation.

Their version bore little resemblance to real lawn bowling. They had to throw, not roll, the "ball." It was almost impossible to knock down more than one pin at a time, so the idea was to knock one down with each throw; you kept throwing as long as you knocked down a pin. Miss, and it was the other guy's turn. You got a point for knocking down all eight pins on the same turn, and game was six points. Since the rock was only fairly round, pitching it accurately was tricky, and it took a solid hit to knock a pin all the way down. A game could last for hours, if they wanted it to.

Cullen moved down near the pins. One of their rules was that the person who wasn't pitching retrieved the rock. This placed him where the other could easily watch him signing. Nathan made a show of warming up his arm.

Dyf caught me last night, Cullen signed.

Nathan scowled at the rock in his hand. Shifted his grip slightly. Cullen was here, alive and not missing any limbs, so some of the worst consequences of being caught hadn't occurred. Nathan swung the heavy rock back and threw.

One pin down. He made the sign for a question.

Cullen sauntered over to retrieve the rock. *Dyf laugh. Funny I watch won't do.*

Not hurt? Nathan signed.

Hurt no damage, Cullen signed on his way to Nathan.

One type of body magic caused excruciating pain without damaging the body. Nathan didn't let himself grimace or otherwise show his sympathy. *Dyf touch to hurt?*

Cullen nodded.

All elves possessed some body magic and some ability to use illusion, but the two Gifts did not arrive in equal balance. Some were innately better at illusion, others at body magic. Before he became a god, Dyffaya had been an adept. Like most adepts, he'd been able to use both Gifts very well—but he'd been a true master at illusion, not body magic.

The question on their minds had been whether Dyffaya needed to touch people to use body magic. Some adepts didn't, and Dyffaya didn't even have a normal body. Yet he seemed to need to use his version of a body when performing body magic, didn't he? Sex was a deep way of touching another body.

Now Cullen said that the god had touched him to cause pain. It wasn't proof that he had to touch, but . . . *How you spotted?*

Mary wandering saw me.

Mary Boyd had wandered away from the site where Dyffaya kept his guests? *Mary okay?*

Punish Mary hurt no damage.

Touch Mary to hurt?

Yes. Cullen handed the rock over to Nathan. "Lucky pitch." And signed rapidly, *Dyf no Sight. Touch to hurt. We try it yes?*

Nathan's heart beat a little faster. What Cullen had proposed was risky, very risky, but . . . *tomorrow yes,* he signed back.

"See if you can get lucky again," Cullen said. His voice was bland, his movements normal, and his eyes gleamed with wild amusement. "You're going to need it."

That was likely true, in a perverse way. Nathan had just agreed to let Cullen stop his heart in the middle of tomorrow's fight . . . if he could. That's where their wishing turned perverse. The spell only worked for Cullen half the time. With luck, this would be one of the times it did.

THIRTY-FIVE

ACKLEFORD had an old-fashioned paper map in his car that was very helpful for laying out a three-mile grid for searching the city. To Kai's surprise, Ackleford wanted José to drive. She understood why when the brand-new Unit 12 agent took a laptop out of the trunk and settled into the back seat with it. He meant to treat the car as his mobile office.

"Before you get too involved with whatever's on that laptop," she began.

"Reports. You said this might take a while."

"It probably will. Before you start in with your reports, I need to tell you something. I think I've figured out what Dyffaya wants. Look at what he's been doing—staging big, splashy events. Extravagantly weird stuff, scary stuff that's sure to be featured on every news show in the nation. He wants attention, and he wants—"

"Hold on a minute." He grabbed his phone, tapped the screen. "How long has it been since Hunter destroyed that knife?"

"Three weeks and . ." She counted quickly. "Six days."

"But nothing happened until day before yesterday. That's what we thought, but maybe he's been acting like a damn stage magician, keeping us focused on the splashy while he grabbed people left and . . . Ackleford here," he said into the phone. "I need you to get the city's missing person reports for the last twenty days. See if there's been more than usual. Especially look for any doubles—for people who might have vanished two at a time. I need—what?" he snapped at Kai, who'd twisted around in the seat to get his attention.

"Fires," she said urgently. "Have them look for missing people who have some connection to a fire." Like the one at Franklin Boyd's house last night. Maybe Dyffaya could snatch people without a big, showy event. Maybe he had some way of storing the excess magic to use later, but he'd still be using chaos motes. Even a god was likely to spill some of that energy—and fire was tied to chaos.

"Look for any connection to fires," Ackleford repeated. "Hell, just get the reports of fires for that period while you're at it." A pause. "Hell, no. I need this yesterday. Pull in Dunn if you need to . . . No, not yet. Call me when you know something." He disconnected. "What were you saying about what this Dyffaya wants?"

"Worshipers. That's the reason he's spent magic so lavishly—to create these big, splashy events. He wants to be worshiped. To get that, he plans to scare the shit out of everyone. He's undermining people's confidence in the police, the FBI, in every kind of authority. He wants everyone scared enough to try anything, even worshiping him, if that will save them."

"Huh." Ackleford's eyes narrowed. "And yet he's been doing fine at splashy without those four. Now all of a sudden he needs them, and he needs Stockman out of the way at the same time. And we can't be sure who else in the SDPD has been co-opted by that asshole god." He thought some more, nodded, and picked up his phone again.

"What are you doing?"

"Agreeing with you. Brooks wants a Unit agent on the spot to deal with whatever's coming. Something big, he said. I can't do the woo-woo shit like Stockman, but I'm a goddamn Unit agent now, so maybe I'd better do what only a Unit agent can." A short pause. "Yeah, it's Ackleford again. I need to talk to Brooks."

"But what are you doing?"

This time he grinned—a real, mouth-stretching grin. He looked like a sour, middle-aged shark about to chomp down. "Calling in the goddamn Marines."

"You've got to be kidding."

He'd already tapped his phone. "Hell, no. Got a hunch. Besides, can't call in the locals, not with Boyd—Ida. Ackleford here. Need Brooks again."

Kai listened, fascinated, to the conversation between Ackleford and Ruben Brooks. Ackleford was just as rude and sarcastic with his new boss as he was with everyone else. After some back-and-forth, he handed her the phone. "He wants your input."

She took it. "This is Kai."

"Derwin tells me you believe Dyffaya's goal is a religious protection racket."

"Uh . . . I hadn't thought of it that way, but yes." What else could you call it when the god used fear to force people to turn to him for protection from him?

"He believes Dyffaya has something spectacular in mind that requires the four people who've gone missing. Since I have a strong hunch that something big is going to happen soon—probably within a few hours—I agree. Being unable to rely on the local police force is a problem, but bringing in the Marines is a rather extreme solution. Is that your idea or Derwin's?"

Kai glanced at the man in the back seat. "His."

"Ah." A moment's silence. "Lily tells me that Derwin has a slight patterning Gift. Very slight, she says, and he prefers to believe it doesn't exist, but it's not blocked. It does explain why an otherwise by-the-book agent occasionally leaps off a cliff—and lands on his feet. I suppose if I'm going to give him the status of a Unit agent, I'd better allow him to act as one. Thank you. I'll speak with Derwin again now."

Kai had given the phone back to Ackleford—who was a patterner. That blew her mind. It was a very slight Gift, Brooks said, but still . . . she glanced at the rune she'd drawn on José's cheek. With a patterner in charge, that rune might not be entirely meaningless, after all.

Ackleford got his Marines—two full companies from 1 Marine Expeditionary Force based in Pendleton, with air support if needed. He would, that is, as soon as he knew where to put them.

For the next two hours, Ackleford worked, José drove, and Kai kept an eye on the charm in her palm. Like most charms, it needed skin contact to work. Ackleford smoked five more cigarettes. He accepted calls and made them. He spoke with Major Joseph Simmons of the U.S. Marine Corps—the CO for the two companies that were standing by to deploy—several times.

From one of his calls, they learned that the fire at Franklin Boyd's house had been reported by a neighbor, not Boyd. The fire truck had arrived at 2:15 A.M. and was met by Boyd in his pajamas. He told them the fire had been started by a lighted candle that got knocked over. It had been small and he'd put it out. The firefighters confirmed that the fire was extinguished and left.

"Where was Mary?" Ackleford demanded of his subordinate. "Mary Boyd, his wife. Kids are grown and gone, but Mary should've been there. She wasn't mentioned in the report?" A pause. "Find out."

Another call was about missing persons reports. The agent hadn't correlated the reports with fires yet, but in the past four weeks, twenty-seven people had been reported missing in San Diego County due to "unknown circumstances." That was a significant uptick. The agent had found several reports that might be pairs—people who'd gone missing on the same day. And one of the missing person cases had been closed when the man's body was found several miles from his home. He'd died without a mark on him—just like Britta.

Kai's job—aside from watching the charm—was to keep track of their progress on the map. She distracted herself by talking to José. Turned out he was the oldest of four children. He had two half-sisters and a half-brother, all of them born to his mother after she moved back to Mexico and married. He'd been raised by his father and hadn't met his siblings until he was an adult because of his stepfather's prejudice against lupi. His brother had bought into that prejudice and didn't want anything to do with him, but he saw his sisters occasionally and obviously valued that contact. One was married and had three children; the other was quite a bit younger, something of a late-life baby. She was attending university in Sonora and would graduate this year. José was clearly very proud of her. Kai had a suspicion he'd helped her financially, but he didn't actually say so. "You grew up at Clanhome?"

"Nearby. Back then, my dad worked at an engineering firm in the city, so we lived there and went to Clanhome most weekends." He smiled. "I loved weekends. Growing up clan is like having dozens of cousins, aunts, and uncles. More uncles than aunts, but still, plenty of family."

"When I was growing up I wished for a big family, but I was an only, and so were both my parents."

"Coming up on an exit," he said. "Do I take it?"

"Yes, that finishes the last leg of this section. You'll need to go south on—stop the car."

José didn't quite stand on the brakes, but they stopped dead in the right-hand lane of Kumeyaay Highway. Which the cars behind them didn't appreciate, but no one hit them, so Kai didn't care. The charm in her hand was glowing. Faintly, but it was glowing.

She swung her arm left as far as she could. Then right. No perceptible change. She unclicked her seatbelt and leaned over into the backseat. The glow dimmed slightly. At least she thought it did. "We're right on the edge of its limit. Keep going straight, but not fast."

She got herself straightened out again and watched the charm intently. In the realms she'd be doing this on foot or the back of a horse. Plenty of time to adjust at that speed. Not so much at highway speeds, though José was going slower than the rest of the traffic.

"That's what you get?" Ackleford said. "It lights up?"

"Like a game of hot and cold. The closer we get, the brighter it glows. When we get really close it starts blinking."

"Huh." A moment later he spoke again. "All right, Major, start rolling. We don't have an exact location yet, but we've narrowed the area and those ICVs of yours aren't exactly fast, so . . . section Two-Nine, as discussed. Generally speaking, you'll be heading toward Old Town."

Old Town. Where the hobbit house was. Kai's heart began

beating faster. "In Faerie, if you wanted to stash four people where no one could get to them, you'd put them behind a good, strong ward."

"Yeah, so what? We aren't—shit. Fox said there was a ward on that place, didn't she?"

KAI stood in the open-air mall that connected the two buildings belonging to the Café Coyote. The charm in her palm was blinking madly. José stood on her right, watchful and wary. Ackleford was on her left.

The streets and businesses in Old Town had reopened today, though the ones immediately adjacent to Whaley House remained closed. Ackleford's ID had gotten them through the barricade, though it had been a near thing. One of the cops had tried to detain Kai. Ackleford had told him no, only with rather more words—words like "fucking" and "goddamn." It had worked, though it might be only a temporary reprieve. But temporary might be enough, if they could figure out how to get past that ward.

The hobbit house looked like it had yesterday—green and gaudy with flowers—only with not so many cops surrounding it. The weather was different, too. Low-hanging clouds had moved in, covering the sun.

"I don't like it," José said.

"I'm not crazy about the idea," Kai said, "but we're low on options. It's probably a fire ward or a keepaway. Arjenie said it was using a lot of power, and those are the most common high-power wards. They're also some of the quickest to set, and this one went up fast. If it's a fire ward, the amulet will protect me. If it's a keepaway, that's mind-magic. Either my shields will block it and I'll be able to go through, or they won't. In which case I won't be able to pass, and we're no worse off than we are now."

"There are other kinds of wards," José said. "And sometimes Cullen sets multiple wards."

Kai was trying hard not to think about some of the wards she'd heard of. Like mind-wiper. That was a nasty bit of business. "But keepaway is quick and the others take longer. Building wards in layers takes a lot longer. One day isn't enough time for layers." A sidhe lord who wanted to keep something safe might set several layers of wards—simple repulsion, keepaway, fire if the keepaway didn't work, with maybe a mind-wiper or heart-stopper as the last resort if the others were breeched. But wards often didn't play well with each other. Setting up multiple layers might take that lord weeks, even months.

Of course, they were dealing with a god, not a sidhe lord.

"Marines will be here in about ten," Ackleford said. "We'll wait on them."

"Are you going to have them shell the hobbit house? Because I don't see what they can do about a ward other than . . ." Suddenly Kai's skin crawled. The hair on her arms stood up.

"What is it?" Ackleford looked around, scowling, as if he felt it, too.

The air swam with magic and imminence, the certainty of something about to happen. Like standing right where lightning was about to strike, or watching the curled mountain of a tsunami wave hover over you. Dread woke in the pit of her stomach. It was a sensation she recognized. "Someone nearby is performing a Great Rite."

"What the hell does that mean?"

"It means we just ran out of time." Kai drew Teacher and started forward.

Both men stepped out from the shelter of the open-air mall with her. "Neither of you can cross that ward," she snapped. "You won't help me by burning up."

Ackleford grunted. "Maybe not, but I can shoot through it. It didn't stop that paper Fox slid through it. It won't stop bullets. Speaking of which, you need a gun."

"I can't shoot one."

"You can stick someone with that oversize knife, but you can't stand to fire a gun?"

"I could fire it, but I wouldn't hit anything. I've never even held a gun. I'll stick with what I . . . oh, shit." The imminence suddenly cracked open, freezing Kai in place.

A face appeared in the sky directly over the hobbit house. A beautiful face, startlingly so, with dusky skin, full lips, Asian eyes. The cheekbones were Slavic. The nose was as

Roman as Nero. The face glowed, as did the mist swirling beneath it. Mist that grew solid, or solid-seeming, until a man the size of a high-rise stood amid the lowering clouds. A man with the face of a god.

"My people," the god-man said, and his voice was the wind, heard everywhere. He smiled sweetly, lovingly. "Though you do not yet know yourselves to be mine, you will. I am called Dyffaya áv Eni. My realm is chaos, and I am here to make you mine.

"Oh, but I am besotted with you—your love of change, your delight in the new and the different! I would court you like a lover, if you allow it." The clouds framing him turned golden, swirling into fantastic shapes—castles, flowers, birds. "I bring dreams and dance, song and story, the electric arc of change. I have much to give, for all things flow from chaos—the joy of discovery. Delight in the odd or peculiar. And darker things. Your city has had a taste of chaos now. I can do more." The clouds darkened. "Dreams may be nightmares. Do not turn me aside.

"I am not a jealous lover. I long for a place in your hearts, but I don't need to be your only one. Attend your church or synagogue if you wish, but don't turn me aside, my lovely ones. I insist. You *will* worship me."

He knelt up there in the air and held out two vast, cupped hands, as if offering a drink of water. Opened them—and spilled out monsters.

"Call on Me," he said, and his voice was thunder now, not mere wind, as creatures rained down on Old Town—red-skinned beasts like hairless hyenas. Two-legged lizards with saber-toothed grins. Scaled creatures with enormous claws. They floated down as the god spoke. "If one of My pets finds you, fall on your knees and ask for My protection. Call on Dyffaya. Call on chaos. I will hear, and you won't be harmed. You may be marked, but you won't be harmed. Afterwards, look for My sign."

One finger moved, tracing a lightning-bright sigil shaped like a backwards C with the arms almost touching. "*Look for my sign!*" he thundered—and vanished.

Kai wasn't paying much attention to him by then. She was busy.

The creature charging her had red eyes and a lot of slobber around its toothy muzzle. It was the size of a St. Bernard. The one José was firing at was the size of a small pony, with scales and great big claws. Maybe Ackleford was shooting at that one, too. She couldn't see, but she heard his gun go off.

Fortunately, the beast was as slow as a St. Bernard, too, and a lot dumber. It all but ran itself up on her blade. Which in turn slowed her a moment. She barely got Teacher free in time to deal with the pair of red-skinned monsters coming up behind it.

They had the massive chests and sloped backs of hyenas, mottled red skin, and the teeth of crocodiles. And they weren't as stupid as the first beast. They dodged her blade and split to circle her and the others, looking for an opening.

Maybe they'd never seen guns before. One of them charged José. The other went for Ackleford. It didn't work out well for them.

"Pull back!" Ackleford yelled, moving in front of her with his gun extended.

Something really large and hairy had spotted them. It looked like a cross between a lion and a woolly mammoth—lots of fur, short legs, massive body, tusks. And big. Fifteen feet at the shoulders. It lumbered toward them at a fair clip for something so large. Ackleford fired. It didn't seem to notice.

Kai reached for the beast's mind—a seething turmoil of angry reds and oranges that scarcely qualified as thought, but was the product of that mind, not under someone else's control, and so available to her.

The great beast's front legs folded. It sank slowly down, fast asleep.

"Cool," José said.

A fusillade of shots sounded from the police barricade, out of sight due to the curve of the road. A scream.

Kai spun just as Ackleford shouted, "Incoming!"

A damned battalion of the hyena creatures streaked around the curve of the road, heading straight for them. Too many, way too many to send into sleep, but she could get a couple of them. Kai reached out quickly and touched the mind of the one in the lead, sending sleep. It faltered and collapsed.

"Fall back," José commanded tersely, and began retreating

backward, firing steadily. Ackleford kept pace with him. One, then another and another of the creatures fell—but there were too many, and the tide of beasts was splitting as they ran, aiming to surround them. Smart beasts, or controlled? She didn't see the signs of control she'd seen in the chameleons, just lots of maddened, red-orange fury.

They weren't going to make it to cover.

"Take this," José said, handing Ackleford his gun. "I need teeth."

As he began the Change, the beasts charged.

Kai set her feet, made sure her body was loose, relaxed. *Teacher, I'm going to need some help.* That was her last clear thought for a while.

She took the first one through the neck before José completed his Change. The second and third fell to Ackleford's gun and to her blade. She lost track after that, though she remained aware of the enormous wolf—bigger than the red beasts, and faster—who kept them off her back while she shifted and spun and coated the street with slippery red blood.

At some point Ackleford's gun stopped firing. Out of ammo. She closed up automatically, keeping the beasts away from the unarmed man. One of the animals got through, but he blunted his teeth on her vest. And then she split his skull open.

She did not notice when the Marines arrived until they started firing. Whatever they were shooting was very, very loud. And effective. After a few seconds of that devastating fire, the remaining hyenas took off.

Abruptly Kai was back in charge of her body again, panting for breath, her arm aching—but from exertion, not a wound. Everything the vest didn't cover was covered in blood, but none of it was hers. She was amazingly intact and about to ask if the others were okay—when the lion-mammoth stirred and shoved to its feet.

She gathered her focus. She'd sent sleep twice, but she wasn't tapped out. She could—

"Now that," Ackleford said, "is just not right."

She was about to tell him it was okay, she'd handle it—when a peculiar gust of wind, some swish of sound, made her look up.

Another battalion of monsters had arrived, this one air-borne. Bats. Giant bats, their wingspans longer than a pickup, and two of them were stooping down on Kai, Ackleford, and José. "Come on," she said, grabbing his arm. They needed cover—and to get out of the line of fire so those Marines could fire whatever-it-was without hitting them.

The lion-mammoth was between them and the Café Coyote. Ackleford, jarred into motion, did a fine job of dragging her toward the hobbit house. With its overgrown, vegetative wall at her back she stopped, turning to look for José.

Something smashed into the back of her head. Pain blinded her, swarmed up from the depths and swamped her, carrying her down into darkness.

THIRTY-SIX

KAI had woken from a head injury twice. The first time, after the crash that killed her parents, she'd come back in bits and pieces, knowing a terrible grief but not the reason for it. She'd been in a coma that time, which was why she'd come back piecemeal, bits of memory tangling up with the present, words elusive at first. The second time had been in Faerie. She'd awakened pretty much all at once, her head sore but her mind clear.

This time seemed to hit somewhere between the two. She floated up into pain, bobbing along on its surface for some timeless interval, aware only of the pain. . . and failure. Failure so deep and terrible it made a weight she could barely breathe through.

Eventually she realized that pain must mean she'd been hurt. But she wasn't in a hospital. It didn't smell right . . . though she did smell blood, the rest of the smells weren't right. And she was lying on her side, not her back, and whatever she lay on did not feel like a hospital bed.

Monsters. There'd been monsters, yes, she remembered now. And Ackleford and José and . . . she got her eyes open.

Her vision was badly blurred. She blinked a few times . . .

oh. Not a damaged retina. A dislodged contact. When her eyelid moved she could feel it stuck up high on her left eyeball, which felt dry and scratchy. She had drops in her pocket. She started to reach for them—only she couldn't move her arms. Either of them. Her hands were fastened behind her back.

She closed her left eye and the room came into focus, though what she saw didn't make sense. She lay on a too-short couch in a nineteenth-century parlor. Where in the hell . . . oh. Whaley House. She'd been outside it. Now, apparently, she was inside.

Or maybe she was still unconscious and having the weirdest dream ever.

"There's no point pretending you aren't awake," a smooth, light voice said from somewhere behind her. "I can tell the difference between waking and sleeping thoughts, you know."

Kai jolted. Which hurt her head enough to wash away most of the shock from hearing that voice, though the sense of failure persisted. How had she not known? Not guessed? Not had one bloody clue . . . "Not pretending anything. Not moving because my head hurts. Someone cracked my skull."

A woman moved slowly into view. She was beautiful, of course, long-limbed and ethereally slim. It wasn't a human beauty, though the dress she wore was a human style. Her eyes were too large and widespread, and no human ever had irises of such pure aquamarine, or hair in that soft, pale shade of yellow. Her limbs were overly long in proportion to her trunk, her shoulders too narrow—but that's how elves were built. Soon you stopped seeing those proportions as odd and saw only the grace.

"That was I," Eharin An'Ahedra said languidly. "I wasn't sure how hard to hit, and it seemed better to err on the side of too much force than too little. Why are you keeping one eye closed? It looks odd."

Kai's mindhealing teacher was speaking excellent English with a hint of Midwestern twang. That had not been true the last time Kai saw her. "My contact is stuck in the wrong place. Would you mind untying me so I can put some drops in my eye?"

"Yes, I would. What is . . oh, a lens you put into your eye.

How primitive." She sat on the coffee table and tilted her head. "I had expected to be bombarded with questions. You've always been so dreary about that—questions, questions."

"Where are José and Ackleford?" She'd failed them. Failed everyone.

"Who?"

"The two men who were with me. Well, one was a wolf at the time you cracked my skull."

"I don't know what happened to the wolf. Probably he was killed."

No, José couldn't be dead. Couldn't. It would be all her fault and—and that dreary gray bubble clinging to her temple wasn't hers. She didn't see her own thoughts. "Stop that," she snapped. Rather clumsily—it was hard to focus when her head hurt—she shoved Eharin's malicious thought bubble away.

"It took you long enough to notice."

"Have you ever had a concussion?"

"I thought you were claiming your skull was broken?"

Kai lay quiet a moment, gathering her resources. Trying to think about something other than how much she'd like to kill Eharin. The desire was almost pure, it was so vivid. She'd always believed that anyone could be driven to kill, under the right circumstances. She hadn't known that a split head and betrayal were her own triggers.

"Is it my death you're contemplating?" Eharin asked, mildly curious.

Kai's teacher might not have much power, but she had two centuries' more experience than Kai did at interpreting what she sensed. She couldn't read Kai's mind, but she could make uncannily good guesses about what she sensed. "Oh, yes. What about Ackleford? Is he all right? And those four people, the ones you brought here—where are they?"

"They died happy, providing the fuel we needed to enact today's script."

Kai felt a sudden spasm of grief. If only she'd been faster, better, able to detangle the mess Dyffaya had made of those minds. She thought of the young woman who'd struggled briefly against the compulsions. It hurt.

Eharin made a *tch* sound. "If you were going to live long

enough for it to matter, I would counsel you, as your teacher, to abandon your absurd sensitivity. It interferes with the detachment necessary for careful work."

As if her counsel meant anything now. Kai's throat was thick. "Ackleford?"

"He's busy telling everyone what to do. I believe he'll succeed in getting that woman out of jail. She's supposed to be good with wards. He hopes she'll be able to lift the one barring them from this floor of the house."

"Will she?"

"Not in time." She smiled faintly. Eharin did everything with exquisite restraint. An all-out smile would probably crack her face. "Your Ackleford is destined to disappointment in another way as well. One of those Marines he's ordering around is not going to do as he says. Instead he'll do my bidding."

Kai's head hurt too much for all this elliptical shit. "Why am I lying here with a cracked skull?"

"Do you think it's really cracked?"

"Hard to say. Why are you here?"

"I felt sure you'd get around to asking that eventually." She shifted, tucking one leg up under her in a way that should have looked awkward and crudely revealing, given the snug sheath she was wearing. It didn't. "Dyffaya wants you."

"I guessed that much. Though he seems to have trouble deciding whether he wants me alive or dead."

"No, he's quite clear on the subject. He wants you alive. I'm the one who wants you dead."

That was direct enough. "And yet I'm not."

"You will be." This smile was no wider, but her eyes glittered with real emotion—one that turned her thoughts a biting, acrid yellow. Bitterness, long-held and consuming. "It would have been simpler to kill you with that blow to your head, but simpler isn't always interesting. Dyffaya expects me to keep you stashed here until he has time to retrieve you."

"He isn't going to get what he expects?"

"He believes I am under his control. Silly of him, really. I am far too good at my work to leave his compulsions in force. I couldn't remove them completely—he would have noticed that—but I could and did tie his additions up in tidy little knots. They don't trouble me at all."

Kai sorted through that and came up with, "He's got a hook in you. Probably he can see and hear what you do, when he wants to. So mostly you have to look like you're obeying, but you don't obey if he isn't watching. That's why you tried to shoot me. He wasn't watching."

"He gave me such a great opportunity. He was using my eyes to show Nathan that he could have you killed at any moment. He didn't intend to, of course, but as soon as he turned his attention elsewhere, I took my shot." She sighed. "Such a shame that didn't work."

"And at the moment he's preoccupied, keeping track of all those monsters he dumped on the city. You believe you can speak freely." But why talk at all? Why was Kai still alive?

"That was almost clever," Eharin said. "It reinforces my decision to kill you."

"I suspect Dyffaya will notice that."

Eharin gave her a familiar, contemptuous look. "He'll notice your death. He won't know my part in it. Soon, a young Marine is going to shell this house. He'll believe he's destroying the source of all those monsters. Sadly, I won't be here to stop him."

"Soon, but not now?" Funny how her mind caught on that one word. Such an optimistic word, "soon." She'd like "tomorrow" even better, or "next month," but anything that wasn't now, right this minute, gave her something to hang her hope on.

"We wait for my other little surprise to catch Dyffaya's attention. An explosion in the building where I've been holding services for his worshipers. He'll send me to deal with that, leaving you here alone." Her smile was as restrained as ever, but the sharp spike of red in her thoughts announced her bloodthirsty pleasure. That faded into the cool gray of intellectual curiosity. "You don't seem as frightened as I'd expected."

"Surprise dulls fear sometimes, and you've really surprised me. I could have sworn you thought too highly of yourself to break your sworn word."

"If you refer to my agreement with the Hound, I haven't violated one word of it."

"And yet you swore not to harm me." Kai might not have

been a party to the deal Nathan struck with Eharin, but she knew he'd included that.

Smugness smeared itself over those lovely features. "No, that was the wording the Hound suggested. Much too broad. How could I know for certain what a human considers harm? And of course I couldn't swear not to defend myself, should you try to harm me. So I swore not to use my Gift or other forms of magic on you, save in those ways a teacher must in order to correct or inform. I have not done so."

She believed what she said. That bit of nastiness she'd attached to Kai's thoughts while she was unconscious—no doubt that had been a training exercise, in Eharin's mind. "So . . . why? Why are you here instead of in Aléri? You must know you can't return. You aren't part of court"—and that was a jab, yes, because Eharin resented that, convinced she'd never been properly appreciated—"but Winter samples thoughts widely at times. One stray thought at the wrong moment, and she would know what you've done."

One eyebrow lifted in delicate scorn. "You believe the Queen cares what happens to you?"

"She cares deeply about what happens to Nathan."

"Oh, yes, she cares about *the Hound.*" For a moment, her careful masks—the tight control of both face and thoughts—slipped. On her face was naked hatred. Her thoughts roiled with sulfurous yellow. "She spoils her pet, encouraging him to believe himself above the true people of the realms."

"My God. You're a Firster." That was Kai's name for the phrase that, in elfin, meant Elves First, a tiny group who had a lot in common with the KKK here on Earth. They believed that every evil of their worlds could be traced to the mingling of the races that diluted the purity of the elfin soul. "How did you hide that from Nathan?"

Eharin ignored Kai's question in favor of what she wanted to say. "He had the gall to force me—me, a daughter of Ahedra!—to teach one such as you. The insult was too much. I will have my revenge."

There had been no force involved. Kai knew that. Nathan had offered the woman a deal, and after some dickering, Eharin had accepted. But Eharin believed what she said. Her thoughts were twisted into distorted patterns by that virulent bitterness—the distortion of serious self-deception. "All of this is about taking revenge on Nathan?" she said incredulously—and then, thinking of Winter's reaction: "You are going to die so slowly."

Eharin's face twisted so that, for a moment, it matched her thoughts.

"Eharin will be famous," another voice said smoothly—another *familiar* voice, this one as much of a shock as Eharin's had been. "She is composing a masterwork, though in a genre you may not be familiar with. Have you heard of *p'tuth*?" Malek asked as he moved into view.

Malek was a small man. He looked as trim and tidy in Dockers and a nicely fitted sports jacket as he had in the robes of court. The little dab of mustache beneath his pug nose looked just as affected here as it did there, too. She gaped at him.

He smiled at her. "You're surprised to see me. That's natural, though you must have realized Eharin had someone to help her with the little things. She couldn't have carried you in here all by herself."

Elves were stronger than they looked, but no, Eharin probably couldn't carry Kai down a flight of stairs without help. But Malek was surely the last person she'd expected to see in that role—especially since Eharin had just revealed herself to be a Firster. "She couldn't have traveled here all by herself, either," Kai said slowly. "You can, though. You brought her."

He gave a little bow, acknowledging that. "*P'tuth* is the art of revenge. Eharin composes a work such as has not been known for centuries. To take such subtle and complex revenge on one as powerful as the Queen's Hound—it will be spoken of forever."

He was just as slimy here as he was at court, too. His thoughts were coated in pus green. The color of lies.

Either Eharin didn't notice, or she took his statement for the sort of empty courtesies commonplace among elves, especially at court. But it wasn't. He was outright lying. Kai could see that . . . but Eharin's way of sensing thoughts didn't give her the kind of detail Kai got. Maybe she couldn't tell the difference between a deliberate lie and the everyday insincerity of a flatterer.

"You've set the explosives?" Eharin asked him.

Another little bow, this one with a touch of flourish. His thoughts were gleeful. "Everything is ready. Do you wish to see the trigger?"

"I wish to have it," she said sharply, and held out a hand.

He stepped closer, reached inside his jacket, pulled out a little snub-nosed gun, and shot Eharin in the face.

THIRTY-SEVEN

BRAINS and blood exploded out the back of Eharin's head. Her legs kicked—quick, jerky motions with no grace at all. She toppled over—first onto the coffee table, and from there onto the floor.

"I've been wanting to do that for so long," Malek said. He glanced at Kai, smiling. "I'm sure you have, too, and I do apologize for robbing you of the pleasure."

Kai thought she might be sick. The smell, his smile, the fact that a few minutes ago she *had* wanted to kill the elf bitch . . . she swallowed.

"Made a mess, didn't I?" He clucked his tongue. "Ah, well. We won't be here too long, I hope. One more thing, and then I'll see if I can make you more comfortable." He took off his sports jacket, removed something from the pocket, and moved to the other side of the coffee table, where Eharin lay in an ungainly heap. He draped the jacket over what was left of her head.

When he turned around, she saw what he'd removed from the jacket. A hypodermic. Kai squirmed, but between her aching head and the ropes tying her wrists and ankles, she couldn't do a thing to stop him. He pushed up her sleeve, which was stiff with dried blood—"You are something of a mess, too, aren't you?"—jabbed the needle in her arm and depressed the plunger partway. Then, to her astonishment, he unbuttoned his own sleeve, pushed it up, and injected the rest of it into himself. "What is that? What did you just do?"

"A harmless virus. Nothing to worry about. But it's alive, and so can carry the—I think you've been calling it a hook? The element that will let my lord bring us to him when he's ready. Much simpler this way, isn't it? Less painful, too."

Not until hope broke apart on the hard ground of reality did she realize she'd let herself hope. She ought to know better than to have thought for an instant that slimy Malek was here to rescue her. No, he was here to collect her. She closed her eyes as a wave of defeat crashed over her.

"Head hurting?" he said sympathetically as he buttoned his sleeve. "I'm afraid I can't do much about that, nor can I untie you. Is there anything else I could do to make you more comfortable?"

Kai blinked rapidly—which reminded her. Why not ask? "Eye drops," she said. "They're in my pocket."

"I believe Eharin emptied your pockets, but the contents should be . . ." He moved out of her range of vision, reappearing a moment later. "Is this eye drops?" He held a familiar little squeeze bottle.

She started to nod, winced. "Yes. It's my left eye. The contact's stuck where it shouldn't be, but with some lubrication it ought to slide back down."

"Contacts." He grimaced. "Many things here are delightful, so innovative—television, for example. Quite remarkable. But the healing sciences do leave something to be desired. If you'll forgive the intrusion, I'll have to apply the drops myself."

He did so briskly. Again she blinked rapidly. This time, the contact slid back where it belonged. "Thank you."

"Would you like to sit up, or would that make you dizzy?"

"I would prefer to sit up, yes."

He huffed a bit—Malek wasn't strong—but he got her upright, though she had to sit slightly sideways to accommodate her bound wrists. It did make her dizzy for a moment, and she swallowed bile at the increased thudding in her head, but it was worth it. "Thank you," she said again. Courtesy cost little and sometimes paid dividends. She's learned that much on her quests.

"I'm glad I could assist you," he said solemnly. Surprisingly, that wasn't a lie.

"Do you know what happened to José? The wolf who was with me."

"Not precisely, but he was alive the last time I saw him. That was perhaps three hours ago. You were unconscious for quite awhile. Excuse me a moment. I believe I'll get a chair." He went to fetch one, a wooden chair with a needlepoint seat, and set it across from her. "There. Now we can chat. We may have a bit of a wait. My lord is extremely busy just now." He sighed with what looked like happiness. "It will be so good to see him again."

That wasn't a lie, either. And . . . studying his thoughts, Kai had to conclude that he wasn't compelled or beguiled. "You're a genuine believer. In him."

"I worship with my whole heart," he said simply. "You'll see why—soon, I hope, but if not, eventually you'll understand and serve, too. I know you've felt rubbed raw by the elves—their condescension, their arrogance. You haven't been exactly discreet. I did caution you about that, but in the end, it won't matter." He gave her a conspiratorial smile. "You'll see. Dyffaya isn't like that. He said he was besotted by us, and it's true. He's eager to claim us—to claim humans—as his people."

He meant every word. He scared the shit out of her. "Um . . . do you know what he plans to do with me?" Not that she didn't already know. He wanted to use her against Nathan. *Nathan, I'm sorry.*

His eyebrows lifted. "Haven't you guessed? You're to replace Eharin."

She blinked. And couldn't think of a thing to say.

Malek didn't mind. He enjoyed having an audience. "Such a pathetic woman, so convinced of her superiority when she was really rather stupid. It never occurred to her that when Dyffaya wasn't using her as a locus he might be using something else. A dog, a bird, a mouse—he isn't limited to sentient loci, you know. He's been aware of her plan to betray him for some time, but he couldn't act until he had you in hand, so to speak, to replace her. And all that nonsense about him being too busy keeping track of his creatures to notice what she did!" He shook his head sorrowfully. "Eharin knew that Dyffaya controls the flow of time within the godhead, yet she failed entirely to see what that means."

"My head hurts," Kai said. "I'm not seeing it, either. Could you explain it to me?"

"Simply that he has all the time he needs to act. It wouldn't do to have one of his creatures fail to honor their lord's word, you know. Any who call on him must be spared."

"He accelerates time in the godhead, you mean? So what happens here on Earth occurs very slowly for him, giving him time to respond."

"Exactly. It's tedious for him. For today's events, he set one portion of the godhead to a vastly accelerated rate, and most of him will have to stay there until most of the creatures are killed or have expired. Still, some portion of his attention must remain with his guests—those like you whom he's invited to the godhead—so he's reset the guests' portions to make this easier. They're currently experiencing a very slow time rate, much slower than on Earth. I don't pretend to understand that, but he's a god. He can do much that is beyond my comprehension." He sounded as proud as a father contemplating his infant's newly acquired crawling skills.

"I see." Malek was astonishingly willing to answer questions. Kai didn't understand it. He was treating her as a colleague, aside from the little detail of keeping her tied up

No, as a future colleague. He was cultivating her now just as he'd done at court—because he thought she would have pull with the source of all power and authority. There, it had been the Queen of Winter. Now it was Dyffaya. "Uh, what do you mean about the monsters expiring?"

"Those that aren't killed—and you took care of quite a few! A remarkable display, I must say, if unnecessary. They wouldn't have killed you, you know, simply planted a hook. Though I suppose they might have bloodied you a bit, and they probably would have killed your companions. You'd have regretted that, so perhaps it's just as well you fought so fiercely . . . but as I was saying, those that aren't killed will expire within a week or two. Whatever Eharin did to incite such ferocity in them shortens their lives."

"What Eharin did? I thought Dyffaya—"

"No, my lord has many incredible abilities, but he is not a binder. That's why he needs you."

Dyffaya thought Kai was a binder? Gods, but that was going to make for problems when he learned the truth. Only Dyffaya also thought Eharin was—had been—a binder. And he'd been using her, so . . . Kai spoke slowly as she absorbed the implications. "Eharin was a binder."

"She was quite sure she'd kept that from you. Apparently she was right about that much."

"She kept it from the Queen, too." Which would be considerably harder.

"It was fortunate she was never at court. Though once she crossed the line from mindhealer to binder, she knew she'd have to leave Iath, so when I approached her . . . oh, dear. You look distressed."

"She started out a mindhealer. And *became* a binder."

"Of course. Did she never warn you about—no, I suppose she couldn't, or you might have guessed. And there are so few mindhealers, and they're watched so closely—I suppose you never learned why. Most at court don't know, either, and those who do wouldn't speak of it. Apparently the Queen didn't, either? No? But it does seem you might have guessed. Mindhealers *are* the only ones who can permanently alter a mind, you know."

Kai could only stare. All this time she'd thought binders and mindhealers were separate—the Gifts similar, but distinct. Mindhealers were the good guys. Binders were bad. But mindhealers became binders if they crossed some line . . . "What's the line?" she asked urgently. "What turns a mindhealer into a binder?"

"Well. I don't know if I should say. My lord wished me to answer some of your questions, but I'm not sure he wants . . ."

Malek's voice faded. Everything faded. Her senses. Her body. She felt nothing, no sensation whatsoever. No sight, sound, no sense of her body, of space around her—and yet she experienced motion. Motion that went on and on and she would have screamed if she'd had a throat or lungs or—

THIRTY-EIGHT

KAI arrived standing, and promptly fell to her knees. Nausea roiled and her head pounded so much she didn't know if she was going to throw up or pass out. Then she was sure she'd throw up . . . and then she wasn't. The nausea seeped out. She swallowed.

The sky was black. Utterly black, without a speck of starlight. The ground was glowing. So was the man embracing Malek . . . and so were the thoughts woven into everything. Absolutely everything. She looked around, awed. Sparkly, shimmering thoughts—roils of darkness—lavender struts and lace twining through tall black trunks that weren't really trees, but massed thought. Great pillars of thought thrusting down deep into the stuff of this place and up to what passed for sky.

Motionless thought. Frozen. Thought was always in motion, yet the black tree-thoughts were utterly still. Yet they weren't compulsions or remnants. She didn't know what they were, but they disturbed her deeply.

All this while, Malek and the man—no, the god, for surely that was Dyffaya, even if he was using a human body—had been greeting each other, hugging, exchanging a lover's kiss. She dragged her attention away from the not-trees and dialed down her Gift.

Or tried to. It didn't work. Panicked, she tried again, but her Gift was so damn stimulated by this place she couldn't make it respond. Or maybe her own fascination was the problem. The thoughts were so large and strange—

"My dear friend." Dyffaya spoke with a resonance that drew her attention. "My loyal and faithful Malek." He looked as he had in the enormous projection he'd sent to inform San Diego residents that they were to start worshiping him. Human, in other words, though as beautiful as any elf. The god—or the embodied portion of him, that is; the thoughts she saw everywhere didn't originate with that body, but many of them were anchored in it—kept one arm around the small, tidy man who'd helped him abduct her. He patted the beaming Malek on the cheek. "You deserve so much more than a quick embrace. We will take time to be together, but just now I am pressed."

"I understand, my lord." Though he looked crestfallen.

Dyffaya gave him a last hug and released him. "You have done well, Malek. Very well. I am pleased with you. You may remain here to watch the last of the games, and after, we'll have that time together. Just the two of us."

Malek brightened.

"Take the path." Dyffaya gestured and a path of pale stones appeared. "It will lead you to the game-place. There's a seat reserved for you, my faithful one, at my left side. Go now. When I finish here, the game will begin."

Malek hurried away. And the god turned to look at her. "Kai." He smiled. It was a beautiful smile, warm and welcoming.

She realized she was still on her knees and managed to shove to her feet, though she wobbled a bit. Her head wasn't getting any better.

"Eharin hurt you. I'm sorry for that."

"Did you see her bash me over the head? She was sure you weren't using her eyes later, after I woke up."

He ignored that. "You are not at all happy to be here, but I am so happy to have you."

Her Gift was tugging at her. *Not now*, she told it. "So I understand. You want me to become a binder."

"So direct," he murmured. "It is a common quality in my

new people. I have not grown accustomed to it. I will, with time."

Don't piss off the god, she warned herself. She might have to in the end, but courtesy cost little and was important to elves. And Dyffaya was elf, even if he wasn't portraying himself that way at the moment. "I've been at court, but I'm not good at the courtesy practiced there. Forgive me if I err. I have questions. Is it okay to ask them?"

"You may ask."

"Why are those thoughts frozen?"

His brows shot up in startlement. "What thoughts?"

"The ones shaped like trees."

"They *are* trees. Not precisely the same as those you are used to, yet still trees."

He said that quite reasonably. And . . . he meant it. No pus green coated the thoughts anchored in that elegant body. And he was wrong. How could he be wrong? How could he not know?

He moved closer, still smiling in that warm, intimate way that made her want to step back. She held herself still, but it was an effort. "You don't believe you'll accept my offer. I understand that. I understand you better than you believe. You think I'm your enemy, but I'm not. It's true that I don't share your fascination with 'good' and 'evil.'" His voice shaded those words in such a way as to make them sound like intellectual abstractions, of importance only to those interested in a particularly esoteric topic. "Yet if you accept my offer, you'll be able to influence me more toward 'good.' You'll help so many people, Kai, if you . . ." He stopped. Frowned. "I am also not accustomed to people looking away when I speak to them."

She'd been studying the way thoughts both anchored Dyffaya's body and were anchored in it, and had suddenly realized that his "body" was nothing more than an extremely complex intention. Startled by that realization, she'd tried to trace that intention where it vanished in the glowing ground. She ought to be able to see into the ground-stuff if she dialed her Gift up high enough, but so far . . . she dragged her gaze back to him. "My apologies. I've never been *inside* thoughts before, and these are so vast and fascinating. It's distracting."

He was silent a moment, then said, more to himself than to her, "I had not given sufficient consideration to what your odd form of mindhealing would mean here."

Instinctively, she knew she didn't want him to think about that too much. "I don't know how to address you. There are so many forms I might use. Not being sidhe, I don't understand all the nuances. I hope I haven't shown disrespect by failing to use your proper title."

"Titles are a bore. You may call me Dyffaya, as you and the others have been. I hope you will call me lord one day, but you are not yet ready for such a commitment."

Again he brought out that smile, a claiming sort of smile, as if they already knew each other. A sexual smile, and yet the thoughts she saw everywhere weren't sexual. They were . . . yearning. Oh. Oh, gods. She turned slowly, staring at the not-trees—the yearning in them! Endless, frozen yearning—eons of it, unchanging, incapable of change, their blackness a lack, a loss so profound—

A familiar and beloved sensation broke in upon her preoccupation. She gasped with delight as an ecstatic Dell raced out of those not-trees toward her. A moment later Kai went to her knees again, but on purpose this time, so she could put her arms around her familiar.

Dell purred madly, an expression of love she didn't use often. She licked Kai's face with her too-rough tongue, making Kai laugh. Oh, it was good to be close again! Even as she purred frantically, Dell sent a chiding thought about Kai allowing herself to be injured and her intention of fixing that.

"She is certainly happy to see you."

Dell immediately sent a sense of warning and a complex gestalt that included Dyffaya's jealousy, his neediness, and his belief that he'd tied Dell to him. Kai straightened and looked at the chameleon instead of simply reveling in her nearness. The shiny lavender beguilement she saw shocked her into stillness—but it wasn't anchored. It looked dense, as if a great deal of power had been used, but it slid through Dell's thoughts like oil, not affecting them. Kai could dislodge it with a single soft—

No, Dell sent sternly. *Fool him.*

Of course. Kai sat back on her heels. "What have you done

to her? She's glad to see me, but she's thinking of you." True enough, though not in the sense she wanted Dyffaya to take it.

Dell promptly went to Dyffaya and rubbed her body along his leg and hip. As she did, she sent Kai instructions in a complex gestalt. Kai frowned, unpacking them. "She . . . she wants me to tell you it's good that you brought me here, and that the bond is much eased now, with me closer."

Dyffaya caressed Dell's head with one hand. "Your familiar and I have grown fond of each other. Does that surprise you? I don't mind sharing her with you," he said generously—and that was a whopper. He minded very much. "I hope you won't feel badly about sharing her with me."

"You've said you weren't accustomed to some of my ways. I'm not used to—to Dell being attached to someone else. Some people amuse her, like Cullen, but . . . I'll get used to it." She let herself sound grumpy about it.

Dell had been right. Her grumpiness pleased Dyffaya because he took it as an acknowledgement of his bond with Dell. Did he not see a difference between beguilement and real affection? He gave the chameleon's ears a last rub. "I don't mind sharing," he repeated, and it was still a lie, but less virulently so.

"Then maybe you'll allow her to do something about my head. It hurts."

"Of course." He gave a gentle wave.

Dell came and sat in front of Kai. Again she sent a gestalt bundle, but this one was so dense and layered Kai couldn't unpack it. She recognized the scent-sight-emotion blend that meant Nathan—who was alive and well. She got that much. She thought the blended sense of strong-male-blood-gift—which arrived with the flavor of the blood and a distinct scent—was Benedict, and Funny One was Cullen, both of whom were alive, thank God. But there was something about the male chameleons and . . . a plan? Something about the future, anyway. Those parts of the gestalt lacked scent, which was how Dell thought of the future. A time that hadn't happened yet had no smell. But she couldn't untangle things enough to be sure.

Dell huffed once and gave up. *Dots him,* she sent, along with a mingling that meant pride-not-earned and a familiar instruction. Dell wanted Kai to keep Dyffaya talking—bragging?—while she fixed Kai's head.

Okay. Kai sat down with her back against Dell's side. It didn't matter where they touched, only that they did. "The male chameleons," she said abruptly. "I wondered why I'd been able to break that link, but if it was Eharin controlling them instead of you . . . but Nettie was sure she sensed you."

He shrugged and settled onto the ground with her, sitting cross-legged. "I used the link, but Eharin set it. Which is, as you say, why you were able to break it. She was never as good as she believed herself to be. She certainly lacked your power, and how she resented that, poor dear! She was so greedy for power. But also, though she would not have admitted this, she was not as good as you will become. More skillful than you are now, yes, but don't worry. At this point, your raw power will serve me better than finicking delicacy."

Kai's head seemed to be vibrating. It wasn't unpleasant, but it would get that way. "What is it you want me to do?"

"Why, make worshipers for me." He smiled at her gently. "Nothing as terrible as you'd imagined, is it? You'll be able to return to your world and live much as you like. Eventually you may not be needed. It depends on how long you live."

"Ah . . . it does?"

"Once I can go there myself, I expect finding worshipers won't be a problem." The thoughts around him glowed brighter. That was a happy idea.

"I was told you couldn't enter Earth."

"Not now, no." The glow dimmed. "Eventually, I will. It will take time. I haven't yet managed to make the necessary adjustments to a mortal body. I suspect it will take just the right body, and when the time comes, I may need your assistance to . . . but that's all well in the future. I hadn't planned to go into it with you yet. Where was I? Oh, yes. Your duties won't be onerous. You won't have to handle any of the organizing—others will deal with that—only be present at services so you can influence the thoughts of those present. I'll let you know which ones I want you to make into my worshipers."

That's all she had to do—remake people's thoughts so they worshiped a mad god while he looked for "just the right body" to take over. That's what he meant, wasn't it? He hoped to find or make an avatar. Kai spoke through dry lips. "I thought you were only fed by true, heartfelt worship, such as Malek offers."

"That's the beauty of using a binder. It's not like compulsion. After you're through with them, the chosen ones will genuinely worship me. Your influence—that's another ability of binders, dear Kai, though I'm sure Eharin didn't teach it to you. You'll catch on quickly, though, I'm sure. You can influence thoughts of those around you in a temporary way, as well as making permanent changes. Your influence will draw many to return to services until their hearts open to me, even without you altering them. Eharin had been doing this, but she had so little power. She could only influence a few at a time, and making even one genuine worshiper left her depleted for days. I could and did feed her power for other things, but for some reason she couldn't use it to fuel her Gift. Odd, isn't it?"

The vibrating was reaching a peak. "Yes. I don't understand that." Any of it.

"Still, she did her best. Had she remained faithful, she would have always had a place with me, even though she was never fully mine. But she wasn't as stupid as my loyal Malek believes. She knew why I wanted you and, little though she might have admitted it, she knew you would become much more important to me than she was. She couldn't stand that." He sighed. "Poor thing. I'll miss her."

He meant it. Kai closed her eyes so he wouldn't see how horrified she was. The vibration crescendoed and popped, much like the *pop* when a swimmer's ears suddenly clear of water.

"You don't like the idea."

Her head felt fantastic. She sent Dell a wave of gratitude and reluctantly opened her eyes. "Making people worship you takes away their free will."

Abruptly the thoughts around him darkened—a darkness that spiraled out, churning the air into ominous patterns, as foreboding as a thunderstorm about to hit. "We were wrong about that."

"Uh—who was?"

He waved impatiently. "It was a long time ago. It doesn't

matter. The point is, free will doesn't matter as much as happiness. You have it in your Bill of Rights—that people are entitled to pursue happiness. My worshipers will be *happy*. They won't have to pursue it because I will give it to them. I'm good at that."

He would compel them to be happy. Beguile them into it.

He was insane.

Kai had known that. He was the god of insanity, after all, as well as the god of chaos. But now she saw it. The darker the patterns grew, the more clearly she saw their distortion, what should have been beauty twisted into grotesquery.

Her Gift tugged at her again. Tugged hard.

A sidhe phrase ran through her mind—*behi'yeli absore né:* the mad gods laughed. She understood that phrase with a new and terrible acuity. Her Gift wanted to heal the mad god. Heal a mind a thousand times more vast and complex and powerful than her own. A mind that her Gift insisted could not heal itself.

Dyffaya was speaking. Kai hadn't heard a word he said. "I'm . . . please excuse me. I'm overwhelmed." Deeply true.

"Also reluctant," he said dryly. The darkness thinned. "Ah, well. I knew you would be." This smile was sly. "You haven't asked about Nathan."

"Dell assured me he was alive and well."

"She is right—at the moment." He sprang to his feet. "Time to go. Take the path I created for Malek. When we meet again, I'll show you why you'll do as I wish, however reluctant you may feel now."

The god vanished. His body did, anyway, as his intention was withdrawn, and most of the thoughts that had been anchored in it slipped away. After a moment's hesitation—and a nudge from Dell—Kai did as she'd been told.

The pebbled path led through the tall trunks of the not-trees. On impulse, Kai stopped and laid one hand on what felt to her skin like smooth bark. She saw—but her Gift leaped up and swamped her before she could begin to process what she saw, nearly pulling her into fugue. She jerked her hand back and dialed down her Gift and the imperative died back . . . some. Not entirely.

Shaken, she proceeded slowly down the path. And as Dell

walked beside her, she sent a sense of agreement and: *No-blood-no-scent stuck. Broken. Bad-sad-stuck. Fix.*

Kai looked at Dell, surprised. No-blood-no-scent was clearly Dyffaya. What startled her was Dell's effort to use words—and the emotion accompanying them. That wasn't pity as Kai experienced it, but it was similar, a strong and pungent emotion, and not one Dell felt often. Kai looked closely at her familiar's thoughts, wondering if the beguilement was affecting her after all. It wasn't.

You fix. Nathan kill.

Again she sent words, even using Nathan's name. That effort meant this was important to Dell. Oddly, the fixing and killing were linked in Dell's mind, not opposed. Kai sent a sense of questioning.

Dell replied with a dense gestalt. Parts of it were too alien to register properly; that was often the case when a lot of memories were involved. Kai had long since concluded that the chameleon experienced memory very differently than she did. But she had the sense that Dell had been expecting Kai's arrival, with that expectation connected to Dell's ability to fool No-blood-no-scent. Dell had—overheard? Yes. Apparently Dyffaya believed Dell wasn't sentient, so he hadn't guarded his words around her.

Kai did her best to assemble a thought-stream. It was nothing like the complex ones Dell sent, but closer to Dell's "language" than words would be. She sent an impression of the vastness of the god's mind, its complexity, and how much power would be involved in changing any of it.

She received in return a smug sense of great fullness, followed by another gestalt.

Kai sorted that one out slowly. Dell had acquired a harem. She'd mated with both males, which somehow allowed her to draw from their stores of power, which meant Kai could draw on it, too. And, as Malek had confided, time passed differently in the godhead. What for Kai had been a couple of days had been weeks for the chameleons—weeks spent in the most high-magic place they'd ever been. All three were full to bursting with magic, and Dell assured Kai she could use all of it, if necessary. The Queen's gift Dell wore was also full, and it held ample power to sustain Dell and her two mates.

Tangled in with all that was a hint of wild joy and completion. The mating mattered to Dell. Mattered greatly. Kai touched her familiar's head and sent a strong wave of grateful happiness for Dell's good fortune. In other words, congratulations.

Dell accepted it with a short burst of purring, then sent again, strongly: *fix No-blood-no-scent.*

Kai's Gift certainly agreed. Both Gift and chameleon had a lousy sense of reality. It was like asking her to fix a nuclear reaction. She couldn't fix what she didn't comprehend, and she couldn't even see all of Dyffaya's mind, much less understand it. A single close encounter with one part of it, when she'd touched that not-tree, had nearly sent her into fugue. She sent Dell the memory of that moment.

Dell slipped in front, stopped smack dab in the middle of the path, sat there, making Kai stop, and stared at Kai: *must fix or . . .* followed by a series of emotions/images/complex thought configurations—an overwhelming onslaught that spoke to Kai of death, being trapped, more death, all of them forever trapped in this not-place of no-scent.

Too shaken to form a mental response, Kai muttered, "Okay, sure. But no pressure, right?"

THIRTY-NINE

NATHAN waited at one end of the clearing where he would fight and wished for a breeze—some natural stir of air across his body that carried the scent of grass, the myriad whisperings of a world busy and varied and living. He wanted a sky breathlessly blue, spotted by clouds. And Kai's voice. He had never felt less ready to die, but if he must, he wished it could be in a world that held the sound of his Kai.

But this was the world he had at the moment, and it was death he faced today. He hoped it would be one of the small deaths and not the final one. Nathan shook his head. How funny that the final death might arrive now, when he wanted it so little, instead of in the days when he would have welcomed it.

Or so he'd thought at the time. Now he understood that he hadn't been paying attention. Hadn't been able to pay attention, crippled up inside as he'd been by loneliness. How many millions of people over the centuries had said and believed they were ready for death, when really they'd simply been unable to pay attention? Perhaps the malaise in elves and depression in humans were different faces of the same problem—an inability to pay attention to life.

Life was sweet. All on its own, without any of the wished-for additions, life was sweet and good. If he couldn't have a breeze or grass, he had the feel of his toes digging into the sand and the memory of breezes, of wind pushing piled-up clouds across the sky. Of Kai.

If there was no breeze to whisper, the people assembled as audience supplied a similar sound, murmuring at each other. Nathan glanced at the little man who'd joined them a few minutes ago, his mood darkening. Malek's unexpected arrival had explained much. Likely he wouldn't be able to kill the man, and he regretted that. Nathan didn't see any chance that Malek could have been beguiled back in Iath without his Queen knowing. No, Malek was simply a traitor, forsworn. He'd chosen Dyffaya over his vows to Winter.

Dyffaya's other guests were fascinated by Malek, asking questions, hanging on his every word. The little man clearly enjoyed that. There were fewer guests now, and two were reclining, too tired from the magic sickness to sit up. Still, they looked happy and excited. No doubt the god had told them they were, so they had little choice . . . all but two, that is. Cullen sat beside Mary Boyd, who was trying to hide desperation behind sternness. Nathan wished he could do something to help her, but at least Cullen was there, chattering away at her. Suddenly she laughed, startling herself.

Nathan smiled. Cullen was a good man.

Across the clearing from him was another good man, one in whom honor ran deep and true. Benedict met his eyes briefly and gave a single nod.

Neither of them had weapons yet, but the god might change that when he appeared. They didn't know what type of combat Dyffaya would decree. He liked to make that a surprise. Nathan was hoping for blades of some sort. That would make it easier to—

The audience cheered. Some of them stood to applaud. Nathan turned to look where they were looking. The god had arrived.

Dyffaya seemed to have settled on his mixed-race body. That's what he wore today, as he had ever since these games of his began. He stood at the edge of the graveled path Malek had used on the border of the black-tree forest, smiling over his shoulder at . . .

Nathan was on his feet and running before he finished the thought. Kai. Kai, was *here,* in this terrible place—

Dyffaya frowned and waved a hand. Bars shot up from the ground, imprisoning Nathan so quickly he couldn't stop in time to keep from running into them. He got his hands up, though, and they smacked into what felt like iron, but wasn't. *"Kai!"*

Her eyes were dark and anxious. "I'm sorry, Nathan! He snatched me after killing Eharin—having Malek kill her, that is. She was holding me prisoner and—"

"Silence!" Dyffaya's voice roared out from the air itself, not from the body he was using. The next words were issued more normally. "Nathan, how impulsive you are all of a sudden! That's a new turn for you, isn't it? Really, the two of you are quite touching, but your reunion will have to wait until after the game. Assuming Nathan survives it, that is. I think he will, but it wouldn't be a game if the outcome were certain."

The way he smiled at Kai made Nathan want to howl, layered as it was with multiple emotions. Anger, yes, and gloating, but also a hint of triumph. "This is why you will agree, Kai Tallman Michalski. You are in love with the Hound who killed Nam Anthessa, and with it, any chance I could ever reclaim my own body." Rage quivered, barely in check, in Dyffaya's voice. "I want my revenge, but I'll settle for the taste of it I've already had, if you agree to my offer."

Kai had an odd expression on her face. An absorbed expression, one he knew well. She was studying something no one else could see. "You wanted to be in your own body so much. More than anything."

The god went still in a way that terrified Nathan. He thought Dyffaya would strike her down then and there. Instead, after a moment, he shrugged and spoke lightly. "There are other bodies. Sooner or later, I'll find the right one."

Other bodies? What did he mean by that? Gods—could that be what he was doing with his body magic—making an avatar? The first step toward it, anyway. He'd need the body he appropriated to be immune to magic sickness.

"What will you do if I don't agree?" Kai asked. "Will you kill Nathan?"

"That would be wasteful. No, assuming he survives today's

game, I'll keep you both here and use him to persuade you to change your mind. You will eventually, you know. What I'll do to him will be more than you can stand. Once you agree, I'll allow him to return to Earth with you. As long as he doesn't act against me, the two of you can be together, all snug and safe."

Suddenly Nathan wanted to howl again, but with laughter—though not the happy sort, for this was a cruel joke. All this time he'd expected the god to try to use Kai to hurt him, but Dyffaya had no intention of killing Kai. She'd been his real target all along. Nathan had known the god might want to use Kai. He'd spoken of her being a power, but he hadn't acted as if he believed that, had he? No, he'd gone on expecting Dyffaya to do what both of them were used to: use Kai to get to Nathan.

Instead, it was the other way around. He'd wanted Nathan in his power so he could use him against Kai. Oh, the joke was on him, all right, but such a cruel joke, when Kai would have to pay the price.

Kai was regarding the god gravely . . . the way she might look at a patient, he realized with a chill of fear. One who posed a major challenge. *No,* he wanted to yell at her. *Don't even think about it, don't try to help this one—he'll know, and he'll hurt you so badly. You have no idea how much pain he can deliver.*

But Kai couldn't hear his thoughts. She spoke quietly, still with that intent look on her face. "What is this game you keep referring to?"

"Oh, that." Reminded of the upcoming treat, Dyffaya was genuinely cheerful once more. "Do take my arm, and I'll explain it to you."

KAI desperately didn't want to take the god's arm. What if that touch sent her into fugue, the way touching the not-tree nearly had? But there was no way out of it.

This particular aspect of sidhe courtesy was similar to that practiced in medieval courts, and for good reason. Humans in Europe had had more contact with elves than anyone else, and some of the courtly behavior popular a few hundred years ago had been copied from them. Among elves, however, it wasn't the man who offered an arm to the woman, but the elder to the younger. Such an offer showed favor, and the younger had better accept the offer. To refuse was to offend deliberately.

She tried again to dial her Gift down. Still couldn't. Gingerly she laid her fingers on what looked like a lean, muscular forearm. To her relief, that didn't excite her Gift at all.

"I was beginning to wonder if you were as fearless as you looked," Dyffaya said lightly as he started toward the people he'd assembled. "But your heart is racing and your palms are damp. You're quite good at concealing your fear otherwise," he said in a kindly way. "Come with me, now, and I'll tell you about the game."

He escorted her toward those poor people, so heavily beguiled, pausing to speak a few words to each of them. All but one, that is—the dark-haired woman next to Cullen. She wasn't beguiled. Traumatized, yes, from the look of her thoughts, but not beguiled. The rest were painfully grateful for each smile, each second's attention, their god bestowed. And in between those benisons offered to his guests, he explained his game.

By the time they reached the central, flowering mound—higher by a good three feet than the others—Kai had lost all desire to be courteous. She snatched her hand back. "You can't be serious."

He grinned. "Not always, no. What would be the fun in that?"

"You said I'd have influence with you. Stop this horrible game."

"I couldn't if I wanted to." He leaped lightly to the top of his mound, settled cross-legged, and smiled down at her. "And I don't want to. Relax. The werewolf is good, but your Hound is better. You may sit here." He gestured at the low mound on his right.

Damned if she would sit and watch while—

Dell bumped Kai's leg with her head. The chameleon's desire was obvious. She wanted Kai to sit and wait. The time to act was coming. It was not yet here.

Kai swallowed fear, pride, anger—everything that made her want to explode, including the growing urgency of her Gift—and sat. She hoped Dell knew what she was doing.

The chameleon leaped up onto the tall mound and settled

beside Dyffaya. He stroked her head, his expression fond, then stood and started talking. He had a beautiful voice. He spoke about the glory of single combat and how privileged they all were to witness combat between two who were truly masters of their art. Kai tuned him out, struggling to keep her Gift in check, and looked at Nathan. He gripped the bars, staring at her with the same longing she felt. Dyffaya could have let them touch or at least speak to each other. Had he refused because he thought it put more pressure on Kai to agree?

But if she understood him correctly, even if she agreed right this moment to turn herself into a binder, he couldn't stop the game. He was bound the only way such as he could be bound. By his own words.

What was Nathan going to do? He had something in mind. Kai had picked up that much from Dell's attempts to explain, but she didn't know what.

". . . in recognition of his courtesy to his enemy by failing to take that death-stroke, I will grant Nathan of Faerie the right to choose the form of combat today. Nathan? What will you have?"

A moment's silence, then Nathan spoke firmly. "Swords."

"An excellent choice. Since you don't specify the type of blade, I will choose." Dyffaya clapped his hands.

The bars surrounding Nathan vanished and a sword appeared on the ground in front of him. Kai glanced quickly at Benedict at the far end of the field. He'd already bent and retrieved his weapon.

Gods, was she really going to have to watch this? No, she decided. And shut her eyes.

"Do you think that's a good idea?" Dyffaya was annoyed. "Open your eyes. I don't want to have to punish someone for your inattention. I'm fond of all my guests, and they don't deserve that."

Kai knew he'd do just that, hurt someone else to punish her. She knew it because, even with her eyes closed, she saw his thoughts—the dark glow of them here, the iridescent sheen over there, the complex and horribly distorted tangle leading into the not-trees. She shuddered and opened her eyes.

"That's better. Really, Kai, if you can't bear to watch this, how do you think you'll handle seeing me slit open your lover's gut and tickle it with flame? You might as well agree." He paused, giving her that chance. "No? Ah, well—begin!"

Benedict and Nathan advanced on each other. Each held a curved sword, the sort she associated with samurai. When they were just beyond the reach of the swords, they stopped and bowed. It was so formal, as if this were a practice bout that one would win, one would lose, and it wouldn't matter.

This mattered. It mattered in the most terrible way, yet there was no outcome to wish for. All possible outcomes were horrible.

A long strand of ebony thought unreeled from the flowery mound where Dyffaya sat, heading for the not-trees, commanding her attention. Ribbons of lavender twined around it, dragged along by some part of the intention that was forming. Something connected to those not-trees. If she could just see inside one of those black columns of frozen thought . . . Kai bit her lip. Hard. She could not go into fugue now.

Slowly at first, Benedict and Nathan began their dance. Steel flashed as they parried, spun, each man stepping so light and quick. Again and again the swords rang as they clashed. Swords and men alike began to pick up speed. It might have been beautiful. Kai couldn't tell, gripped as she was by fear . . . distracted despite her fear by the rising imperative of her Gift. *Look,* it commanded her. *Look deeply.*

She didn't know if she could hold it back much longer. She didn't know how. Need mounted and built in her much as the swordsmen's dance was accelerating. She had to—had to fix—

Wait, Dell sent, and with it a wave of reassurance that she could do this, she could wait a little longer. Just a little . . .

There was a sudden flurry of motion too fast for Kai to follow—ending with Benedict stepping back, his sword red with blood. And Nathan on the ground. Motionless. His eyes open in the blankness of death.

Kai was on her feet. "No!"

"Hush," Dyffaya snapped. "He isn't dead. The godhead won't hold dead things. If he were dead, his body would have been expelled."

There was no expression on Benedict's face, but in his

thoughts she saw tightly controlled satisfaction. "As he refused the coup de grace with me, so do I refuse it now. Not that it's necessary. His heart has stopped beating."

"He's not dead," Dyffaya said more loudly.

"His heart stopped. I won."

"He'll heal it. He's a *Hound*. He'll heal it."

He could. Of course Nathan could heal it. He wasn't dead. Kai still saw his thoughts—pulled in tight, they were, dark and shadowed and coiled around his head. But he could live without a heartbeat for much longer than it would take to heal his heart. He'd once survived without oxygen for three hours. He . . .

All at once Kai understood. Parts of what Dell had sent earlier suddenly made sense. Added to those were the way Dyffaya had commented on her dry mouth and damp palms, plus her heart's certainty of who and what Nathan was. What he was capable of. "He won't!" She turned to Dyffaya. "He won't heal it. He's opted out of your game. He doesn't want to be used to control me, so he won't let himself heal."

Yes, Dell sent.

"He can't do that." But finally Dyffaya looked worried. A dead Nathan would interfere with his plans. "No one can control healing when on the edge of death. He isn't conscious enough to control it."

"I can see his thoughts, you fool! I know what he's doing. He's shutting down. You have to start his heart beating!"

"It will. In just another moment—"

"It *won't*. You've got body magic. Use it! Get his heart going again, or you'll lose him—and if he dies, you have to kill me. He'll have lost your stupid game, and you're bound to follow through."

That got through. "He wouldn't. You matter too much to him. He wouldn't lose on purpose."

"To save me from torture, or a life of slavery to your whims? Oh, he would. He is more than capable of that."

Thunder boomed in a place with neither clouds nor sky. An expression of anger, she thought. Or fear? "What absurd histrionics." But he stood and leaped down. "Get back," he ordered Benedict. "All the way back to your starting point."

Benedict obeyed.

Dyffaya advanced on Nathan's body. He stopped about ten feet away, studying it. His expression changed and he moved forward more quickly. Maybe he'd confirmed that Nathan's heart was stopped. Maybe it was too badly damaged to heal. Maybe—

Dyffaya knelt and stretched out a hand.

Nathan rolled onto his side, his arm swinging in a smooth arc, with Claw in his hand. And buried the blade in Dyffaya's chest.

The world screamed.

FORTY

THE air, the ground—everything screamed along with the god. Including the people behind Kai. Behind her, because she was already running toward Nathan and the being—the *intention*—impaled on his knife. The very large knife that had been made from a dragon's living claw, freely given. Made with a dragon's knowledge of death to carry the Gift Nathan had been born with.

Which was also the knowledge of death, freely given.

Thoughts roiled around Kai as she ran, streaming clouds of color and agony. She raced through the darkest violet and a tattered mist of white, instinctively ducked to avoid a snapping pattern in furious red. She landed on her knees beside what had never truly been a body, propelled by her Gift.

Dyffaya's not-body had changed. Gone was the form she'd seen. The body Nathan's blade pinned to the ground was larger, more muscular. A Greek Adonis with shining blond hair snarled up at Nathan, reaching for him even as his body began dying.

Kai waited. Now that she was here, ready to act, her Gift no longer pushed, but waited with her. This was not the right moment. Not yet.

Nathan twisted the blade. Dyffaya and the world shrieked.

And he changed again—this time to a youth, maybe ten years old, his arms slim and lovely. His legs were slim and lovely, too. And dying.

The next body wasn't human. It wasn't elf, either. It was huge and hairy, with arms like tree trunks ending in claws that could have ripped out a rhino's throat. He swiped one arm at Nathan.

Who held on grimly to Claw, even as blood splashed from a deep wound to his chest.

Dyffaya wasn't bleeding. With a huge knife in his chest, he didn't bleed. No-blood-no-scent, Dell had called him. He changed again. This time, as he died, one of the great trees nearby came crashing down. Kai was suddenly certain each death had brought down a tree, but the others had been too distant for her to hear. She gasped as this enormous trunk smashed against its neighbor, splintering as if it were glass—the patterns, oh God, the patterns, broken now into crystalline fragments, each shard a fragment of—of—

The world groaned.

Dyffaya began changing faster. From hairy beast he flipped into a race Kai had never seen before, one with blue-green skin and gills. The aquatic being had no time to suffer for lack of water before dying. Then to an old man—an elfin man, his white hair streaming around his face and shoulders, which were bare now, for the god was forgetting to add clothing, his face lined and bewildered. "Why are you doing this?" he whispered. "I can't die."

With every change—every death—another tree came crashing down. Some distant. Some closer by.

Dimly she was aware of Dell coming up beside her as Dyffaya cycled through yet more forms—another human shape, then two that were grotesque, then a new one that was female. That was . . . her. Kai looked down at her own face, distorted by pain. Saw herself gasp Nathan's name. Quickly she looked up at Nathan.

The determination on his face didn't falter, but sweat poured down his cheeks, wetted his hair, dripped down his chest to mingle with the blood from his wounds—one from a sword, one from a beast's claws. Still bleeding, those wounds, and they shouldn't be. His healing stopped bleeding almost immediately. Had he lost weight? Even as she watched, did his cheeks become more hollow?

Another death. Another tree came down. And Dyffaya changed again.

This one was different. She saw that or sensed it in the turbulence of thought around them. He was a boy again, but an elfin boy—slim and more beautiful than any of the other forms he'd worn, for this one was true. This was how he'd looked once.

This time, he looked at her, not Nathan. Tears shone in his eyes. "Please," he whispered. "Make him stop killing me."

Now. This moment. She reached for the boy's face and laid her hands on his cheeks. Touched him, too, with her Gift. Lightly, lightly . . . "Nathan," she said. "You must stop."

"Kai, he's tricking you. He isn't—"

She looked at him. Met his eyes. "I know what he is." And she did. She knew what shapes were frozen in those terrible not-trees. "I know what I have to do."

His eyes were pools of terrible strain, an effort she could see in his thoughts, as rigid as his shoulders as he held to his purpose. Trust eased in. Trust in her. He didn't know what she knew, had no proof . . . and needed none.

He withdrew Claw.

Nathan couldn't call back the death he'd already sent, but he'd stopped sending more. She had time. A little time. The patterns around her, those huge, tumbling patterns, so incredible and majestic . . . and furious. Tortured. Distorted, and growing worse.

Broken sad-bad, Dell had said. Yes. "What is your name?" she asked the boy.

His throat worked as he swallowed. "I can't . . . I lost it. A long time ago, I lost my name. I looked and looked, but I couldn't find it again."

Crystalline sorrow surrounded her. She was in his thoughts, not reading them, yet somehow understanding much of what she saw. He referred to the moment of his first insanity, she knew, the one that started the rest. He'd been an adept. He'd known his true name. And yet he'd lost it. "What did your mother call you?"

"Sandetti." A little boy's voice. "It's a love name, not a—a true name. My mother loved me, but she's gone. I have been alone so long. So very long."

Three thousand years or more. "Sandetti, will you let me help you?"

"I'm so *afraid* . . ."

The world shuddered with his fear.

"I know what's wrong," she told him gently. "You told us, didn't you? You *can't* die. Yet death has entered you. Death is here, and it can't stop killing you, yet you can't die."

"Yes." Tears wet his cheeks.

The black not-trees reaching from deep in the ground of this place to the blackness above . . . black, frozen pillars of thought. Of denial. Deep and total denial. He hadn't wanted to die, so he'd denied death—and, being a god, he was the only one who could bind him.

That was his second insanity. He'd banished himself to his mind, used the power of his own words to trap himself, forever alone in his godhead and his delusion. That insanity gripped what was left of him, this broken god, yearning endlessly for the one thing he could not have.

Life. "Let me help you," she said gently.

He looked at her for a long moment. His voice shook. "Will I be alone? I am so very afraid of being alone again."

Before she could answer, Dell did. The chameleon moved up beside the boy-god and lay down, touching him. And purred.

He reached up weakly and stroked her fur. "She does love me," he said in a marveling voice that, for a moment, sounded like the adult Dyffaya. "I was never sure . . . yes. You may help."

Kai sank into trance. Quickly, easily, her Gift eager.

And saw everything. There was no ground. No flowers, no endlessly tall trunks. Only patterns. And there, buried deep, the tangled roots of those not-trees, the denial that had distorted that great mind. Thick and knotted and huge, they were the binding he'd laid upon himself when he refused to accept reality: that he'd been killed. For over three thousand years, everything that remained of him had been built on untruth.

Carefully she formed the purest white thought bubble and poured power into it. More power. It would take so much power to shift those roots, but she knew where to begin prying . . . there, where the shock and pain of death were true, at the very base of the roots. Before they became twisted into other shapes.

She shaped her thought bubble and sent it where it was needed. And began to pry apart that first, tight twist. As she did, something else became clear.

She knew how binders were made, what line had to be crossed. To turn into a binder, she would have to impose falseness on another mind. Falseness like *this*. But to do that, she'd first have to knowingly embrace the false, take it into herself. She couldn't give what she didn't have.

Like Dyffaya—like everyone?—a binder's first victim was herself.

Perhaps it was because she was *in* the thoughts this time, instead of merely observing them. Perhaps it was because he was a god, however damaged. But this time, she heard thoughts. He spoke to her, whispering of events long past. Sometimes she saw the memories, moments of life flashing by . . .

"Tell me," she said as she pulled and pulled at the next great knot. "Tell me what happened."

His voice grew clearer. It was a boy's voice, not a man's. "When they came for me, Winter and her sister . . . she was my friend, and she'd promised. I'd asked her to promise before . . . before a lot of things happened that made me lose my name. I don't remember that very well, but I know what happened when they came for me. I'd changed my mind. I didn't want to die! I told her and told her but she wouldn't *listen*."

The word he used for *friend* was elfin, and meant true intimacy. . . . "She'd promised to kill you?" So much power already used, but she needed more. She drew it and kept working.

"Yes, because I thought something bad would happen to me. Or was happening . . . I don't remember what."

"Yes, you do."

"I don't want to remember." But he wept now, for he did. She'd untangled too much for him to keep forgetting. He wept and wept, first for the deaths that he'd caused. Some he'd meant, for they'd been at war. Some he hadn't, but they'd happened anyway, for in that long-ago time, which was also happening now, chaos was becoming his master instead of his servant.

Somewhere, in all those deaths, he'd lost himself. Whatever was meant by a true name, he'd lost it. But he'd retained chaos and all its incredible power. And so his friend, a true friend, the Queen of Winter, and her sister of Summer, had come for him as she'd promised she would if he lost himself in the madness of chaos. She'd come and . . .

"They killed me," he whispered. "I . . ."

"Yes." Almost finished now. Kai felt weak. It was hard to keep pulling at that last, terrible knot, but she had to.

For a moment, a face wavered in front of her—the face of the elf boy she'd seen earlier, changing slowly into the face of a man. An elfin man, beautiful as they all were, but with something more. Something she couldn't name. His eyes—startling eyes, a turquoise as bright as crystallized laughter—opened wide just as Kai undid the last knotted root.

He looked at her, astonished. "I died!"

"Yes," she whispered. And wondered if she were dying, too. She was so weak, and she didn't know how to get back. How to find her body again, when all she saw were patterns. Fugue. She'd fallen into fugue, and she was lost here in the thoughts of a dying god.

"Tell Winter," he said, his voice growing fainter as he died . . . it took time for such a vast mind to fade. "Tell her to remember Sandetti, and forget that other one. The god. He didn't do well for himself. For anyone."

How could she? She was lost in his thoughts and would die with him. She wouldn't see Winter again. Or Nathan, who would grieve so terribly. Or Dell, who might die when she did, because the familiar bond—

The dying god gripped her suddenly. Not with hands, which he lacked, just as she lacked a body to feel them—yet it was much like being held in strong hands. And that—the brush of a kiss? Something very like that, and the merest whisper of a name that reverberated through her with such *truth*. And then he shoved her, shoved her hard, spending the last of his power.

Shoved her away from him. Out of his thoughts.

And back into her body. She drew a deep, shuddering breath.

"Kai, Kai." Nathan was holding her. She was half in his lap. Dell, who'd lain down next to Dyffaya so he wouldn't be alone, was next to her now. She figured out all that from feel because she hadn't managed to open her eyes yet.

She made the effort. It was worth it, because there he was, bent over her. His cheeks were wet.

"Your heart stopped," he told her. "You were gone so long, and then your heart stopped."

"So . . . did yours." She reached up to touch his wet cheek.

"That was just Cullen. Yours . . . I thought I'd lost you."

"You still could," Cullen said dryly. "This place is coming apart. We have to get out. The question is, how?"

Some of his unspoken urgency carried over to Kai, gave her a spurt of energy. She couldn't quite sit up, but her effort to do so got Nathan's attention. He propped her up higher against him.

Dell was beside her, yes. And next to Dell were two more chameleons, smaller and leaner—much leaner. And Dell was skinny. Her ribs showed. Kai had drawn too much power. Alarmed, she sent a quick question, and Dell huffed and returned the knowledge of hunger. The Queen's stone was almost empty, too, but there was enough to hold the three of them for a time.

Relief shuddered through her and she looked around. The not-trees were gone. All of them. The stuff that looked like ground still glowed, but it was cracking. Cullen was near, his arm around the dark-haired woman who hadn't been beguiled. Benedict was carrying someone, a woman too weak to stand. A young man was held up by two of the others. "Where's Malek?"

"Dead. The body vanished."

She looked at Nathan.

"No," he said. "Not me. He killed himself when his god died. He didn't want to face the Queen's justice."

"No," she said, "that was grief." Malek had been a small, slimy man, and when he'd found something larger than himself to serve, he'd chosen badly. But his devotion had been real.

Not so for the others gathered around them. Some of those

who'd been kept by the god were weeping. Some looked dazed as they woke from the beguilement that had vanished with the god . . . who was not here to hold things together.

Or to send any of them back.

Kai wanted to weep, too, from sheer frustration. To have come so close, done so much . . .

"Wait," Benedict whispered. He cocked his head. Some emotion broke over his face, deep and painful, cracking the grimness, revealing the man inside the warrior. Hope. "Do you hear that?"

A moment later, she did.

Drumming. Coming from—"Thataway," she said, drunk with exhaustion and a burgeoning joy. She'd survived. As had Nathan and Dell and all who'd made it to this last, terrible day. They'd all survived, and someone—or Someone, or more than one?—had come to help them get home. She couldn't see Them, but as she listened to the drums, the breath of those Presences stirred her hair and her soul.

Kai lifted one limp arm, pointing in the direction of the drums. Down. The drums were beneath the cracking not-ground. Many drums, she realized, beating in unison. Many, many drums. "We go that way. Down, toward the drums."

"What drums?" Nathan asked.

He couldn't hear them? Well, he wasn't Diné. She grinned like an idiot. "The drums of thousands of the People. Grandfather's drums."

FORTY-ONE

NO two people reported exactly the same experience of that strange return. They all saw the not-ground lose its glow. As it did, one of the cracks widened, becoming a wide hole spilling light into the dark, crumbling godhead.

Kai had gone down a steep slope where tough grass mingled with rock. Cullen and three others had seen slopes, too, but their descriptions didn't match hers. Nathan had seen only light, but that light formed itself into a ramp leading down. He remembered carrying Kai down that long ramp, while Kai remembered him carrying her down that short, rocky slope. One of the women swore she'd ridden down an escalator. Stairs were the most popular version. A couple people reported walking endlessly through mist or fog, and Dell had the simplest descent. She'd leaped down the hole and landed directly in the Ordinary World.

Benedict wouldn't say what he'd experienced. When asked, he only smiled and shook his head, though something in his eyes made Kai wonder if he'd actually seen the Presences she'd only sensed.

She didn't ask. Such experiences were too personal.

They'd all descended in whatever manner to emerge on a real slope, that of Little Sister. At the base of that small, unprepossessing mountain, gathered around it in the thousands—sixteen thousand and ninety-five, she later learned—were those of the People who'd answered Joseph Tallman's summons. They'd been drumming for eighteen hours straight.

It had taken several days for all of those thousands to arrive at Clanhome. They'd had time, though. On Earth, ten days had passed since Eharin opened a hole in one grassy wall of the hobbit house so she could bludgeon Kai with a cosh she'd purchased online.

Three days after Eharin knocked Kai out, Karin Stockman had taken down the ward at the hobbit house. She'd had to call in a Midwestern coven to help. Turned out the ward had been a keepaway, just as Kai suspected. Once it was gone, Ackleford and his crew had found bodies—Eharin's, and those of his four witnesses. They'd also found all sorts of evidence cops love, like that cosh.

Cullen hadn't come up with a way to destroy the chaos motes. He had, however, come up with an alternative. At the last minute, as they were leaving the godhead, he'd stuffed his pockets with handfuls of the sandy ground. The motes were strongly attracted to the godhead-stuff, and he was using that attraction to gather them. Kai and Nathan would ask the Queen to send an adept to retrieve the motes. Nathan agreed with Cullen: a number of adepts would be eager to get their hands on such concentrated power, however hazardous. The problem would be deciding who could be trusted with it.

All of those who'd returned with Kai had lived. Most were physically recovered. The two who'd been the most ill from magic sickness—Penny from the beach and a young man named Frank, whom Dyffaya had called Liu—were still pretty weak, but they would get back to full strength eventually. Emotionally, none of those he'd beguiled were back to full strength. Kai had treated some of them. Others had refused her help. They didn't want anyone messing with their minds ever again. She understood that.

"It's weird how little it's changed, isn't it?" Arjenie said.

Kai looked around. The vines covering the walls of Fagioli's patio had lost their blooms, but they were making new buds. Otherwise the place looked just as it had when all this started. In Earth time, that was less than four weeks ago.

She'd spent the first week of her return with her grandfather. The second week, she and Nathan came back to San Diego so she could help those who wanted it. "It is. They still serve the best mocha coffee in the universe, too."

Arjenie grinned. "Spreading that net pretty wide, aren't you? I heard you arguing about mochas with Rule last night."

"I'm pretty sure I won that one." Mostly because Rule Turner didn't sully his coffee with chocolate, but still. She'd won.

Rule Turner and Lily Yu had long since returned, and last night the lupi had thrown a party. A big party, intended to combine "welcome home" with "yay, we won!" and a send-off bash for her and Nathan. There'd been music, dancing, and food. Lots and lots of food.

José had been there. He'd danced with her. Doug had attended the party, too, but it would be a while before he danced again. And Ackleford had been invited. To Kai's surprise, he'd come—and he'd brought Karin Stockman. At one point Kai had been mostly alone with the special agent. Surrounded by people, yes, but none of them had been talking to her at the moment. She'd taken advantage of it. "You like Karin," she'd said.

He'd scowled. "Won't anything come of it. She's based on the other side of the goddamn country."

"Yes, but you like her. A lot."

He'd shrugged. "She's smart, she's mean, and she's solid. What's not to like?"

Kai had laughed at Ackleford's romantic criteria and assured him that Karin liked him, too.

"So." Arjenie set her mocha drink down and leaned forward. "We've talked about Ackleford's possible love life, and mine—which is entirely satisfactory—and all sorts of other things, but we haven't talked about your decision. You said you were pretty sure what you were going to do, but you didn't want to tell me until you were a hundred percent. How about it? Have you made up your mind?"

Kai smiled. "I'm going to get my eyes fixed."

"At the surgical center?"

"Nope. I'm going for the surgery-free option."

Arjenie's eyebrows went up. "You're going to take service

with the Queen of Winter. Wow. That's good. I think that's good." She frowned. "I'm not sure. But you are?"

She nodded. "Nathan was right. I couldn't make up my mind before because I didn't know what I wanted. But that wasn't all there was to it. There were two things I had to learn, and I couldn't make up my mind until I did."

"You okay telling me what those things were?"

"I've been wanting to. The first thing . . . until all this happened, I kept seeing myself as lesser. Less than the elves, and worse, less than Nathan. He was the power. I was just this nice girl with an unusual Gift that he'd fallen for. He didn't see me that way, but I did."

"You don't now?"

Kai shook her head slowly. "I hadn't realized how much my attitude about elves was really about me, not them. I wanted them to be more human, which is silly, but I was afraid I'd lose myself in their—their magnificence. I hadn't realized how much Eharin had poisoned my attitude, either. Oh, everything I disliked in her is common in other elves, too, but those things were so exaggerated in her, almost cartoonish. It's like Europeans saying they don't like Americans because we're so loud and brash. Sure, some Americans are loud, and culturally we're more about the brash than the meek. But plenty of Americans are neither of those things. Reducing an entire people to a stereotype is always dumb."

Arjenie grinned. "You like elves now?"

Kai chuckled. "Some of them, no. But others . . . I liked some of them all along. I just insisted they were the exceptions." She was silent a moment, thinking of what she'd learned in that final, intensely private time with one who had been a god. Most of it she couldn't speak of, but how it had affected her—that was okay to talk about. "Elves are so beautiful and powerful and graceful that all I could see was how much better than us they were. But they aren't. Better at some things, yes, but . . . Arjenie, I think many of them are lonely."

Arjenie's eyebrows shot up again. "Poor, lonely superstars?"

Kai laughed. "Something like that. They're so good at all the surface things that I thought that was all they valued. I was wrong." She thought of a trapped, desperately lonely mind . . . but he'd been lonely before he became trapped. That's part of what went so badly wrong. Being visible to lots and lots of people is not the same as connecting with others, but the man who became a god hadn't known any other way. And in that, he was typical of his people. "Then there's those status games they play. I was pretty contemptuous about that, but now I suspect that's how they connect with others. Through their games. They need connections as much as we do, but I don't think most of them know how to make a friend over a cup of coffee. And that's kind of sad, isn't it?"

"I guess it is." Arjenie fell silent, contemplating an inability Kai suspected she didn't really understand. Kai hadn't, either. "What was the other thing? You said there were two things you'd learned."

"Oh, that. Well. The thing is, I've become a power." It sounded silly. Pretentious. And yet . . . "That's very sidhe of me, putting it that way, but the point is that I *have* power. Lots of it, especially now that Dell's taken a pair of mates. Before, I was hiding from that, scared of the responsibility that goes with it. I wanted to go on being lesser so I didn't have to face up to that responsibility—which means, among other things, that I'd damned well better get the best training I possibly can. To do anything else is irresponsible."

"And you can get that if you take service with the Queen. I understand. But you have to vow to her for life, right?"

"Yes. But I feel okay about that, because I know what I want. That might change, so I'm going to ask that some of the clauses be open for renegotiation after some fixed time. Maybe ten years. Otherwise, I'll negotiate the best deal I can—"

"You will, not Nathan?"

"I'll certainly want Nathan's advice. He's the expert at negotiating with one of the sidhe. But it's my life. I have to handle that particular deal myself."

Arjenie grinned and lifted her nearly empty plastic glass. "That calls for a toast. To negotiating our own deals!"

Kai grinned back, tapped her plastic glass against Arjenie's, and drank the last of a truly delicious mocha.

"You want to tell me what kind of clauses you're talking about?"

"Splitting my time between Earth and Faerie, for one. I've realized that I enjoy wandering, but I need a home base, too." She wanted more time with Grandfather. She wanted to get her things out of storage, and have a place to put them. "Nathan's okay with that. He likes a lot of things about Earth."

Arjenie perked up. "Here? I mean, not just here on Earth, but maybe you could make your home base in San Diego, or nearby?"

Kai smiled slowly. "Nathan really likes hanging out with lupi, and San Diego isn't that far from Grandfather."

Arjenie shrieked and did the happy dance sitting down.

Kai laughed, and of course had to hug her friend, and then they talked about possibilities. Kai had figured out a lot, but she didn't yet know what she wanted for a home. A house in the mountains, or one in the desert? Something near Clanhome, or halfway between it and Grandfather's beloved mountain? Maybe even a place on the beach . . . when Arjenie pointed out how much even a tiny beachfront condo would cost, Kai admitted sheepishly that price wasn't much of an issue. The Queen had supplied them with gems to finance their stay here. Rather a lot of them, including three of a type that weren't found on Earth. *Tétel an bo,* the sidhe called those stones, meaning eye-of-the-sky. They were lovely, rather like a star sapphire but a brilliant turquoise color. It turned out that collectors really, really wanted one of the new gems. A single one would pay for almost any house, even in high-priced San Diego; two would buy a mansion.

But Kai was sure of that much: she did not want a mansion. Something small and homey, with a comfortable guest room in case Grandfather agreed to leave his mountain for a short visit. And who knew? They might have a guest from Faerie from time to time, too. Something outside the city, too, because Dell didn't do well in cities. Neither did Dell's mates.

When Nathan appeared in the wide doorway to the patio, she realized guiltily that she'd lost track of time. She was supposed to have been out front thirty minutes ago so he could pick her up. He paused, looked around—and a smile broke over his face when he saw her. One of *those* smiles, the ones he invented on the spot to say that he'd found her again.

There was a flurry of hugs and goodbyes, promises between Kai and Arjenie to see each other again. Then Kai was outside Fagioli, looking around. "Where's the car?" They were supposed to head back to Clanhome one more time. Nathan could cross realms from anywhere, but it was much easier for him near a node, so Dell waited for them at the one on Little Sister.

"Eh." He rubbed his nose. "I thought we'd walk a bit first. Do you mind?"

She cast him a puzzled smile. "No. Something bothering you?"

He took her hand. "Let's walk."

He didn't say another word for the next three blocks. Finally she did. "Are you still upset about getting things backward?" That's how he'd put it. He'd been "backward" about who Dyffaya wanted, but worse, he'd been "backward" about who was needed to deal with a mad god. He'd started out all right, he said, following his instincts, which told him to keep Kai close. Then he'd gotten all sidetracked, thinking he could go fix things himself, without her. Without even consulting her.

He'd been shaken when she told him what would have happened if he'd stuck Claw into Dyffaya and she hadn't been there—because Dyffaya couldn't die, but his mind could. Over and over and over. The god would have lost any trace of rationality, even his sense of self, yet he would still have had the power of chaos—chaos unleashed, driven by the impossible imperative to live and a terrible craving for company. Neither of them knew for certain what that would have meant for those trapped in the godhead, but "hell" was a fair guess. And that hell might have lasted a very long time.

Who had been needed to deal with a mad god? Not Nathan alone. Not Kai alone, either, but both of them together.

"Yes," Nathan said firmly, "but not now. The thing is, I don't know how to do this right."

"Do what?"

"I even read some women's magazines. I was right," he

said darkly. "They didn't help at all. Muddled my mind up, they did, with all their advice."

"Hmm." Deeply curious, but willing to let him play this out his way, she didn't ask any of the questions bubbling up.

They reached a little pocket-size park, one of those small islands of green in the city. This one held trees, with a narrow concrete path so you could wander among them without getting your shoes dirty. "Here we are," he said with relief. "This is the best I could come up with. Mostly I just gave up," he admitted. "It seems I'm not good at romance."

"I can't agree with that."

"This one," he said, drawing her over to a tall oak that looked older than the other trees. "Its roots go deep." He placed her up against the tree. "Kai, you are sure about taking service with the Queen?"

She nodded, bemused.

He expelled his breath in a gusty sigh. "Good. That's good." He pulled something out of his pocket. A jewelry box. A small, square jewelry box. He opened it.

There were two rings. One was white gold or platinum, she wasn't sure which—a wide, silvery band set with turquoise chips in the shape of a simple rune. The one that meant *always*. The other was made of some dark metal she didn't recognize. It was larger, but had the same turquoise chips set in the same rune. "They aren't the usual, but neither are we, and I thought—but if you'd like something different, we can do that. Do you want one of the diamond ones? The engagement kind? I didn't think you would, but—"

"Nathan—"

"I couldn't ask you before or let you know that I wanted to. Vowing to my Queen, that needed to be your decision, freely made, so I didn't want you thinking about this decision instead of that one. But now you'll be made a legal adult, able to make agreements in your own right. It's forever I want, like humans try for and Wild Sidhe do, not the sort of contract elves make, which can mean almost anything. Though we may want to make up a contract later, something they'll understand—the elves, I mean. We can talk about that. And you may want a ceremony with the dress and your grandfather and all, but we can do that later, too. But this . . . among my people, you see, it's just between you and me."

"Nathan—"

"If you don't want to, you'll still be my Kai. You can't stop being mine, and I don't need anything to show *that*, but this ring says that I'm yours, too, and I . . . I would very much like that."

"Nathan, you haven't *asked*."

Light shone at the back of his eyes, a glow turning the winter sky luminous. "The asking and answering, that's the whole thing, for my people. The rings aren't part of it for Wild Sidhe, but I thought you'd like them, and I liked them, so . . . but once I ask and you say, and you ask and I say, it's done, and there's no changing it."

"Nathan. Ask."

He handed her the dark ring, the one sized for his finger. He took out the other one—the silvery ring that, like his, said "always"—and held it in one hand and her hand in the other. His voice was husky. "Will you marry with me, Kai?"

She smiled—a fresh-minted smile, one invented just for this moment. Just for him. "Yes."

EPILOGUE

IT was a small room. Not cozy—elves didn't do cozy—but as close to that as they came, with large, soft cushions scattered invitingly on the gleaming wooden floor and a small fire burning merrily in an ancient stone trough. No wood needed for that fire, of course. It burned air and magic and someone's intention.

Kai didn't dare sit on one of those cushions. She was terrified of wrinkles. Or smudges or dust, though it was highly unlikely any dust was allowed here, in one of the most private places in Winter's court. She wore white, pristine, glistening white, draped around her in a way only an elf could pull off properly. The color and style of the dress were obligatory. In a short time she would leave this room and go to the Great Audience Chamber. There she would make her vows to the Queen of Winter in view of her entire court.

There had been a moment when she thought the offer might be withdrawn.

She and Nathan had made their report to the Queen, but Winter had known the key fact before they returned: the one they called Dyffaya was finally, fully dead. She knew this, she told them, because "chaos has returned to Faerie."

"Oh," Nathan had said. "I suppose it would. I hadn't thought of that."

Kai had needed that explained. For over three millennia, Dyffaya had occupied the godhead, but his worship had been utterly banned. For over three millennia, therefore, chaos had been severely limited, its spiritual power unavailable.

And now it was.

Change was coming to the realms. To the elves, who loved stability almost as much as they loved beauty. The Queen had not been happy about that, but after a moment she'd sighed. "I cannot regret it. Sandetti is at rest now. If the rest of us are due for unrest, perhaps that is fitting."

Kai thought about that conversation, alone in the almost-cozy little chamber. And then she wasn't.

"I am here, as you asked," Winter said in a crystal-pure voice, "and I am curious."

No door had opened to admit the Queen, not that Kai had seen. Startled as much by the Queen's beauty—she simply could not grow used to it—as by her sudden appearance, Kai was slow in making her bow.

"No, don't. We leave our stations outside this room. Here, it is just you and I."

"Thank you for coming," Kai said. "I have a request. This isn't part of our deal, but separate. A favor, I guess, though I'm told I shouldn't ask for favors—but maybe this one goes both ways. It's about the token of your service I'm to accept. I . . ." She was making a mess of this. "Let me show you." She held out the ring she'd had made—a simple circle framing one of the *tétel an bo* gems the Queen had given them. An eye-of-the-sky. "If you don't mind, Lady, I'd like to wear this as your token."

Winter glanced at the simple ring—then looked up sharply at Kai's face. She said nothing.

"It's the color of his eyes," Kai said softly.

Winter's eyes went dark as night, but a quiet night, calm and ancient. And grieving. "He was a great man."

"He was."

"We asked too much of him," she said abruptly. "We were desperate. The war was not going well. But we asked too much."

We . . . ? But—

"Surely you knew that? You didn't." Winter shook her head. "Child, he was on our side in the Great War. He fought those who would have taken choice away from us. I don't know if we could have won without him . . . but we did win, and he lost. He lost everything." She fell silent, caught by memories Kai had no part in.

Little part in, anyway. A few snatches of memory shared by a dying god didn't give her the right to intrude on someone else's memory of those events.

Finally the Queen stirred and looked at her. "Why that for your token?"

"Because it will remind me . . . you aren't human, and it's good to remember that, so I don't expect human things from you. What you are, I can't see clearly, but I know you were a true friend to Sandetti. Your promise to him cost you dearly, both in the giving of it and when the time came to honor it—but you honored it. And I want to carry a reminder of him, too. Of what he once was, before he was broken. And what I learned from him about myself."

Winter's lips turned up ever so slightly. "Your name."

Kai stared.

"Come, did you think you could discover your true name and I wouldn't notice?" She smiled, suddenly impish. "I suppose I ought to tell you. You became a legal adult the moment you learned your true name, no matter how absurdly young you might be. You humans—always in a hurry."

"I don't see how you . . . I didn't realize it myself. I just kept remembering what—there at the last, the very last moment, he whispered it, but it was weeks before I could call it up clearly, and understand." Though when she told Nathan, he'd known. Without her saying a word, he'd known. "Actually, I still don't understand. I know, but I don't understand."

"I will tell you a secret." Winter leaned closer and whispered. "Understanding your name—that is the work of a lifetime." She straightened, looking quite pleased with herself for no reason Kai could see. "Are you still minded to take service with me?'

"I am. Yes." The legal-adult part of the deal had never been what mattered most. And she didn't distrust Winter anymore. She might not see the Queen clearly. There was so much of her, and she was not human. But something in Kai recognized something in this Queen. Something worthy of service.

"Good. You belong in my domain, you know. You are as ruthless as I in its service."

"I am?"

Winter's eyes were now as pale and hard and bright as stars. "Of course. That is how I know you will never become a binder." Winter was probably reading her mind again, for she nodded. "Yes. You serve truth, as I do. You killed a god with it. As did I." She glanced down at the ring in her hand—and when had it moved from Kai's hand to hers? "The answer to your question is, yes, I will use this as your token. You are right. It is a favor that runs both ways. Come," she said, and held out her arm. "Let us amaze my court by entering together."

Kai grinned, thinking of how shocked some of those elves would be at the sight of a human shown such favor. And placed her hand on the Queen's arm.

GLOSSARY

PLACES

Aléri: city in the Queens' realm (Iath); Winter's court spends time there

Adelsfrai: a region in one of the sidhe realms

Angorai: a sidhe realm

Annabaka: city in one of the sidhe realms where Kai was attacked by a mind-controlled assassin

El Cahon: a small town near San Diego

Fagioli: coffee shop in San Diego

Iath: home realm of the two sidhe Queens, Winter and Summer

Kakkar: an especially nasty region of one sidhe realm

Kumeyaay Highway: one of the main highways in San Diego

ELFIN/SIDHE WORDS AND TERMS

Alath: a trio of nonmaterial beings (there are only three, or possibly one being in three parts) that Nathan mentions; they/it are called Alath by the sidhe but do not have a word-name for themselves

adit: a handmade honor gift

behi'yeli absore né: "the mad gods laughed"—a well-known saying or quotation among the sidhe

birith: that spectrum or range of magic which includes healing magic, body magic, and transformational magic

Dei'ri het Kai ahm insit?: "Will it make Kai sick?"

- dei is the uncertain form of "it," used when the object isn't known well enough to specify gender; used here with the suffix *ri* to indicate a question about the future. In the most common sidhe tongue, subjects, not verbs, are modified for tense.
- het = verb form of cause
- ahm = a linking verb similar to "to be"
- insit = physical malaise

Devrai: a sidhe race

Dirushi: a sidhe race

eriahu: poison

Jisen dá, oran-ahmni: "shut up, dot-eater"

kish: an innate, unalterable ground that determines the form someone's magic takes; a matrix

liarda: rather like leather jockstraps. Worn by gladiatorial slaves in one region of a sidhe realm.

Nathveta: no clear English translation, though "blessings" comes close; to call *nathveta* on someone means to actively desire good fortune for someone whose actions altered events in one's favor, even if that favor was not intended. Elves consider this an obligation.

One-off: English translation of a sidhe term for someone—almost always of mixed blood—with a rare or unique Gift that is unlikely to be inheritable

Osiga: one of the Hundred Names (sidhe families or clans)

p'tuth: revenge as performance art

tétel an bo: eye-of-the-sky, a beautiful turquoise-colored gem with a white, star-shaped incursion

NAVAJO WORDS

Azhé'é: Father

Hataali: medicine maker

Doko'oosliid: Abalone Shell Mountain, one of the holy mountains

Diné: the People

Diné Bizaad: the Navajo language

Bilagáana: white person

Yázhi Atsa: Little Eagle

OTHER UNUSUAL WORDS

Sukhasan: a yoga term

Ent: a tree-being (from Tolkien)

marbligpot'th: (unknown derivation) a magical configuration

Nokolai: a lupi clan

Rho: the leader of a lupi clan

Rhej: the memory of a clan; Lady-touched

Keep reading for a sneak peek
of the next Lupi novel
by Eileen Wilks

MIND·MAGIC

Coming soon from Berkley Sensation!

THE guards came as a shock.

She knew about the alarm system and exterior lights. Those had been in use when she lived in the big farmhouse. She knew about the perimeter alarm they'd added, too, having checked the updated schematics through her back door. No problem. There wasn't a tech system yet invented that she couldn't subvert, given enough time. She'd crossed the perimeter with no problems.

Maybe she'd been cocky. No, definitely she'd been cocky. Tech wasn't the only way to keep people out.

Or to keep them in.

Demi pressed her back against the big oak as if she could get it to soak her up if she pushed hard enough. Her heart pounded. Her mouth was dry. Nausea stirred in her gut. She didn't deal well with surprises, even the happy sort. This one was not happy. Her mind was a mess, thoughts shooting off in all directions like accidental fireworks. Her fingers began moving in an automatic pattern, fingering an imaginary flute.

Sensei said once that her mind was her biggest friend and her most terrible enemy. Sensei could say stuff like that and no one laughed at him. It wasn't because he was right, either. He was, but you could be right and people would still laugh at you or get mad. She understood the getting mad. It's like Mama said: people don't like to feel stupid, and sometimes if you're right it means they're wrong, or else just you being right makes them feel dumb, and that makes them mad. She knew how that felt. She didn't understand the laughing, but it always made her feel stupid.

She missed Mama so much.

The tree refused to absorb her. Her fingers kept moving repetitively. Gradually her mind calmed down enough to be useful again. The situation wasn't what she'd expected. She needed to evaluate it before deciding what to do.

Demi was in a small copse of trees about a hundred yards from the big farmhouse. There was some cover between her and her goal—a dip in the grassy meadow that she knew from experience would conceal her as long as she crouched low. That would take her to the barn, which would block her from view of the house as the dip petered out. She'd planned to slip inside the barn, climb to the hay loft, then out the window at the back and into the big elm. From the elm she'd go to the roof of the detached garage; from there to the patio. The motion sensor aimed at the patio was tied into the security system, so that wasn't a problem. She was already hacked into it.

She couldn't hack into eyeballs or the brains and bodies that went with them. The guards had been wearing camo, as if they were soldiers. Maybe they were. Mr. Smith could probably get soldiers if he wanted some.

Why would he want soldiers? What was going on?

She drew a shaky breath. That's what she was here to find out, wasn't it?

The knot of determination in her chest tightened. She wasn't giving up. Nicky was in there. She was ninety percent sure he was. If she was right, all kinds of things she'd thought true were fake and false, lies created to get her to help them do . . . whatever dreadful thing they were doing. Because you didn't lie in order to get people to do wonderful things, did you?

First things first. If Nicky was here, she had to rescue him. Which meant she had to figure out not just how to get in without being seen, but how to get both of them out again. Slowly she sank to the ground, sitting with her knees drawn up. She needed to think. To get her mind pointed in the right direction. If she didn't get all hurried and frantic, she could do this.

First question: should she abort the mission? Not give up, but gather more data, come up with another plan?

She tried to weigh the risk of continuing against the risk of postponing, but she didn't have enough data to make reasonable estimates. What she needed, then, was more data. How many guards were there? Were they armed? Were they really soldiers? Did they stay put or move around?

She didn't know any of that. She'd seen two guards and panicked and kept backing up until she bumped into this tree. She must have been quiet because they hadn't come after her, but all she really remembered was being scared. She still was, but she was thinking again.

It was three o'clock on a sunny September afternoon. The sun would be up for hours. She had time and a tall tree at her back. She stood, crouched, and launched herself at the lowest limb, grabbed it, and scrambled up.

Climbing was Demi's one athletic skill. She went up that tree like an oversize squirrel, stopping when she reached a convenient fork that gave her a good view of the house and grounds. She straddled it with her back to the trunk and looked out.

Still two guards, one at the east end of the house, one on the west side. Those sure looked like Army fatigues, with their billed caps and the pants tucked into combat boots. There was some kind of insignia on the sleeve of the closest guard. That made her stomach unhappy. So did the holstered gun.

Grimly she pulled out her phone and tapped in the data: *3:05 Guard 1 by fountain; Guard 2 25 ft. fr. west wall (dining rm).* Then she took pictures of the guards using the phone's zoom feature and got a fairly good shot of the insignia so she could check it out later. She couldn't do that now. The phone was in airplane mode so it wouldn't ping any nearby cell towers. That was probably excessive caution on her part, but why take a chance if she didn't have to?

Right now the guards were staying put. She set herself to watch. While she watched, she thought about minimum force.

When she first began taking lessons from Sensei, he'd talked about how minimum force was the idea behind every martial art. You learned how to spend the least possible force, often using your opponent's own force to defeat him. This, Sensei said, was what everyone tried to do in every aspect of life: use the least effort possible in order to achieve a goal. No one used one bit more effort than he or she thought was necessary. The trick was in figuring out what that minimum was and how to apply it. That's what people got wrong. That's what they would learn to do in his class.

Demi had been fascinated by the concept. For the next few months, she'd tried to find examples of people intentionally using more effort than was needed. The first one that occurred to her was studying for a test. Some people crammed like crazy, going way overboard. But that, Sensei had said, was because their goal wasn't to ace the test, but to reduce their anxiety about the test. Because they couldn't control what was on the test, they could never eliminate that anxiety entirely, so they kept trying to memorize more and more facts.

Another time she'd suggested that suicide bombers broke the rule. Sensei agreed that they appeared to do so, because giving one's life to achieve a goal could be considered spending the maximum possible to any person. But if your goal is to be a martyr, death *is* the minimum requirement. And those who sent a suicide bomber out to kill strangers were obviously expending the minimum force. They exchanged one life for several of those they considered enemies and caused fear in hundreds or thousands more.

She'd come up with lots more examples, but after a while she could shoot them down herself with a little thought. People mostly weren't very good at estimating the amount of effort needed. Mostly they underestimated it, which was why diets failed so often. People tried to make sweeping changes without allowing for how difficult, how against their nature, this was. Incremental change worked better because each step felt like the minimum necessary. On the other hand, when people were scared they often overestimated the amount of force needed. That's why police departments had rules and training for when it was okay to use deadly force. You couldn't rely on instinct when you were scared. Your instinct might be to shoot whatever was scaring you, and that could be a terrible mistake.

Demi had also come to realize that when people seemed to

use disproportionate force, she'd probably misidentified their goal. As she sat high in the tree watching the guards and brooding, she fought valiantly to persuade herself she could fix this, could find some way to avoid being seen by those soldiers. Nicky had been missing for a week now. She didn't think they would actually torture him, but he must be miserable and frightened. Who knew what kind of pressure they were putting on him to do—well, whatever it was they wanted him to do? Given the nature of his Gift, it must be something awful. She had to get him out.

Only she couldn't. Not yet. Her chest ached with the knowledge. She hung her head. *Nicky, I'm sorry. I'll be back.*

The dreadful truth was that she'd overlooked the obvious.

The amount of force people use is always in proportion to their goal. She'd been ninety percent sure that Mr. Smith had lied about his goal for the enclave, yet she hadn't reevaluated the amount of effort he might employ to secure it. She'd acted as if nothing had changed, trying to sneak into the enclave the same way she used to sneak out of it.

She had been downright woolly-headed. That stung.

Demi's eyes watered. Angrily she rubbed them. Much as she hated it, today's plan was a bust. She was going to have to go back to campus and come up with another one. She began making her way down the tree, going a lot more slowly than she'd climbed up.

A stick cracked. She froze in an awkward crouch, one foot firmly placed on a thick branch, the other foot reaching below it for the next one. Her heart pounded. That might have been anything—

Faint but clear, she heard the rustle of feet. Coming this way? She thought so. Oh, God, oh God, now what? She was going to be sick. No, she wasn't. She refused to throw up and give herself away. She'd get herself firmly planted on this branch and hold extremely still. She was still fairly high up, with branches and leaves and all between her and the ground. Maybe whoever it was wouldn't see her.

Slowly, careful not to make noise, Demi made herself secure and held very, very still. Even when the pair of soldiers moved into view, heading right for her tree, she didn't move. She may have stopped breathing.

The soldiers carried rifles slung over their shoulders. The man with them did not.

He was a round little man. Not fat, but with a bureaucrat's round little tummy and gray slacks. His cheeks were plump and pink, his head round as a bowling ball and almost as bald. Even his glasses were round. He stopped at the base of her tree and looked up. Those glasses winked at her as light glinted off them.

"Demi." Mr. Smith shook his head sadly. "You might as well come down."